DAWN FALCON

Books by Ann Moray

DAWN FALCON
GERVASE
A FAIR STREAM OF SILVER
THE RISING OF THE LARK

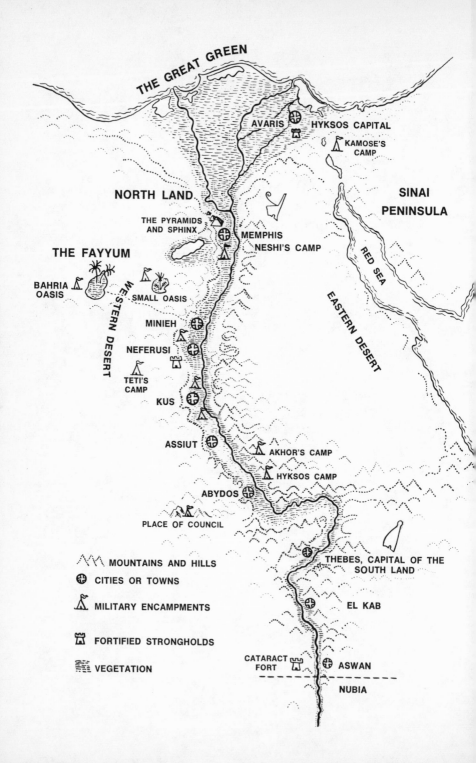

DAWN FALCON

A Novel of Ancient Egypt

by ANN MORAY

William Morrow & Company, Inc.   New York   1974

Map and illustrations by
Mark Hasselriis

Printed in the United States of America.

1   2   3   4   5   78   77   76   75   74

Library of Congress Cataloging in Publication Data

Moray, Ann.
  Dawn falcon.

  1. Egypt—History—To 332 B.C.—Fiction.
I. Title.
PZ4.M83Daw3 [PR6063.0673] 823'.9'14 73-12019
ISBN 0-688-00217-X

Dawn Falcon is gratefully dedicated to the late Professor William C. Hayes, formerly Curator of the Egyptian Department of the Metropolitan Museum, with the deepest obligation for his scholarly generosity—which included an invitation to work daily, for almost a year, in a room in the Department, with access to his own notes, articles and pertinent writings and translations not readily available to the lay researcher—and with the hope that he would have found some small merit herein worthy of his interest and encouragement.

I would like to thank my publishers, John Willey for his patience, Minda Tessler and Susan Courtney for their unfailing interest and enthusiasm, and most especially my editor, Joni Evans, for her encouragement in the beginning and her invaluable and constructive criticism of this book in manuscript.

List of Principal Characters

Ahmose
: Who tells the tale. Younger son of Seken-en-Ra II and Queen Ah-hotpe. Prince of the South Land, Neophyte-Priest. Deviser of Kamose's secret weapon.

Ahmose-Eb
: Son of Ebana of El-Kab and Unique Friend of Kamose since boyhood. Later, Captain of the Royal Fleet. One of Kamose's Company.

Ah-hotpe
: Daughter of Queen Tetisheri and Seken-en-Ra I, regal and beloved Sister Queen of Seken-en-Ra II. Devout High Priestess of Hat-hor and Spouse of Amun-Ra.

Ak-hor
: Son of Neshi the Nubian and Unique Friend of Kamose since boyhood. Later, Chief of the Nubian Scouts. One of Kamose's Company.

Aknere
: Grandson of Pery-em-Wah and a loyal admirer of his work. Grew up in the Court at Thebes. Later, Chief of the young spies. One of Kamose's Company.

Anat-neby
: Beautiful daughter of Piopi of Neferusi. Raised with the Royal children from the age of three, beloved of Kamose.

Apophis
: Tyrant Hyksos king in Avaris, capital of the captured North Land.

Atu	Beloved of Ahmose-Eb. Escaped from the Hyksos to work in a kitchen-ship of the Theban Royal Fleet.
The Chief Scribe	Avaricious father of thin Sittek.
Ebana of El-Kab	Unique Friend and Fan Bearer to Seken-en-Ra II, father of Ahmose-Eb.
Princess Herath	Courageous and beautiful daughter of Apophis. Princess in the Hyksos capital of Avaris, who refused to marry the cruel Hur.
Hir-ty	Loyal messenger to Kamose.
Hori	A captain of the Royal Fleet under Ahmose-Eb.
Hor-min	Refugee from Memphis, a goat-herd in Thebes. Ka-friend of Ahmose in the House of Life and battle-scribe to Kamose.
Hur	The Cruel One, Chief of Apophis' Treasury and Collector of Taxes for the Hyksos in the subjugated South Land. Despised even in the North Land.
Ina	Village Maiden. Secondary Wife and beloved of Kamose. Mother of his natural daughter.
Inhapi	Daughter of Ameni, Nomarch of the Wall Nome outside Memphis. Beloved of Ahmose.
Ita	Betrothed of Nome's son. Raped by Hur the Cruel One.
It-yu	Chief Scribe of the tyrant king Apophis and his trusted counselor. Unwisely gives his confidence to Pery-em-Wah.

Kamose	Elder son of Seken-en-Ra II and Queen Ah-hotpe. Warrior Prince, Dawn Falcon, who succeeds his father as King and after three years' planning leads his hosts to battle against the Hyksos tyrants.
Kheri-heb	Lector-Priest and Adept. Master and Mentor to Ahmose in his preparations for the spiritual ordeals of the priesthood.
Mayebre the Libyan	Envoy of Apophis from the Hyksos to the Court of Thebes. Insulter of the King and defamer of the God.
Mer-neb	Twin brother of Per-neb, nephew of Queen Ah-hotpe from Ed-fu, who grew up with the Royal Family in Thebes. Later, Captain of the King's Archers. One of Kamose's Company.
Miutu	High Priest and Chief of Visions through three generations of Theban rule.
Montu-Thoth	Young Adept and Healer-Priest among the Theban battle-wounded.
Nefertari	Natural daughter of Seken-en-Ra II and a half-Nubian concubine. The dark half-sister to Kamose, Ahmose and Rai. Favorite of Queen Tetisheri. Desired to be honored as Queen and worshipped as High Priestess of Hat-hor.
Neme	Servant of the Royal Family.
Neshi the Nubian	Unique Friend and Fan Bearer to Seken-en-Ra II. Ever faithful to his King. Chieftain of the Nubians in Egypt.
Pen-aati	Loyal Vizir and trusted Grand Administrator of the Theban Court. Cousin of Pery-em-Wah.

Penekheb	Called Pen by his comrades. Son of a southern nobleman. Later, Captain of the King's Chariots. One of Kamose's Company.
Per-neb	Twin brother of Mer-neb, nephew of Queen Ah-hotpe from Ed-fu. Grew up with the Royal Family in Thebes. Later, Captain of the King's Foot-soldiers. One of Kamose's Company.
Pery-em-Wah	Chief spy through three reigns of Theban kings. Disguised as a Hyksos in Avaris he gains the confidence of the king Apophis' chief counselor, It-yu.
Piopi of Neferusi	Prince of Neferusi, father of Teti and Anat-neby. Closest Unique Friend of King Seken-en-Ra II.
Rai	Young sister of Kamose and Ahmose. Royal Daughter, Kamose's intended bride and Queen.
Res	Childhood friend of Rai and Sen-ut. Daughter of a temple administrator. One of Sen-ut's young spies, successful in infiltrating the city of Neferusi before Kamose's battle. Beloved of Penekheb.
Seken-en-Ra II	Son of Queen Tetisheri and Seken-en-Ra I. King in Thebes, during whose reign the battle against the Hyksos was begun.
Senseneb	The Old One. Teacher of the Royal Family through three generations and companion of Queen Tetisheri since their escape from Memphis.
Sen-ut	Of the Lotus Hands. Childhood friend of the Royal Family, born in the King's House. Beloved of Thure. Leader of the young women spies.

Sittek	The thin one. Daughter of the Chief Scribe. Betrothed in childhood to Ahmose-Eb.
Tetaky	Young poet and boyhood friend of Kamose, warrior for the King. One of Kamose's Company.
Teti	Son of Piopi of Neferusi and brother of Anet-neby. Beloved god-son of the King, Seken-en-Ra II. Lusted after Sen-ut.
Tetisheri	Widow of Seken-en-Ra I and Queen Mother in Thebes. Escaped as a child from her family home, Memphis, holy city of the Apis bull, pillaged by the conquering Hyksos.
Thure	Son of an exiled Prince of Assiut and boyhood friend of Kamose. Warrior at the King's left hand. One of Kamose's Company. Beloved of Sen-ut.
Thuty	Natural son of Seken-en-Ra I in his old age. Royal Treasurer under Seken-en-Ra II; later, Overseer of the household of Tetisheri and lover of Nefertari.
Tui	Overseer of the Royal Animals.
Weset	Tui's son; also keeper of the Royal Animals.

Author's Note

The Two Lands is the name most often used in the inscriptions and writings of the ancient Egyptians to describe their land, and the word *Per-aa*, from which "Pharaoh" is derived, means Twofold Great House. The Two Lands, each having its own crown—the North Land the Red Crown and the South Land, the White—were, for most of their long history, under the authority of the king, who wore the Double Crown.

The name of the Two Lands together was Ta-mery, *Ta* meaning "earth," and *mer*, "beloved." Ta-mery: the Beloved Land.

The ancient name for the Nile was *atur*, "the River." The god of the River was Hapi, who was worshiped at the time of the yearly inundation that began in the summer solstice and ebbed in October, leaving on either side of its banks the long strips of fertile earth that is Egypt. This rich land, stretching from Assuan to the Mediterranean, between mountains and two vast deserts, was called by the ancients The Black Land.

I have used the familiar names for the cities.

Certain priests in ancient Egypt had wives and children, and some priestly offices were hereditary. When they wrote of ancient Egypt, Herodotus, Diodorus, Iamblichus and others described both priests and initiates. The initiate, or adept, would from choice and vocation be celibate. The king was highest priest of all. Various other functions of the priestly hierarchy will become familiar during the course of the story.

Though the ancient Egyptian theology involves mystical aspects of the psyche, the soul and the spirit, I have used only the word *Ka*, as we use "soul."

The Temple, throughout the thousands of years of this land's history, was called The House of Life, and within its vast precincts, priests, scholars, keepers of the ancient canon, scribes, artists and even craftsmen were trained.

At the time this tale begins, the usurping Hyksos had ruled Egypt as despots and conquerors for more than two hundred years. They had captured all the cities and nomes of the North Land, and those of the South Land as far upriver as Assiut. They had made a vassal kingdom of Thebes, Hawk City of the South Land, though the beleaguered Theban kings of the XVII Dynasty (according to Professor Hayes's chronology, 1660? to 1610? B.C.) still held titular authority.

The Hyksos ruled from their capital in the North Land, Avaris, and they worshiped Set, the dark enemy of Horus, Falcon of the South Land, with the orgiastic rites of their own god, Baal. They had sacked Memphis, massacred the people of Abydos and desecrated the shines of the ancient gods.

By the reign of Seken-en-Ra I, the Elder, and his tiny and beautiful queen, Tetisheri, who had escaped from her own captured city of Memphis when she was a child, the vision of freedom had grown.

At the death of her husband, Tetisheri became Queen Mother, and their children, Seken-en-Ra II and his sister-queen, Ah-hotpe, ascended the throne. With their reign, and the growing to manhood of their two sons, Kamose and Ahmose, the battle for the freedom of the Two Lands was joined.

From the XVIII Dynasty (1567 to 1304 B.C.), which was founded by these two young Theban princes, and of whom this story tells, comes the first picture discovered to date of a man on horseback. Professor Hayes, in the second volume of his *Scepter of Egypt,* which deals with this period, writes, "We are not, however, justified in assuming that every mounted Egyptian was a groom. Many shown in the later reliefs were archers, spearmen, and mounted scouts. . . ."

These words added the necessary impetus to an idea for Kamose's secret weapon that was already in my mind.

Ann Moray

New York, 1973

DAWN FALCON

THE BEGINNING

Nine scrolls, loosely rolled, lie to my left hand on the long, wide Council table. Though I am no scribe, through two Nile rises, two spring seasons when the River ebbs leaving the black earth rich and damp to nourish the seed, and through two arid summers, the story in these scrolls has poured through the beaks of my rush pens in Cataract spate.

I look at the niches bored out, to house them, in the granite side of this long room, deep underground and secret since my father's reign. At dawn, with Holy Ritual, four Overseers of the Royal Stone-masons, old and tried through years of work concealed beneath the ground, will wall up this hidden place, and I, Ahmose, younger son of Seken-en Ra II, and his beloved Sister-Queen, Ah-hotpe, will at last, in my fortieth year, become full Priest.

The name Ahmose means "Born of the Moon." "My Young One," my mother once said to me, "you were conceived when the River was a shining silver sword in the womb of the Black Land, and the moon was full." I always knew when my father and mother had been night-sailing together: Ah-hotpe's eyes were bride's eyes, and her beauty a diadem.

The two who gave me birth had loved since they played as children. Brother and sister, growing up together to know that Kingship is a goodly thing, so that when the time came for them to rule in Thebes, justice was sealed on their tongues, and their hearts were enthroned in the Temple of Truth.

I look at the strip of yellow parchment still spread out in front of me. It is weighted down with a golden statue, one half-arm's length in height, of the Goddess Maat, who is All Truth.

"Osiris, Lord . . ." my whisper echoes in this silent place. I gaze at the shrine niche in the granite wall. The small black basalt statue of the God glimmers in the light of the tall wick lamps and the wall torches. "Osiris, Lord, let this my scribe's work be acceptable to Maat . . . and to my Master, Kheri-heb . . ." I sit back, looking again at the scrolls, the fruits of the work he laid upon me. Kheri-heb! Lector-Priest and Initiate, he is wise beyond mortal knowing, and has been my beloved Mentor since my youth.

The water in the alabaster Hour Bowl has almost dripped away. In the world above me it is sun-set. I test the black ink on the scroll spread out in front of me. The last words I wrote are now quite dry. It is my mother's scroll.

With the sun-rise this morning, in answer to my message, eager as a girl she came. Followed by our faithful Neme, carrying a platter of honeyed milk and grapes, she made deep obeisance to Osiris, then rose and turned to me.

"Ahmose . . ." She walked toward me across the stone-flagged floor, and I stood up, my hand on my heart. "My Young One, your work for Kheri-heb? The nine scrolls?

They are accomplished? On this day, the appointed day?"

"By twelve hours, my Mother."

"And your message to me?"

"I have written a tenth scroll." I had put my hand on the parchment spread out in front of me. "For you!"

"Ahmose . . ." Her smile had the wise and innocent joy of the God's true Votary. "By Thoth, from whom all words do flow! You have become a true scribe for Kheri-heb."

"It seems I have been many things for Kheri-heb. Born a Royal Son, I have read for the Priesthood, been a trainer of animals, a River-man and sailor, helped in battle strategy and planning—and now! By Thoth! I am a scribe."

Grave again, she touched the nine scrolls one by one. "So vast a scene—so many men and women, young and old, to tell of . . ."

"These scrolls tell only of those who were bound by the thongs of loyalty and treachery, love and hatred to Thebes, to us and to our fight for the freedom of Ta-mery."

"The Beloved Land," my mother whispered. Slowly, she turned. "And this secret room! Through three Kings' reigns the hub and core of our Theban stratagems and planning. Ahmose . . ." She turned again to me. "How clearly my heart remembers . . . It was in the third month of the second year of your father's reign, that first day we walked down the nine steps, secret steps that led from the King's bed-chamber . . . so hidden they were that a beetle could not have found its way to this room . . . and when our Royal Stone-masons slid the heavy drop-stone door into its place, Kheri-heb and Miutu, High Priest and Chief of Visions, con-secrated the niche of Osiris, and blessed our planning. On that day, your father held his first safe, secret Council. . . ."

"Miutu! How my father loved him. . . . 'Goodness not backed by live energy is blasphemous,' he would tell us when we were young."

"Miutu was long in earth years when I was but a girl." She smiled. "Tall, and spare, and changeless . . . I will sit here. . . ." She looked, her eyes filled with memories, on my father's chair. Of ebony and native woods, fine-worked and inlaid with faience, green, blue and carnelian red, its legs were carved to the slender, strong, cloven feet of the ram. They widened and squared where they joined the purple-dyed leather seat and the ends of the arm-rests were horned rams' heads. fine-carved in ebony. Their eyes were of bright rock crystal that shone in the flickering wick flames. My mother sat down. After a moment she put out her long, slim hand and rested it on the arm of the chair next to her. "Pen-aati . . . I have felt the deep loss of him. As Miutu, Chief of Visions, held the spiritual order of our Land's life, so Pen-aati held the temporal. Our Vizir and Lord High Administrator lived in eternal vigilance for the South Land's weal." She clasped her hands on her lap and looked up at me. "How many long and sleepless nights we spent with him, your father and I when we were King and Queen, seeking ways according to the canon of balance between our water and our earth, to build new dikes and mend the old—and to eke out the grain, so that when the heavy tribute was paid to the Hyksos, all in the South Land had a share according to their needs. . . . Akh! My Young One, you have written of Miutu and Pen-aati, who now know joy in heaven?"

"It is all here, my Mother." I looked at the nine scrolls. "By the Truth of Maat! Here are the eye-held truths of our betrayal and our shame. Of murder, and burial delayed, and of the carrion soul who, to this day, stalks the King's Household, glutted with kindred blood."

"Ahmose!" The gaze of my mother's eyes has ever washed me in the waters of quiet. With a sigh, I sat down in my chair. She smiled again, and asked, "This tenth scroll . . . my scroll?"

"It is the first. In it I have written such scenes of our childhood and our growing as have bearing on the story here unfolded." I looked again, almost unbelieving, at the nine loose rolled papyri.

"Then, my Young One, let me rejoice awhile in these

youthful memories." She rested her hands on her knees and sat straight up in the chair. "Kheri-heb will not emerge from his long fast till moon-rise. . . . We have all day."

"He is too old for these long fasts."

"Have no fear for Kheri-heb. Earth years take no toll of him. Read to me now . . . my patience grows smaller with each drop of water from the Hour Bowl. . . . Akh! My Young One, how your father's Ka will rejoice."

"I have felt his spirit close in these last months here, deep underground, alone. . . ." I leaned forward, and drawing the wide-spread parchment toward me, I began to read the words I had written.

Thebes, Hawk City of the South Land, and Residence of the God, had stood embattled and alone, a vassal City, for two hundred years. Yet, though the tyrant Hyksos had dese-crated our Temples, despoiled our cities and enslaved our people, and though, in the King's House, my home, we had lived for generations taxed beyond mercy, in an austere pride and a grinding poverty, our early years were happy and passed swift as summer lightning. How fair in our early youth were the Feast Day mornings, when our mother, High Priestess by the wisdom of her own God-longing, led her three children, Kamose, Rai and me, to sing and dance around the Image of the God. Rai, my sister, and my soul's love. Rai, who even as a child was moved in heart from ancient days. The grace of her and her joy in the Rite, as she danced with the Virgins around the Barque of Amun-Ra, held high by the priests called Purified of Fingers, and her high, sweet voice would mingle with the cool, clear notes of the Temple minstrels and the whirring wings of the water-birds.

The Virgins were like the clouds in spring as, hand in hand, they danced along the tree-lined avenues and around the Sacred Lake. Their fine white linen cloaks, thin-woven as the wings of the butterflies, opened as they swayed and moved, and against their truth and nakedness, evil had no power. They sang:

"Amun-Ra! O Beautiful Being!
Thou risest as God in the Eastern Horizon
And joy comes forth from the mouths of thy people.
All happy cattle rejoice.
Thou illuminest the earth with thy rays
    of Turquoise Light"

and held out their sistra to the Thebans who had left their fields and boats and fowling-nets, and their dike-digging, to gather in the vast Outer-court of the Temple, and all who touched the Holy Rattles, and all who touched those who had touched them, had heightened life and a fuller joy, and were in health and contentment in the Rays from the Barque of the Morning Sun.

And when the God's Circuit was made, and the Sacred Barque returned to the Naos in the Holy of Holies, how long they stayed, my father and mother, on the Balcony of Appearances. High on the ledge between the pylon gateposts of the King's House they stood together, cooled by the rhythmic rise and fall of the large ostrich-feather fans held with hereditary pride by Neshi and Ebana, my father's close and Unique Friends. Neshi was Chief of the Nubians in Egypt, and Ebana of El-Kab was Captain of the Royal Armies. They walked to the left and right of their King when he went in his chair among the people of Thebes, and their apartments adjoined his chamber. While my father gave judgments on the disputes brought before him, and rewarded the deserving with land-plots, cattle and seed, my mother blessed the new-born children. Ah-hotpe stood God-mother to every child born within her Temple domain, even the children of the lazy ones, the squatters who lived in the shacks piled up against the outside of the Temple walls, and she gave a parcel of her land to each. The love of her was throughout the Land, and the loyal Egyptians living as slaves in the captured cities breathed her name as an amulet. . . .

I looked up at her. She was quite still, her eyes gently closed. Quietly, I read on.

I was five, and Rai had lived four years on earth, when our father and mother told us of Amun-Ra. It was sun-rise, and the season of harvest. The early birds sang, and my mother's garden was bathed in Ra's rising Light. Only the young of us sat around the feet of my father and mother—Kamose, already for a year, had been at battle-play with Neshi and Ebana of El-Kab. I felt close to my father. I wanted to sit on his knee, but he had lifted plump Teti up, and I squatted cross-legged at his feet. Teti was the son of my father's closest Unique Friend, Piopi of Neferusi, whom he so esteemed that he stood God-father to his infant son, bereft of his mother at birth, and took him and his three-year-old sister, Anat-neby, to live with us in the Royal Household. Anat-neby, now seven, and already showing promise of more than ordinary beauty, was lying on her belly beside me, gazing at her own face in the cool, sunny pool water, while Rai and her friend, Sen-ut, sat close together, near to my mother on her stool at my father's feet. Sen-ut, the daughter of a Nobleman murdered in the massacre of Abydos, had been born within an hour of my sister, and since babyhood she had lived in the King's House. They were close as twins. Rai was laughing at the young hoopoe larks that like to be with humans, strutting and tossing their crests, while Sen-ut stretched her hand down to the water to touch the morning-spread petals of the sacred blue lotus flower, and my mother said, "Your hands are perfect as the flower of the lotus," and she leaned forward and took Sen-ut's hand in her own. "My child, such beauty is the Gift of Hat-hor."

Then in the bright stillness my father, gazing away to the

Eastern Hills, unshadowed and unhazed, whispered, "Amun-Ra."

Rai echoed his words. "Amun-Ra."

"The First-born Son of the Nameless One," my father said, "who created heaven and earth and all that is therein." And holding Teti in the crook of his arm, he looked down at my mother.

She smiled at him, then turned to us. "My Little Ones, Amun-Ra made the green herb whereon the cattle live, and the wheat and barley that are the staff of life for men. He gives Life to that which is inside the egg. He made the fish that swim in the River, and the reptiles that crawl. He makes the rats to live in their holes and his life is in the son of the worm, and"—she looked down at Rai—"and in the small birds on every green twig." Then she called softly, "Anat-neby, come, come child, and listen." But Anat-neby, pouting, sat up, curled her legs underneath her and pulled out her small pointed tongue at her brother. My father smiled.

"Listen, children, to my words. Each dawn, Amun-Ra rises in the Eastern Horizon in a boat, called his Atet Boat, and he sails upward across the heavens to the height of his noon-day Fire——"

"And then, Little Ones, he is the Lion! You are used to symbols," my mother said. "And the Lion is the symbol of Ra's Fiery Power, of the Flame that destroys the evil of Set, who is Lord of Darkness."

"And when the noon-day passes?" I asked.

"The God changes boats!" Rai turned to me. "You should know that."

"And what is the name of the boat in which the God sails down to the west?"

"His Sek-tet Boat," Rai answered.

"And each day that dawns . . . Children, it is a miracle!" My mother clasped her hands about her knees and looked up at my father, and, holding Teti close, he said,

"After each night when Amun-Ra steps into his Atet Boat to rise behind the Eastern Hills, the huge Fiend-Reptile,

Apopi, and his foul spawn of monster serpents, bred of darkness, dearth and death, and swollen strong with the evil thoughts and deeds of living men, and the obscene unfulfilled desires of wicked souls, are massed, and in array to slay him." He paused and looked at us, each one. "To slay the Sun-God . . . and thus, to bring Eternal Darkness to the world."

"But till this day"—our mother laughed and held up her arms in praise—"Amun-Ra has been victorious, and with the Utterance of his Word of Power, the God has cast a spell upon the Fiend Apopi, and he and his foul and monstrous spawn have been as fish thrown out of the River onto hot embers and they have been consumed in his Light, as he rises, triumphant, in the east."

"To light the faces of men to a new day," my father added.

"And so you see, Little Ones, how every day is a miracle? And we should live it as though it were our last day on earth. . . ."

"Akh!" My mother's voice startled me. I looked up. She had leaned forward in her chair. "How often I felt that our last day had come! Ahmose, you have not told how our sacred River had become an embalming-place. How the crocodiles sank down into the mud with what they had eaten, for our men went to them of their own accord, and our women wakened to turn their faces to the wall . . . Akh! My Young One, I ask your forgiveness. . . ."

"Mother, while writing this last scroll, your scroll, my thoughts have been as the thousand birds in your garden, alighting where they would, along the paths of our youth and our growing. . . . Your garden-house . . . the green trees and the vine-trellises, the pool . . . it was ever a place of joy and frolic."

Easing a little, with a deep sigh, she sat up straight again. "The words you have written bring memories flocking like homing birds to my heart. . . . Read on, my son."

When my brother, Kamose, had twelve years, and still wore the side-lock of youth, the only older boys in the King's House were the sons of my father's Fan Bearers. Ak-hor was the son of Neshi the Nubian, and the father of Ahmose, my namesake, was Ebana of El-kab. His son was known as Ahmose-Eb, and he and Ak-hor were Kamose's close friends. They were always together, in study, working with the Master Craftsmen, wrestling, learning the use of arms with Neshi and Ebana, mock fighting and playing leap-frog. In our mother's garden, they would stand on each other's shoulders to amuse us, tottering and balancing till they fell away from each other, laughing, while Teti would be chasing Sen-ut around the date-palm trees with his thin switch till she climbed up to the highest branches and gathered the dates and played with the chattering monkeys, and Rai would be jealous because she was the Royal Daughter and must not climb trees lest she fall and bruise her small, perfect body.

"Why should I not climb trees? What matter if I bruise myself? I shall not be Queen. Kamose's eyes are large as Thebes when he looks at Anat-neby, and hers when she looks at my brother. Piopi of Neferusi and my father have agreed, I know, that she will be the Queen. Let Anat-neby take care not to bruise or mar her pale body." Rai would stamp her small foot. "I want to climb trees like Sen-ut."

But for all her tomboy energy, Sen-ut was deep of thought. She had her own small plot to the left front of Queen Ah-hotpe's garden, and my mother taught her to plant bulbs and seeds at the moon's first quarter. Their fragrance filled all the garden and Sen-ut made fine delicate wreaths for us all to wear at the evening meal, and Rai would tease her to make one for Thure, the solemn young son of the Prince of Assiut, who could not see the food on his plate for looking at Sen-ut. Thure lived with his father in a small house on the edge of the King's parkland, and the murder of his mother and the rape of his city by the armies of Apophis, the Hyksos king, clouded the joy of youth in his dark gray eyes, except when he gazed at Sen-ut. But she ran away, blushing, when he came near, and he never played with us. He was between us and Kamose in age. Teti was youngest of all. Though he was a fat little boy, Teti of Neferusi was agile as a monkey and he could juggle four balls at a time. He was a tease, and Rai and Sen-ut would not let him play with their kittens, but my father loved him. He would tell him King Tales and smooth his swollen rump with unguent of flea-bane when the Nile-goose had pecked him and sent him, swift as his plump legs could carry him, to the safety of my father's arms. The King would laugh and chide him that a wise boy adds not to the burden of others with his wild lamenting.

"He goaded the goose! I saw him! Teti flicked his thin switch behind it all around the Animal Court." Anat-eby would point at her brother and pull faces at him, while our mother sat combing and braiding her fine, softly curling brown-black hair. Sometimes Ah-hopte tried to tell the beautiful child of the life in sleep, and of how she could learn to meet Kamose in her dreams, so that their Kas could grow close in spirit against the time when they would rule together in Thebes. But Anat-neby would wriggle and squirm on her stool, and, soon tiring of any pastime, she would push away from the Queen and lie down by the pool and gaze at herself, till we all jumped in, splashing and chasing the butterflies that hovered on the pale blue petals of the sacred lotus. And Teti would follow Sen-ut, who loved to touch the strong petals with the tips of her fingers, and come up behind her and push her down. Then he would grab her hands and hold them, hidden by the lotus flowers, tight-pressed to his groin. Sen-ut would stand up to her waist in the water, pale with anger and shame till he let go of her hands. But when he laughed his high, jolly laugh, all of us, even Rai and I, in our merriment and play, would forget. Sen-ut stayed away from the pool, and soon we young ones were too old for childish games, and we spent whole days in the animal pens with our pet gazelles and our tall, tame crane birds.

As we grew older, we had a Healing Place behind the vine trellis in our mother's garden. She taught us to distill herbs that soothed, and to make healing salves. Rai, when she was seven, could send a small bird, or a hare, or a young gazelle, wolf-mauled, to sleep while Ak-hor stitched the torn flesh with a fine bone needle, or set a broken wing with a strip of wood. Ak-hor the Nubian had tender hands, and Kamose loved all animals. He loved the beauty and grace of them, moving. Bounding antelopes, high-jumping hares and the lions leaping from ledge to ledge in the mountain wadis, but of all the creatures of Amun-Ra he loved best the young horse-animal bred from our grandmother's First Horse, "The Golden Fiery One."

How rapt we were when, after lessons, we came to the garden of our grand-mother, Queen Tetisheri, to sit at her feet and listen to her tales. Curled up like a kitten, tiny and beautiful, she would sit in her big painted chair, while Senseneb, the Old One, fanned her with a large and ancient feather fan. Senseneb! He had been tutor to our mother and father and he taught us all. He had escaped from pillaged Memphis with our grand-mother strapped to his back in a reed basket, and how she loved to tell of it! "Akh! By the Thighs of the Sky Woman!" she would swear, "his back was thin and bony then!" She would wrinkle her small straight nose. "But I was only eight when we escaped, and small for my years by the Grace of Hat-hor, in whose care are virgins." The Old One had brought her, hidden in a honey boat, upriver to Thebes. The small daughter of a Memphian Nobleman was welcomed at the Theban Court, and so loved, as she grew to maidenhood, that she married our grand-father.

True stories our tiny grand-mother told, of our people in the Days of Splendor, three thousand years ago. "Our farmers then," she would say, "when the harvest was garnered and the Nile flooded our fields, would turn with joyful hearts to building in stone for the God. Singing hymns in his praise as they mined gold for his shrines, in the Eastern

Hills, and the granite for his statues in the quarries of Elephantine . . . And when the day's work was ended, after the Evening Rite, they would eat their fill of antelope and hare, baked on spits, while the children, laughing and tasting and burning their fingers, turned the spit handles. There were honey-cakes and barley beer!"—her eyes would shine and she would make a small noise of relish with her lips—"and they were paid for their work of worship and Ka-health in cattle and goats and seed, while they waited for the Perit season, the spring and the River's ebbing, and the rich black earth, to go back to their fields, and their sowing. . . . In those days," Tetisheri said, and her high sweet voice was a low quiet sigh, "the King in Thebes wore the Double Crown; the Red for the North, and the White for the South Land, and the Two Lands were One, and free." Her small face would glow with an ancient pride, till she told again of the Hyksos tyrants, sly-encroaching when they need not fight, rapacious and deadly cruel, and she would look down at my brother, pull his side-lock and say, "You have my blood, Kamose, my Young Warrior, and a belly hard toward battle. You will free the Beloved Land from the tyrants in the North." She would look at him with pride and love, but Kamose would be smiling and gazing at Anat-neby as she played with the jeweled bracelets on her dimpled arms.

Since first she came at the age of three to live in our House, Kamose had played with her, giving her the bright beads and small colored balls that brought merry gurgling laughter to her baby mouth, and when he was twelve, and Anat-neby eight, it seemed that his play had burgeoned into a boy's adoration. Her skin was pale as ivory and her eyes shone black as a raven's wing. Her long lashes made shadows on her cheeks, and the blood would come with a rush to Kamose's face when she came near to him, or happened to touch him, and though she was not of Royal blood, and Rai was the Royal Daughter, as we grew older it seemed to be known and accepted that Anat-neby would be Kamose's bride: Wearer of the Beautiful White crown, Royal Wife and Queen.

My sister, who had no desire to be Queen, would turn laughing green eyes to me when Anat-neby, restless and having no patience with Tetisheri's stories, would pick the tiny jeweled flowers out of our grand-mother's wig, till our half-sister, Nefertari, who was twelve, and but four months younger than Kamose, would chide her,

"Anat-neby, be still. You are only eight." But always Nefertari smiled when she spoke.

She was our father's one natural child. Her mother, a concubine with both Egyptian and Nubian blood, had died in childbirth. Tetisheri had taken the infant girl and her old Nubian nurse to live in her own apartments, and from that day our grand-mother had doted upon her. Nefertari's skin was as polished bronze. Her eyes were long and dark, almost black, the whites of them pale blue and clear. "She has afrits' eyes," Rai once said, and I chided her. The afrits are malicious spirits who live inside our mountains. Then Rai had said, "But a very beautiful afrit," and she laughed.

Except when we gathered around Tetisheri, for all Nefertari's bronze beauty we rarely saw her, and in truth we seemed to forget her. And Thuty! Somehow we thought of them together. They both lived with our grand-mother and shared tutors. Thuty was our natural uncle, though only nine years older than Kamose. He was tall as his half-brother, our father, but his eyes were close-set and his nose was long, and he had the ambition that is stronger than pride.

"He has the small, clear-sly eyes of the hippopotamus," Rai once said. "He is viper-cold, and keeps his sting hidden." I had learned not to chide Rai when she saw to the inside of people. She spoke the truth, without malice.

"Thuty's eyes are not viper-cold when he looks at Nefertari," I had replied. "And he showers her with gifts."

Although Nefertari's stool was always closest to our grandmother's, it was Teti of Neferusi who urged Tetisheri to talk of the tyrants. He would lean toward her, put his plump hand on her fine-pleated skirt and ask for the tale we all knew was closest to her heart.

"Queen Mother, tell us again of Khian, who was king of the Hyksos when you were Queen in Thebes."

"Khian!" She would sit up straight and taut. "Khian! He dared to come himself to Thebes! It pleased him to travel in state through the Two Lands, the nosy carrion hyena! And with a hundred larded curs as retinue." She had burned incense for seven days in the rooms he had used, the hated Hyksos king, and doubly hated guest, and Miuti, High Priest and Chief of Visions, had purified every place where they had been with water from the Sacred Lake. "Wily and cunning as a desert dog, he was, and he dared to use the ancient manner of our greeting and to pose as an Egyptian. Akh! The grandeur of him, that clothed his cruel and crafty rapings, and his teeth were big and yellow!" She shuddered. Then she would draw up her slender body. "But I was Queen in Thebes, and must behave with grace. Akh! Always he would whisper in my ear. Akh! That evil-smelling beard!"

He had left the Theban Court at last, with long and flowery messages, and a gift for the Queen his ravening hoards had driven from Memphis, her childhood home: the gift of a young, wild golden-colored horse.

"He was the first horse-animal I had ever seen! I loved him. How I loved him." She would clasp her hands close to her breast and shake the hundred tight curls in her wig, so that the tiny jeweled flowers would glint like stars. Then her face would change as a desert shadow. "Though Memphis fell to beasts like him, with chariots. Our Foot-soldiers and our Archers with their long, old-fashioned bows, they were helpless before the onslaught."

"Tell us how you tamed the wild young beast," Teti would urge, "and of Tui, who became Master of the Royal stables."

"And still is! And still trains our young horses. What

courage and patience he had! Tui is brother to all animals."

Together they had tamed the beautiful horse, and a stable had been built for him near Tetisheri's garden. She named him her Golden Fiery One.

But the Hyksos king, for all his flowery messages and his gift, had, when the harvest burgeoned once again, sent his tax collectors led by Hur the Cruel, and his soldiers, armed with their deadly double bows, to ravage and to kill if tribute were not paid in time and to the full.

"Memphis was tribute enough!" Tetisheri's voice would harden and the knuckles of her small hands clench whiter than the pleated linen of her kilt. "Our Memphis men were killed in sleep, their throats slit in the beds, and while their blood ran warm, our women . . ."

"Tell us, Queen Mother, how you stole the she-horse from the Hyksos camp?" Teti of Neferusi knew how to melt my grand-mother to merriment again. "My little ball of castor-wax," she called him, and she would laugh with him and raise her hands into the air. "Akh! The she-horse! Khian never knew! The King, my husband, never knew! None of them ever knew! By the Eater of Shades! How I enjoyed that foray."

"You waited for the harvest . . ." Kamose would prompt.

"A grain-ship . . ." Rai would smile at me.

"A grain-ship heaped with corn stoops . . ."

"But with a hollow place . . ."

"Large enough for a she-horse . . ." We all abetted her, till she held up her hand for silence.

"We pulled out from shore under a full moon. The King, your grand-father, was closeted with his counselors. Their hours were heavy with affairs of state, for the River had been low that year and the stock of barley and corn, after tribute, was scarce enough for a third of our people. That year we were eating the flesh of the pig, and we made bread from the roots of water plants that we gathered in the swamps and grew in our garden pools. Akh! How we saved and planned! And how it pleasured me to hoodwink them! The scabrous, stinking scavengers!"

She had dressed in the long black robe of a village woman, and she boarded the ship with Tui, five trusted sailors from the Royal Yacht and seven of the animal keepers who had joined the rowers. They had all donned false beards and put on wigs of greasy curling hair,

"So that they looked as those Egyptians who had taken to Hyksos ways, the renegade traitors!"

Rowing with the current they had come to the land held by the enemy, and had crept ashore to the camp where the chariots were housed and the horses stabled, a few miles to the north of Kus. "There were many more than we suspected." Our grand-mother's eyes would open wide, then she would shrug. "But I was left on board with five stout sailormen to keep watch over me."

Appearing as traitor Egyptians, Tui and his companions were doubly welcomed when they shared their barley-beer and the drugged wine they had brought with them. For a while all in the camp made merry. But soon the Hyksos were fast asleep and snoring. With a cake of poppy-seed to quiet her, they had lured away the first she-horse they saw, and had stolen her!

"And no one ever told, and no one in the King's House ever asked how, one day, there was a she-horse in the stable with my Golden Fiery One." Tetisheri's eyes were wide and innocent. "She gave no trouble on the homeward voyage." She looked at Kamose, then at Rai and me. "Your father and mother, when they were your age, would sit together on her back, and she would carry them."

"Were they not too heavy?" Kamose once asked her.

"They were very thin children. There was not much food." Then she laughed. "But my Fiery One! He kicked out his back legs, then stood up on them, and he would not have any thing, nor any being, on his back. How he amused your grand-father!"

"He might have carried them had he been trained," Kamose said. Almost fourteen, though he still wore the sidelock of youth his young mind was keen and reckoning.

But we all jeered at him, and Anat-neby pulled his sidelock, laughing.

"What need of sitting on a horse?" Tetisheri smiled. "We have many chariots," she added softly.

"And we shall have more, and more—and more!" Kamose said, pulling Anat-neby's shining hair so that she begged for mercy, and he promised a gift, while Teti asked, "How many horses have we bred?"

And his sister whipped around and, teasing, said, "Hot mouth with all your questions!"

"If you use your little dagger tongue so many times, Sister, its point will blunt."

"But we must have more than a hundred horses now?" Teti was a stubborn little boy, and full of curiosity.

"Teti-poke-his-nose," Rai called him. "Someday a crocodile will bite it off."

Then Anat-neby would jump to her brother's defense and call Rai "Prickle-tongue!"

And Grand-mother would raise a hennaed fingertip to her pursed lips, look at us with gay conspiracy and say, "Children! You know the number of our horses is a secret."

"Secrets! I love secrets," Anat-neby lisped. Her small mouth was red as a full-blown poppy. "Teti, come on! Let's make up a secret." She would be turning to her brother, but beneath her long black lashes her coy gaze would be for Kamose, who in his fourteenth year could pierce a dom-palm leaf from the farthest arrow-flight away, and fight Ak-hor and Ahmose-Eb together and win, with wooden sword or hand-ax.

"The Young Lion," Senseneb, the Old One, called him, and often he complained, as Kamose grew toward manhood, of his pupil's rages and desires.

"Akh! Let him be." My mother used to shake her head, and laugh.

"There is yet time, Senseneb." Our father smiled at the Old One's fears.

But when Kamose grew to manhood, and was shaven of his side-lock, the Old One was beside himself with worry.

"Since he wears the loin-cloth, the Prince has lost no time! Wine-bibbing in the taverns with Ak-hor, and whoring in the villages. Risking his life in the Eastern Desert hunting the mountain lions." The old tutor was like a dog with a bone. "Kamose forgets that he will be King."

"By the Disc! Let him be! My son is lashed by the thongs of his destiny to the chariot of the South Land. He will find wisdom."

Ah-hotpe agreed with her husband. "At the acceptable time, the Fire of Ra will descend upon him. Have patience, Senseneb."

"I have more need of it than ever, my Queen." The Old One made a melancholy face, but his shrewd black eyes shone young, for with Kamose's manhood, his class had grown. Six youths, chosen for their salient traits and carefully nurtured, by Miutu, High Priest and Chief of Visions, and Kheri-heb, Master of Wisdom, had been summoned, on the day my brother put on his loincloth, to live with us in the King's Household. They joined in our battle-play with Neshi and Ebana, to become, each according to his bent and prowess, Captains in the South Land's fight for freedom. They shared our studies with the Old One, grew ever closer to us and came to be called Kamose's Company.

"I see them all!" My mother rose with the words and came to sit on the edge of the table. "And memories crowd my heart to bursting. . . . I loved them all. Thure! Quiet Thure from Assiut, who had loved Sen-ut since childhood, he was the first one chosen." I nodded. "Then the Twins, Mer-neb and Per-neb, my nephews from Edfu, and Pen-aati's grandson, Tetaky, our poet. . . . They were all as sons to me. Penekheb, who loved to work with wood . . . and Aknere, thin and of few words. Akh! How Senseneb rejoiced in his new larger class! The Old One who looked so frail and was so strong."

"He would not wear a wig." I smiled. "His thin, straight hair fell over his eyes when he leaned to scan our work. . . . He was a merry teacher, Senseneb. He could explain the hard things in the ancient writings as though he had written them himself. He showed us how the sound of words, and their position in a script, gave them double and triple meanings—I have written of this. . . ."

"Ahmose, I feel young again. . . . The old Court of Learning. . . . Akh! . . . those age-old, torn, ragged scrolls . . . but read on. . . ."

When we studied an ancient papyrus for the first time, the Old One would say, "Write out the lines that appeal to you most." Then he would leave us to study and think and write. Later, with laughter and quips and talk, we would read aloud to him what we had written, and grow in our knowing of each other and of ourselves.

"You, Tetaky? What have you in that fine script of yours?"

Frail Tetaky, our poet, whose lips foamed when he fought, whose smaller weapons had to be made for him alone, would blink his eyes. "'None is impetuous who practices excellence.'" He had the wit to laugh at himself, and none knew better than he how hard he worked and sweat for his prowess at arms.

"And you, Per-neb?"

The twin brother of Mer-neb thought before he acted. He had written, "'Do not join in wrangling with a hot mouth!'" And he looked at his brother as he read it aloud, for Mer-neb spoke and acted quickly, perceptively.

"They are as like as two beans to see, unlike as cat and dog to know," Kamose once said to me. "Except in courage! When it comes to the use of battle weapons, Mer-neb loves his new double bow as a man loves his woman, and Per-neb is a god with shield, long sword and javelin. And Penekheb —Pen—he is my chariot man."

Tall Pen, son of a Southern Nobleman, was as skilled in letters as he was in arms. He had not written anything, though he had read the ancient script. He looked up and said, "If a tree is cut after the sap has ceased to rise in it— then the fibers will be dead, and the wood will deform with heat, or time. When I work with wood, I feel the life in it."

"And I see the form," Aknere said. "The true proportions that give stability and beauty."

Aknere, cool-eyed and angry for the right, was grand-son to Pery-em-wah, who had been, since my father was a boy, the Chief of our Eyes and Ears in Secret. The chief spy had reason to be proud of his grand-son. Aknere was a true scholar, thin and wiry and contained, and since early youth he had trained to follow in his grand-father's secret and perilous work.

Ahmose-Eb was always hungry, and of great appetite. With his tongue in his cheek and a wry glance, he read out his words: " 'It is the eater who tastes.' "

"And the dreamer who dreams." Thure had not written down one word. His mind was swift and sure, his memory a scroll spread out in front of him, even in dream. Thure cried out his hidden terrors in his sleep. "But," my brother had said from the first, "I would have Thure at my left hand in every battle." Since childhood, Sen-ut had been his lode-star, and Thure said that when he wakened, sweating and shaken with terror, from the nightmares that ever plagued him, he would think of her hands, like flowers, and be at peace, and cool again. Sen-ut, with girlhood, had lost her child-shyness, and after lessons she and Thure would walk hand in hand in the parklands. He would help her to plant the bulbs, to weed and care for her garden. Then they would sit under Hat-hor's sycamore tree and hold hands again.

The girls, Rai, Sen-ut and Anat-neby, were often quicker than we to learn, and each year Anat-neby grew more beautiful, and Kamose more desiring. On the day of his manhood he led her to the Throne Chair, and the King, happily, gave consent to their betrothal. I remember the jewels she wore, and my father's simple pleasure in them.

"Befitting a maiden who will be bride of Kamose, the Hawk Prince," Piopi of Neferusi said, and looked on his girl-child with fatherly pride.

And on a day, in his house, he told us that even in Avaris, the Hyksos capital, Anat-neby's beauty was renowned, and he laughed. "Hur the Cruel One has brought, along with our tribute, the knowledge of her loveliness to ·the tyrant Apophis."

"How know you this?" our father asked.

"From Pery-em-wah, who else?"

"Who else, indeed." My father joined in the laughter as Piopi poured out more of the good North Land wine.

"From the Dwellers in the Desert," he explained. "They bring us, for a price, the sweet Delta wines."

"It seems my subjects have more riches than their King." My father often teased his life-long friend. . . .

I looked up at my mother. She was nodding her head slowly, and her eyes were wet with unshed tears. Without speaking, she went back to her chair, sat down and waited for me to read again.

My thirteenth year was a brooding year. All through the green months my father was sad, and my mother's eyes were shadowed. They had not sailed together, drifting with the current, or strolled, when Council hours were over, in the green canal-watered parks of our home, among the animals they loved, their tame antelopes and long-horned cattle. Nor stayed to drink a cup of wine with Thure's father, who never left his small park house. The King, in those days, stayed in secret Council with Miutu and Pen-aati, Neshi and Ebana, till the hour of the evening meal.

When my mother did not join them in their planning and

inquiry, I walked with her in her garden, and on an evening when the corn was golden ripe, she said, "Ahmose, your father has turned his face toward battle." I stood still, staring at her in unbelief. "He has not yet secured his heart in this, but we have disturbing news from Pery-em-wah."

"Since my childhood we have had such news from the Chief of our Eyes and Ears in Secret."

"My Young One, this last year, having lived so long at the Court of Avaris, posing as a traitor to us, he has, at last, become Sole Friend of It-yu, Apophis' Chief Scribe. . . ."

"I know of him . . . a servile man, arch-flatterer. . . ."

"And confidant of the usurper king in Avaris. It is a chance sent by the Gods. . . . But Ahmose, my heart fears for Pery-em-wah."

"What is the news he sends?"

As we walked on again, she sighed. "Pery-em-wah's Eyes and Ears in Secret have come upon a thousand chariots, battle-ready, in a rocky cleft across the river from Kus."

"Then they would now take the city of Kus away from us?"

"And we are not yet prepared to fight."

"Nor ever will be! For all their guilt, my Mother, we shall be the guiltier if we turn to slaying."

This time my mother stood. She put her hand on my shoulder. "My Young One, you will not fight. Though you are tall, you are but thirteen. Kamose is seventeen, strong beyond normal men, and skilled in the use of arms—yet he will only watch this battle. He will not be in the forefront— your father will lead our hosts. My Moon Child, Pery-em-wah has heard from It-yu that when our harvest is safely un-laded in the North Land ports, Apophis will send an envoy with a gift, and a message to your father, of such deep insult that no Theban wit could answer it—they mean to goad us into fighting. Ahmose, your father may come to the place beyond which honor will not bide."

And when, to the last grain, the harvest was laded onto the waiting ships, and Hur the Cruel One and his locust crew had sailed with their booty to the North Land, Pery-em-wah's dire and secret message was brutally fulfilled. The Hyksos envoy and his minions, in their rattling chariots, cracking their whips and shouting, clattered across the Courtyard to the door of the King's House.

My father granted a Royal Audience, and full. In front of the Thirty Great Ones of the South Land, the Nobles and the exiled Princes, he received Mayebre the Libyan. With the merest pretense of a bow, the strutting foreigner dared to stand with his foot on the Royal Dais, and, stroking his curled and oily beard, he said in a loud, harsh voice,

"Your hippopotamus pool! Destroy it! For their bellowing fills the ears of all in Avaris, and keeps the king, Apophis, awake both day and night."

A dog barked. It was the only sound. Standing behind my father's Throne Chair between Neshi and Ebana, I shuddered. They had used with ridicule and foul intent the sacred myth of Horus, Hawk Son of the South Land. The huge, dark hippopotamus was a form that Set, the Lord of Darkness, took upon himself, and in our sacred Ritual, Horus the Hawk Prince, on the day before he is crowned, must entangle the feet of the great Set-beast in a golden chain, then thrust his huge, dark body through with the Spear of Light. And Apophis' message! The Dark Power of Set is so strong in Thebes that the roaring of his beasts can be heard five hundred miles away!

And Kamose? Horus-Son of the South Land? Tall and golden-skinned he stood, the Fisherman's Circlet about his wig, the silver Hawk Belt around his waist, disinterested. The Hyksos envoy's thought of him was in his crass presuming stare. "Whoring, wild young stripling! What menace he to the Set power of the North Land?" The Libyan's face was an open sneer at my brother.

Then I heard my father say, "We must arrange that the king in Avaris sleeps soundly well both day and night," and he would have ended the audience, but Mayebre the Libyan stood, both feet now planted firmly on the ground and wide apart, and raised his hands and clapped them! Loud! Clapped his jewel-bedecked fat hands before the Theban Throne!

My father was still as his own Ka statue. Kamose was looking past the pillars of the Court out to the gardens. He seemed bored. Neshi and Ebana had ceased the movement of their fans and held them, still as rocks, above my father's head. Of the Great Ones and the Princes there, not one man moved or raised his eyes. Only the summoned minion, his sandals flapping loose from swarthy heels, made sound in all the Court of Audience.

Slowly, with an arrogance equal to his master's, he swaggered toward the Royal Dais. He held a rich-embroidered cushion bound with golden threads. Red tassels hung from it, swinging to his gait. He held it high and forward in his outstretched arms.

The Libyan took the ingot from the cushion, held it in his hand and looked at it with lewd and smiling gaze. My father's eyes were away from thought, quiet as the still heart of Amun-Ra. Kamose touched the Hawk clasp on his belt, then scratched his neck with a gesture of irritation, still gazing out to the gardens. I was surprised, ashamed of him. I should have better known my brother, and been ashamed myself, that I allowed my gaze to rest upon the golden thing.

It was twice as big as a warrior's hand, and carved on it, in crude and clear relief, was a lion with a human head. I rolled my tongue back into my throat, as I had been taught to do when the calm of a Royal Son must not be broken, for the head of the lion had a curling beard and wore the the likeness of Apophis, the Hyksos king, and in his tearing claws he held the maimed and mangled body of a tall Egyptian, and the face was the face of Seken-en-Ra II, my father.

Mayebre the Libyan took the loathsome thing and held it up for all to see, and then, amid the stricken murmurings, he gave it to his minion to lay at my father's feet, turned his back to the Throne and raised his voice to echo against the Theban Hills.

"Apophis-Ra, king in Avaris, the Northern City! Living Image of Ra on earth! Lord of the Two Lands! Life, Stability, and Health, Apophis! Living Son of Ra since the Day of Creation!" He shouted the blasphemy before the Throne Chair of the true King.

With a scorn to flay the soul, my father ended the Audience.

The Hyksos messengers had been well housed and fed, and while their barbarian needs were satisfied, my father went alone to the wall-room beside the Inner Shrine of the God and stayed there, in the Holy of Holies.

At noon-day he returned to preside at the Council, judge the petitions brought before him and make due showing of his person on the Balcony of Appearances. After performing his manifold duties he came, in the saffron quiet of Ra's descending Light, to Ah-hotpe's garden. Limp and weary, he sank into his chair and stretched out his long legs by the pool.

Scarlet-and-yellow lilies were closing with the day, but the clear blue petals of the sacred lotus were still open, wide and pointed, as I dipped the shallow alabaster washing bowl into the pool and filled it with the sweet Nile water.

My mother brought her stool and sat down close to her husband, her head against his lean thigh, and as I untied his sandals, he stroked her hair. His eyes were cool and held authority. Even our tiny grand-mother did not speak, but sat in her chair under the acacias at the other side of the pool while Senseneb fanned her quietly. A male hoopoe-lark, red as rusted iron against the yellow flowers of the acacia trees, opened his beak and called, then flew to perch on my father's shoulder and peck his ear.

Rai was lying on a reed mat, trying to catch the small red-darting fishes and laughing as they slipped through her slender fingers. "Rai, I am the pool in which your hand has dipped. . . ." She felt my gaze and turned to smile at me.

Kamose was sitting on his haunches pulling the ears of his lioness cub, Sek-met. She was his grand-mother's gift to him on the day of his manhood. "May she bring the strength of Ra's noon-day Fire to your spirit, and her own strength to you in battle," she said, as she placed the two-months-old cub in his arms.

"And may she guard your sleeping body when your Ka is away in dream," Rai said, and he had lifted her up and kissed her nose to nose.

Kamose was chewing on a reed. "They think me a whoring, reckless princeling," he said through his teeth. "And that is well! Let us nurture this thought in their Set-darkened hearts."

When my father's feet were washed, I put the bowl aside. He did not move, but looked up and said,

"How is it with the Beloved Land when the plowman must go to the field with his shield upon his arm?"

"The Hyksos swine!" Kamose's ready anger flared. "They seep in as thieves, without noise, and are there."

"Without noise? Their hairy messenger was loud enough!" Senseneb's voice was clear and young for all his years.

"That harsh and strident sound, I hear it still," my father said with quiet distaste.

"The filthy Libyan!" Kamose swung around, with crossed legs, on his haunches. "Screaming his nonsense through his larded beard."

"Dung-fed crocodile with crooked jaws!" Our grand-mother hissed, and Kamose laughed at her. Then he told her what he and his Company had been doing since the Audience.

"While the greasy sons of unwed mothers were slaking their thirst and carousing, we probed the armor of their chariots—Pen, Ahmose-Eb, and the Royal Carpenter, three artisans in metals and I! Ak-hor and the others kept watch about the King's House, and around the chariot sheds." He turned to our father. "Their wheel rims are made of Lebanon pine, and the wheel spokes bound with birch straps, and the pole!—Pen was full of envy—it was made of elm wood."

"And why not?" the King asked. "The strong woods of Syria and Lebanon are theirs for the taking."

"May the Breath of the Serpent blast their evil eyes!" Tetisheri's merry voice was low and hard on the still air and Kamose turned to her again.

"Pen made a discovery! 'Should not this part,' he said, patting the front of the Libyan's chariot, 'cover the thighs of the Bow-man? Should it not be higher?' 'Ra-en-Ra!' I answered. 'And covered with cow-hide, seven layers thick, and oiled!' And we all laughed together. Their workmanship was shoddy, for all their fine wood and metals. . . . Father, we learned nothing we cannot improve upon, and our native woods, well-worked, will have the strength we need!"

"By the Great Strider!" our grand-mother said. "When do we fight?"

My father looked up with a faint smile for his mother, and Senseneb, fanning her quietly, said,

"In the North Land, even among those who pander to the tyrants, brother spies on brother, sons on their mothers, and no man has a friend, for one sits in a corner and turns his head while another is killed."

"And yet with vile apings they make to be Egyptians." Tetisheri was quieter but her lips were tight and thin. "Khian did, when I was Queen, and now! This foul Apophis! Living Image of Ra on earth . . . How dare he!" Her voice dropped to an unbelieving whisper.

"Apophis . . . Mayebre the Libyan . . . and Hur." Kamose spoke the loathed names slowly and with cold anger. "When I have had my way with them, then let the desert hyenas eat their stinking flesh." He pulled the lioness' ear. She nuzzled him. He looked up. "But Father, we are not yet prepared to fight. We need more horses . . . more of their double bows . . . Ak-hor and his Nubian Scouts have more raids planned, and——Tetaky! Ra-en-Ra?"

Tetaky came running into the garden and knelt at my father's feet.

"My King! Piopi of Neferusi . . . and Teti . . ." He stood

up and looked around at us all, his eyes wide. "They have rowed with such haste upriver from Neferusi that four of their sailors have burst their hearts while their hands still clung to the oars."

"Piopi!" My father stood up as his Unique Friend came, stumbling, his hands to his face. "Piopi?" My father embraced him, and took him to a chair near Ah-hotpe's stool. Piopi sat down and covered his face with his hands. "Speak, Friend! What brings you here in such desperate haste? The insult to the South Land? You have heard?"

"Worse . . . worse!"

Teti was weeping openly. "My sister! My sister!" He flung himself down on his belly.

"Anat-neby!" Kamose leapt up as a sand viper, his face pale as marble.

Piopi groaned and swayed from side to side in his chair. "A virgin sacrifice . . ." He raised his head. "To save our city, Neferusi, from the Hyksos . . . Kidnapped!"

"A virgin sacrifice!" Teti was rolling on the ground in his wrath and grief.

"Anat-neby is taken hostage?" Ah-hotpe asked.

"Hostage? Sacrifice, I say! Apophis desired her. . . ." Piopi's voice was hoarse with strangled weeping. "She is aboard a Hyksos ship, captured by the soldiers of Apophis' Body Guard."

Kamose had not spoken. He looked huge standing there. His eyes were cold and hard as malachite.

"When? How?" my father asked.

"Last night . . . they stole her from my house in Neferusi . . . came upon her while she slept . . . Akh! That I should live . . ."

"How wide-seeking are the Hyksos spies," my mother said, "when the betrothed of the Hawk Prince can be so abducted."

"And Neferusi's walls are strong," Rai whispered to me, but Teti heard her words.

"Not strong enough! My sister, my beautiful sister." He was on his knees, wringing his hands.

"I will cut them to pieces." Kamose's lips scarce moved. The King stood looking at his son. His eyes were calm. "There is no safety in all Egypt. This black-souled Apophis——"

"At last! We fight! Ra-en-Ra! We fight!" Tetisheri came running around the pool to stand between her son and her grand-son, her small body taut with an ancient rage.

"By the Flaming Disc!" Kamose threw back his head. His eyes blazed. "We fight!"

I looked up at him, towering above us, from the reed mat where I sat with Rai, and I heard my sister's loving murmur,

"Our brother is Hawk of the South Land."

"And it is war," I said, still watching him.

"We will cut them to pieces, my Father! Throw them to the Flames where their limbs will never come together." He spoke the dire curse softly, but he took the dagger from his arm-sling and flung it, a streak of bronze-gold fury, at one of the acacia trees. It missed the back of Tetisheri's chair, struck and drove deep at the joint of branch and trunk. The big branch sagged.

"Kamose, my Son," the King said, "do not hate. To fight with hatred is to lose the strength of Ra."

And our mother ended the ancient saying: "To fight with hatred is to turn away your face from the Fortress of the Ways of Horus." Ah-hotpe looked on her older son with love, and would have spoken further, but his grand-mother swung around on her heel to face him.

"Nourish your hatred, Grand-son!" Her gray eyes were bright and cold. "Nourish it well! Let it burnish your shield, and be the death-thrust of your dagger in their bowels."

Piopi rose and embraced my father. "Neferusi is strong," he said, and my father, returning his embrace with all his heart, replied, "My Friend, Neferusi is the hope and bulwark of the South Land."

"My little daughter . . . my virgin child . . ." Piopi bent his head. His tears flowed. "Neferusi still stands . . . Anat-neby . . ."

Silence fell. I walked slowly around the pool and wrenched the dagger from the tree. The fallen branch was bright with yellow flowers. "Osiris, Lord of the Acacia Tree," I prayed, "bathe my brother's heart in the waters of thy peace." I pulled the flowers one by one from the broken branch and looked across the pool at Rai.

With the flowers in my left hand and the dagger in my right, I went back around the pool.

"Give it to me, Little Brother." Kamose embraced me swiftly. "It looks strange in your hand, Ahmose," he said, and slipped the dagger back into his arm sheath.

The King took his wife's hand and held it in his own. Then he looked at us and said, "Damaged indeed are the good things. The Two Lands are prostrate. Our store-houses are stripped bare, and the cattle of Ra are branded as they graze in the Temple fields. The Builders of the Everlasting Hills are vassals and slaves. But all these things we, and our fore-fathers, have known." For a moment, he held Ah-hotpe's hand to his cheek. Then he stood up, naked except for his loin-cloth and the Royal Cobra on his brow, and said, "They have blasphemed. And with their blasphemies they have let loose those Fiends of Darkness who strike at the Ka of a man and possess his soul, as their war-lords have possessed the Two Lands." His voice was deep and clear.

"My Lord." Ah-hotpe rose from her stool. "Were the massacre at Abydos and the accursed and brutal ingot not enough, they have desecrated our Holy Altars with the black ritual . . . and now, they have ravished the King's Household. My Lord, this is an honorable field."

He drew her arm through his and held her hand. They stood tall together gazing into the fiery radiance of Ra's last Light, and their eyes were cool as the wind from the North. In the silence, my father said, "The darkness of Set has drawn too close to the Shrine of the God."

I looked up at my mother. Her tears were falling now. She clasped her hands under her chin. "That day your father stood wide of gait." I rose and went around the long wide table. "Ahmose, it was an honorable field." I took her hands and held them for a long while in my own. Then she said, "Pour for me a cup of honeyed milk—and for yourself." I went to the platter left on the small table each morning by Neme, who had looked to my brother and me since childhood, and poured out two cups. Then I sat in the chair that had once been Pen-aati's. My mother drank slowly, gazing the while at the parchment spread out on the Council table. She smiled through her not sad tears, and said, "Kamose's Royal rage! How it fired the hearts of the Thebans! With the speed of a bird flock they gathered as one, one-pointed toward victory and the rescue of their Prince's betrothed."

"Within a moon's span they were marching, ten thousand strong, to Kus."

"Akh! Those long days and nights of waiting. . . ." Her mood changed. Joy shone through her tears. "Ahmose—tomorrow . . ."

"Before tomorrow, there is tonight, and Kheri-heb! Osiris grant that the work is acceptable to him."

"By Thoth, from whom come all words that are." My mother laughed. "I have learned to know the false words from the true. Kheri-heb will rejoice in the fruits of the work he set in front of you." She held up her hand with the palm toward me in love and blessing. "Tomorrow, cleansed and hairless, clad in new loin-cloth woven by my own hands, and new-made sandals anointed with myrrh and blessed, I shall lead you to Kheri-heb, and he, at last, will lead you to your Place of Initiation."

"Akh! My Mother, am I ready for that vault? For the Tomb Chamber beneath the Inmost Shrine! My Ka shudders. Should I fail . . ."

"In the Place of the Silence, my Moon Child, you will meet all that you are—face to face. You will fight with your naked will. Lock up your Heart-case. Be not distracted. The Essence of all things is One." She rose in tall beauty, High Priestess and Queen, and I, too, stood.

After a moment she went to the small table, put her empty cup on it and held out her hand for mine. We walked across the flagstones to the hidden door. She put out her hand to press the place on the wall that no eye could discern, then paused. "Ahmose, you have not told how, since you were seven, your brother would leave Ak-hor and Ahmose-Eb and his battle-play, to ride with you, alone, sometimes for three days and three nights, into the Eastern Desert."

"It had no bearing on the story." I turned my head toward the scrolls on the table. Then I sighed, remembering. "He would take me along the paths our ancestors trod, three thousand years ago, through the wadis to mine gold and quartz stone . . . and they left drawings! And writing on the face of the rocks that we scrambled over . . . on foot! Kamose let our donkeys loose to be serviced by the strong wild asses . . . and, my Mother, a King, two thousand years before, had written: 'I gave a leather bottle, a carrying pole, two jars of water and twenty loaves of bread to each man every day. . . .'"

"Your memory, my Young One, it is the God's gift."

"And the reason Kheri-heb put this scribe's work upon me. Mother, imagine, the bakers! Sixty thousand loaves of bread each day . . ."

"Those were the Days of Splendor," she said.

"And my days in the desert with my brother were golden days . . . and all too few."

She smiled, and now she pressed the hidden place and the drop-stone door slid open with soft sound. She put her arms about my neck and we stood for a moment, cheek to cheek. Then, drawing away from me, she said, "What have you called the tenth scroll, that is first, and is mine?"

"I have not named it—nor any. They are numbered."

"Even though they will be sealed away for a thousand years, and perchance forever?"

I laughed and kissed her. "There is space. I shall, before moon-rise, inscribe: 'This scroll, with the love of the children she bore, and loved, is for Ah-hotpe, Wearer of the Beautiful

White Crown, Royal Daughter, High Priestess and Queen, Beloved Wife of Seken-en-Ra II, the Brave."

"My Moon Child, that is pleasing to me," she whispered, and, laughing a little, she was gone.

I pressed the place on the wall. The door slid down, and I came slowly back to my chair. I picked up the least stunted of all the rush pens I had used through these months of writing, and inscribed the words I had promised. I looked at the scroll and leaned back in my chair, thinking of my mother. "The Essence of all things is One." I looked at Osiris, obsidian-bright in the torch light. "Osiris, God and King, mutilated Lord, who is born again in all living creatures, that they may know regeneration, and resurrection with him . . . Osiris Lord, help me . . . Give me strength in my soul trials tomorrow . . . Lord, grant that this, my work, is found to be good in the eyes of Kheri-heb."

Since boyhood I have longed to be as Kheri-heb. To have the Opened Eye, to wear the Shoulder Scarf of Wisdom, and to know, as he, the meaning of the sacred words inscribed in the Scroll of Utterances it is his sole right to carry.

My thoughts full of my beloved Teacher, slowly I rolled up the parchment in front of me. Double-pressed to endure, it crackled in the silence like small drums. I glued it, tightly tied it and went to the niches in the wall. As I put it in the first smooth socket, Kheri-heb was in the chamber, and although he was at the end of a long fast, his body and step were lithe as he made deep obeisance before Osiris and left the bright armful of flowers that he carried on the floor at the foot of the wall shrine. Then he turned and came toward me.

"Ahmose, my son. It is the night." His eyes were clear and joyful. I walked to him, and, with the courtesy that seemed to flow from him as a fresh spring in the wadis, he put his right hand on my brow, and his left hand on my heart. I looked into his fine-boned, fine-skinned face, unchanging through all the storms and assailings of our lives, immutable, grave and tender.

Without seeming to move, he stood by the table looking down at the nine scrolls. "You have done well, my son—and I see one, tight-rolled, in its niche—you have ten scrolls."

"Nine, my Master, as you commanded. The tenth is the first—and is for my mother. It tells of our childhood and has bearing on the story."

"You have given as the gods give, Ahmose, more than is asked for—full measure and running over." Sitting down in the chair set for him since my father's day, he said, "Bring me a half-cup of honeyed milk if you will, and a small bunch of grapes."

As, in silence, we broke our fast, each sparely, I was lost in looking at him. Initiate and Sage, aloof yet full of grace, he had loved me all my life. Yet I knew that others came to him with open longing for the Knowing, and they felt, each one, the self-same surety of being loved. There is a state of love on earth that goes beyond earthly love. A companionship, calm, serene and ever-fresh, yet stable and strong as the pylons and Temples that are built to the ancient canon of measures to last for a million years.

Kheri-heb, his light meal ended, looked again at the scrolls. "Nine, for the nine gods . . . then Silence and the consecration of this underground Council Chamber, the place of manifold secrets and now, to house, perhaps for all time, these secret parchments sealed away in their niches. Go back to your chair across the table from me, and read. It is the hour." As I rose from Pen-aati's chair, where I had sat to eat, he drew his own closer to the table, and when I was seated I saw he was smiling at the large pile of stunted rush pens at the side of my palette. "My son," he said, "splendid actions and great deeds are worthy, and precious to the gods. But the tasks the gods alone see—they surpass all." He spread the first scroll out in front of me. As he moved the statue of Maat to hold it, he said, "Ahmose," and the gaze of his eyes pierced my marrow as a Master Joiner testing new wood, "after a long period of darkness we have gathered once more the threads of our ancient wisdom. Ahmose, my son, there will be no invaders of our Land for the last centuries of the Age of the Ram . . . that what was written in the beginning may be fulfilled and 'The Answer given in Thebes' and so that the wisdom appropriate to our time may be taught in our Temples. That is the reason I asked of you this scribe's work . . . the story of the men and women who opened the way to what in later days will be called the New Kingdom, in our Beloved Land." While he was speaking, he sat back in his chair, his hands on his knees. His long white robe and shoulder scarf glowed yellow in the torch and wick light. His shaven head shone smooth and golden. I was held in the gaze of his eyes. "Read, my son, till your tongue gives sound to the last word you have inscribed in these scrolls. After that word . . . the Silence."

I lowered my eyes. Then I looked up and gazed for a while at the statue of the God. "Osiris, Lord . . ." I murmured, and began to read.

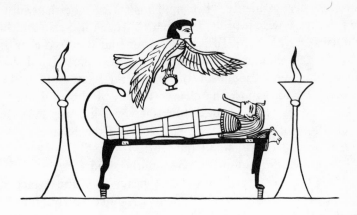

CHAPTER I

For two moons' span Thebes had held vigil. Old men and boys manned the walls, and at dawn and sun-down the vast Temple Fore-court was thronged with our women, praying for the men who had followed their King to hold the city of Kus for the South Land, and to rescue the bride of their Hawk Prince.

Messengers had come and gone. "The opposing sides outside the city have not yet joined in battle . . ." "The King's hosts have recaptured half the city . . ." "The Thebans are holding their ground . . ." "Two thousand chariots are on their way from Neferusi . . ."

Our Eyes and Ears in Secret had told us of the stubborn valor of our Egyptian soldiers, with their ancient longbows and their heavy shields. Then the King's Messenger had come, and the news was joyful! Seken-en-Ra II, with Neshi and his Nubians and Ebana of El-Kab with our four hundred chariots and the ten thousand Foot-soldiers of the South Land, had thrust the invaders out of the city, and were holding beleaguered Kus against the chariot hordes of the Hyksos.

"By the Eater of Shades!" Tetisheri was jubilant. "At this hour, Piopi of Neferusi will have relieved the King with his two thousand chariots and the battle is ours!"

"All praise to Amun-Ra," my mother said.

"The tribute? It will not be as heavy—by the Grace of Amun!—no tribute at all?" Pen-aati spoke softly, but his tired eyes were alight. "Through three reigns of Theban Kings I have not allowed myself this hope."

My mother looked at him with the understanding of long devotion.

"Pen-aati, you know that the King will thrust on, to Abydos."

And though, since childhood, the thought of battle-slaughter, filth and blood-stained spoils, children orphaned, mother-loss and wailing in the houses of the dead had filled my soul with horror, in these days of vigil-waiting all my prayers had been for the South Land's victory. I sat up on my bed, my back against the reed matting, in praise and thanksgiving that the darkness of Set had drawn no closer to the Shrine of the God. After a while, at peace for the first time since my father and brother set forth for Kus, I fell into a deep and dreamless sleep.

"Ahmose . . . Brother . . ." The hoarse whisper, close to my ear, pierced my heavy slumber. "Ahmose, our father . . . dead . . . murdered . . . Brother!" A hand gripped my shoulder almost crushing the bones, shaking me awake.

"Kamose!"

He fell on his knees by the bed, his face pressed against his fists that pulled and tore at the linen cover till it was in shreds. I scrambled up against the head-rest. Names retched through his stiff, cracked lips. "Piopi of Neferusi . . . Teti . . ." he raised his head and looked at me, his eyes glazed dim with rage and pain. "Piopi of Neferusi and his Set-spawned son . . . Neferusi . . . Neferusi . . ." He buried his face again, and wept.

I sat up, cold with fear and staring into the jewel-gold eyes of the lioness, standing above us both, her fore-feet on the bed. I saw the side of her head, swollen and raw. Her eyes gazed at my brother. The shoulder-strap of his battle tunic was hanging loose. On his left arm, in the sheath above his elbow, the golden haft of his bronze dagger gleamed in the moon-light that streamed through the roof-slits. His dark, war-grown curls were matted with sweat and dust. I could not move, nor put out my hand to touch him. Sek-met dropped onto all fours and leaned against him, growling softly. I watched, I know not for how long, as she fell to licking his nape. Slowly the soft hairs stretched, thin black threads along her rough pale red tongue. My skin stretched. The hair-roots in my side-lock cringed and hackled and I heard my own thick, shuddering breath as horror caught hold of me and coiled my entrails into a knot. I leapt from the bed and ran across the floor. The water basin was empty. My knees sagged, and, sick, I stayed there, limp against the low stone rubbing slab.

When I moved, my legs were cramped. Slowly I stood up and wiped the wet from my eyes. I poured water from the ewer into a red Nile pottery cup, and drank it thirstily. After a moment, I went back to my bed-room. Sek-met growled. Each night a jug of wine was left on the small square table. I poured out a full cup.

"Kamose . . . drink."

My brother moved. Slowly he looked up at me, his weeping spent. His tears had left dry salty rivers down his dusty cheeks. As one in a dream, he rose and sat down on the bed, took the cup of wine, silently drank and put the cup on the floor. Then he eased himself up against the cool reed matting on the wall behind my bed and sat for a while, his face drawn and ageless.

"The day was ours," he said. "Our long-trained, eager Foot-soldiers fought as lions against the Hyksos chariots, and though thousands fell to the poisoned barbs of their deadly double bows, our Egyptians battled on, buoyed by their own long urge to fight, and the thought of the chariots from Neferusi . . . Neferusi . . . Neferusi!" Rage shook his whole great body. Clenching his grinding teeth, he waited a while. Then he took a deep breath and let it out slowly. When he turned to me his eyes were cold. "Come, Little Brother, sit up here on the bed with me, the reed matting is cool. Our father spoke of you . . . 'Ahmose, my Young One,' he said, 'has the heart that thinks. . . .' He said you were a 'booth of rushes, and a shelter. . . .'

"Ahmose, we were alone together after the evening meal, my father and I, in his tent. He had sent Neme away to sleep, and we were drinking honeyed wine while waiting for Ebana to join us. Earlier in the evening a welcome messenger had come from Piopi and Teti, asking that 'The King of the Two Lands' and the 'Captain of the Royal Armies' should await them in the King's tent 'to plan the morrow's essay.' The messenger told us that the Hyksos chariots would be in the camp by dawn. Our father was at peace. 'Amun-Ra be praised,' he said, 'for so Unique a Friend as Piopi.' Then he spoke of our mother, and Abydos. 'When I have freed the Holy City,' he said, and he smiled as a boy, 'Ah-hotpe shall share, with the Priests of Osiris, in the Rite of shriving the God's Altar of the dark rites of Set. It will be her life's joy . . . and you, Kamose,' he said to me, 'though you have not fought in this battle, you will have your chance at Avaris. I shall send you, with Piopi, and Teti and two-thirds of our hosts, to rescue——' " My brother's voice stuck in his throat. His body shook again. He pressed his fists to his brow. I could not speak. With a thin sigh, he straightened, saying, with a voice empty as that of a child reciting a poem but half understood, "I was dipping a bunch of grapes into the bowl of water on the table when we heard Sek-met's roar of rage. I looked up at my father. 'Your lioness is in trouble again,' he said. 'Sek-met finds trouble as a fly finds honey.' As I left him in the tent he was pouring second cups of wine for me and for himself, and one for Ebana.

"After Sek-met's one great howl, all was quiet. Men were asleep around the embers of the campfires, bone-tired and exhausted from the day's fighting. I went about the camp searching and calling to the lioness. I saw Ebana come out of his own tent, and walk to the King's. It seemed we were the only people awake in the whole camp. I went among the stacked chariots, passed horses feeding and walked through the kitchens. Then I heard a small animal sound. I went, in the star-lit darkness, slowly toward it, calling, 'Sek-met, meri . . . Sek-met . . .' and heard the sound again, closer. I found her beside a weapons cart. She was lying stretched out, tied by her neck to one of the wheel-spokes. She did not raise her head. In the darkness I could not see her wound. Cold with rage, I untied her and gentled her. Who? Who in the King's camp could have done this thing? I lifted her and stroked her legs. She staggered, and fell. I went to a dying fire, lit an almost-burned-out reed torch that was lying there, came back to her and saw the wound on her head. Blood oozed from the bash. She was stunned. They meant to kill her! The thought was cold as the north wind in my heart. I picked her up. She was limp and heavy. Who? In our own camp? Why? Slowly, for the weight of her and not to jog her head, I carried her back to the King's tent, and, pushing the large reed curtain aside with the lioness in my arms, I said, 'Father . . .'"

Though my brother's cracked lips scarce moved, his voice was clear. "I laid Sek-met down on the ground. Then I turned and looked again on the sight before me. Our father lay dead. His tall body was ax-hacked, and stabbed. Then I saw Ebana. He was lying against the side of the tent. He was still alive. I went to him and, kneeling beside him, lifted him up in my arms. He had been stabbed through the heart. 'Kamose . . .'—he could scarce speak for the blood in his mouth—'my Ka pulls away from me. . . .'" My brother closed his eyes. "Then, Ahmose, he told me . . . 'Piopi of Neferusi stabbed the King from behind . . . a dagger thrust through his left ear into his throat. Swift as an adder's strike, Teti slew me . . . Mayebre the Libyan, he clove your father's head . . . and Teti of Neferusi . . . laughing, he swung his ax again and again into the King's body as he lay.' " Kamose opened his eyes. "Ebana's head fell on his breast. I whispered his name. He lifted his head again, and said, 'My son . . . Ahmose-Eb . . . all my heart's love.' Then he looked straight at me. 'Kamose, my young warrior, your boyhood's, your manhood's love . . . She is queen in Avaris.' Then Ebana of El-Kab, Hereditary Fan Bearer to his King, and Captain of the Royal Armies, raised a hand to his brow in his last allegiance. 'Kamose, Hawk Prince of the South Land, avenge your father, and free the Two Lands . . . Ta-mery . . .' he breathed, and his Ka left him.

"I laid him down, and slowly stood up. There was not a sound in all the camp. It was as though I saw a painted scene in front of me. I watched our father's lifeblood soaking into the dried earth of the tent floor. Then, as I stood, I heard chariots at the northern end of the camp. The sound grew fainter. They were riding toward Kus. Why had they not waited to murder me? A wild young stripling Prince is of no danger to them?" Kamose sat up and put his hands flat on his knees. "I am Horus, Falcon of the South Land's Dawn . . . I will avenge . . . and I will prevail." He closed his eyes again. Sek-met crept up and put her head on his chest. His body sagged as he held her cradled. "Our father knew victory," he said softly. "We drove them out of Kus. Had we not been betrayed, the day was ours." The grief in my soul was an ache in my body. My brother turned to me. His eyes were dark in the moon-light. "Neshi ordered our men to retreat from the camp before dawn. To scatter and make their way as best they could, and as secretly, back to Thebes. . . . Let us pray," Kamose said, "that they use their native subtlety in this retreat, for we shall have need of them, every man, to train my new armies." Then he told me how, with Neshi and the Anubis Priests, he had taken our father's body, and Ebana's, to the south of the camp, and there, ringed around by a Company of Nubian Scouts and a few Bow-men, the Anubis Priests had slit the King's side with the flint knife, taken out his viscera, stuffed the void with saw-dust and put his body into the wooden coffin.

"Without the true Ritual! Kamose!"

"Brother, there was no time."

We sat silent, Sek-met, her wounds healing, was asleep. Without moving, my brother quietly finished the telling. They had put the two coffins, my father's and Ebana's, together in an ox-cart, stacked weapons around them, covered them with green reed matting and set out, secretly, for Thebes. Traveling by night along the paths made safe for them by Neshi's Nubian Scouts, by day they stayed in the huts of loyal farmers who hid the ox-cart and its Royal Burden amid the trampled earth and dung of the cow stables. As he talked, my brother's breath came slower and his eyelids drooped. "During these days of stealthy travel," he said, "Neshi and I have not closed our eyes. We have planned. He will train all the Captains of the Royal Armies. Ak-hor will lead the Nubians, and Ahmose-Eb will be Captain of the Royal Fleet and the Sailor-soldiers. . . . The rest of my Company, Thure, Pen, the Twins and Tetaky, will, without delay, take up their quarters in the Battle-court and under Neshi's tutelage will apply themselves day and night, each to the warfare they will lead in our battles . . . and you, Little Brother, who would be Priest . . . I may have need of you. . . ." He stroked the wound on Sek-met's head. "At dawn, I shall speak with Miutu and Kheri-heb, that the two High Priests will decree but thirty days of mourning for our father. . . . Ahmose, the tyrants feared him! They were afraid of Seken-en-Ra II, and of our square-faced Ebana of El-Kab. They drove us to war that we might show our

strength . . . and lose two-thirds of our long-trained army."
He sighed, and shook his head slowly. "The South Land
tribute is vast. They think that the South Land will stay
quiet and willing under its feckless young, wild and lusty
King. . . . They do not fear me, and that, Little Brother, is
our strength! They will taunt and bait us, ravish our crops . . .
and our maidens, but they will not yet attack us. And mark
my words, Brother, their first insult to me, to Thebes and to
the South Land will be to send an envoy to the Funeral Rite
of the King they murdered." His head fell forward till his
chin touched the head of the sleeping lioness, and suddenly
he was asleep.

I stood naked, chill in the mist that comes with the hour
before dawn, staring at my father's coffin. The flickering
light of the tall wick lamps in the Hall of Audience played
tricks of living laughter with the painted mask of his face.
On this last day of his Funeral Watch, the horror still
festered in me. "Osiris, Lord of Breath, his tall flesh lacks the
Ritual. . . . No natron bath, no myrrh! No cedar oil to
soothe, nor fragrant herbs, nor beeswax scarab-sealed, where
they had slit his side . . . Osiris, Lord . . ." The ancient funeral couch on which he lay was too short by three hands'
length for his long coffin. The gold leaf on it looked yellow-
green and the colors of his painted collar crude and bright.
I knew the feel of every bead and amulet. Learning their
meaning at my father's knee had early turned my heart
toward Priesthood. "The God-Knowing is good for the
soul, as barley for the body," he would say. I looked at the
painted vulture wings, red and blue and black-tipped green
painted along his coffin, and his soul name in a golden rope
between them. "When a man's soul leaves his body," he once
said to me, "he finds himself with all his deeds piled up
beside him." As I stood in this last hour of his vigil I thought
that my father, for all his mutilated body, would meet with
fair mien the company of the gods. "Mutilated . . . hacked
and stabbed . . ." The blood rose to my head. "Teti of

Neferusi!" My thought had hung on him for the whole moon's span of this Funeral Watch, as raw fish hangs in the sun till it is dry and hard as rock. I, who could not kill a scorpion, could wish a human dead? Teti of Neferusi! His black eyes darting: "How many horses have we bred?" As a boy he would ask my grand-mother questions. Were his eyes sharp and probing then? His smile a mask? His heart an acrobat? "Teti-poke-his-nose," Rai called him, and always she stood away from him. And Sen-ut! She would hide away from Teti. As a youth his eyes would glitter as he watched her lotus hands. Once, during lessons he had passed a new rush pen to her and put his own fat hand on hers. "A toad upon a butterfly," Rai had whispered, and I chided her! Had they seen then, so young, the traitor seed in him? How clear to me now the things that to the eyes of innocence were simple mischief. The branch he always carried, thin-whittled of acacia wood, to sting the young gazelles to higher leaps. His high-pitched laughter . . . we had thought it merry then, as he made puns about his sister and Kamose's love for her.

"Anat-neby . . ." My brother had not said her name, nor ever would. Anat-neby of the ivory skin and raven-dark blue eyes. How she would press her pointed breasts against Kamose, lift her face to his and stroke his cheek with her long black lashes; a moth-touch to rouse his passion and bring worship to his eyes. Anat-neby, her father and Teti . . . for months they had known well the tyrant king's desire for her. Piopi of Neferusi, with wild lament telling of his virgin child "captured from our house by the soldiers of the Hyksos king!" On that same long, fatal day when Mayebre the Libyan rattled up to the door of the King's House with blasphemy and insult, Anat-neby was sailing in queenly state downriver in Apophis's barge. With what double cunning our ruin had been planned. How could we all, and for so long, have had the eyes that see no day? How, for all these years, believed in the Neferusians? And loved them! My father, he was Priest, my mother Priestess. She had the Gift of Looking. Kheri-heb, standing now at the head of my father's coffin with Miutu . . . the sons of Light . . . they had not known! They had not sought to know. Piopi was my father's Unique Friend, Teti and Anat-neby as brother and sister to us. Those whose allegiance is to Set are subtly clothed! Treachery has a smiling face, and the Priests of the Shadow have foulness on their brows and are strong in the dark magic. The Darkness of Set! It was thickening, and whelming us. "Amun-Ra! Lord of the Flame! Grant that Kamose avenge our father. . . . Grant, O Lord of Light, that my brother prevail. . . ."

I looked at him standing in front of me, Sek-met at his feet. The Ritual Panther Skin was onyx-black against the gold of his skin. The cording muscles swelled in his arms and shoulders, in his long, strong legs. Kamose, who could shoot a dom-palm date from the longest arrow-flight away, and swing the stone-headed mace to break a granite rock. He is King, I thought. And he is changed. He had gone out beside our father, hot-blooded, with his heart's love-rage and a high pride to recapture his betrothed and thrust back the tyrants from Kus. He had returned to tear the strong linen of my bed, and to weep.

Remembering, I felt sick. The years of patience, of careful planning, had failed through betrayal. Our long-trained soldiers were returning in stealth, taking to the desert, stealing by night from farm to farm, hiding in cattle-boats and grain-ships, that they might not be taken by the Hyksos. On this dawn of my father's Funeral Rite, shame and grief hung as a pall over the Thebans who, the day before, had gathered in the Outer-court of the Temple to mourn their murdered King, the Captain of their Armies and their men who had died in vain. Each day of the Watch those of our soldiers who had escaped found their way, weary and beaten, back to Thebes.

A sharp prickling in my nose brought me back to myself. It felt as though a fly walked there. "Akh! The cheap brown resin!" A web-priest walked around the coffin, censing it.

Milk-white tears of frankincense should have sent their burnt-sweet fragrance to the nostrils of my father's Ka. I almost sneezed. Terebinth! They use it in the privies, and to free the granaries of vermin. As the acrid smoke of our native tree filled all the air with the smell of our poverty, the Hyksos envoy to my father's Funeral Rite stalked into the Hall where the King lay in state. At the sight of him I felt my scalp shrink. Mayebre the Libyan! "Their first insult . . ." my brother had said. Mayebre the Libyan, who clove my father's head! In the silence his rich cloak, dark red and heavy with golden braid, swept the tiles with slithering sound. "Like snakes," I thought. His high Hyksos cone of a hat was studded with jewels, and on his right big toe was an amethyst ring. The sick bile rose into my throat. Then I saw the Libyan's companion: Pere-em-wah. I whispered his name and gathered myself. The Chief of our Eyes and Ears in Secret had come from Avaris to the last Rite of the King he had long loved and served. I watched him as he slowly walked toward the coffin, his arms outstretched in adoration. It was the first time since early youth I had seen Pery-em-wah, though we had heard much of him through the years. He fell on his belly and bit the ground in fealty and deep love. Though he was tall and strong, he was old as Senseneb, and had known my father's birthing. To Mayebre, who had not bowed at all, Pery-em-wah's homage seemed a gesture of supreme ridicule. Contempt for us all oozed from the Libyan as the yellow water from a putrid sore. He stood, his feet wide-planted, as he had when the obscene scarab was laid at the foot of my father's Throne Chair.

The blasphemous thing had lain there. After my father had ended the Audience, Miutu and Kheri-heb had spent a day and a night in the Inmost Shrine, seeking the will of Amun-Ra. For though gold is the metal of the God, this ingot had been carved with a dire curse on the South Land, and charged with the dark power of Set.

When the two Illumined Ones had emerged from their fast, the golden ingot had been melted down, shriven and glorified in the Fiery Beam of Ra, at the noon-day, and the Anubis Priests had beaten the horror into four flat golden rings, smooth and shining, to encircle the eyes of Seken-en-Ra II, and his Queen, Ah-hotpe, when their time came to travel the Way of Osiris.

A dawn breeze cut the mist. Fresh and strong from the River, it revived the dying wick flames, and blew the dark veil that hung from my mother's head into billowing folds about her slender body. Since the fifth hour of the night she had not moved from her place at my father's feet. Her eyes were glowing and tearless in her drawn face. "Isis, Lady of Heaven," I prayed, "let your star-strewn cloak fall around my mother. . . ."

Then a shudder that was not of the dawn wind, nor the stinging smell of the incense, crept up my spine. Nefertari had come into the Court. She had her arm about the shoulders of my tiny grand-mother, and looked even taller in her long black robe, and strangely beautiful. Since boyhood I had felt unease when she was near, and guilt for that unease, for my half-sister's words were soft and always she smiled at me. Tetisheri patted the hand on her shoulder and looked up with loving pride at the natural grand-child she had raised since babyhood. But Nefertari was gazing at Kamose! And her dark, long-lidded eyes were a flame in the gray dawn. "She desires him! Our half-sister, birthed by a concubine, not wholly Egyptian! She would be Queen? Kamose is King! She desires him!" My heart leapt to the knowing in sudden fear. "Nefertari aspires to the Beautiful White Crown. . . ." For a swift moment the whole Court of Audience and the people spun around me as a playing-top whipped to whirling stillness. "Rai, who sings with the birds and weeps with the reedy water . . . Rai is the Royal Daughter." My breath returned as, with my thought of her, she came, tripping over the hem of her long dress, and gathering it up in folds too big for her small hands. At the sight of her, the chill in me was a noon-day warmth. She felt my gaze and, without turning, smiled at me. I wished I were not still wearing the side-lock, naked of my first loin-cloth and four years younger than my brother.

His stillness was of the God. He had not moved an eyelash when the envoy he had foretold brought desecration to our solemn Rite. My mother turned to him. With a whispered word to Sek-met, who would have followed him, he went to the Queen. The lioness stayed where she was, her chin resting on her paws, her golden gaze watching Kamose's every movement.

Together, as the first pale vanguard Light of Ra in his Atet Boat rising pierced the mist, my mother and my brother, Isis the wife and Horus the son, stood at the feet of my father, the dead Osiris, and a swift presaging thought touched my heart, and was gone.

Ah-hotpe, Queen and wife, held her arms outstretched in front of her, the palms of her long, slim hands upheld in adoration, and spoke the ritual words:

"Your wings are as the wings of geese."

"You rush toward the Sky as a heron." Kamose's voice was calm.

As the sem-priest censed the coffin again, Miutu, High Priest and Chief of Visions, bowed and chanted:

"He rises on the smoke of the incense burning."

"He kisses the sky as a Falcon." Kamose spoke with the voice of authority.

Kamose, High Priest and King! I felt young and bare and shut away from this grown man who had been so close a brother.

"You steer your Barque to the Fair West," the two High Priests chanted as the pallbearers, first Neshi the Nubian, in his ceremonial cloak of vulture feathers, and Ak-hor, naked except for his warrior's loin-cloth of plaited leather and the twin dagger to Kamose's in the papyrus sheath on his left arm, took the dark blue shoulder-pads from the web-priests, and after them Kamose's Company, Thure, Tetaky, the Twins and Pen, each took his place. Two were absent. Aknere was already working in the North Land. Kamose had appointed him Chief of our Young Eyes and Ears in Secret, and Ahmose-Eb, the shroud of grief around his heart showing in the sag of his strong, square face, had sailed with his father's Funeral Barque to El-Kab.

As a web-priest censed the King for the last time in his earthly House, I moved to my place behind Kamose, and to the left of the Royal Women. Pen-aati, who loved his cousin Pery-em-wah, and knew his long, quiet bravery, looked at him with seeming disgust as he, with Mayebre the Libyan, took his place behind me, and I, in this last moment of the Watch, smelled the tardy presence of the Royal Treasurer and heard the arrogant tapping of his Staff of Office on the tiles. I could smell the scent that Thuty used, as he took his place beside Pen-aati, and I thought the harsh burnt terebinth more pleasing to my nose.

Kamose made a sign to the lioness. She lay down where she was, her tail a golden mace, black-tufted, along the floor, and as the pallbearers lifted the coffin high, the two High Priests came to stand in front of me and behind Kamose, who today was Highest Priest of all.

I looked at the wrinkles where Miutu's thin neck joined his shaven head. He had been High Priest in my grandfather's reign, but his shoulders were square-straight and his body sinew-thin under his white Priest's robe. Kheri-heb's neck was smooth as polished stone, and his shoulders sloped. He was lithe as a young man for all his Temple cell vigils and his fasting.

Slowly we moved past the bright blue pillars of the Audience Hall, and as the first beams of Ra in his Atet Boat ascending touched the faces of men, the high doors of the King's House swung open on their huge bronze pivots, silently.

We made our measured way down the wide steps to the brick-tiled Court-yard. While the Royal Women were taking their carrying-chairs, I saw, with surprise, among the Thirty Great Ones and their families, the Chief Scribe and his thin and haughty daughter, Sittek. She had urged, with tears, to sail with Ahmose-Eb, as his betrothed, to El-kab, and I thought that, bereaved and sorrowing as he was, our friend still held his quiet strength. He had twice postponed the wedding his ailing mother had arranged when he was a child. She had died before Sittek grew up, and Ahmose-Eb had avoided the final step with a logic and politeness so cool and pleasant that Sittek had felt no insult, and even her father had not balked, though the Chief Scribe felt the smallest slight. I was happy for Ahmose-Eb that he had sailed alone in his grief.

The Royal Women were all seated in their chairs and I saw that Thuty had left his place and was standing beside Nefertari, his silver-headed staff thrust out to show the golden Seal-ring on his finger. I thought of Miutu's words when my father, in his gentle grace, had conferred the high title on his natural brother. "Though you feed him corn on a golden dish, my King, the hyena will always prefer to eat carrion." And Kamose, after a desert lion-hunt said to me, "Thuty is a hunter who slakes his ardor." As slowly, we moved out of the Court-yard into the vast Outer-court of the Temple, I thought that when Kamose was crowned, Thuty would no longer be the Royal Treasurer.

Every Theban who was able had gathered along the wide avenue of the Temple Fore-court, their faces streaked with dust and their clothes rent, singing the ancient dirges. And when they saw the coffin of their murdered King, they moaned and bowed their heads, their arms across their breasts. Then they raised their heads and the clear air was full of wild and grieving sound as our father was borne forever from his House of Earth.

There were no washer-men at work, no linen, white and pumice-clean, lay drying along the River banks, and no village girls came to fill their earthen jars with the sweet water, as we walked the wide and mournful way to the Temple wharf. But the birds were everywhere, and as we came to the Quay, we could see flocks of pin-tails gathered along the ropes and beams and on the upper masts of the waiting ships.

Not a single bird call broke the gleaming silence of the stately Funeral Barque. In the brightness of early day, green-bronze, blue-and-gold, she lay at anchor. Her prow and stern curved inward with tall grace to golden papyrus umbels at their tips that caught the risen beams of Ra, so that the funeral couch in the center of her deck was bathed in a golden haze. It seemed that no Theban breathed as the pall-bearers laid their King's coffin down on it, and as my mother took her place at the foot of the couch, a tall, somber figure in the brightness, I could hear the lap of the water against the wharf stones. I watched the ancient scene: the tall Overseer of the King's Household, with order and scarce a sound, leading our porters and pages and our flower-girls, their head-baskets full to brimming and spilling flowers along their way, the Temple dancers and the acrobats of Thebes, to follow the Two High Priests and the Nobles onto the long Temple Barge. The Royal Women, sitting under the canopy of the King's Yacht, were still, dark figures in the yellow-striped, red-masted pleasure boat. I was lost in the solemn beauty of the age-old pageant, the Theban Hills, the Western Crags and the unchanged shapes of the ships that had sailed the green-brown River since the dawn of time. Slowly, I walked up the painted ramp of the yacht to join my sister and the Royal Women.

One sailor, Kamose, manned the Funeral Barge. As the ungainly tow-boat loosed her moorings and swung around westward toward the Necropolis Shore, I could see him on the prow. In his right hand he held the sounding pole of ebony and gold. Horus the Son; Osiris, mutilated King; Isis, his Sister-Wife. Once again, as during the Funeral Watch, the deep thought touched my heart that we were led by Fate. The Rite of Osiris was diffused to earth in beleaguered Thebes. Once again the battle would be fought, and Horus the Son would avenge his father's murder and betrayal. I felt

Rai's hand in mine. She rose from her chair and stood beside me, gazing at the shining Funeral Barque.

"And the company of the gods rejoiced at the coming of Horus, the Son of Osiris, whose heart was firm," she whispered, and the Knowing was clear between us, and our love for the Ritual words. We stood silent awhile, then she linked her arm in mine and we walked to the splash rail together.

"Ahmose, when will you go to the House of Life? To live there in the Temple, and truly learn?"

"Soon . . . When Kamose is crowned, and I am shorn of this side-lock, and gain my manhood. . . . And you, Little Sister, you are the Royal Daughter, and you will be Queen." Suddenly, I shivered. Nefertari . . . Nefertari . . . I could not shake the cold her name left in me. Then Rai was saying,

"Yes, I shall be Queen . . . at the Harvest. . . . It is arranged. And I will be as a cool shade to my brother, and Ahmose, you will be as an acre of sweet-smelling herbs to us both." She smiled, and her smile was the dawn breeze in the papyrus. Rai, where light and shadow meet, in your smile is gathered all our lives and all fore-loving.

For a while we watched the oar-churned water. Then Rai looked up. "Ahmose . . . the sun on Mentu-hotep's tomb . . ." I followed her gaze. Ra's risen rays lit up the magnificent, pure stone, high-rising tomb. We turned to each other, thinking of our childhood when, on Feast Days, we would cross the River with Senseneb and hundreds of Thebans, and while the ceremonies were taking place we would play in the shady gardens around the tomb chapels. "Our father told me that Mentu-hotep had more inspired men working for him than Kings for hundreds of years." Rai turned to the west again and we did not speak till the rocky ledges of the Western Crags loomed close, barren-rising, yellow–dust-red, to the yellow sky. "The Firmament is crossed," Rai whispered. "May the Blessed One who knows all things be gracious to our father."

"How quiet it is," I said. "How strangely quiet."

There were no Necropolis sounds of building and restoring, sawing, hammering and pounding. No chanting of Mortuary priests in tomb temples long endowed, or children playing ball and leapfrog in their well-tended gardens. There were no potters squatting; no makers of clay statues, beads and amulets, singing as they worked under their small square tents; no scribes writing out pages of the Ritual; and no Necropolis officials on their donkeys, bumping busily up and down the winding paths, their palettes underneath their arms. I looked at the cluster of stone houses where the workers lived, open-doored and empty, and at the people who lived in them, the people of the Western Town, gathered silent, on the shore, waiting to pay homage to their King.

We moored at the wharf called Opposite his Lord, where the Priests of the West were waiting with the ox-drawn sledge, and as the Queen stepped down, and walked ashore, she raised her hand to bless the babes their mothers held toward her, and the crowd made deep and reverent bow. Then they rose and waved their palm branches as, with slow and halting step, their chins bent on their chests, the pall-bearers carried their King through the close-pressed ranks of his crowding people to where my mother waited on the ox-drawn sledge, and laid their beloved burden on the jackal-headed couch.

"Remember the picnics here, in Mentu-hotep's tomb?" Rai looked up at me.

"And how the Western women leave their doors wide open, yet tie their heavy house-keys to the ends of their long plaits?" We watched the house-keys swinging as the women walked the crowded quay.

Kamose followed our father's coffin, and stood behind the ox-cart. Senseneb helped Tetisheri to her chair. Rai leapt up into hers as light as a goose-feather in the breeze, and sat down in the curtained cool. I went to Nefertari, who was waiting. I saw that she had refused Ak-hor's hand, and Thuty's, and must have a Royal Prince to aid her. She leaned against me as she stepped inside. Her full, firm breast cool-touched my shoulder, and, sitting, she held the curtain back and looked at me, her eyes unblinking bright as snake's eyes, long and beautiful. I felt again the shiver cringe my spine and, hard-pressed not to run from her, I walked with slow steps to my place behind the two High Priests, as the procession moved slowly up toward the dusty heights.

The Necropolis people had joined the throng, their sing-song voices chanting and their heads bare in the sun. There would be flat honey-cakes, and barley beer, feasting, and games, acrobats, dancing and telling of the ancient tales when the door of my father's tomb was sealed forever.

Higher and higher we climbed along the steepening way. Lizards, rock-browsing, scurried to their crannies. A late-prowling wolf with a long, scraggy tail slunk to his day-light lair, and bullfinches, sand-colored, hundreds of them, huddled on the fallen boulders, filling the early day with their flute-thin trumpeting. Without moving my head I looked up at the cliffs in front of us, grim, misshapen, angry and huge beyond believing, their high ledges piercing the green side-wings of light fading toward the north.

The way grew harder and more rock-strewn as we walked the last scrubby slope to the wide clearing in front of my father's tomb, pillared and brick-built to a high point, at the foot of the crag. As we slowly filed into the shade I saw, across the clean-swept stretch of sand, the Sacred Mound. I knew that hidden in its center was a stone well, shaped and measured, wherein to wedge the coffin's foot, so that my father, when his Ka returned to him, would be standing tall, on the Primeval Hill.

Kamose helped our mother down from the sledge, and the Royal Women descended from their chairs beside a dark green canopy that had been stretched across four wooden pillars, which were carved and painted to seem like bundles of papyrus stalks, cool-growing out of the hot sand. The women then took their places in the shade.

The Queen, Isis, walked forward and stood alone, her fists clenched on her breasts, and in each hand she held a golden circle. She watched as the pallbearers raised her husband's coffin from the jackal-headed couch, carried it across the clearing and placed it, standing upright, on the mound of earth and sand. And when it stood there, tall, the flower-girls tipped the blossoms from their baskets at the feet of their King: peonies, chrysanthemums and myrtle, leaves of the budding lotus that opened to the sun, ivy "for eternity," lilies and jessamine. Nearest of all to him they strewed the poppies and the cornflowers that he had loved. Then slowly, in a line, their empty baskets on their heads, they came back across the clearing to their place.

The crowd was gathered in the shade, silent. Even the children of the Necropolis workers sat quietly on the sand, sucking their sweetmeats in the shadow of the boulders.

I looked at my mother. Her hair shone, black as the shell of a beetle, through the thin dark veil she wore, as, with measured step, the flat gold circles on her outstretched palms, she walked toward the Mound, and bowed. Then, gazing up into the painted mask of her husband's face, she raised her arms.

"Hail to thee! Gold of my Heart," she said, and pressed the golden circles around his eyes. "Hail to thee! Thy two eyes are decked! Hail to thee, my Gold." And she fell on her knees and clasped the foot of the coffin in her arms.

She stayed there long, her brow against the hard, hot wood. Then she rose, stepped backward to the ground and, bowing in adoration, said:

"Grant that I may see you as each day breaks.
And know the smell of you in the Flame of the Morning."

She walked backward from the Mound and stood alone. The two High Priests walked slowly across the gritty, rock-strewn sand, and parted, bowing, at the Sacred Mound. Miutu stood to the right of the King, and Kheri-heb, holding the Scroll of Utterances, to his left, and awaited Kamose. Horus the Son.

Barefoot and holding the narrow ewer of Holy Water, he

came and stood in front of the upright coffin. Then he poured the Holy Water over it, stepped back and called out to his father:

"Horus comes! He recognizes his father,
    Youthful in the Name of Fresh Water . . .
The Divine Fluid in thee cries out . . ."

And my heart cried out and jarred my body to a salty sweat.

"Osiris, Lord," I prayed. "Osiris, Lord . . ."

The people were silent as the sand-ground scarps. The children sat still, holding the sun-dried sweetmeats in their hands, unlicked. Miutu took the ewer from Kamose and gave it to a web-priest. I wondered how long he could stand the burning heat after the long climb. "Yet he looks cool as a gourd skin, and pale. . . . Pale?" I looked at him more closely, screwing up my eyes. "It is the sun-light playing tricks." I scarcely breathed. The web-priests, with prayer and incantation, had taken a young white calf. The sweat stiffened on my skin as they cut off its right fore-leg and brought it to Kamose. As the calf was slain, Kamose held the fore-leg to his father's mouth and called out to him, and his voice was deep and clear. "Father! Father! Father! Father!" Four times he offered the young flesh, then knelt and put the fore-leg, dripping warm, fresh blood, among the flowers on the Mound, then rose from his knees and held out his hands together. Miutu handed him the Adze.

Kamose approached his father and held the shining copper to his painted mouth, and called out:

"Ur-heka!" He held it there and called again. "Ur-heka! I have opened for thee thy mouth! Horus has opened the mouth of his father, Osiris! Ur-heka! The dead shall speak!"

He laid the sacred tool beside the fore-leg.

I was trembling. The silence in the clearing was a living silence as Kheri-heb unrolled the Scroll of Utterances, and I could not believe my sun-blind eyes, for he was paler than Miutu as he read.

"The Sky moves for thee.
The earth trembles for thee."

I held my breath. The air brightened as though to vision, and the high crags, lost in the glory, rose in pride. The Lector-Priest was rigid as the coffin. The sun blazed down and light plunged into Light. I stared and could not close my eyes, for the brown of Kheri-heb's skin was shining white.

"The mountains divide!
The God becomes!"

Empty and cleansed, I watched, all thinking gone. The web-priest ran across the clearing with the Torch. The flame of it was pale blue in the dazzling, magnified Light; the smoke a gray-black pennant, solid in the shimmering air. He gave it to Kamose. My brother stood with it, his arm a golden pillar held up to his father's face.

"I am thy son, Horus.
Ur-heka!
Ra is filled with joy to see the face of his son."

Kamose's voice rang clear and full of virtue in the silence, but it was his own voice. The sound that came through Kheri-heb's still lips was no man-sound, and as he spoke he grew more holy radiant, as from a white fire within, and the words poured forth like thunder.

"The stars rain down!
The bones of the hell-hounds tremble.
The Keepers of the Doors are silent,
When they see Seken-en-Ra dawning as a soul."

Sound and light mingled as he spoke, overflowing the earth and the heavens. White sand, sky and towering rocks were one as—O Great Hawk of Gold!—the golden rings around my father's eyes caught noon-light and God-light both, outblazing them. All there fell forward on their faces, and I was flat on the gritty sand.

"The Living King is departed to the Fields of Celestial Grain." Kheri-heb's voice was a golden gong. The noon-day sand was silver cool. I plunged into the horizontal yellow and, through curves of living light, looked up and saw my mother. She raised her arms, Ka-square, and all the vast throng, young and old, even the children, lowly and noble, servant and lord, rose as one and raised their arms with her, to the glory of my father's Ka. The noon-day Fire of Amun-Ra was cool and in the resounding silence the great cliffs moved as the stars move, seeming still. I knew my mother and the Lector-Priest could see the living Gods around us. I did not need to see. I was out of my loosened clay. Celebration, bliss and praising were all fused in me.

The smallest lizard's scale I was, a hair on the shaggy tail of the wolf. I heard the River's Song, and the laughter of the Imperishable Stars, and in brimming emptiness I knew that pain and fear, and horror and the blackest doubt, are part of light, and the Light is not consummate if it lacks the darkest ray.

CHAPTER II

Kamose carried the reed raft on his shoulders. His brown hands holding it, and his bare feet, were all we could see of him, Rai and Sen-ut, Ahmose-Eb and Thure, Ak-hor and I, as we followed him past the gazelle pens and birdhouses. After three months of planning since my father's Funeral Rite, tomorrow, in the burning Flame of Ra's noon-day Fire, Kamose would be crowned. Today, his last day as Horus Prince, he must fulfill the Ritual and slay the hippopotamus. Rai was laughing at him striding ahead.

"Our brother looks like a giant afrit from the mountains," she said, matching her steps to mine as we came to the old granary. Then she frowned. "Why don't they pull it down? Or make a cow-stable of it?"

"It is used for storing things," I said.

"What things?"

I had wondered myself why it still stood there, empty and old, a gaunt symbol of Theban poverty. As we came closer, I saw that the door was locked with a heavy cross-bar.

"That is strange." I pointed to it, and Rai asked,

"Why does it need so strong a lock? What have we to store?" Her green eyes were bright with curiosity. "There's something more in there than durra for the cows."

Ak-hor turned and looked at her through the lattice of harpoons and throwing-sticks strapped to his back. "The woods and skins for the chariots are there, and what metals we can collect."

"Collect? Ak-hor!" Ahmose-Eb eased the tackle on his own back, and Rai laughed.

"You weave ferryman's words, collect! You and your Nubian Scouts go a-raiding at the dark of the moon."

I looked down at her, amazed that she knew. Since our father's day, the Nubians had, under Neshi, raided the Hyksos forts. Swiftly, silently, they hied up the walls of the enemy stronghold, climbing the tough papyrus ladders let down for them by one of Pery-em-wah's Secret Army, working inside, to strangle the guards with their long, strong fingers. Then they looted the fortress of tools, axes, spears and mace-heads all ready and ground, to descend again with their cache, and with the strong double bows threaded on their arms like beads.

"Ak-hor"—Rai ran to him and caught hold of the strap that held the harpoons to his back—"when was the last raid? Was it a good one?"

He smiled down at her. When she was a child and he a youth, he would throw her high in the air, catch her above his head and hold her there: a golden lotus in an ebony vase. He was taller than Kamose, and as broad of shoulder. His slatted leather loin-cloth looked light brown against the shining black of his skin. He wore his arm dagger and, like all the Nubians, he wore a bracelet of cowry shells, as a charm against night-spirits.

"It was a good raid," he said. "More than six hundred strong double bows."

Rai wrinkled her nose at him, and came back to me. She took my hand and came close. "That is a very strong lock for so old a granary," she murmured.

It was the seventh day of Spring, and the ebbing River left sheets of water, silver-gray in the gray dawn. As we came, each with our burdens, singing, to the fields, I looked at my brother and felt the inmost meaning of this day, the Eve of his Crowning. On this day alone he must fetter and destroy the Set-beasts. I thought of Mayebre the Libyan and his sneering insults, his rude ignorance of the ancient Rite the Hyksos tyrant, Apophis, had ridiculed. The Rite of Horus and Set, the fight between Light and Darkness, that Kamose would perform with the sun-set.

"Trample not the furrow of another," my brother called back to us, as we came to where the farmers were plowing, making our way under clumps of trees that rustled with waking birds. Kamose led us along a new furrow. I watched him as he steadied the raft with his left hand and plunged his right hand deep into the basket that hung around the neck of the farmer, and scattered the seed, singing, "This furrow is too long, too long . . ."

We were all singing with him, Rai's voice soft and high till she broke off in laughter at the wide-loping strides of the buff-backed herons that flocked round the plow team.

"Look at them! Bobbing their heads up and down, up and down, so busily pecking."

We watched their quick spurts as, fighting and squeaking, they stabbed for the grubs thrown up in the overturned soil.

"Hold! Rest for a space!" Pen called from the edge of the field, and came running, his feet all muddied and gear all a-jangle.

"Better late than never at all," Kamose called to him.

Sen-ut said, "He won't dare to be after tomorrow." She and Thure were walking side by side. Thure put his arm around her shoulder.

"That he will not, nor any of us." He put his head close to hers for a moment, then they walked on together and the plowman alongside us, bending over his wooden handles, wailed:

"Downward! Downward! Let's start all furrows downward . . ." and though he stretched up with a groan and put his hands to the small of his back, his eyes were merry.

Rai linked her arm in mine. "What a beautiful boy comes my way . . ." she sang, and Sen-ut joined in, taking my other arm, but looking at Thure. He put his arm round her waist, Pen and Ahmose-Eb linked onto the line and, all up to our calves in the soft-churned earth, we walked in a row behind Kamose and Ak-hor.

Under the tree-clumps, already, before the sun had arisen, officials and the older farmers argued the land-parcels, shouting and waving their hands, disputing the measures of this year and last year, and even those of the year before, while their dogs ran barking and yapping around the plow-teams, chasing the white wag-tails, cheeky and friendly, in the depths of the furrows, to retreat, their tails flattened down! For the wag-tails fear neither man nor beast, but only the shadow of the hawk or harrier.

We plodded through the soggy mud close to the River. To live is a wonder, I thought, as the cool ooze seeped in between my toes. Then, a yellow cow stumbled. Rai and I went to help her, lifting the yoke from her forehead. Her lashes were straight and white, and her eyes rolled under them as she struggled to get up. She seemed to glance sideways at Rai, and her eyes were brown-red like jasper. Hat-hor! I thought, who comes in the moon-light, a milk-white cow, to bless young lovers. Rai put her cheek against the cow's face.

"Rai . . ." I whispered, and in my heart said, I bathe your palms in milk and honeyed wine. The cow's head was between us. We were lost in each other's eyes, and I knew we had loved each other aforetime.

"What are you today, Little Ones?" Kamose called from the top of the dike. "Plowmen, or fishermen?"

I stroked my hand along the cow's wide-spreading horns. The plowman touched her side with his stick, and Rai whispered,

"Strive again, Beautiful One, the north wind blows and it is cool."

With a last pat on the cow's sweat-damp neck, she took my hand and we ran to Kamose, slipping and sliding in the thick black mud.

When we came to the top of the dyke Kamose was standing knee-deep in the bright green rushes. He heaved the long raft over his head onto the water. "Stow the gear," he said, and Ahmose-Eb, with a sailor's salute, waded out to it.

"Look!" Rai pointed upriver. Three rafts were sailing toward us. "The Twins and Tetaky, and he has the picnic basket! And Tetaky's towing the pole-raft—why?"

Ahmose-Eb turned from stowing his gear on Kamose's raft, and echoed her question. "Why the pole-raft?"

"Hy!" Kamose waved to the rafts upstream to come into the shallows. Then he turned to Ahmose-Eb. "The Great Black Belly," he said, and stood with his hands on his hips like a fisherman.

"But why? Surely the slaying of the Set-beasts, the Rite you perform on this day, is enough . . . Why the Great Black Belly?"

"For good measure." Kamose grinned, and waded to the Twins' raft. It had been made for them and had two paddles astern. "Hy! Spotted One," Kamose said to Mer-neb's hunting cat, Pu. Then he pulled her ears and she nuzzled his hand.

"Sek-met was angry to have been left behind," Rai said. "I was almost afraid of her."

And I thought of the lioness, of her great bronze-gold eyes in the white moon-light, her gentleness as she had licked clean the matted curls in my brother's nape while he knelt, weeping, beside my bed.

"Lash the pole-raft to mine," Kamose said, as Tetaky untied the tow-ropes. Ak-hor was already aboard the wide raft, sitting with his back to the pole unstrapping the weapons. He laid them out on the solid deck, while Kamose and Tetaky lashed the two rafts together. Then Kamose said to Thure, "You and Sen-ut, go with Tetaky, and Thure, you paddle. Keep astern of the Twins, and Pen, we need you to paddle the pole-raft." He turned to Rai. "Come, Little Sister." He picked her up in his arms and put her on the deck of his raft. She sat with her legs curled up under her and held out her hands to me. I leapt up. "Cast off!" Kamose leapt after me on to the raft as Pen and Ahmose-Eb pushed deep into the reeds and paddled us out toward midriver.

We slid downstream through the broad-leaved sedge, tuberoses and the creep-rushes, stiff and pale green, in the dark green water, slowly moving toward the papyrus clumps. I sat cross-legged at my brother's feet. Rai was lying on her belly, peering into the water. The shallowing River was teeming with fish.

"The Great Black Belly has not foraged here," she said, as I joined her and watched skeet-fish curled between the wide-spreading roots, and the thin-snouted bulti, silver and green, flashing in and out of the reeds. I sat back on my haunches. Ahmose-Eb and Pen paddled in silence, without seeming effort. Kamose looked down at the water.

"He is about, the Great Black Belly," he said, and for a moment it seemed as though a desert rain-cloud had passed before his eyes. "When shall I have time, ever again, to hunt him down, this cannibal fish?" I leaned over to the pole-raft and picked up a harpoon reel. "He lurks," Kamose whispered. "I know he lurks, the huge prickly one!"

The River was flat and a lighter green now. I looked at the two rafts behind us. The Twins were silent, pulling as one man, with Pu, lithe and feline, obedient and alert, stretched out on deck. Sen-ut sat with Thure, astern of their raft, as he paddled, and Tetaky squatted amidships with the basket and the reed mats. We were all watching, waiting, gliding and quiet, our paddles making scarcely a ripple, as Ra, in his Atet Boat, rose behind the Eastern Mountains, and the marshes wakened to rustling life. The Nile-geese drummed the dawn, and the donkeys in the fields brayed the sun-rise, and suddenly our rafts were set a-rocking. We held on, as from behind the tall rushes, brown teals took off from the water, showing us their yellow undertails as they passed us in slanting flight.

"They are dancing their dawn dance," Rai said, watching them soar.

Kamose stood up. His skin was as polished cedar wood against the milk-white linen of his loin-cloth.

Rai and I gazed at him, golden and white, blue-striped headkerchief and green-gold eyes.

"Tomorrow," she whispered, "our brother will be crowned."

I felt the loss of him: riding our donkeys out into the desert to stay for long white nights in the cool quiet; training his curd-yellow horse in the evening behind the cow-stables. He will have little time now, I thought, for Minirt; taller than the other horses, he had a lion's shoulders and was descended in a line from the Golden Fiery One and the she-horse our grand-mother had stolen from the Hyksos. Kamose was training him to the chariot.

Rai put her hand in mine. Her hair stirred in the breeze, and her eyes were deep as she looked up at our brother, and wise beyond her earth years. She knew that, for all our merriness and joy, and our picnic, the hunting today was the end of our carefree youth.

"Akh! Yeh!" Ahmose-Eb snorted as his paddle caught in the glossy black bog-rush.

"Quiet, Sailor!" my brother whispered. "You'll scare off our prey. This great Nile-fish is sly as he is voracious." He held out his arm to me, and I tied the harpoon reel I was holding to his wrist as, quietly, Ahmose-Eb and Pen nosed the two lashed rafts amid the leaping, darting frogs, into the shade of the papyrus. Kamose held out his hand for a harpoon. He set it, felt the sharp tip of it with his thumb and leaned on it, deep in thought. He looked down at me in the gloom.

"Ahmose," he took hold of my side-lock, "tomorrow you will be shorn of this!" he said, and pulled it, and pulled again, so that I almost fell into the water. But Rai held on to me, and I righted myself and stood up. He laughed, and the full deep sound startled a hen-bird on her nest and set the dim quiet alive with moving creatures. My brother turned and looked at me from head to foot. "By the Disc! It is time that you wear the loin-cloth," he said, and put his arm about my shoulder. "Akh! Little Brother, if you would fight beside me." He took his arm away and unwound a length of string from the reel on his wrist. "No." He looked at me again. "I shall not ask that of you. But there is one thing I shall require of you. The time is not yet ripe, but when it is, my Brother, you will perform one great, secret duty, for me and for the South Land." He turned away, and peered into the thicket. The hen-bird had settled, still wary. The other two rafts were close astern, silently gliding. Without turning his head, my brother said, "There is stress ahead, and long months of dissembling, and secret planning. . . . Two years . . . Three more tributes . . ." He was almost talking to himself. When he looked around again, his face was stiff and cold. "We must be more stealthy than the cat-fish, and our seeking, searching feelers in the North Land more luring silent." As he spoke, the reed growth thinned out and we saw the Eastern Hills, bright-edged and shadow-ringed. "Little Brother, the Dawn Light of Ra ascending shall feed my rage till I am the Fiery Flame of Ra at the noon-day." He took the harpoon from Ak-hor. The bones of his hand were white through the gold of his skin as he clutched it beneath the spear-point. He stood, granite-strong, and his eyes were green as polished malachite as he gazed at the Eastern Mountains, full-bathed in sun-light. He stood for a while. Then he sat down, tailor-wise, and laid the harpoon on the deck.

Ak-hor was untying the throwing-sticks, and the Twins and Tetaky were close alongside as, silent again, we pushed against the tough stems to a small sunless clearing in the middle of the next big clump of papyrus.

Kamose took five of the throwing-sticks in his left hand and waited while Mer-neb unleashed Pu. Then he whistled softly between his teeth, and she sprang into the thicket. The air was filled with the whirring of wings as flocks of birds rose, and Kamose, with a strong, deadly twist, hurled one stick after the other till the five had been thrown and the bird-flock—mallards, herons, cormorants, plovers, a pair of clumsy flamingos and hundreds of others, in swift and curving flight—was away, out of reach.

Five birds had fallen. Swift as an arrow, Pu brought them to Kamose's feet. Two were mallards. I looked at their purple-blue wings, and Rai stroked the smooth feathers with the side of her finger. Pu slid away again, faint-stirring the marsh plants, and came back with a sad-faced spoonbill. She put it beside the mallards and stood over it. Kamose leaned down and stroked her head, then pulled her ear.

"Find the lost ones," he said, and she swam out again, seeking.

The bird flight had disturbed the marshes anew. Cobra and chameleon slid up the reed-stalks seeking the eggs of small birds, and a python lay curled around the scaling roots, to uncurl and slither away at the sight of Pu. An otter, too far from the Nile banks, was whistling to his lost mate, his squat head and spike whiskers just above the water, brown against the green.

Tetaky stood up on his raft and in the flashes of two small spears, two hungry genets fell with splashes into the water and a bird host rose again with noise and crying.

I sat by the dead mallards and the spoonbill, and Rai said, "Ra makes to live the rats in their holes, and the birds that are on every green twig."

"Our mother's words," I said, and I listened to the myriad sounds of marsh life around us and thought of my father. "The Universe is a living presence," he would say, when the smell of small birds, on a hot summer day, filled all the dry air.

A streak of bright sun-light through the thick papyrus stalks almost blinded me, and touched the green-faded yellow of the roots at the water-line to gold. The spreading umbels above us glowed like wick-flames filtered through Temple linen. Pu swam back with a plover, its black-striped breast bulging from her mouth, its long thin legs limp. She laid it beside my knee in the curve of the spoonbill's neck, returned to Merneb and licked his lean thigh. I saw that the plover was still alive. Its eyes were red, and round with fear. Ak-hor leaned over and with a deft turn of his strong wrist wrung its white neck. He looked at Rai, and at me, and his eyes were sad. Then he stiffened, alert.

"Sh!" He put his finger to his lips. Silently, Ahmose-Eb and Pen took up their paddles. "Akh! Quiet!" Kamose crouched. "Aha! The Great Black Belly," he whispered.

We waited. The frogs had gone stiff as though Kheri-heb had put the Looking on them. The birds twittered and were silent, then twittered again. Quietly, Rai and I crept onto the pole raft with Ak-hor and Pen. Mer-neb whispered to Pu. She stayed still as a stone. I held my breath. Rai held my hand. Kamose rose slowly from his crouch and took the harpoon. He stood poised. Rai looked at me, her eyebrows raised with a question. Her lips moved but no sound came.

"How did they know?"

I shook my head. I had not heard a sound. None of us moved.

"By Hapi!" Ak-hor said under his breath, as a faint wind ran like spring rats through the reeds, and the Nile-Forager swam into view. It was huge.

I heard Rai gasp. Eight full arms' lengths at least, I thought. Kamose watched. I saw its brown-green, blood-colored, sharp-pointed spine in the sheaths of bog-rush and sedges. We glided out of the reed-clump toward it. Kamose stood now, tense and ready. We seemed not to breathe. Kamose was trembling still. Then, when he saw the red-gleaming eye of the cannibal fish,

"Istr . . ." he breathed, and with a slight hiss in the air, the harpoon found its mark.

With a great lunge the foraging Nile-fish rose toward us, its teeth all showing though its mouth was closed on a large gray mullet. I thought it would founder us but, with great lashing and splashing, it turned and, taking another spear-head in the crest of its spine, dove downstream. Kamose let the line unwind and our two rafts were towed, swift as a water-bird, streaking past the thick-grown clumps, out into the wide, full River, the other two rafts paddling behind us and everyone shouting and laughing as the Twins threw a tow-rope, caught our pole and lashed on to it, then threw a rope to Thure and Tetaky, and the Great Black Belly pulled us all downstream.

Slowly, Kamose wound in his reel. His straining muscles were hard and bulging.

"This is an afrit fish," Ak-hor said. He was kneeling, watching every move of the fight. "A glutton and a killer!"

"Soon now, we will tow him," Ahmose-Eb said, as Kamose pulled his catch closer, still fighting and lashing the River to clouds of spray. The Twins, Thure and Tetaky leapt from their rafts onto ours, and it took all of them to pull the monster alongside and bind him with ropes.

Breathing fast, Kamose stood up straight. Then he took the dagger from his arm-sheath, and knelt down.

"Aha! Ra-en-Ra!" he murmured, and stabbed the Nile-perch through the gills.

We had been towed far downstream at high speed. Fishermen were staring, aghast. We pulled into a small village on the east bank. Two of the fishermen waded out to meet us.

"They are brave," Rai said. "There are crocodiles here about."

But their companions were paddling a raft out after them, and pulled them aboard. Rai heaved a small sigh. They came close, chattering like magpies, their black eyes sparkling. Then they raised a great shout:

"It is the Afrit Fish! The Black-Bellied One! The Bane of our waters!"

My brother stood looking down at his catch, as Ak-hor lifted the pole from its socket and held it in his hands, high over his head.

"Now, by the Grace of Osiris," one of the fishermen said, "we shall have plenty of fish again in our waters."

Thure and Tetaky loosed all but one rope, and, as we drew into shore, Ahmose-Eb and Ak-hor thrust the long pole through the gills of the fish. Then Ak-hor cut the last rope, and he and the fishermen hoisted the pole on their shoulders and waded ashore. The fish was taller than Ak-hot by an arm's length, and made a wide wake in the water.

Thure went to Sen-ut, lifted her from the raft and they climbed up the bank.

"Hy!" Ahmose-Eb called out to them. "Ask the fishermen if they have mullet roes."

"Ra-en-Ra!" Kamose spread out his arms and took a deep breath. "I have a desire for fresh mullet roes," he said, as our two steersmen brought the bows of our double raft against the bank like a ramp.

"There are mullet roes a-plenty," Thure called down to us.

"Thirty roes for these game-birds," Ahmose-Eb pointed to the birds on our deck.

Thure nodded. He loved to bargain. His teeth were whiter than ivory in his brown face, and he was laughing as we scrambled ashore with the napkins, the reed mats and the large linen cloth, while the Twins carried between them the large picnic basket, followed by Pu, and Pen came slipping and sliding after them with the box of cheeses and fruit.

The fishers were squatting again. They rubbed their chins

and, shrugging, pulled down the corners of their mouths, deciding.

"Twenty-five roes!"

"Thirty roes." Sen-ut added her voice to the bargaining.

"Twenty-six." Their voices were softer.

"And what of Great Black Belly?" Ak-hor stood tall, looking down at them. Shrugging again, one of them rose, went down the bank, boarded our raft and, tying the feet of the birds, slung them, a bundle of bright-colored feathers, over his shoulder.

"Thirty roes," Thure said, and helped Rai up the bank. Then he said to Tetaky, "You wait for the roes, and don't let them cheat you."

"Kamose will like them with his wine, before we eat the cold goose," Rai said, as we came to the top of the dike bank and unrolled our reed mats. The small ones we put around under the trees, and the big one in the center, while the two girls spread out the cloth, the napkins, the spoons, knives and platters. We always worked ourselves when we went into the desert, or along the River banks.

Thure took two mats and put them close to the center cloth, and Tetaky came, full of smiles, holding the roes heaped up on a palm leaf.

"Thirty-two!" he said, and Kamose looked at them with relish, then turned to Ahmose-Eb.

"You are good with old women," he said. "Go to one of those houses and borrow a cooking stove . . . and Pen, open the wine if you will, my throat is as dry as cow-straw. . . . Hurry, both of you! Great Black Belly is no more! I deserve my reward."

Smiling, Ahmose-Eb turned and walked, with his slow, rolling gait, across the soft, sprouting earth to the row of small houses that nestled amid acacias and date-palms.

"We'll go to the Tavern and drink the cool beer," Merneb said. "And some fresh milk for you!" He pulled Pu's ears, and she purred, rubbing against his bare legs. "Wine makes us sleepy."

"It makes you sleepy," Per-neb disagreed. "Nothing makes me drowsy during the day."

"Then stay here and drink wine."

"I prefer to drink beer."

"So be it."

Ak-hor watched the Twins walk away. "How they hate to be parted," he said, "and yet there is no peace between them." He sat down on a mat and leaned his back against a palm tree.

"Except in battle," Kamose said, and smiled as he watched them. "In a crisis they think and fight, as one man."

Ahmose-Eb went into the third house along. It was washed dull yellow. Each house had three air-slits high in the front wall, and pigeons and laughing doves cooed and fluttered in the palm-branch fences that bordered the jutting roofs. I climbed up into a dom-palm. I could see two women on the roof of the house, and, after a moment or two, Ahmose-Eb's head came into view, then his whole body.

The women looked surprised, then the older one bowed in greeting, her hand on her heart. The young one looked at him, then she, too, bowed.

"What do you see, Little Brother?" Kamose stood at the foot of the palm tree.

"Two women, and Ahmose-Eb, on the roof."

"Women? Young?"

"One is."

"And the cooking stove? My sides are cleaving together."

"Then have some cold goose."

"When my desire is for mullet roes?" He climbed up beside me, and peered through the trees.

The maiden had turned away from Ahmose-Eb, walked past the linen-curtained sleeping place and returned to feeding the doves. As the dark blue robe fell away from her raised arm, I saw that her skin was almost as white as the birds' feathers, and her hair was straight and long, the color of polished copper. The doves flew about her head, and took food from her palm.

"My health and my joy! By Hat-hor! Beauty may be found among the maids who draw water." My brother whispered the ancient saying.

"And on a rooftop in a Theban village," I said, and saw that for the first time since the night of our father's murder, my brother's eyes were warm.

"Wait here," he said, and leapt down. He ran barefoot through the trees to the house. I heard his deep voice calling Ahmose-Eb as he came to the house door. I saw my namesake speak into the ear of the older woman, who bowed almost to the ground. Then, her arms above her head, she ran to the young one, as Ahmose-Eb disappeared down the stairs.

The girl listened to her, still feeding the palm doves, then she walked to the edge of the roof.

My brother came up the stairway. The old woman bowed again. He sent her away and, stepping onto the roof, he stood silent, watching the girl, who seemed not to know he was there. After a while, she turned to him. Her arms dropped to her sides. My brother did not move. With her arms crossed on her bosom, but with her head high-held, slowly she walked toward him. They stayed for a long moment, close, gazing into each other's eyes. Then he picked her up, carried her to the sleeping shelter and laid her on the soft reed matting. He stood tall above her, holding the thick linen curtain.

I climbed down from the tree as Ahmose-Eb came back with a small round stove in his arms. The old woman followed him.

"We'll put it under this palm," he said, and put the stove down.

Ak-hor piled the dung-and-wood fire he had kindled into the bottom of it.

I sat down beside Rai. I was happy. Kamose had hunted and killed the Great Black Belly, and he would find release, and a passing joy, in the arms of the strangely white, coolly willing girl.

Rai looked up at me. "I am happy, too, for our brother,"

she whispered. Then she wrinkled her small nose as the smell of roes in the hot pan filled all the air, and Ahmose-Eb poured out a cup of wine and handed it to her. She leaned over and took it from him, and he poured another for Sen-ut, then for me, and, holding the wine jar out, he said:

"You others may help yourselves."

Thure took the jar and poured a cup for Tetaky, who was lying full-length on his stomach, his elbows on the edge of the linen cloth and his chin in his hands, on the other side of Sen-ut; then he poured his own.

"The roes?" Rai asked. "They should not be overdone."

"Not yet, my little Princess." Ak-hor looked up from stirring them around in the pan. "Underdone, they are not appetizing."

"They need some leeks and some spices." Sen-ut stretched out her hand to the basket and I felt, as I had since child-hood, a thrill of pleasure at the beauty of her fingers, slim as reeds. Then I thought of Teti of Neferusi, traitor and murderer, who as a youth had lusted after the touch of her hands on his flesh. "Let them cook a little longer with these," she said, getting up and going to the stove. She emptied the leek-strips and spices into the pan, sniffed, looked up and said softly, "Only small portions for us . . . The lion's share for Kamose." Her brown eyes were warm and ardent. "To-morrow, our King . . . Manifest on his Throne."

We were silent while she picked up her wine-cup. Then together we stood up, lifted the cups to our lips and drank to the dregs.

We fell back to our places and were silent again. Pen had his back against a tree, and Tetaky was sitting cross-legged now, his elbows on his knees and his chin in his fists.

"Tomorrow, the Grace of Ra will descend on him," he said, and closed his eyes. After a while, his eyes still closed, he asked, "Will he have patience to wait and plan?"

"I think he will fight, and fight soon," Ak-hor answered.

"I know his vitals are churning to fight," Rai said softly. "But I know, too, that he will have patience; more perhaps, than our gentle father had, for Kamose's rage is cold, and he has a warrior's heart."

"And this time we must be prepared." Ahmose-Eb was helping Sen-ut to serve the roes, passing the shallow red dishes to her one by one, as she scooped them up with the copper ladle.

"We planned long and well, the last time," Ak-hor said.

"But our Unique Friends of Neferusi . . ."

"The traitors!"

We could not bring ourselves to speak the abhorred names.

"They forced us into battle before we were ready. They knew each detail of our preparing." Thure's eyes were somber.

"We were not secret enough," I said, and felt the muscles of my face stiffen.

"Teti of Neferusi," Rai whispered the name in my ear. "When you think of him, Ahmose, you are no longer Priest."

"This time we shall be secret as desert foxes." Tetaky, always restless, was lying on his belly again.

"And as wily," Ak-hor said. "The King has plans even now, for next year." We all looked at him. "The Fort, at the First Cataract."

"The Cataract Fort?" Tetaky sat up straight. "It bristles with Hyksos soldiers and arms!"

Ak-hor wiped his lips and put his plate down. "My father has already sent two Companies of his Nubians to live with the Dwellers in the Desert, behind the Cataract Fort, and thirty of Pery-em-wah's tried and seasoned Eyes and Ears, dressed as merchants from the North Land, are camped along the River-road beneath the Fort. They will infiltrate the garrison, slowly . . . and with time . . ."

"And this year"—Ahmose-Eb looked up from his plate of roes—"the King has planned a Royal Circuit in the South Land nomes that we still hold to the north of Thebes."

"When?" I asked.

"At the time of the Cattle Census, my Prince."

Rai's eyes brightened. "That is an idea with merit," she said.

"After the Crowning," Ahmose-Eb lowered his voice, though no one was near, "there will be a secret Council to finally plan this Royal Circuit." He turned to Ak-hor. "The name of Neshi the Nubian is known throughout all the South Land. . . . It is natural that, as Captain of the Royal Armies, he himself will protect the King's person . . . and the ox-carts of the Royal Treasurer . . ."

"Not Thuty!" Thure's low voice had risen sharply.

"After Kamose's Crowning," I said, "Thuty will no longer wear the Royal Seal Ring."

"He will be Overseer of our grand-mother's Household," Rai laughed.

"Thuty will be watched," Ahmose-Eb said, sniffing with delight the roes that were left for Kamose.

"Eschew the foods you love!" Sen-ut teased him. "Self-denial is but for a moment."

"Thuty will be watched, and others," Ak-hor murmured, and Rai knew his thought. Though Nefertari was half-Nubian, he distrusted her.

"They are not traitors to the South Land, our half-sister, and half-uncle"—Rai sat up, and leaned forward—"but they are traitors to Maat. There is no truth in them."

"Nefertari is more than my nose can bear." Tetaky's narrow shoulders shrugged up to his ears. "And Thuty is a wolf's whelp in the farm-yard."

No one spoke for a while. Ak-hor bent over and cut a piece of goose-meat from the leg on the platter. I watched him, remembering how he had taught me arms while Neshi and Ebana were teaching the older boys. "He lacks nothing as a warrior but the will to fight," he had told my father, and Tetisheri had been angry. "Akh! By the Flaming Orb! He will fight. He is my grand-son." But when I could hold my own with him, and with Kamose's Company, Ak-hor sent me back to Senseneb to study the ancient works that I loved. He was biting his strong white teeth into the goose-meat with deep satisfaction. When he had finished it, he looked up and said,

"No one will suspect that a Royal Circuit would cover recruiting and spying. . . . The King must have a retinue, and my young Nubians, they will guard the ox-carts with their lives. . . ."

"What will your Nubians be guarding with their lives . . . in the ox-carts?" Rai asked.

Ak-hor smiled at her, and Ahmose-Eb broke into the talk. "Aknere is returning."

"Aknere?" I liked Pery-em-wah's grand-son. He was the same age as Kamose and, though not unfriendly, he did not invite companionship. "Where has he been?" I asked.

"In Memphis." Ahmose-Eb saw my surprise and his face crinkled into a rare smile. "He and six other Young Eyes and Ears have been there for four months. They have made firm friendships with the chariot-builders and bow-makers of that City, who, though they are forced to put locks on their lips and work for the tyrants, are loyal to a man, to the true King in Thebes."

"And to our grand-mother," Rai agreed.

"So many loyal to us!" I murmured, and they all looked at me. "Could we not find some way to agree together? Without the shedding of blood—Egyptian blood, or that of any man? Could we not negotiate peacefully? With true understanding, there could be a way . . ."

They sat around me, silent. I wondered why they loved me, and did not abhor me and name me coward. Tetaky voiced my thoughts.

"Had we not learned weaponry with you, my Prince, and did we not know your soul strength, we might judge you to have the heart of a tame gazelle."

"The musician recognizes the musician," Sen-ut said, and grinned at me.

"To break this tyranny, my Prince, we must fight." Ahmose-Eb shook his head. "To be free to come, and to go, and do, or not do . . . to be . . ."

"You won't be free to do, or not do, if you marry your venom-tongued Sittek." Sen-ut could not help teasing Ahmose-Eb, who looked her full in the eyes with serious mien and said quietly,

"I am not yet married to Sittek."

"And you, my Prince"—Tetaky smiled—"will strengthen our Kas in prayer and ritual. You will join us in sleep when we are in battle, and be refreshment to us."

"That is a strength of which our foes are ignorant," Rai said.

"You will be with us in our fight, Ahmose." Sen-ut looked at me with loving in her bright dark eyes. "And we shall have need of you. Remember how your side always won when we planned mock warfare?"

"Your brother knows he will need your counsel in our strategy." Ahmose-Eb wiped his lips with his napkin. "And this time we shall fight with all planning, and in our own time," he said, and cut a large piece of goat's cheese, though his eyes were on the roes in the pan.

"A trifle serves in the place of much," Sen-ut quoted, laughing and looking at the large piece of cheese. She piled lettuce onto a flat cake, then looked up and asked, "Where is Aknere now?"

"He is on his way to the Crowning and the Council . . . and he, and you, Thure, and Sen-ut will all be in the King's retinue for the Royal Circuit."

"Sen-ut?" I looked at her in her short kilt, her young breasts bare and her soft black hair curling around her ears as Kamose's in battle, and I asked, "Sen-ut, why you?"

"To recruit young women to train for the secret work. Ra-en-Ra!" She grinned. "Much can be done under the cloak of a Royal Tour."

"I wish I could go," Rai said, pushing back her hair from her brow.

"But you cannot," I said, too quickly.

"And you would not."

I looked at her and slowly shook my head. I was thinking how deep I had been in preparation for my Temple studies during the thirty days of my father's mourning and the plans for Kamose's Crowning—and Rai? I looked down at her. She had known all that was happening in the quiet of the King's House.

Ahmose-Eb broke into my thoughts. "How old are you, my Prince?" he asked.

"In one month, fifteen years."

"And Kamose is right! It is time this was shaven!" Rai pulled my side-lock, hard.

"Yeh!"

She gave it another hard tug, then turned to me, suddenly grave.

"The enemy laughs at the ruin and poverty of Thebes with the laughter of sickness," she said. "And now, even in the Theban nomes brothers are enemies for a basket of grain."

"And Unique Friends are traitors." Tetaky sucked in his breath with an aware hiss, and looked at me. He knew. The gall in me, when I thought of Teti, was stronger than thoughts of God.

"There will never be another Piopi," Mer-neb said. He and his twin had come back to us. They sat down on two of the small mats next to Pen, who was fast asleep with a kerchief over his face.

"How can you be sure?" Per-neb carefully cut some goose-meat with his pocketknife. "You are too sanguine."

"It is our duty to make sure."

"How my father loved Piopi and trusted him," Rai murmured.

"With his life," Thure said, and for a moment his face was the face of an old man. "Teti . . . he and Anat-neby were as the King's own children."

"More than any of us," Sen-ut added.

"Anat-neby itched to be queen in Avaris." Rai's soft voice held cold contempt. "There was no love in her for the

South Land. She craved the riches, the ostrich feathers and the brazen opulence . . . cloaks heavy with golden threads and jewels large as figs . . ."

"She always loved baubles." Sen-ut shrugged.

"She is a whore." Thure made the simple statement without feeling.

Sen-ut nodded, and Tetaky said,

"Then she must be happy now. How many come in the darkness to clasp her honey-belly in the Set rites?"

"My father believed she had been captured and ravished."

"Captured!" Sen-ut blinked her merry eyes, and poured out more wine for Thure, who handed it to her to share with him.

"For once," I said, "our father did not even believe Pery-em-wah!"

"Nor would Kamose . . ." Rai sighed. "He loved her with all his heart."

"And still loves her," Mer-neb said, but Tetaky shook his head and at last began to eat the small portion of spiced roes on the plate between his elbows with one hand, leaning his cheek on the other.

"They must be quite cold," Sen-ut said.

"They are cool." He ate them in silence. Then he said. "Anat-neby, queen in Avaris!"

"For two moon's span while we gathered the Thebans to rescue her," Per-neb said slowly, "she was living in lust and luxury with the Hyksos king."

Tetaky looked up, his eyes wide. "By the Disc! She had sailed to the North Land and her father and brother had already full plans to murder their King when I led them to the Queen Ah-hotpe's garden, moaning and lamenting . . ."

"Teti weeping, and rolling on the floor," Rai said quietly.

"What play-acting! What treachery beyond belief . . ." Thure looked sick. "Always I loathed Teti . . . he followed Sen-ut . . ."

"Thure . . ." Sen-ut kissed him.

"When Kamose conquers the North Land, he will avenge

his father, and Anat-neby will be sent to the wharves and handed from drunken sailor to drunken sailor," Tetaky said.

"I await the day!" Sen-ut laughed, but Ahmose-Eb shook his head.

"The King will not insult her. He will kill her."

"Our sailors are too good a bunch of Nile-men for her filthy wares." Mer-neb got up to serve himself some food, while Ak-hor stretched out his long ebon legs and said with a heavy sigh,

"Unbetrayed, we could have pushed on from Kus."

"We could have avenged Abydos!" I said, and Rai gave me a swift, surprised glance.

"Our longbows are ancient, and our body shields still far too heavy and clumsy." Tetaky pushed his plate away and lay flat again, his arms behind his head.

"We've stolen hundreds of their new double bows and we're making thousands more"—Mer-neb pressed his lips together—"but still our bows are not as good as the ones we steal. The woods they use in the making of them are supple and rare."

"And the enemy have become more wary," Ak-hor said, "our raiding more dangerous and likely to fail." He stood up, ebony cool in the heat of the noon-day. "We must make more of our own. And now I shall go to the raft and sharpen harpoons for the Set Rite at the sun-set."

"To sleep in the shade of the bank, you mean," Mer-neb laughed. "Look for my hunting-cat, will you? Pu wandered down to the fishermen to cadge scraps of the mullet."

Ak-hor nodded, and leapt down the bank.

I looked at the ardent young faces around me. Then Rai sat forward away from me. Thought was bright in her green eyes, and the sun streaming through the branches of the trees dappled her bronze hair to gold. Her nearness was my well-being. She was looking at the eager faces of our child-hood friends.

"Beyond what my mother calls, 'The honorable field," have we, each of us, who have been born to tyranny and grown up in its shadow, have we, each one, our own dream for Ta-mery? For ourselves?"

They all began to speak at once.

"We know that Ahmose-Eb fights for his freedom . . . to do, or not to do," Pen said, waking up quickly.

"To marry, or not to marry!" Sen-ut laughed, and Ahmose-Eb threw a fig at her. Thure caught it and bit into it. "And Tetaky will fight for beauty. He is a poet." She looked at him with her head on one side like a bright, inquisitive bird.

"And Ak-hor for loyalty," Ahmose-Eb added.

"And you, Thure, you fight for your own," Mer-neb said. "To avenge your mother . . . for what was wrested from you . . . your lands, your cattle . . . Assiut, your home." He lay down, his hands behind his head. Thure smiled with tight lips.

"We all seem to know what the other one fights for . . ." he said. "Let us speak for ourselves."

"Then you begin, Thure." Rai curled her legs up under her and leaned back again, half against the tree and half on my shoulder, and I thought, So intense her feeling, and so light her body.

Thure looked at her, thinking. "No, Rai, I am not fighting for my own, not wholly. I am angry. I am fighting a power that seems so encroaching-strong and unassailable that to be against it is of less value than the flutterings of a desert bird against the hyena that raids her nest. I loathe this power . . . but I do not loathe . . . power. There is a might that is right, but then?—it is not might, and is right. I would fight for the might that is right, and is not might."

"By the Sacred Ibis!" Pen sat up. He put his kerchief in his sporran. "Thure, I did not know you for a rhymester." He laughed. "Though your punning has merit, if punning it is, for a man from Assiut."

"Strange for a man from Ed-fu to recognize wit."

"The might that is right," Rai mused. "The true might, that builds for all. For every man and woman in the Two Lands, that they may be free. . . . The might that raises majestic Temples of bright stone in accordance with God's aspect, that those whose original nature is, as yet, small and mean, may gaze and be uplifted. . . ."

"We men"—Tetaky looked at her—"we open our hearts to beauty, as the lotus to the beams of Ra." He paused. "But where beauty is not, and ugliness reigns, we grow to be as the world around us." He looked at Thure. "The might you would fight for is here, in Thebes. Only here, in the Residence of the God, for all our poverty, do the ancient glories abound."

"This Black Earth is holy ground," Pen murmured. "Only here may each child in our Land learn of Ra each day by his Light and his Warmth, his Land and his River; and in his Temple grow a spirit transparent to the gods. I fight for Thebes."

"And I, to wash our Land clean of the filth of tyranny." Per-neb looked around him. "If we do not fight, our children will not know the Living Beauty of Ra."

"The living of Life is not to do, but to be," I said, and they all looked at me again. Then Tetaky shook his head.

"Though we fight, and may die, what we are ever outweighs what we do, my Prince. Therefore, we are."

"You weave words, Tetaky," Rai said. "But you are right. Each one serves in his own place."

"We all have our being in the Creator of all things." Tetaky pursued his thought. "Since I was first able to think I have known a beauty that was not mine, is not mine. Has my Ka in dream met with an immortal God? Is it for this unknown beauty that I fight with all that is in me? Or in spite of it?"

"This immortal God, Tetaky, finds a void in you to fill." Per-neb looked on our frail friend with love. "You always say you are an empty ewer."

"Well, whatever it is, you fight for it." Mer-neb gave a little laugh. Then he said, "It would be simple to hold and keep our Land with prayer and contemplation . . . if we were all Lector-Priests."

"To be a Lector-Priest has to be fought for," Tetaky said.

"And we would not all be Priests," Thure added, gazing with tenderness and desire on the beauty of Sen-ut's small breasts.

"Yet Priests may help in the secret work," she said, and for a while they were lost in each other.

Rai looked up at me. "You would help in this secret work?" Her eyes were close. I could see each eyelash, golden-brown, and longed to feel the touch of them on my face.

"I would." I thought with wondering of my brother's words. "A secret duty . . . for him, and for the South Land . . ." I said for the hundredth time to myself.

"I fight that we may have cedar wood for our coffins," Pen said. "That once again we may mine our own gold, and pound our own granite, and raise obelisks to the One in One, our God, who, it seems to me, is ill-served if we do not fight."

"The God of the Hidden Name is stronger than granite. All trees that grow are his, and he is more shining than gold," I said.

"That is so, my Prince." Sen-ut turned from Thure to wink at me. "But it is a holiday for all of us when the Dwellers in the Desert come to the edge of the Black Land with their wares, their welcome wines and figs . . ."

"And the goat's fat with which we temper our weapons." Ahmose-Eb nodded.

"And tell our fortunes in the sand grains." Rai leaned forward. "Sen-ut, do you remember the old desert woman with rings on every finger?"

"And all precious stones they were, too. I remember her."

"She saw you in a huge tent, richly decked, with palm trees around it."

"Then she stopped." Sen-ut's eyes opened wide with the memory. "She stopped speaking and took my hands and held them tight, between her own. . . . I shall have left my body before I forget the look in her eyes."

"She could not believe their beauty," Thure said.

"The Dwellers in the Desert . . ." Ahmose-Eb leaned back

against his tree. "Most of them are loyal to Thebes. But Kus was barely held before betrayal. We must keep constant vigil. Nubia is with the tyrants." He sat up again, impatient. "Constant vigil . . ." he repeated.

Sen-ut nodded slowly. "Res tells me," she said, "that Neferusi, apart from being a breeding place for their chariot beasts, is an arsenal! Hundreds of carpenters, weaponry makers and builders of chariots are gathered there."

"Res?" I asked in amaze. The daughter of the Temple Administrator was sixteen and scholarly.

"She works with me," Sen-ut said, "and we have a plan —the King knows of it—to salt antelope flesh and water birds, as the fishermen salt and press fish to keep it for months."

Ahmose-Eb's eyes opened wide. "Can this be done?"

Sen-ut nodded. "It has been done. It is as flat as fish and easily hidden."

"Where?" Tetaky asked.

"In caves, and in storage bins made of brick deep in the sand along the routes that our soldiers will take."

Thure was looking at her with adoring wonder. "Our soldiers will be better fed than ever before," he said.

"And where the Hyksos have been, it is as though the locusts have plagued the Land," Sen-ut said, and added, "It was Res who thought of the antelope flesh."

"She is lovely," Pen said, and his stern face came alive.

"She is both lovely and brave," Sen-ut answered.

"The Two Lands will be free!" Tetaky sat up straight. "And in the Eternal Life of Ra, what more than to offer these our young bodies, and breathe out our last Holy Breath to nourish our Kas?" he asked, and we all seemed to lean forward, drawn to a center, as though the strength flowed in and out and through us, from one to the other. Rai held my hand.

"The God is among us," she whispered.

I closed my eyes. After a while I looked at her. She was asleep.

"Her Ka is winged," Sen-ut whispered, and Thure, looking at me, said,

"My Prince, your love for us all shines deep as mother-of-pearl." Silently, he poured more wine into my cup and gave it to me.

There was peace among us. The Twins had wandered down to the rafts, and Thure's head was on Sen-ut's lap. They were two hearts of a single Ka. Thure's courage was the true courage, that knows fear and conquers it. I looked at Tetaky, frail Tetaky, who must carry a lighter shield and lighter-weighted arms. How he fights! Kamose's Company, trained, each one of them, since childhood for their high destiny: the King's Captains.

I looked down at Rai. Then, as I leaned my head against the tree, pipe-notes, high and sweet, filled all the bright hot afternoon quiet with silver-cool sound. I heard the quick patter of goats' feet on the soft earth, and the sharp plaintive bleats of the she-goats. Then I saw the young goat-herd.

Happily piping, he came toward us between the houses and the palms and sycamores. The fishermen looked up from their nets and sang to the music.

"The goat-herd is in the water with the fishes . . ." and they laughed at him.

> "The goat-herd speaks with the mullet . . .
> And talks with the pike,
> Our goat-herd is out of the West . . ."

Rai stirred but did not waken. Tetaky, interested, put his chin on his hands and watched, but Thure and Sen-ut were lost in each other, and Ahmose-Eb was watching the mullet roes, to see that those left did not burn.

The young man ceased his piping as he drew close, and greeted us with a slight bow, his reed pipe held over his heart. He had curly brown hair, and a white loin-cloth, and wore a wide bronze bracelet on his left arm. His searching look was upon what was left of the cold goose and cheese, the honey cakes and greens.

"The mullet roes are for my brother. There is nothing much left of the other food." I asked his pardon.

"It is the sight of what is left of the goose that gives me the prickles of the twig-rush in the back of my mouth," he said, and squatted against a palm a hare's leap away from us.

Rai opened her eyes, and like a bird she was wide-awake.

"The greeting of Ra to you," she said, and poured wine from her own mug into another and handed it to him. He stood up and bowed, while I cut pieces from what was left of the goose, and piled sheep's curd, goat's cheese and greens onto the plate.

"What is your name?" I asked.

"Hor-min." He took the plate and sat down again, nearer to us.

"You speak with the speech of learning," Rai said. "From whence are you?"

"I was born in Memphis, but my father fled that city, to Kus. I escaped from Kus."

"Alone?" I asked.

He nodded. "My father and mother were stabbed in their beds while they slept, when the Hyksos attacked. The people of our household were taken as slaves."

"To the quarries?" Tetaky was interested.

"I do not know. But I have heard that they are building new forts, and need Egyptians to dig and pile the earthworks, for their own people have grown soft and even the peasants will not till the fields, let alone quarry or build, and they have little skill . . . and less of art," he said, and bit into the goose-flesh, chewing with relish.

"Hor-min," I said. "I would like to see more of you."

"That will be simple. Here in Thebes I am a goat-herd, but I am free!" He stretched out his arms holding the almost-bare goose-wing in his hand. "Here, I am not watched by the secret men of the enemy. By the Disc! They are everywhere, like gnats in the summer dark."

I cut the last pieces of meat from the goose. The copper knife shone, greasy-bright. Hor-min rose again and brought his plate. He was tall and thin. His thick brown hair was cut straight across his brow. "What would you have been . . . a scribe?" I asked as I refilled his plate.

"A Temple scribe I desired to be." He looked away from us and, with his finger in the side of his mouth, he whistled, sweet and high. Thure and Sen-ut wakened up with a start.

"And who is this disturber?"

Hor-min bowed. "Your pardon." A small dog came running. "Aja! where have you been? Scavenger, come here!" The short-eared, sharp-nosed little animal came to the goatherd's feet wriggling with joy, its rump on one side like the ill-steered stern of a river raft. He jumped up to the plate his master was holding. "Down, Aja!" Hor-min went back to his place.

"It takes many years of learning to become a Temple scribe," Ahmose-Eb said, and Hor-min, giving the goose-leg to the small dog, replied,

"I would have been a Priest of Ra."

My heart leapt. I turned and met Hor-min's eyes. This goat-herd would be Priest! My heart spoke the words deep inside me: I have found my Ka-friend. Aja was barking for more food. Filled with a strange joy, I thought: Today is a day of the Gods. I have been close to my sister, my Love. My brother has found for a while the beauty and pleasure he needs; and I have found my Ka-friend. Hor-min was telling Aja to bring the goats back. The small dog was well trained. In a few minutes the stray goats were eating the new green shoots with the rest of the herd.

Rai held my hand. "I shall never forget this day," she said. We sat silent, and close.

Ahmose-Eb had a kerchief over his face against the flies, and Aja was asleep on Hor-min's lap. Even restless Tetaky slept, stretched out on his belly with his head on his arm, and Pen, eternally sleepy, had his head on his drawn-up knees. Rai's head fell against my waiting shoulder. She sighed, and closed her eyes, but I knew she was not asleep. I thought that

Ak-hor and the Twins must be asleep down by the River. The fishermen had ceased their chatter. Only the buzzing of the bees among the acacia flowers, and the faint rustling of the birds, broke the silence. I closed my eyes, and after a while, leaning my cheek against the fragrant softness of my sister's hair, I, too, fell asleep.

"Wake up! Wake up!" I opened my eyes. Rai sat up, laughing. Kamose stood tall above, looking down at us. "Come! I have my Horus duty to perform. It is the hour. The Set-beasts will be browsing." Ahmose-Eb snatched the kerchief from his face and began to ladle the still warm roes onto a plate. "We must lessen the number of these foes of our farmers, before they spawn more of their lazy huge breed." My brother looked down at the linen cloth. "The locusts have swarmed here, I see." His gold-flecked eyes were bright.

"Cool wine for my King." Sen-ut leapt up, held the cup for Thure to fill and brought it to Kamose. He quaffed it with joy.

"And the roes? My gray mullet roes?"

"Here, my Lord."

"That's my Unique Friend!" He accepted the plate, and said, "Take the round stove back, my Sailor, if you will."

"My Lord." Ahmose-Eb grinned and turned to Hor-min. "You can help me." And together they carried the cooking stove back to the yellow-washed house.

Kamose ate leisurely, and with enjoyment. His eyes glowed brighter than the westering sun. Then he handed the plate to Sen-ut, thanked her and said, "I know who added the coriander and leeks." As he finished the wine, Ahmose-Eb came back with Hor-min, who, as he approached us, was suddenly still, his eyes wide with wonder. He stared at Kamose with awed recognition. Then he looked at me, and his mouth formed the soundless words,

"The King."

I nodded. Hor-min stood for a moment longer, then took three steps backward and bowed low, his arms outstretched, palms upward, in the ritual bow.

"Ra-en-Ra!" Kamose handed the wine cup to Thure. "What have we here? A goat-herd who does not fall flat on his belly? Who knows how to approach his King?" Aja was barking about his master's feet. "Come closer," Kamose said, and Hor-min came forward to the ritual distance. "When you face your King, speak boldly."

"To hearken is better than anything there is, O Divine of Existence."

"What is your name, Goat-herd?"

"Hor-min," my new friend answered, and bowed again.

"Well met, Hor-min." Kamose turned to us. "Up and about! All of you! Let us be away while the River is high and the Set-beasts are ripe for the spear. Thure! You stand as one in a dream"—he smiled, and put an arm about Sen-ut's shoulder—"a beautiful dream." He released her. "Tetaky! Off your belly! Pen! Uncurl yourself . . . Rai, up with you." He held out his hand to her. "And you, little Brother . . . Where are the others?"

"Down by the River," I answered, patting Hor-min's small dog, Aja, who was licking my feet.

Rai and Sen-ut were gathering the last of the plates and cups, knives and spoons.

"Come and help us," she said to Hor-min, who had been standing at a loss, not knowing whether he should walk backward, or wait for dismissal. Sen-ut closed the lid of the basket. "Come and help me to fold this," Rai said, taking hold of a corner of the large linen cloth. They folded it, while Thure and Sen-ut took the basket to the River. "Now the reed mat," Rai said, and together, laughing, they rolled it, and she gathered the small mats while Hor-min and I tied the large roll tight, and hoisted it on our shoulders.

Kamose was watching. "Goat-herd with the speech of learning, and the manners of a Nobleman, will you come with us?"

"My herd of goats, O Lord of the Two Lands," Hor-min said, bowing again.

"There are others to be goat-herds."

"Yes, O Bright on the Throne of Ra, but today this herd is in my care, and must be taken safely to the fold."

Kamose smiled and, nodding slightly, turned to me. "I would see more of this youth."

"That will be simple," I replied. "In Thebes, we are free." And I looked at Hor-min. He bowed to Kamose, as Ra on earth, then turned to me with his hand on his heart. He bowed to me, then to Rai, who held out her hand to him.

"Ra's Blessing on you, Hor-min," she said, and he bowed again, then was about to pick up his end of the roll, but Tetaky picked it up, smiling, and said,

"Your herd of goats, Hor-min."

My new friend walked a few steps backward, almost tripping over Aja, and turned to gather his flock.

We stacked the roll and the mats and cloths on the Twins' raft. The basket and the spice box were already on the deck of Tetaky's, and the fishermen, wide-awake now, were teasing Pu with a large piece of mullet. She was jumping high, making darts at it. At last, with a graceful leap, she caught it and held it fast in her paws, tearing it through the side of her mouth, her eyes watchful.

Kamose put one arm around Rai's shoulder and the other about mine, and we stood at the River's edge. Hundreds of pin-tails were gathered under the bank and I remembered how they had lined the ropes of the ships moored behind the Funeral Barque on the day of my father's funeral. Their scout saw us and gave the alarm, and the drowsy birds flew up and away as one bird. At the whirr of their wings the other fishers looked up from their slicing and salting, and called us farewell.

We waved back to them. Stray dogs had gathered and were barking and growling and making quick sallies at Pu, who hissed and spat at them but stayed there, tearing and chewing, till the mullet was gone and Mer-neb called to her.

She swam to his raft, jumped onto it and sat up straight by the rolls of matting. Kamose swung us around still in his arms, and looked at his friends standing there on the bank.

"You, my Little Ones, may go in whose raft you wish, and watch from the shallows. Only my double-lashed raft will make this attack." He held Rai and me close for a moment.

"And Horus who avenges his father shall make the poison to retreat," she spoke the ancient words and looked up at him, her green eyes grave. He lifted her with a swift strong hold and held her face to his, then gently put her down.

"Off with you! Now Tetaky, you . . . and Thure, and Sen-ut, that will be four of you, don't drown my little sister. You two," he said to the Twins, "you take Pu, and keep her on leash! And now, Brother! Let us rid our farmers of this lumbering evil, and shrive our Kas of the black mists of Set." With his arm still about my shoulder, we walked along the old jetty to where Ahmose-Eb and Pen were already squatting astern of the two bound rafts, their paddles held upright between their knees. Ak-hor knelt in the bow of the pole-raft stacking the harpoons he had ground sharp as razors.

I leapt to the solid deck with Pen, and gathered myself as small as I could.

"Cast off, Mariners of Ra!" Kamose said.

This time we were paddling upstream and it was harder work. Marshy islands were appearing everywhere the River had ebbed. Soon we approached the papyrus clumps, weaving in and out of the tall reeds till we came to a wide stretch of open water and saw hippopotamus heads all so close together that they seemed like another island. When our raft glided into view, they turned to stare at us with cold, outjutting eyes. Kamose stood looking at them. Then he pointed.

"Akh! Hiy!"

A great bull hippo rose like a mountain out of the water. Ak-hor gave a sharp gasp.

"He looks dark red as dried blood."

Ahmose-Eb and Pen turned to face the beast.

"Not yet!" Kamose murmured. "He is the last one! Stinking Face will be the last one."

A cow dived under the water astern and the lashed rafts heaved up, sideways, and turned full around, almost capsizing.

"She-put!"

I heard my own short, hard laugh at quiet Pen's using the name of Set's wife as the curse that it is. We had righted ourselves.

"Sta-ur! Face to the east!" Kamose commanded, and the raft slid by the other two cows toward a mound where two of the huge beasts were belching at each other and fighting in a haze of spray and foam, their open mouths two arms' length wide, and the great fangs in their lower jaws boring each other's necks, till the huge bull came between them, and the mound gave way under their weight. The three of them disappeared under the water, but our raft was besieged by the angry beasts. A bull lunged toward us. Kamose threw his harpoon. It almost found its mark, but went into the side of the animal's throat. "Ra-en-Ra!" he muttered. "Love makes the arms languid." He waited till the bull came up to breathe. Then, with a small scudding sound and the flash of sharp metal, the spiked blade sank deep into its throat, and this time the shaft broke and left the gaff where it had found its mark. The bull roared and fought. The River was a moving mass. The bull swam away, pulling the raft after him. At last he weakened. The spume and splashing of his fight settled, and the River bloodied.

Time and again, we dragged our enormous kill to the shore and left it in the hands of the jubilant farmers, who would barter the hides to make shields and helmets for the South Land's soldiers.

I saw the other two rafts in the shallows, but not clearly. My Ka had shifted. I was in a world of huge, dark aggressors, rearing up over us, belching up water and filth from their bellies and spewing it out of their yawning jaws onto our naked bodies; the stench of blood, the rafts whirling and as lightning shafts, the bright-tipped javelins speared through the spray. Through my half-closed, sweat-filled eyes I saw that my brother's face was the Falcon's proud face: Her-bak! Then it was his own face again. But the Falcon, Horus, hovered above his head! Amazed at my own Ka-sight, I stood in awe amidst the bulging, heaving chaos.

"Out astern, Sailors of Ra! Stinking Face, he is there!"

Swiftly, our Mariners turned the lashed rafts, dodging the swarming beasts like light-footed wrestlers.

"Hiy! Ra-en-Ra!"

To the left of our bows Stinking Face had come up to breathe.

Ak-hor put the long chain in Kamose's hands. We were close. The rage of the animal was a living thing. Its eyes were cold stones. It was huge beyond imagining. I felt a thrill of fear, but kept my gaze on Kamose's legs. His straining calf muscles looked as though they had grown out of the reeds of the raft. I saw the sinews flex. His feet seemed glued to the solid deck. He raised his arms slowly. Then with his left hand he threw the chain. It straightened out to its whole length, then seemed to coil as it fell on the water, sank and entangled the feet of the monster beast. Its head disappeared under the water, seeking this new menace; then it reared up again, howled battle and charged. At the sound, all the other beasts spat and spumed, lunging in fury and lashing the River to the rage of the Cataracts. As the rafts turned, the bull charged again, its mouth agape and its fangs in the reeds of the deck. I thought we were lost, but Kamose jumped onto its back, struck between its fat shoulders with his dagger and struck again and again. With a bound it went under the water and the swell almost whelmed us, but Ahmose-Eb and Pen turned the rafts toward Kamose as he leapt back again to the deck. The River was red with blood and the churning spray the color of rust. My stomach heaved as the rafts rose, rocking. I almost fell overboard, and lost my sickness saving myself. Stinking Face rose out of the water, his sides streaming blood, and, lumbering, charged us again. Kamose struck twice with his dagger. The rattle of the chain was loud in my ears, and strange. Ak-hor stood tense. Kamose fought on, the chain in one hand and the dagger in the other. The vultures had gathered, dark shapes against the green-gold of the sun-set sky. Alone, Kamose brought the Set-beast in closer. Then the rafts heaved up on end, an angry cow under them, to fall onto the water again; calm, blood-streaked water, and the dark beasts seemed all turned to stone, as the huge bull reared up over us spewing filth. As lightning, Kamose struck. His arm was deep-thrust into the gaping throat. He leapt back. Then he plunged deep again, and the chain slackened. With a last great lurch that sent spray to the tops of the papyrus umbels, Stinking Face fell dead in the River.

Kamose pulled the huge carcass close in, flung the other end of the chain around the flesh-rolled neck and held it firm as we paddled ashore to the waiting farmers, who were shouting now, and waving their knives that shone gold in the rays of Ra, westering.

Breathless and spent, we left them to their work and pulled out again. Ahmose-Eb and Pen paddled through the reeds, away from the bloodied River, and soon the water around us was calm and green-gold in the sun-set. A few huge heads rose, black against the gold of the sky, and the tall reeds were flame-edged. In a quiet pool, an ibis stood silent among the water plants, its pure white plumage golden-pale, alone and brooding.

"The Thoth-bird awaits a fat frog," Ahmose-Eb said, and his voice was tired.

"Or is waiting to write with its golden beak the defeat of Set, by the Falcon of the South Land." Pen was solemn, and I thought, as he lay down his paddle, that he spoke true words. For my Ka had seen.

My brother slid quietly into the water. We followed him. It was deep and clear. We swam and laved ourselves till we were clean, then climbed back and turned our rafts to the Eastern Shore, to the place where we had embarked at the dawn.

Slowly we pulled in. The other two rafts had come up

alongside. Kamose waded to Tetaky's raft. He picked up Rai in his arms and carried her ashore.

We left the others to bring in the tackle, weapons and baskets, and walked, one each side of our brother, barefoot along the new-plowed furrows. The plows lay about, but the cows were stabled, resting and fed. Only the farmers and fishermen who were skinning our kill remained in the darkening fields.

"Press in the seed, Little Brother. Press it in deep with your feet," Kamose said and, bending down, he took up two handfuls of the rich earth and looked down at them, his face stern and terrible. Then he clasped his hands together, and raised them, clenched, toward us, and opened them. The earth was solid and black in the center of his right palm. "Thus will I bind the Two Lands." He stood, tall against the turquoise sky, his bare feet sinking into the black earth, and his face toward the Western Crags, purple-dark with earth's shadow, their summits ablaze with Ra's golden Light. "Amun-Ra, Who is Yesterday, is Today, and knows all To-morrows! Let thy Rays encompass me." Rai held my hand. "I will sear the scum of Set with the burning Flame of Ra, and scorch their gross and arrogant bodies till the stench of their oily flesh fouls all the winds of Byblos. . . . Cover your face, Set-Apophis." He almost whispered the words, but the sound held all the winds and typhoons and the sand-storms of Ta-mery. "The Silence has covered your name."

We fell, for the majesty of him, flat on our bellies, and there, in the new-plowed field, we paid homage to our brother, and our King.

"Lord of the Two Lands, Whadj-Kheper-Ra, Kamose, Neptaui."

CHAPTER III

Kamose was manifest on his throne. All the South Land had,
for three days and three nights, held Festival. The soul of
Thebes had been ravished by Kamose. On this last night
of rejoicing, on the risen tide of jubilation, no one in the City
of the God would sleep, but snatch small naps in the heat
of the afternoon, and waken to new revelry.

During these days of celebration, after the Crowning, there
had been quiet in the King's House, and I came, on the third
day, at sun-set, to the summer house in my mother's garden.
The birds were drowsy in the vines and acacias, and only
the sun-birds twittered and plunged, to strut the tiles and
chase the small lizards that basked in the last warm rays of

Ra in his Sek-tet Boat descending, on this, the day of my manhood.

After the Morning Rite, in the Inmost Shrine, Miutu had tied on my loin-cloth, my *dayu*, and tomorrow, at dawn, I would enter the Temple, The House of Life, to begin my longed-for studies toward Priesthood.

I leaned against the cool painted wood of one of the pillars feeling young and lack-wit, and my shaven head felt bare. Four new wigs, feather-light and lined with the finest linen, lay on the chest in my dressing room. Two of them, for wearing at all times, were cut to the lobes of my ears and straight across the brow, and two were fuller, to wear with the Fisherman's Circlet for State occasions.

The breeze that comes with the sun-set played about my naked ear. I missed my side-lock. I had twirled it, twisted it and pulled it while I was studying, or thinking, or sitting alone, or standing, as now, in a strange unease. I had not seen my brother since the Crowning. "Kamose, Whadj-Kheper-Ra . . ." I whispered the words. His stillness had been a void, pure and unmeasured, and his gold-flecked eyes held the apartness of the God. The Thebans who had filled the vast Outer-Court of the Temple, and beyond to the banks of the River, had fallen on their bellies, and as they rose to gaze on him, they fell on their faces again and a great breath was born, and as they stood up straight, it gathered to a murmuring like distant thunder in the Eastern Hills, and grew into a surging wave of pilgrim sound that met and joined with the whirring of wings as a thousand doves for the Thousand Stars soared skyward, white-golden in the blue, to fly with the Four Winds to the earth's Four Corners. And as though she, too, were winged, Sek-met, held in leash by Ak-hor, tore away from his grasp and, with a long wide-curving leap, landed on the platform of the Throne Shelter.

Kamose, his hands crossed on his breast, holding the Crook, for Service, and the Flail, for Authority, with the Fiery Cobra on his brow, was apart, and unaware. The lioness raised up, her fore-feet on the arm of the Throne Chair. Then she stood down, bent her head and licked his feet, and a different sound rose from the throats of the Thebans. Their necks swelled, and their whole heart's loyalty, the hope of freedom and the will to die, came forth in a vast human roar.

My mother's eyes had been bright as the light all about us, and her tears did not fall, but washed her face in beauty.

With my thought of her, she came into the garden and gave me her hands, in silence. I saw that though, since the Crowning, she had stayed in the Innermost Shrine, in prayer, there was no peace in her eyes.

"Ahmose, I am afraid," she said, echoing my own unease. She paced, began to speak and paced again. "I am afraid because Kamose knows not the meaning of fear."

I thought I knew the reason for my mother's disquiet: Nefertari! She had stood, tall and shining-skinned, with Teti-sheri. Her full, firm breasts were bare, and bronze-smooth between the rich faience and lapis lazuli belt that held her linen skirt, and the hundreds of gleaming jewels in her collar. All earth's embellishments, I had thought, and shivered at the glitter in her long, half-closed eyes watching Kamose as a snake watches, and subtlety hung on the curve of her thick black lashes.

My mother clasped her hands to her mouth. Her lips were pale.

"My fear is thin as the air, Ahmose. When I try to clothe it in thought, it dissolves like clouds in the wind. . . . Yet my soul is caught in its dark web. Akh! No! Ahmose, no! Help rid me of these thoughts that crawl like lean ants foraging." She unclasped her hands and leaned against a pillar, her shoulders sagging. "Flames eat Nefertari, and her fists are clenched on dark desires. . . . Ahmose, the half-sister desires to be Queen."

Our eyes held in the silence. Then I said, "My Mother, I have known her desire since my father's Funeral Rite. I was

shocked cold standing there. But it is of no matter! Rai is
the Royal Daughter. She and Kamose will wed at the harvest. The preparing is already afoot. . . ."

"Nefertari is like a snake coiled." Ah-hotpe shuddered.
"And Tetisheri abets her. Ahmose, how is my mother so
blind?"

"She loves Nefertari. It has always been thus."

"She sent a message to me an hour after the Crowning,
but these three days I have spent in the Inner Shrine . . .
till this moment." She sighed, and looked out toward the
Western Crags. "If your father were here I should be fearless
as a hawk." She turned to me, her head high. "But Kamose
is the Hawk! His mind grows wings from which the lightning glances as a Flame that falls on easy men and seres the
stagnant rust in them to ashes. With him to lead them, our
men will grow broad again with the will to fight." Her body
softened. Her eyes were warm again and we embraced. "My
Three!" Her voice was hushed. "King-Warrior, Priest and
Queen." She lifted her head and looked at me. "Strange,
that Anat-neby turned traitor to Kamose's love . . . At the
harvest he will marry, according to our ancient ways, the
Royal Daughter."

"Rai," I whispered.

My mother put her hand on my shoulder. "It is seemly,
and just, Ahmose. It would seem that the God does not
consent that we stray from the age-old custom. Anat-neby
had not one drop of Royal blood."

"She is queen in Avaris."

My mother shrugged and shook her head. "It was only for
Kamose's love of her that your father and Miutu gave consent
to their marriage."

"And his own love for . . ."

"For Piopi . . . I can speak the name." She smiled. "He will
not escape Kamose."

I put my cheek to hers. "You are not still afraid . . . for
the King?"

She put both hands on my shoulders. "My Moon Child,

my tall, thin, solemn and new-shaven man-child, no! Forget these fears that are born of what is beyond my heart, and even my believing." Her eyes were bright with tears. Then she smiled, as dawn-light through the mist, and kissed me nose to nose.

Dogs were barking as I walked slowly back. They are freed from their leashes, I thought, and the farmers are hunting the marauding hyena at the desert's edges. The pillars of my room were darkening to purple-blue in the last long-hovering wings of dusk-light. The basalt statue of Osiris glowed in his niche. He seemed to breathe. "Osiris, Lord . . ." In silent praise, I stretched myself belly-down on the cool floor, thinking of my brother. "Osiris, Lord . . . his will is a two-tongued flame. He would destroy, and he would build . . . and he will marry Rai . . . Osiris, Lord, whose Plumes shed Light," I prayed, my arms outstretched, and my brow pressed against the cold tiles, "may my brother and my sister, on the Throne of the Two Lands, cause a state of reverence to enfold the earth . . . Osiris, Lord of Peace . . ." For all my prayer, each dull thud of my heart against the tiles said, "War! War! War! Osiris, Lord, who would not have us in array against our fellows. . . . Lord Montu, of the Animals, our chariot beasts . . . our horses! Kamose's white-gold horse, Minirt . . . trained to the chariot . . ." Behind my eyelids I saw him, spear-thrust, slashed with swords and pierced with arrows, his blood flowing red rivers down the white of him, his bronze eyes dimming. "Osiris, Lord . . . Akh! Lord Montu . . ." I lay in a cold sweat, brooding.

After a while I rose, bowed to the God and went to the small room next to the bathing-room, where Neme dressed me. A short, fine-pleated kilt lay on the low wooden chest. I put it on, then took up my father's first man's sporran, put there for me, beside my kilt, and, with pleasure and remembering, fastened it to my belt. My groin was stiff. Miutu's hand was firm, I thought. The sharp flint knife cut clean. I looked across the room and saw on my small stool a golden arm-bracelet. I went and picked it up. Inside, my name was carved. It was from Kamose, and had a lion's head on it. My heart leapt. Filled with joy I clasped the golden gift around my wrist and, sitting down on the chest, looked long at the finely wrought lion's head: Kamose's symbol. I pushed the bracelet up to its place on my upper arm, and held my hand around it.

As the first gray hint of day-light paled the stars, I was bathed and dressed, too early, and as the first bird sang, I came to our childhood Court of Learning, and sat alone on my own low stool, thinking of Senseneb, and loving him. The Old One! He still teaches us, I thought, and we listen. "Never cease to strive, my Young Ones, for no man yet in a million years has developed his full skills." How often did he tell us that the limits of our learning, our endurance, can never be attained? Nor the full limits of our seeking, I thought, remembering Kheri-heb's answer to me, as we waited in the King's Chamber before Kamose's Crowning. "When the Golden Cobra is placed upon his brow, the Fire of Ra and the latent God-fire in the spinal marrow of Kamose meet and join in the center of his brow, between his eyes. The Golden Cobra is more than a symbol. It is the Spirit revealing Itself in fusion with Kamose, no longer Kamose alone, but Kamose Whadj-Kheper-Ra, Nebtaui . . . But this cannot be explained, my son, in a few moments' words. We shall have long hours to meditate on this in the House of Life."

The birds in full song brought me back to myself. I stood up. Then I walked along the wall, fingering the niches that bulged with ancient scrolls. I saw that most of them sadly needed mending. Then, impatient and wondering when Neme would come to say my chair was waiting, I went to the pillars and leaned against one of them. "The House of Life . . . today." I was shivering with eager joy as Ra, rising, flooded the old Court of Learning with his Light.

"So I find you here . . . I should have known." My mother came across the garden. Her hair was loosely held in an amethyst fillet, and she wore a simple shift, off one shoulder, like the girls from the bakery. She came between the pillars into the room. "Today, my Young One, you begin your life in the Temple." She took both my hands and held her cheek against my own. "Learn well. . . . Perhaps I will lead your first steps myself, while Kheri-heb is away. I will ask him. He is to go with Kamose on the Royal Circuit."

I looked at her in surprise, and would have asked questions, but my grand-mother came toward us across the garden.

"Ah-hotpe! My Daughter, for three days I have been searching for you! All this time you have been in the Temple. What, by the Tears of Isis, do you find to do there? And now I find you in the children's Court! There is much to talk of, plans to make . . ." She was talking as she came close to us, the fine pleats she always wore flicking with each quick step. "She's here! At last, Senseneb, I've found her. My daughter is here," she called over her shoulder to the Old One. "And by the Phallus of the Apis Bull! Our young Princeling, too!" She came, stood on tiptoe and put her hands on my shoulders. Her fingers were strong as metal. "You are thin with growing, but you are tall as your father, and sturdier flesh will come with valor. There's warrior blood in you."

"Ahmose has learned almost all I can teach him." Senseneb smiled, and embraced me. "Your first day in the House of Life," he said, and turned to the women. "Our young Prince will, with time, and devotion, become true Priest."

"After the Two Lands are free he may be Priest if he wills," Tetisheri said. "Now it is the time for him to learn of battle."

"Let him learn the True Knowing, my Lady, while he has the leisure, and the desire"—he looked down at her, smiling —"for rarely do the two come at the same time."

Tetisheri laughed up into his face and shook the tight curls in her wig. "And the Young Lion? Kamose? He will have the desires he has always had . . . but not the leisure." She wrinkled her nose. "At least, not until he marries." She turned to Ah-hotpe. "And he must marry at once! The King must marry!"

"At the harvest," my mother said, and Tetisheri looked up at her with raised brows. "Kamose will take his bride, according to tradition," my mother repeated, and her voice was gentle, "at the harvest."

"By the Great Strider! To wait all these weeks! These are times of crisis."

"My Mother! You know well that our strategy is to appear at ease with the North Land . . . and to give no sign of crisis. You know that in the Two Lands the people expect their King to wed at harvest time. It would be unwise to give the least hint of change."

"Until we, ourselves, are ready," the Old One added.

"Kamose should marry now. He spends far too much time with that white-skinned girl of the people. He is King. He must marry." She stood stiff and straight, her head high, her eyes bright as quartz stones. "He must marry Nefertari."

My mother stood quite still. With a swift glance our eyes met. Cold sweat chilled my nape. Senseneb, stretching his stiff neck, walked to the other side of the small pool and stood with his head bowed down and his hands behind his back. My grand-mother drew herself to her full height. Her voice cut the silence like a spear-thrust.

"He will marry Nefertari." She swung around on her heel. "Senseneb!"

"My Queen." He bowed, and stood silent.

"Speak! Have you lost your tongue? Are you not in accord with me?" Senseneb shrugged his thin shoulders. Tetisheri turned back to my mother. "And you, Ah-hotpe, why have you avoided me in this?" Without waiting for an answer my grand-mother turned to me. "And you, Grand-son? It is rare that our young scholar has nothing to say. Though, for all your shorn head and your covered manhood, I doubt if your chatter is any less childish."

"Then, Grand-mother, it is better I do not speak till my words match my shorn head."

"You are insolent! And you have not answered my question."

"I did not hear you ask a question, Grand-mother."

"You are right! By the Crusher of Bones! I did not! I spoke!" She looked again at the Old One, then at her daughter and again at me. "This silence irks me! Ahmose, speak!"

"He who is cautious of speech has a broad face," I teased her. Then, seeing her fury, "I had thought the matter settled," I said.

"Of course it is settled."

My mother stood still, tall against the early light, and said,

"The King will marry the Royal Daughter."

"The Royal Daughter!" At the scorn in my grand-mother's voice, I felt anger grip me.

"You would shape all to your own desiring," I said, and held my breath.

"By the Everlasting Devourer!" She stood in front of me. Her linen skirt seemed carved in stone. "Must I listen to the babble of children?"

"No, my Lady." Senseneb spoke quietly, bowed and held out his arm.

After a moment, she put her hand on it, her small face set as in a mask of clay. She looked up at her daughter.

"You, my Child, are wrong in this. Kamose will marry Nefertari. Though on a concubine, my grand-child is kingly got! She has the Royal warp. She is strong and beautiful . . . and clear of heart. . . . She loves the King."

"Clear of heart?" I murmured.

My mother did not move. When she spoke her voice was quiet.

"Kamose will marry the Royal Daughter."

Suddenly my grand-mother stamped both her tiny feet in rage, clenching her fists and shaking them. Then she stood still as a stone.

"I have been thrust out of my own city, exiled. I married a King. I have given birth to Kings and—by Ptah, The God

of my City, and Shaper of All Things!—I have shaped!"
She swung around to face me, her eyes narrow. "Would that
I could re-shape my younger grand-son! Make him a warrior!
Not a puny priestling, mooning. calf-eyed after his punier
sister. . . ." I felt my nostrils stretch. My face froze, then
flamed. "Akh! By the Cruncher of Bones! He has a temper,
the Young One. . . . Come, Senseneb, it is all said that must
be said." She shook her curls, and with a slight, graceful
bow to us, smiling, she whispered, "Kamose will marry Nefertari. What a glory they will be on the Throne of the
Two Lands when we have won our battle! And, my
Daughter, perhaps you are right about the season of the
marriage. I agree. It shall be held, as is our tradition, at
the harvest." And as though we had passed a pleasant and
unruffled space together, she placed her hand again on the
Old One's waiting arm and, still merrily chatting, she left us.

My mother watched their two figures disappear through
the pillars at the other side of the garden, then she turned
and came to me.

"Ahmose, on this morn you will enter the Temple. On
this morn, your God-ward studies will begin."

Amazed at her calm, I said, "I am still scourged with anger,
and far from God-thoughts."

"My Young One, you know that when your grand-mother
is thwarted and enraged, the strong words that spate from
her small mouth ease her fiery spirit. She means but half of
them . . . and Rai, in her own self's joy, is beyond the hurt
of words, as she, the Royal Daughter is beyond the plans of
mortals." She smiled. "May Thoth prosper your studies, my
Moon Child."

"These studies? For so long the desire for them has filled
my whole heart. My Mother, what is this heart that thinks
and feels and desires?"

"It is the carnelian vessel that holds the Divine Fire of
Ra within us." She put her hands on my shoulders. "And
may Ra's blessing, and the blessing of your beloved Osiris,
go with you." Her hands were firm and cool, and gentle.
"My Young One, harken to Kheri-heb. You will be given to

learn of things that seem strange, sometimes wrong, to you, and you will balk." She smiled at my gesture of unbelief. "Kheri-heb is Adept. He is wise. All that he commands and wills for you is good. . . . And now, my Moon Child, your chair is waiting to take you to the House of Life."

I went across the garden, through the House and out onto the pillared porch. The wide Court-yard was almost empty. I walked down the steps, the heat of my anger still lingering, watching my sandaled feet, and when I came to the bottom step a small dog came barking and jumping about me.

"Aja!" I looked up, and there, standing beside my chair, with a smile on his face as broad as Thebes itself, was Hor-min. He bowed, his hand on his heart. Then he took my outstretched hands. His long eyes were so full black, there seemed to be no white in them at all.

"The King sent Ahmose, son of Ebana, to my dwelling, to bring me here."

"My brother sent for you?" He nodded. I stepped into the chair. "Come with me." He followed and sat down beside me. Aja jumped in after us.

"My Prince, I am to share your studies in the Temple," he said. "I am unable to believe what has happened to me."

And I could not believe. Amid the ceremonies of his Crowning, the daily Temple Rituals, his judgments and appearances and his secret Councils, my brother had remembered Hor-min. I could not wait to tell Rai how our brother had found again the friend who had wakened her sleeping with his pipes, and come to us leading a herd of goats.

With slow, measured step, the bearers walked the wide Temple way in time to their singing. Hor-min and I talked together, then we were quiet, our souls praising and joyful.

"Thebes," he whispered, as he gazed at white sails half-seen above the low-washed banks, and a heron on a mound left by the shallowing River. Tears filled his eyes when five tall maidens moved from their waists in a circle, but could not bow for the water-jars they held on their heads. "My Prince, I am in Thebes. The City of the Hidden Name! The City of the Lord of Eternity!" Then a shadow fell across his face. I waited. "Yet even here, within the limits of the Holy City, there are spies. For five moons I have lived in the outskirts, among the people, and some of them, for a bag of corn, will shed their virtue as young cobras shed their skins. The people were dull of heart and hopeless again after their King was murdered and we lost the battle for Kus. The Hyksos came to further forage and rape, though the full tribute had been paid. . . . But since the King was crowned . . ." he murmured.

"Hor-min, my brother will unite the Two Lands. Our people will rally again."

"I saw him crowned." Hor-min's eyes were bright. "With all there, I fell on my belly, and rose to shout with all my breath and strength. He is Ra on earth."

We came to the Great Pylon Gateway in the outer wall of the Temple. I looked up at the huge bronze sockets of the flag-poles, and upward to the banners of the gods, rippling in the early morning breeze. As we drew closer, up the wide shallow ramp, the great gold-studded bronze doors opened silently.

We walked along the wide way to the bustling Peristyle, where Temple scribes hurried, artisans worked, painters and sculptors were decorating new chapels and Priests of Purified Fingers were leading the visitors to the places of their desiring. Three of them came to meet us. They walked swiftly, with seeming slow gait. We followed them across the huge Fore-court and up the wide steps to the vast pillared Hall, and stood, forgetting our messengers, our necks craning upward, gazing at the immeasurable height, overwhelmed by the grandeur, the hush, the immense, incalculable shadow-shafted space.

Slowly, we lowered our heads, feeling as ants. The three Priests were waiting. We came up to them, and followed as they turned eastward, at the end of the vast colonnaded Hall, to an Inner Court, and there, surrounded by the Purified Ones, sat Miutu, High Priest and Great of Visions, and be-

side him was Kheri-heb and his pupil, Montu-Thoth. At the
majesty of these three, we fell on our bellies.

Then Kheri-heb spoke, and touched our heads with the
gold tip of his ebony wand. We stood up. His eyes did not
leave Hor-min's face.

"Name the Door."

"Opener of the Divine Light."

"Name the Upper Hinge of the Door."

"The Lord of Truth is his Name."

"The Lower Hinge."

"The Lord of Strength to bind base desires."

The Lector-Priest then turned to me.

"Ahmose, Prince of the Two Lands," he said, "Hor-min
will spend seven days in the testing. Afterward, you will
meet again." He looked at us both. "Between what you are
now, and what you will be, a Path leads. The Way of the
Knowing is narrow."

We both bowed. Miutu rose, and stepped forward. He
raised his hand above us, in blessing.

"May the Lord of the Winds cleanse your breath. May
your Kas gather strength in the Eastern Horizon."

We bowed low. Then I turned to Hor-min, and Aja,
who had been quiet, began to romp about us and bark. I
looked at the High Priest. His thin lips were smiling. He
nodded to Montu-Thoth, and Hor-min, his hands crossed
on his breast, followed them, Aja at his heels.

I stood alone with Kheri-heb. My long ardor had left me.
I asked in my heart only to be a humble slave of this majesty.
There was a hint of a smile on Kheri-heb's lips as he turned,
and silently we walked together to the small pillared room
where, for two thousand years, Royal Sons had come into
the Knowing.

As he had planned, Kamose used the Cattle Census and
the Royal Circuit as a final means of bringing his plans and
preparation in the South Land nomes, north of Thebes, to
battle readiness. Pen-aati and the Chief Scribe stayed with

the Nomarchs, and made check of the grain and the animals: "Every hoofed of four feet and every hatched of two wings."

The King, with the Royal Guard in their silver uniforms, Neshi and Ak-hor, with their Nubian Scouts in full war dress, and thirty of Pen's chariots, all drawn by the well-known gray-black horses bred in the Royal stables, made a brave and magnificent procession along the dyke tops and through the villages and towns. Everywhere the people, the fishers and farmers, the fowlers and gleaners, the merchants and artisans, left their work and came running, to fall on their faces and rise up again waving their arms and shouting, all along the way.

Each nome was quietly cleared of grafters, of the sheriffs who received and the mayors who took bribes. The honest old men were pensioned. The not-so-old were given work for the South Land: collecting and packing animal skins and hides, sinews and bones from the butchers and hunters; gathering glue from the trees; and taking them, when dark had fallen, to the secret places prepared by Pery-em-wah's Eyes and Ears. Releasing these men enabled the ardent and well-trained young men to revive the two interlocking systems of Royal and rural government, and to be alert to treachery and the stealthy entry of the enemy into the provincial towns and villages.

A war-ship and the Royal Yacht sailed alongside the route of the Progress. Kamose took one meal with the Nomarch they were visiting, and afterward he slept in the yacht, where secret meetings were held and the underground work reported and discussed.

Aknere, the Chief of the Young Eyes and Ears, followed the Progress in secret. He spent the days with his young fellow spies, and under cover of hunting the lean, shrewd wolves that stole out of the desert to harass the herds, or stretching a net across a ravine where the jackals gathered to raid in a pack, or setting traps for the wary hyena, he was planning secret food stores for the dried game and fish that were Sen-ut's and Res' concern. The ox-carts that carried their netting and traps carried, hidden underneath them, dried water-fowl, game and fish, and fodder for the horses to stack in the caves and in brick-lined storage bins deep in the sand, along the route that our armies would take. Pretending to go with the honey-gatherers and the collectors of turpentine, Aknere and a chosen few of his companions would leave them to scout for safe hiding places in the Eastern Hills, and good places for ambush. His nights he spent in the taverns, recruiting men of all ages for Kheri-heb to meet with, to test with his inner vision, and choose. From all walks of life they came, to aid and strengthen Pery-em-wah's old and experienced spies.

Pen-ekheb's Captains, all along the way of the Progress, under pretext of inspecting the chariot-repair stations, left the secret vaults full-stacked with wheels and spare parts, harness and tools for the mending, which they had brought concealed in the ox-carts of the Royal Treasurer, and which were guarded as harvest produce by Ak-hor's trusty Nubians.

The Royal Seal was now held by a cousin of Ahmose-Eb's, but he wore his Seal-ring and carried the staff of his office only when ceremony demanded, and not every day and everywhere he went, as Thuty had done.

Sen-ut and Res had secretly gathered the young of the nomes, and had carefully chosen thirty-six young scribes, two web-priests and seventeen virgins who were versed in the Knowing, to join the ranks of the Young Eyes and Ears by the time the King and his retinue returned to Thebes.

In his chariot, with Set-met at his side, and Pen's Chariot Company behind him, Kamose drove his pair of gray-black horses through the length and breadth of the nomes north of Thebes. He was Falcon of the South Land, and his people adored him, and were refreshed by his presence among them. Courage and hope were born anew in their hearts at the sight of his youthful majesty.

The days of the Royal Circuit had been quiet in the King's House, and I engrossed in my studies. Though Kheri-heb was away with Kamose, he had left enough work for me, and my mother, as she had desired, guided my first steps with patience and joy.

After meditating with her on Kheri-heb's lesson, and talking of it, I told her of my loosened flesh, and the magnified Light I had seen, the awareness I had felt at the height of my father's Funeral Rite, and her eyes glowed deep, and she talked of Osiris.

"Your father told you the legend of Osiris, the God-man, when you were a child at his knee. Now you must delve deeper into the meaning of the ancient myth. Ahmose, Osiris is the God-Spirit in every man; the Eternal Principle, changeless through births and through deaths; the Center of Infinite Peace and Bliss. My Son, be still. If you gaze at yourself in the quiet water of my garden pool you will see your face. If its surface were troubled by the winds or the wings of water-birds splashing, your face would be broken up and distorted, unknown to you. To see our own soul, the Osiris in us, we must still the waters of our thinking." She was silent. Then she asked, "Ahmose, what is your thought on the Dwat? The Realm of Osiris? The Other World?"

"It is the Realm where we find ourselves after we die. The Realm of the Kas."

"It is the Place of Becoming. Your Ka will find itself with the full consciousness it has acquired and earned while it inhabited your body on this earth."

"My father once said that a man would find himself with all his deeds, good and bad, piled up beside him."

She smiled. "We shall all be judged. Osiris will weigh our hearts against the Feather of Maat, who is All Truth. Osiris is King and Judge in the Dwat, the Other World, and Ahmose . . . we cannot escape the judgment of the Highest, the Osiris, in ourselves." She sighed. "It is deep, my Son. Seek your True Self." She rose from Kheri-heb's chair, where she had been sitting the while, and looked down at me. "There will be work for the King, and the South Land," she said, and left me.

I did not see my brother till the fifteenth day after his return, when, my concentration disturbed by a sudden shadow, I looked up and he was there, in the small enclosed Court! He looked down at my palette and my scrolls.

"I need you, Brother," he said. "We know not of the future that is held in the Eye of Ra, and you, Ahmose, Prince of the South Land, should be aware of our Councils . . . and of what we have accomplished during this Royal Circuit. . . . You plan well. I have need, more times than I can count, of your thoughts on our strategies. . . . Come, sometimes to the secret Councils. . . . Later, I shall ask a great task of you."

"Kamose," I sighed, "three times you have told of this task. What is it?"

He smiled. Then he shook his head. "When the time comes," he said.

I was reluctant to leave my Temple studies even for the hours in the Council, but as I listened to my brother's plans and saw how he pierced to the marrow of a problem, then resolved it with vision and daring, I felt a growing excitement.

Pery-em-wah's Eyes and Ears in Secret and Aknere's Young Eyes and Ears came from Memphis, and Abydos, and Assiut and from the Cataract Fort. As was the custom, they would call on Pen-aati. Then they would come by the secret passage that led from his garden-house to the secret Council Chamber, to read their dispatches and join in the planning. In each city where they had been, they had trained men, in groups of five to a house, to shoot their arrows unseen from the roof-slits, standing on rope-ladders already well hidden and stacked. Others they had prepared for special tasks they would perform when our soldiers attacked, to hinder the tyrants who garrisoned their city. Each hour I was in Council, I grew in amaze.

Mer-neb had stationed Captains of his Archers in relays all about the South Land, training our soldiers in the use of the new double-bows. It was arduous work, but our craftsmen were expert, and our young recruits strong and willing.

Ak-hor and his father had devised new means of ambush and assault for their Nubian Scouts, and a team of Young Eyes and Ears went to live in Avaris as friends of the North Land and of Pery-em-wah! When they returned in secret, or sent messages by the goat-herds and other spies, our knowledge grew of the Hyksos armies, or where they were deployed and how many strong, and we had heartening news of the captured Egyptians.

"They are treated as less than animals"— Aknere himself had come to the Council—"but they are not slaves, and they are in touch with my teams. They fight against digging the trenches for the forts, and heaping the earthworks, thus knowing that they will be put to the task as punishment." He laughed. "And they leave faults!"

"Key faults, I hope," Ak-hor said.

"Key faults indeed, and entering places in the base of the walls."

"Well-concealed?" Ahmose-Eb raised his eyebrows.

"Well-concealed, and will be till the day we attack. . . . And my grand-father's legions have grown by the hundreds in these last few years."

"May your grand-father, Pery-em-wah, walk in the Rays of Amun-Ra." Thure made the sign of protection for the safety of our oldest and longest loyal Eyes and Ears of the King in Secret.

"He surely rides the edge of a butcher's knife," Aknere said, and his voice there was awed admiration for his hero.

"It is said that in the house of the Hyksos king, he receives the fattest fowl. . . ."

"And still, after two years, he is the Sole Friend of It-yu, the Chief Scribe."

"And well in his confidence?" Kamose interrupted his friends, and Aknere nodded.

"He is, and without his Chief Scribe's advice the foul Apophis will not make a move."

"Aknere." My brother looked at the map spread out on the long table before him. "We gather each day details of their plans and preparedness. . . . Let them not get the measure of ours."

"They have no thought of it, my King. . . . Better still, they laugh at our merry ways, and your own whoring and roistering are the talk of the Court in Avaris. . . . The stories of the maidens brought from the nomes and the villages to feed your insatiable lust . . ." He shook his head, and smiled at Kamose. "It was a splendid story, my King . . . 'How does the young wolf get them to the King's House?' Apophis asked Pery-em-wah. My grandfather put his finger to his lips and smirked, raising an eyebrow. I wondered what he would say, and held my breath . . ."

"What did he say?" Kamose's eyes were bright with amusement.

"He shrugged, sipped his wine and said, 'In ox-carts! What else? And shorter distances, in carrying-chairs, guarded with their lives by the trusty Nubians.' A dig at the Hyksos king who thinks all Nubia vassal to him."

"Except for Neshi and Ak-hor, and their tribe, who have lived in Egypt for hundreds of years," Kamose said, "all Nubia is!" Then his eyes narrowed in thought, opened wide and narrowed again, and he looked at Aknere. "Your uncle's words have made clear as rock-crystal a plan that has lain clouded in my heart. . . . Already the ox-carts have given us yeoman service. In an ox-cart my father's murdered body was borne from the camp at Kus. Ox-carts have carried our secret supplies through the nomes north of Thebes this last month of the Circuit. And now—Ra-en-Ra! By Montu of the Horses—they shall serve us again." He looked across the long table at Pen-aati. "And you, my loyal Lord High Magistrate! You will be part of my plan." We were all silent and agog, but my brother said, "We will talk of this later."

When all had been noted and written, and the maps and scrolls stacked in niches, Aknere and his young spies would go back through the passage to Pen-aati's garden-house, and out into the darkness to a waiting boat, to sail northward again, and Kamose, at last, would go to his room and call for the tall pale-skinned girl he had found on a roof-top feeding the doves.

She had come to live in the women's quarters, and she was gentle as she was beautiful. She served Kamose's meals and laved his hands and danced for him while he ate, and her name was Ina. Ah-hotpe looked on her with quiet joy, but our grand-mother never lost a chance to find fault with her. Nefertari made no sign. She spoke soft words, and made puns, and Thuty gazed on her, his small eyes aflame, and always, faintly, she smiled, and always I felt the cold touch of her evil, and the guilt for that feeling.

The cool days of the north wind passed swift as a hare's leap. I was not called to Council, and my disciplines of eating, breathing, sleeping and prayer were severe and taxing. But my senses grew keener, and my thoughts more under my will and more lucid. Kheri-heb's teaching was a bride-groom joy. Then, at the hour before dawn, on a day near to harvest, Kamose came to my room and awakened me from sleep.

"Come, I need you." I sat up. "Put this on." I blinked my eyes and looked at the linen-lined leather loin-cloth he held in his hand. "It will fit," he said, "Neme saw to that. . . . Hurry!" While I put it about my loins he said, "I want you to sit on Minirt."

"Sit on him?"

"Sit on him."

"He has been trained to the chariot."

My brother did not answer. Buckling the waistband of the strange garment, I followed him to the stables. Ak-hor was waiting for us, and he held the yellow-white horse with a papyrus halter. I stroked the horse's hard nose. My brother was looking at me. His eyes seemed almost black in the first gray dawn light, and bright with vision.

"My slender Ahmose," he said, and his face was both smiling and grave. "I have a thriving thought that with your help the South Land has a secret weapon."

Before I could reply, Ak-hor, with a quiet chuckle, had

lifted me onto the horse's smooth, broad back. Two straps were attached to the strap around his nose. Kamose put them into my left hand.

"He is strongly built, and will carry a slender man," Ak-hor said.

My brother held out a short whip. I took it in my right hand, and he said,

"Touch him with it. You have ridden a donkey since you were three."

I touched the milk-white side gently. Minirt lunged and sidestepped. I almost fell off, but gathered myself, clutching the straps. The more I clutched them, the more he edged to one side and walked backward. I loosed them. He plunged forward. I pulled them again and he reared up. I found I was talking to him as I would to a wounded bird, and holding the straps easily, neither loose nor tight. He quieted, and I thought, with a strange new excitement, I can teach him signs more easily than I taught my donkey. I pulled the straps firmly toward me, and said, "Stand still." And he did. I laughed with surprise, and kicked his side with my foot. He jumped forward again, then steadied, and I stopped him a second time. "Kamose," I called, "come here."

"No, you come here."

I touched Minirt again with the whip to see what would happen. He jumped twice and I almost fell off again, thinking as I righted myself and grabbed the hair on his neck that the whip was for restrained use. Then, without thought I used my legs, holding them firm, pressing his sides, and he began to put his feet down more carefully. Quiet again, I walked him toward Kamose and Ak-hor.

"He can be taught! Kamose, horses can be trained. They are willing animals." I felt Minirt's muscles, and my own, and the play between them. "He does not mind that I sit on his back," I said, as we came close.

"That was my thought." Kamose gave the horse a honey-cake. Minirt took it with outstretched lips, ate it, nosed Kamose's bare chest and snorted.

Ak-hor took my arm as I jumped down. Then I went to the horse's head. "Minirt . . ." I felt his face against me. His eye was bronze-brown, round and bright. "Minirt."

Kamose looked at me, and with a deep sigh and a broad smile, he said, "This, my Brother, will be the great task I ask of you, and your gift to the Two Lands."

"How?"

"You will teach Minirt. Ahmose, this strength of a man and a horse, together . . . this is my secret weapon! Small regiments of men and horses alone together . . . no rattle of chariots . . . silent and swift!" he said. "My Brother, you are close to animals. You will train this one . . . and you and Minirt together, you will create a new art." He stroked Minirt's neck, following the proud arch of it. Then he took a fistful of the golden-white hair and, holding it, turned again to me. "A man's heart, and this horse's strength and his knowing, for I believe that this beautiful strong creature, like the dog and the cat, like Sek-met, can know . . ."

"And, my Prince," Ak-hor said to me, "only you are able to do this thing."

"It will mean our victory, Ahmose. We are vastly out-numbered in men, in arms, and we are hemmed in by strong forts to the south and the north." My brother loosed his hold on Minirt's hair and patted his neck.

"Where shall I train him that none may see? How can this be secret?"

Kamose turned to his Ka-friend, and they laughed.

"We will show you, my Prince."

"That we will!" My brother was serious again. "Tomorrow night, when the moon is high and the household asleep, I will come for you. Be ready. And now, the last star has faded in dawn's first light, and I must go to the Temple and be shriven for the Morning Rite." The green-gray firstlight gave form to the buildings around us. "And you, Brother, to your bath and your studies."

"Till tomorrow night, my Prince," Ak-hor said, and,

showing his square white teeth in a wide, satisfied smile, he led Minirt away.

Kamose put his arm about my shoulder, and we walked across the Court-yard.

"Little Brother," he said, with a small throaty laugh, "build your strength! For if you knew my will for you, the roots of your shaven hair would hackle."

My heart raced with questions. I felt my brother close. His arm was loosely around my shoulders and his face was cool, remote. I held back my questioning. When we came to the door of the passage underground that led to the Inner Shrine, he said,

"Till tomorrow night, Ahmose," and left me.

As I came back to my room, my heart beating high and my thoughts a-kindled, I saw Ina. The proud white-skinned girl was leaving Kamose's room. Since Rai's chair had been next to his on the dais at the evening meal, Ina no longer served him, but she brought him the moons of her breasts and her lips' sweet cool, and I saw that she was with child.

All through the day, the feel of Minirt's back under me, his sides between my legs and the bright vision in my brother's eyes came between me and my studies. I was impatient for the fourth hour of the night, and I was waiting, already in my leather loin-cloth, when my brother came to my room. Together, we stole through the silent courts, past the animal pens, and, I thought, to the stables, but Kamose stopped, turned and looked about him, then went swiftly, silent as a shadow, to the old empty granary! He took a bronze key from the pouch in his sporran, opened the heavy lock, drew the strong cross-bar and opened the door.

As we entered, Ak-hor joined us. He bowed and locked the door. The old granary was stocked full of woods and wheels, leather and oils and chariot parts, as Ak-hor had told Rai on the day of our picnic.

"Woods and metals for the chariots?"

"Yes, my Prince."

"And the bolt is large and strong! But easily opened? And those who come a-spying will find what we desire them to see?"

My brother nodded. Then he said, "Come, Ak-hor! Let us show the Young One the results of his father's and our planning."

Ak-hor smiled and went to the bottom of the steps and, to my surprise, slid the first two aside. A square opening gaped.

"A pivot!"

"Come." My brother led me to the opening. I looked down. The whole shaft was lined with mud-brick. The narrow step-way led sharply downward. Kamose went first. I followed and Ak-hor came behind me, sliding the steps into place over his head.

As we reached the bottom, Tui came to meet us. He bowed, and I looked over his gray head. In the light of the wick-lamps and torches, I saw an underground world. My eyes stretched. I was speechless, and I found that my head was moving gently from side to side in awe and unbelief. Before me was a space of land wider than the Court-yard of the King's House and twice as long. With a start I looked into the distance. The far end there is under the Court-yard, I thought. Then I looked at the stables lining the walls. Not large stables, but open, with wooden gates and stone troughs for the food, and good chaff for the horses to lie down— for horses there were! Female horses and their young, long-legged and weak, with downy soft coats.

Tui said, "Your Majesty, one was born this last hour," and he led us across the soft earth to a stall, and we looked inside. A new-born horse, still damp and bloodied, lay in the straw. I felt warm tears, and blinked and heard Kamose murmur,

"Ra! Giver of Life."

And Ak-hor said, "Who gives life and warmth to all beautiful cattle."

"And all beautiful horses for the South Land's victory," my brother added, and turned to me. "Well, Ahmose, what do you think of our secret?" I was still without words. "Since the year before our father's murder," he said, "we have bred secretly three hundred and seventy horses, male and female, apart from the gray-black chariot horses bred above ground."

"But where are they all? Where do you keep them? Did our father tell Piopi and Teti of this underground place? They were deep in his confidence." I had found my tongue at last.

"By the Grace of Amun-Ra and of Maat, who guards the Truth, this secret was kept even from our grand-mother."

"Who knows of it?"

"Ahmose-Eb, Ak-hor and his father, Tui and We-het, his son, whom you will train, along with their chosen men, and Penekheb . . ."

"And Pen-aati?"

Kamose smiled, nodding. "And the two High Priests, Miutu and Kheri-heb . . . And the Eyes and Ears concerned in the work. No one else in the King's House . . . excepting our mother."

I looked about me, my eyes clear now and used to the torch-light. There was a large pool at the end of the clearing. I saw slits in the roof. "Air-shafts?"

"You do not observe what goes on around you." Kamose grinned. "And we trust there are many just like you! You never marked the new flower-beds in the Court-yard?"

"Along the south wall?"

"Now that you know, take no more interest in them than you have ever taken."

I shook my head. The smell of these strange and beautiful animals filled my nostrils. I looked down at the new-born horse.

"Kamose, I would like this one for my own."

"He will be small for the sitting upon, but he is yours."

I looked down at the trembling animal. "Ra! Who makes

the fishes to swim, and the winged fowl to fly . . ." I murmured, and turned to my brother. "I shall call him Soker-uff . . . the Earth-god flies."

"He will be a chariot horse," Tui said. "His mother drops them strong, but small."

"I shall train him. He could carry Rai!"

Kamose laughed. "My Little Brother, sometimes you fill me with wonder." He turned to Tui. "Look now to this young creature, or he will not even walk."

Tui picked up the shaking young horse in his arms and took him into the next stall, while We-het cared for his mother. I looked at him, alone and weak on the soft chaff. "Soker-uff," I whispered. I wanted to tend him myself.

Trusted men were guarding the she-horses and their young, and in their eyes I saw loyalty, a steadfast joy in the work they were doing and love for the animals they tended.

"But Kamose, where do you take them all? And how?"

"Have you noticed the new, larger carrying-chairs? Or the ox-carts with heavier curtains?" His laugh was low and husky. "It was Pery-em-wah at the Court of Avaris . . . 'In carrying chairs, and ox-carts,' he said to Apophis. You remember! Aknere told us in Council . . . 'Thus are the virgins brought to the young and lecherous King.'" Kamose's eyes glowed, mirth in the depths of them.

"Horses in ox-carts and carrying chairs?"

"Two and sometimes three half-grown can be carried, my Prince," Tui told me.

"And one full-grown is hardly heavier than I would be," Ak-hor added. "Or a fat woman."

"Horses in ox-carts and carrying-chairs!" I murmured again, unbelieving. Then laughter rippled my entrails, gathered strength and loosed on my breath in a cataract of sound. Tears ran down my cheeks. Tui, bowing, broke into mirth, and all there about us, unabashed, held their guts and surrendered to clamorous laughter. "Kamose . . ." I said, still bubbling with the warm joy, the sound of men's laughter and the wet horse stench, "I, too, wondered, on my way back from the Temple in the evening, who was inside those chairs. . . . I knew it was not the virgins whispered and chortled about, but I was deep in my studies and forgot all about them."

"Wildness in youth is an asset, when there are secrets to be kept," my brother said, "and, Ahmose, the bearers are our most trusted Captains, each wtih his own picked men." He was grave again. "On Feast Days we send a few down to the River side where grain- and cattle-ships are moored. Covered with matting and hidden in the shelters, or amid bags filled with chaff and sere plants, we sail them to our newest and largest underground paddock. . . . On the day of the Valley Feast, we send fifty or sixty horses in chairs and ox-carts, mingled among the vast crowds sailing to the Necropolis Shore . . ."

"The Western Shore?"

"Little Brother, the new paddock is under the magnificent tomb-Temple of Mentu-hotep!" My jaw fell. "Who would suspect any preparations there except for life in the Dwat? Where else are tunnelers and builders and excavators a usual sight? Under those vast pillared levels . . ."

"That filled Senseneb with wonder when he took us there, as children, to play in the gardens . . . and——Akh! Ra-en-Ra! Where on the day of the Valley Feast we all go with offerings!"

"The Little Brother is not slow to perceive. Our tomb builders have been putting their life-long skills to work other than the building of tombs."

"And on Feast Days the Western Shore is full of traffic of all kinds." I shook my head in wonder at the simpleness of the plan. Then I asked. "And I am to use this paddock? This place under my ancestor's shrine?"

"How his Ka will rejoice!"

"I must cross the river." I paused, and looked him full in the eye. "Kamose, I will not neglect my Temple studies."

"By the Great Heart of Horus!" He laughed. "You are as stubborn as our grand-mother. . . . No, Ahmose, you will only cross to the Western Shore on Feast Days, as is your wont."

"But that will not be time enough."

"You will work here, in this paddock. You will train We-het and this company of young men. They, in turn, will be sent to train the new recruits underneath the Temple of Mentu-hotep, and they, again, will be sent to one of the three other paddocks on the way up North."

My eyes widened. "There are other underground paddocks?"

"Three hidden stations to hide our horses. These were built by our father before his betrayal."

"Piopi . . . Teti?" I could scarce say the loathed names.

"That was one secret we did not share." For a few moments his face was drawn, and cold as granite. Then he said, "And there are five, as large as this one, being built along our northern borders. . . . Ahmose, when your work is done, we shall be battle-ready."

"And when the Cataract Fort is captured, my King——" Ak-hor said, but my brother put his hand on my shoulder. "By the Disc! I have held your interest, Ahmose, Prince of the South Land." He put his arm about me, and turned to all there. "Your Prince will train the chosen men, to train the chosen horses. My Loved Ones! Let us set about what our hearts have ordered." He looked at me. "My Lean and Double Lightning! You will form my secret Company." He embraced me. "Your Company, Ahmose. What will you name them?"

"The Sitters on Horses."

"The Sitters on Horses," he murmured. "A just, and a simple name, by the Truth of Maat." He stood back from me. Our hearts weighed themselves and each other's, and they did not lack.

Then I said, so that all could hear, "My King, by Osiris, Lord of Green Fields, this secret work shall bear my seal as the plant that of its seed."

We walked around the pool where some of the youngest

horses were drinking, unsteady on their long, out-splayed legs, but we did not speak till we came to the bottom of the steps. I turned, and shook my head, and my eyes were as wide as Thebes.

Kamose looked at me with a grin. "The Young One is still astounded," he said to Ak-hor.

"This time we shall be well prepared," the Nubian nodded slowly. "And from what we hear from our Eyes and Ears in the North Land," he said, "the tyrants grow soft and too sure of their strength."

My brother shook his head. "They have impregnable forts, and we are vastly outnumbered." He sighed. "Many dogs are the death of the gazelle."

"But my King is a lion!" Ak-hor smiled as the workers of the new shift took their places, bowing low, and Kamose blessed them, and the work, and spoke to them, praising them. Then he turned to me.

"When you feel Minirt is ready to respond to you, I must know his full worth: his speed, his strength . . . how he acts when the wide sky is above him and the green turf beneath his feet. Ahmose, once and once only, he must be brought up into the park lands."

"But then our people, the grooms, the stablemen . . . the gardeners and animal-keepers . . . they will all see me sitting on him."

"That is my affair . . . and have no fear, I have given thought to it." He turned to Ak-hor, who was grinning like a boy. "The dawn is near, and we must not be seen." He paused, one foot on the first step, and looked at us. "A sweet fruit has ripened this night," he said, "and you, Brother, and I, with the help of these creatures of beauty and strength, will swiftly, silently, win freedom for the Two Lands." He went before us up the narrow stone stair-way.

Still astounded by what I had seen, and more, by what I had promised to perform, I let Neme bathe me, and when full morning broke, and Kamose, High Priest and King, had celebrated the miracle of Ra in his Atet Boat rising to give light to the new day, I went, as we had all done since childhood, to our mother's garden to partake of honeyed milk and fruit with her. I stayed but a short space, and, leaving Kamose and Rai with her, I went to seek our grand-mother. I felt no anger now at her scorn of Rai and of me. Her plan to make her half-Nubian grand-child Queen had failed. And she loves Nefertari, I thought, she has always been her favorite. I smiled to myself, feeling a deep love for tiny Tetisheri, and remembering her words: "I married a King. I have given birth to Kings . . ." To assure her of my love, and good feeling, I had a gift for her: some agate pebbles, and some beads of onyx I had exchanged with the Desert Dwellers for a crane-bird.

As I walked to her pool-garden, I took the stones from my pouch and looked at them. The stripes on the agate were of a rare pale blue, and the white on the onyx, straight and clear. Her artisans would make tiny amulets of them. I thought how our father had loved her. How gently he had smiled at her rages. How the small jewels would glitter and shine in her hundred curls as he picked her up and swung her around and around. How could so tiny a woman have birthed two children so tall as my mother and father? With merry and loving thoughts of her, I came to her garden.

She and Nefertari grew herbs here for their salves and unguents and cooling waters. I looked at the small herb-flowers and wondered which of them Tetisheri's jeweler would copy and make from the stones I was bringing. Musing on the herbs at my feet, and thinking of all I had seen underground and learned during the night, and marveling at the vision and planning of my father and brother, I strolled toward her summer-house. Then I swallowed my shadow in a swift-caught breath. Nefertari was kneeling, absorbed, by one of the herb-beds. She was gathering dark green plants and putting them in a string bag on her arm. Her thick black hair fell about her. I moved with instinct between one of the pillars and the wall, and saw an old Nubian woman squatting on the floor in a corner away from the light. Her long, tangled hair was gray and her bare, withered bosom almost hidden under rows of beads and amulets. She was sorting juicy herb-stalks of the same dark green color as those Nefertari was gathering, and with her bony fingers squeezing the juice out of them into a bowl with the figure of a snake coiled round its rim. Dead ravens, four of them, lay on a mat in front of her, at the four corners of a square she had drawn, and as she put the bowl of dark green juice in the center of it, she was saying, and her voice was cracked and harsh-clear,

"Chaach! Chacach! Charcharaachacha!"

My skin crawled at the evil words. I stood still as a stone, then gathered myself to leave the place as swiftly and silently as I could, and hurried, my bare feet making no noise, back along the path to my mother's garden. I leaned against the vinery wall and put the small stones back into the pouch of my sporran, my thoughts as a swarm of bats. The unwholesome hag! The sight of her had sickened me, and the words she had spoken over the bowl of green juice were words of the deepest evil. "Osiris, Lord of Sweetness," I prayed, "lave my heart of these vile suspicions." Omens, augury, magic? They are not evil, and may be nourishment for the Ka, as herbs are medicine for the hurts of the flesh, I thought, and with a few deep breaths, quieted. "Maat, tune the lyre of my heart to truth," I prayed, and looked up. My mother's garden was washed in the bright early sun-light. The hour was fragrant with the scent of lilies new opened to the Light of Ra arisen. I moved, my heart lighter, to the shade of a sycamore tree, and leaned my brow against the cool trunk. Then I heard a soft step, turned and saw my mother.

"Ahmose, you left us. Where have you been?" she said as she came toward me. "But there is still a while before you leave for the Temple." She came close and looked into my eyes. "My Moon Child," she said, "your work in the House of Life will be mingled with your work for the Two Lands." She was whispering, and I thought that our habit of secrecy was a strong one. "Let us sit down." She led me to the granite seat under the acacia. "Your father loved the horses. The thought of sitting on them was born in his heart when we were very young and we rode on Tetisheri's first she-horse."

"I cannot believe all I have learned these last two nights."

"We live in stress, my Son, and we are beset by spies."

"Hor-min made me see that there are pockets of treason even within the City of the God and the villages of the Theban nomes."

"Hor-min's goat-herds are useful indeed. They are gathering their kind throughout the South Land, and . . . their friends in the North. They will be a splendid message corps."

"They can roam at will, and be unsuspected."

"By even the wiliest!" My mother smiled.

"Mother, I knew nothing of this vast underground."

She put her hand on mine. "Ahmose, are you distressed that your peace will be broken for a while?"

I shook my head. "I do not know."

"Kamose says that you and Minirt are as one being when you sit on his back."

"I feel this, too. I was happy to sit on my donkey, but I brim with a strange joy sitting on Minirt. . . . A slight pressing of my knee or heel on his side, or the slightest touch of my small whip on his neck, and his thews and sinews answer beneath me, and stretch to swift power."

"Kamose says that together a man and a horse can be a god."

"It is a strange winged feeling."

"Priestlike, my son?"

"The eagle of my heart flies in widening circles; to be Priest encircles all."

"And my heart grows sweet in the listening," my mother said. "You are to work with Minirt each night for four hours, in the underground paddock."

"And Kheri-heb?"

She smiled. "Had you not a willing heart toward this work,

Kheri-heb would have commanded you. . . . My Priest-child, your Temple studies will not be the less."

I rose from the seat and, walking to and fro in front of her, told her my thoughts. "I must work out clearly, and with care, the movements of my legs and buttocks, so that he will respond without pull on the reins. Thus the Sitters will be free to shoot their arrows, or wield their short-swords . . ."

"Or throw their torches! The short-sword is not in the King's plan for your Sitters."

"Torches!" I stood still. The thought had not occurred to me. "Torches, and perhaps a javelin company. It will come to me as I work with Minirt."

"You are deeply involved, my Young One. I had feared, Kamose, too, that this duty might be painful to you."

"It is not. This work will be its own reward. Mother, I take delight in training men and horses for my King, and for the glory of the Two Lands."

My mother sighed happily. "Leave me now or you will be tardy. . . . Akh! I near forgot . . . Hor-min will now be scribe for the secret Councils."

"My brother is wise." I nodded, thinking how naturally everyone spoke of Hor-min, and how he had become a part of our life and our thinking.

"My Son, Kheri-heb tells me that you drink in his teaching as the parched earth drinks the flood waters."

"I am as the bud of the lotus, my Mother." I put my cheek against her smooth one. "And my learning is small." I left her and went back to my rooms.

That night, when the King's House was silent, I began my work with Minirt. When he had learned to stand quite still in spite of what went on around him, or what I was doing, I spent half a moon trying to leap up onto his back swiftly and surely. I tried many ways, and in the end I held the light reins and a fistful of his long hair twisted around the thumb of my left hand and held the crest of his neck. Then I put my right hand on the bone above his shoulders, and with both feet at once, with my whole weight on my arms, I leapt up. It took five days to perfect, and Minirt stood still as a statue. When I could leap up as a young gazelle, I had a wooden horse built. It had long flax hair, and We-het and his young men learned to leap onto its back.

After a four moons' span Minirt would follow me, without rope or rein, at a word, or a soft whistle, or a click of the tongue, and I soon discovered that what he did not understand at first, after patient and repeated tries, though sometimes he was more stubborn than a hungry donkey, he never forgot.

"These animals remember," I said to Kamose. "They remember kindness and unkindness, and they must be trained with soft voices, and gentle measures. . . ." Of these things and many others, my brother and I talked, and half-way into the sixth month of our training, he told me the time had come to watch Minirt's prowess in the parklands.

"But Kamose, our secrecy?"

My brother held up his hand. "I have chosen the day . . . and the hour. You will sit on Minirt above ground one hour before sun-set . . . tomorrow." He lingered on the last word, smiling.

"Tomorrow? Akh! Ra-en-Ra! The Feast of Hat-hor!" Again, I marveled at the height, breadth and depth of my brother's vision. He had chosen the one day in the year when no man, nor youth, nor boy, be he fisherman, plowman, fowler, or craftsman or merchant, school-boy or apprentice, would put his little finger to the smallest task, after the noon-hour. "The Feast of Hat-hor." I shook my head, laughing for the simpleness of it. When the Priestesses of the Goddess, garlanded and strewing flowers as they danced, led the women, the maidens and girl-children through the streets, no man would incur the wrath of the Goddess, nor of his own women-folk, by his absence. And on that day, the Menat collars they wore, for love of Hat-hor, had deeper power to allay barren women and enhance men's potency. "My brother," I said, when my laughter ebbed, "Minirt and

I, above ground? No torches flickering, no fence around us . . . no other horses! For four moons Minirt has not seen the light. Tomorrow, he will see the Great Torch of Ra, scarlet-and-gold in the western sky, and feel the wide earth beneath him, beneath us!"

"Little Brother, my patience is less than your own. . . . Till tomorrow."

All day the stirring of my blood, up from my heels to my knees and loins, as though I would straddle wide space and not the smooth back of Minirt, veered my heart away from my studies. Kheri-heb looked at me with Knowing, and was silent.

I donned my leather loin-cloth, and an hour before sun-set Ak-hor came to my room and we went out together. When we came to the Stable-court Kamose and Pen were there, with Tui and We-het. There was no one else to be seen. The horses were in their stalls, fed and bedded down, and the animals penned. All except the sacred Nile-geese, who roamed where they would. Kamose was giving Minirt a honey cake. "Hy! Brother!" he called, and I lifted my hand in reply. When I came to Minirt, he was restive, but well-behaved. I gentled him. Then I gave him the word to stand and, losing no time, leapt up onto his back. Kamose and the others stood away.

"My Prince . . ." Pen was lost in amaze. "He stands still as a rock!"

Tui and We-het stood back looking proud and smiling, and I was about to touch Minirt's side with my foot when a Nile-goose rushed squawking, with a huge flurry of feathers, out of a stall to the left of us. Minirt leapt as a hare to one side, reared up and came down hard on his forefeet, lifted his rump and tossed me high in the air. Then he stood still for a moment, reared again and tore out of the stable-yard. By the time I picked myself up, Minirt was streaking across the parkland to the pasture.

"He will stop at the fence," Ak-hor said. "He cannot get to the cows, to scare them." Then he and Kamose and Pen and I raced after the wild running horse. As we came to the parkland we stood still as one man, our eyes wide and our mouths ajar. He had leapt a canal, and raced onward, straight at the pasture fence. We did not move. He was over the fence like a bird.

"He can leap!" I spoke to myself.

"He flies like a bird," Ak-hor murmured.

"What a proud and magnificent sight!"

We all spoke in awe.

"Ra be praised in his Glory!" my brother whispered. "That fence is higher than the tallest shield." We turned and looked at him, at one with his thought.

"The shield fences . . . around the enemy camps . . ." Pen's breath came out in a soft whistle.

Then the cows were running amok, their full udders swinging.

Minirt stood still, then reared up on his back legs.

"What a magnificent sight!" Pen said again.

Then the horse turned, leapt back over the fence and came tearing toward the animal pens. The gazelles were shrieking and the antelopes jumped out of the enclosure and fled with high curved lopes to the park; the monkeys, chittering and screaming, scared up to the top of the palm trees, sending the twi-light birds in fright-crooked flight to the tops of the stables and granaries; and the Nile-goose, for once afraid, fled squawking around a safe corner.

"Soon he must tire," I said to Kamose, as Minirt tore across the Battle-court and into the gardens, ripping the vines and the trellises down, crushing the flowers and herbs and stamping the poppies and peonies to juicy blood-colored pulp. Breathless, we chased him till at last, with the splash of a pylon rock hitting the river, he fell into the pool in my mother's garden and foundered and floundered, bewildered, slipping and sliding on the smooth copper floor, his feet all tangled in the thick-spreading flower-roots.

"Akh! Minirt!" Rai came running from the summer-house.

"He is angry, and full of fear. . . ." my mother said, following her.

The horse was using all of his strength to get his feet free, and when he did, with a lunge he fell into the deep part of the pool where we had learned to swim, and—"Ra-en-Ra! By Montu, of the Animals! Osiris, Lord! He swims!" We all stood there as he struggled, felt his fore-feet on the bottom and scrambled toward the side of the pool.

"Minirt . . ." I called softly. His eyes were rolling, and his hair and his tail were all wet and matted. "Minirt . . ."

Rai came with honey-cakes. "Here, give him one," she said, and I coaxed him, but he shook his head and his neck arched in fury. He slid and slipped and was frightened again.

"Minirt . . . come to me!" I commanded gently, and held out the honey-cake. "Minirt, my milk-yellow beauty . . . My horse that flies as a bird over fences . . ."

"And can swim!" Kamose stood still but it seemed that his feet were dancing, his fingers tingling, and I could almost feel the whirling flames of his thought. Then cool laughter burst from him, and Minirt stood still. I called him again. The reins were hanging, wet. I moved toward him. He jumped back from me and almost sat on the bottom of the pool, as ungraceful as a vulture on the ground. Ak-hor came with a rope.

"Have patience," I said. "He will come to me. I must sit on him again."

"Ahmose?"

"This I know." Kamose nodded, his eyes still alight with thoughts and planning. "Minirt!" I spoke with authority. To my surprise, with a great bound he leapt out of the pool and shook himself.

"By Hat-hor of the West!" Rai said. "Like a small wet dog! Come to me, my Little Wet Dog, I have honey-cakes. . . ." I stood still. She called him again. No one moved. "My Proud One . . ." she whispered, and slowly, with mincing steps, dainty as a young gazelle, he came and gently ate the honey-cake. Rai took the wet straps and held them toward me. "Here he is . . . here is your horse."

"Kamose's horse."

She shook her head. "I shall soon be Queen." She stood to her full slim height and looked up at Kamose. He lifted her up, swung her around and put her down again, holding her close, his arm about her shoulder. "And when you are Queen, Little Sister, what will you do?"

"I shall give Minirt to Ahmose."

Still holding her close, as they stood together, my brother said,

"You will have to think of another gift. Minirt was Ahmose's horse from the first day he sat upon him."

At a soft word from me, Minirt stood quite still. I looked at my brother and sister and my heart beat with a faster beat. My rhythm changed and I was lost in them. I was my brother. I was my sister. I felt a freshness and a pure joy, a releasing love! Does it exist, a state of love still untouched by men? While I was thinking, the rhythm changed again. The swift, charged moment passed.

"I will sit on Minirt now," I said, and grabbed his wet hair and the slippy wet straps and leapt onto his back. His hard feet made sharp sounds on the tiles, but I murmured to him, and patted his neck, and he was quiet. "I am going to leap with him, over the fence."

"Akh! No, Ahmose . . ." My mother rose from her stool. But my brother and sister still gazed on me with wide, clear eyes, and they were one with me on Minirt's back.

I touched him with my heel, and he walked quietly, nodding his head, past my mother, and Ak-hor and Pen, treading daintily on the smooth, hard tiles.

I took him around the park. Without urging, he leapt the canal, and when we landed at the other side of it I found I was holding the reins, but not too tightly. I turned him and jumped again, still lightly holding him and watching for the moment when he moved his head forward and stretched his neck. Five times we leapt the canal, and Minirt wanted to jump it again but, with my heart pounding in my throat and fear beading my brow with sweat, I turned his head toward the pasture fence. He made straight for it, seemed to gather himself and leapt high. I stayed forward on him. His heart and mine were one. "Hy! Minirt!" I shouted, and he switched his tail, and we turned and jumped back again. "Minirt! My winged God-horse!" I leapt from his back and held his head, warm and wet with water and sweat, hairy and beautiful, to my breast. And as I stood there, I saw Rai. She was running toward me.

"Ahmose! Ahmose! You are no longer a man . . . With your legs astride Minirt you are a god!" She was laughing and out of breath. "Kamose was late for the Evening Rite. . . . He ran! He leapt for joy in the air like Minirt! And his thoughts are lions. . . . Akh! Ahmose . . . But first Minirt! Here, you have well-earned these honey-cakes. . . ."

As she fed him, Tui came to take him to his stable underground. The place was deserted.

"My Prince," Tui said, "wonders have happened this day."

Rai rubbed Minirt's nose. I stroked him down the curve of his neck, and my eyes filled with tears. Rai handed the string cake-bag to Tui, and put her arm in mine.

"The last beams of Ra still light the Land . . . let us walk awhile. Ahmose, our brother has told me of Soker-uff."

"He has?"

"And how you agreed that I should sit on him!"

I laughed. I was happy that at last, Kamose had given our secret into her keeping. "He is black as the night," I told her, "and the star on his nose is the Morning Star. You will love him. . . . Rai, Minirt was my brother's gift to me . . . Soker-uff is my gift to you."

"When I am Queen, I shall go with our brother on the Royal Circuits."

"Kamose is too heavy to sit on a horse."

"He will drive his chariot, with Sek-met beside him, and I shall ride Soker-uff alongside."

"With the King's leave. . . . Meanwhile . . ."

"Meanwhile," she looked up at me—"let us walk together."

In the lengthening shadows of the after-glow, we walked toward our mother's garden. The gazelles were drinking at the canals, and the late birds rustled in the branches. The Land was hushed. Rai took my hand.

"Ahmose, are you sad that our brother has asked this work of you?"

"No."

"But you are training these beautiful creatures for battle, as soldiers are trained, to die." In the joy of sitting on Minirt's back I had put the thought from me. Rai knew. She looked up at me. "You have hidden this from your own heart."

"Almost, till this moment."

"These animals will be killed in war."

"Rai, I know! Once, on the day of my manhood, I felt the full horror of it. I saw, in my heart, Minirt yoked to a chariot."

"Before you sat on him?"

"Yes. . . . Rai, I am in honor bound to train these noble creatures for the King, and for the Beloved Land. . . . Our secret bands of Sitters on Horses will rush swiftly through the cities we besiege, firing torched arrows into the stables and chariot sheds, the armories and the chief places of the town, then, as swiftly, leave! And Pery-em-wah's men will build up a legend of our mysterious way of appearing and disappearing. Then the chariots will attack . . ."

"Akh! It is true, few of your horses will be harmed . . . but, the chariot beasts?"

"Rai, by our Lady of the Sycamore! What my heart feels . . ."

"What your Ka feels . . ."

I looked down at her, and though my heart had released her, I yearned for her. "Rai," I said, "I must find my own Knowing."

"You will." She looked up at me. "Your eyes, Ahmose. By Hat-hor, I have loved your eyes since first I saw. Gray, black-ringed and deep, my Brother. Changing as the River in the hours of light, and gray as the River at dawn." I saw myself in her eyes. "And shaped like the Eye of Horus, long and wide." She laughed. "Come, we shall be late for the evening meal." She led me along by the large vinery at the entrance to our mother's garden. The birds held twittering conclave in the leaves, and a coppery sun-bird, perched on the nearest sycamore, was singing his evening song to the saffron sky. "Look . . ." Rai whispered.

"And listen!" I bent my head to hers. "He praises Hathor's beauty in her own tree—on the day of her Feast."

"And he is beautiful," Rai said, for his breast was the color of polished bronze in the red-gold light, and we paused, listening and watching, in the green square of the vine trellis, till the birds, rustling and fussing, settled to rest, and the last beams of Ra in his Sek-tet Boat descending gleamed on the still pool and touched the tree tops, kindling the leaves to fiery-edged splendor, and dappling the vines to gold.

A little wind rose with the twi-light, driving the evening bees to their hives. The sycamore tree threw a shadow, darkening and silent. I looked down at my sister. She was golden in the light. My heart sang celebration. She put her arms about my neck and lifted her cheek to mine. Then she kissed me nose to nose. I held her close. She was tiny and soft, yet strong in my arms. She spoke my name softly, my secret name. Her breasts were cool against me. All Egypt's lovers held court in my heart as I lifted her close to me, and kissed her again. Her tears fell on my shoulders. "My brother is strong with love," she whispered. "And I am my brother."

Still as the night in the desert we stood together, hushed as the wakening stars.

Each night I sat on Minirt, and in the days that followed our leaping together in the parklands he seemed to respond more eagerly to the words, soft touches and leg pressures, and Kamose, watching one night in the underground paddock, said, "My secret weapon is ever more potent. . . . You noble, high-leaping one!" He stroked Minirt's nose. "Creature of beauty and strength, it will be you, swift-footed runner, with a thin Egyptian man on your back, who will destroy the Set-fiends who have profaned the Two Lands, and with the torch-fire that flames in the wind of your passage, you will sear them from the face of Ta-mery!"

We talked long, and worked long, and both the men chosen and their chosen horses exceeded even Kamose's imaginings. Within ten moons' space, in the vast paddock under Mentu-hotep's tomb-Temple there were one hundred and ninety men and their horses, battle-ready and themselves training others.

In the days that followed, I felt no unease. I forgot my mother's fears, and my grand-mother had made her peace with a gift: a small table for my room. It was made of our native sycamore wood and inlaid with ebony, faience and carnelian, tiny pieces of gold and silver, so rare in Thebes, and insets of shining quartz. I had not yet given her the stones I had for her, but the anger between us was wiped clean as drawings on a clay tablet.

Kamose, with kingly grace, had refused to countenance, even to speak of Tetisheri's desire that he marry his half-sister. "And," he warned, "I will have no conflict in the harem." Our grand-mother had accepted her defeat. She was merry as ever, and her language as lusty as Nefertari's was gentle.

When, each evening, the family and courtiers gathered in the Center-court for the evening meal, there was no sense of strain. The guests sat in small groups, on chairs and cushions, and on every small table there were wreaths of flowers.

Exhausted but happy, after long days in the Battle-court, Kamose's Company sat, as they had since boyhood, on their stools to the right of the dais. Sometimes Ahmose-Eb sat with the Chief Scribe and his daughter, Sittek, but, knowing how loath he was, Kamose or I called him to join us for the last two courses. Sittek wore thin pleated linens, and her body was bony and not pleasant to look on, yet for all her thin frame she ate like a soldier. I thought if they agreed in nothing else they would enjoy their food. But, watching Ahmose-Eb, I saw that when he sat beside her, he picked at his food like a sick bird.

Rai and I had always sat on cushions, but now that I was shaven, and a man, and she soon to be Queen, we sat on chairs. Nefertari had, since she was fourteen, shared a double chair with our grand-mother.

Our half-sister looked at Kamose, when he spoke to her, with a smile that was a charm against remembered fears. And speak to her he did! And made puns with her, and I thought in spite of my long distrust of her I should feel some kindness for Nefertari. Her words held nothing of envy or malice. She would smile at Thuty, repeating her puns and daring the guests not to laugh at her wit. But she lowered her eyes, too subtle, to behave in a manner less than wholly Royal.

Then Rai would look at me, and I was a stranger to all else around me. I would watch her as she turned, listening to Kamose, and I thought that her rainbow moods, her swift perception and her love would meet his wild and unyoked heart, his tight-reined rage, and that her Ka would refresh his Ka. As I watched them both, I remembered her words to me as we sailed to our father's Funeral Rite. ". . . and you will be as an acre of sweet-smelling herbs to us both." "Osiris, Lord," I prayed, "bathe us in your Love . . ."

It was a season of fruitful studies. Once more the crops burgeoned toward harvest, and the fields changed from their early blue-green to gold. I lived in two worlds, and I was happy. As I grew in the Knowing, I touched again the charged moment in our mother's garden, with Minirt, and my love for Rai was my love for Kamose. They would marry when the harvest was garnered, and together they would bless the grain, charging it with the Life of Ra. My own heart was joyful because I knew that when Kamose was ready for war, the Sitters on Horses, too, would be battle-ready.

Then, on a night when Kamose had called a special Council and we had been in the underground chamber till dawn, I came back to my room with my heart afire, but my body exhausted. I was about to throw myself, still wearing my leather loin-cloth, onto the bed when I heard hurried steps in the garden. I turned and saw my mother. She leaned against a pillar. I went to her, and saw her face in the dawn-light.

"I paid no heed." Her white lips were trembling. "The gods warned me and I paid no heed to my fears." Her lips were drawn as I had never seen them before, moving, yet stiff and soundless, and she was shaking. I tried to hold her but she pushed me away and stood looking through and beyond me with empty eyes. Her stretched lips formed a word. "Rai."

I ran, barefooted, silent across the gardens to the quarters of the Royal Women. My mother had not wakened the household.

I lifted the colored matting that hung across Rai's door-way, and went inside. She lay naked under the linen cover. She looked as she had looked when we played as children. Her brown hair fell softly about her shoulders. Her lashes made shadows on her cheeks, and her lips were parted, as though she breathed and was smiling in her sleep. I crept close, and knelt down beside her. "Rai," I whispered, and, putting my cheeks against hers, felt the chill of her Ka-less body.

I did not move my face. A speechless, thoughtless, help-less agony filled all my being and I gathered her up in my arms, tight-close, that her small, slender body might take life from my own, till a great shudder passed through me, bring-ing me back to myself, and gently, tenderly, I laid her down again, put my lips to her cold brow and smoothed the linen cover, and as I knelt there looking down at her, my Ka, swept out of me on the crest of a swifter, wider tide, touched hers! "I am my brother." Her words restrung the bow of my heart. "Rai . . . there is an Oasis where time is not, nor space . . . nor barriers, and all who love are One. . . ." The joy of her flooded my spirit. As I rose to my feet, Amun-Ra, with bright command, shed his first pure morning beam, putting his Golden finger, forever, on his beloved, his child.

Kamose had returned, rage-cold as granite, from the Dawn Rite. He stood for a while on the Balcony of Appearances, judged the petitions brought before him, decorated ten soldiers for their valor at Kus and gave a land-parcel and seed to two widowed sisters. Then he came back to the King's House and called for Ak-hor and Ahmose-Eb. Together they left Thebes and went into the Eastern Desert, and they did not return for three days and three nights. Then, in our mother's garden-house, we talked, she and Kamose and I, and she was bereft.

"I am torn with remorse. . . . I gave no heed when the gods warned me," she said, and I did not say how many times I had lain on my belly and cursed myself that I had not followed the threads of my suspicion when I had come upon the Nubian crone in our half-sister's quarters, and overheard the evil words she had croaked. Only Kamose was guiltless. He looked at me, then at our mother, and there was in him an unspeakable tenderness as he whispered.

"Rai . . . Rai . . ." Then he was grave. After a while he said, "Our people have suffered through two hundred years of tyranny, and when their hearts rose to the fight, they were crushed again by the murder of their King, and the loss of Kus. But now! Their hearts are round. Once again they are rising to the fight for freedom." He paused, and looked out through the pillars to the vine trellises. Then, slowly, he turned again to face us. "My mother and Queen . . . Ahmose, Brother and Prince of the South Land . . . our people, they could not sustain, now, at this moment of time, the knowledge of evil . . . of murder . . . within their own Royal Household."

My hair-roots hackled. He will marry the half-sister! With the thought my whole body cringed. My mother, perceiving, said, "At the harvest." Their eyes held. Then she raised a hand. "Kamose, your grand-mother, Tetisheri . . . she had no part in this."

"By the mercy of Amun-Ra," I said. "And she must never know."

"For all her strong and fiery spirit, this knowledge would break her." Our mother's voice almost failed as she tried to say, "Nefertari . . . she is . . . now . . ."

Kamose stood before us, his head high. His face was austere, his eyes cool. "The half-sister is now the one nearest in blood and heredity to be the Royal Wife."

We were silent. My brother was calm and apart. "I am Whadj-Kheper-Ra, Kamose, the Two-fold Great House. The ancient custom will not be changed in the South Land." He looked at us, first at one, then the other. "My Mother . . . my Brother, we shall contain this evil within the inner circle of the Royal Household."

Deep grief and cold horror were close to us. Yet it seemed that the Truth of Maat, that is beyond earthly truth, was in the understanding and the resolve between us.

Rai was buried with the Rites of the Great Royal Wife, and the people mourned her deeply, for her beauty and her joyous gentleness, her mischief and laughter, had been a balm to the Thebans.

Sen-ut, in her long dark-blue linen robe, her face and arms dyed blue, and waving long scarves, green, blue and black, danced before the Door of Rai's Everlasting House. Swaying and bending, rising again and bending backward to the ground, she danced her love to the sound of Hor-min's pipes and the low murmured songs of the people; not dirges, but Theban songs, full of a strange sadness, and a strong, quiet love.

My mother grew stern, and she gave more and more of her time to her duties as High Priestess of the God, spending whole moon spans in her Lodge by the Sacred Lake.

Kheri-heb demanded almost tyrannical disciplines, and with the secret work in the underground paddock, my days passed swift as pool-fish darting through Rai's slender fingers.

At the time of the harvest, Kamose married Nefertari, and together they walked the fields and blessed the grain gathered in the huge reed baskets, and outside the inner rooms of the King's House there was rejoicing again in the land.

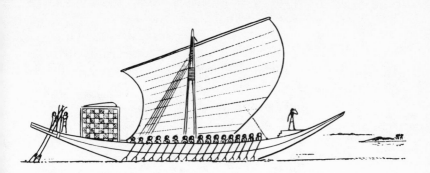

CHAPTER IV

When every grain of the South Land's harvest had been garnered and threshed, Hur the Cruel One came again. He sailed in state from Avaris in the foremost of five newly built tribute-ships, with his tax-collectors, his Bow-men, his scribes, and Mayebre the Libyan. One of Pery-em-wah's oldest Eyes and Ears brought the news, and he was welcome in the Council Chamber, for he had known our father and mother as children. "These five ships," he told us, "are one hundred and twenty cubits long and forty cubits wide, and, my King, more than a hundred sailors man each ship." His old face crinkled into a smile. "Among each of these crews there are twenty of our own loyal Egyptians." Kamose had outlined his plan for those ships.

"The wildest plan of all," I said to Ahmose-Eb. We had left the secret Council Chamber, and were on our way, under the cloak of darkness, to the old granary where, with Tui and We-het, I would choose the young horses ready for final training in the paddock under Mentu-hotep's tomb. "I can scarce give credence to this plan."

"But we need these ships, my Prince."

"My Friend! Dressing up as Hyksos and manning these large ships ourselves? Almost a child's game."

"They have to be captured first!"

"True! And all Kamose's plans seem so simple. . . ." I sighed. "But enemy spies are everywhere."

"I find this plan less wild than the horses in carrying-chairs!" Ahmose-Eb was enthusiastic. "And that one worked!"

"As the River flows northward," I agreed.

"And yet, my Prince, to move the young horses right under Hur's nose! This makes my skin crawl as a cat's before storming."

Kamose had invited Hur and Mayebre the Libyan to stay in the King's House, and to celebrate the Feast of the Valley with us. "It will not choke me to carouse with them," he said in Council, "if it furthers my plans."

I watched Ahmose-Eb as he crept past the birdhouses. "There will also be the virgins our guests expect?" I asked.

"An ox-cart full for their special pleasure," he whispered. "And special virgins! Sen-ut's Young Eyes and Ears."

"Ra-en-Ra!" I murmured, and now my own skin crawled at the thought of their gift of themselves for the South Land.

Ahmose-Eb caught my thought and my feeling. "They will gain potent facts from the Hyksos whose couches they share, my Prince."

"And with their charms hold the tyrants in Thebes . . . that is Kamose's hope and desire. . . . But Hur? He is cold . . ." I let my breath out in a soft whistle. "So much of the King's plan rests in the lap of chance."

We ducked our heads down, and ran swiftly past the

cow-stables, and as we edged along the sides of them I thought of my brother's amused smile when, at the end of our meeting, he said to Pen-aati, "With all your other duties, my Lord High Magistrate, by the Great Hare!—you must now be social, and entertain."

Pen-aati's stern, lined face broke into a smile, his teeth were white and almost perfect, except for the chip out of one of the center ones, and he looked almost young. "These parties are as the breath in her nostrils to my wife. These Feast Day breakfasts in her hands will thrive!"

We crept past the snoring animal keepers, and I thought how each month, on the day before the Necropolis Festival, the young horses I had chosen would be gathered at the north end of the paddock and put to sleep by Montu-Thoth. He went among them with love and power, and with the first two fingers of his right hand, he touched each one gently between the eyes, and slowly they sank to the ground, asleep. As I had watched him, so wise and strong, and but one year older than I, I had thought how small was my own depth of Knowing.

The young horses were then laid in papyrus rope-hammocks, strung onto a long pole and carried by two men along the arm of the secret passage that opened into the vine-trellised arbor behind Pen-aati's garden-house where, working as always, he could not be disturbed. Around it, young Eyes and Ears would be lounging, laughing and chattering like waking birds, and early drunk, it seemed. While Pen-aati's wife's party rose to its height, the carrying-chairs were quickly filled with the sleeping horses, and, with their curtains tight-drawn and a guard inside each to laugh and joke and make puns as though guests were arriving or leaving, they mingled with the traffic. Amid the comings and goings to and from the King's House and the party at the house of the Lord High Magistrate, thirty or forty carrying-chairs passed quite unnoticed in the bustle of the vast Court-yard. Their bearers, young Eyes and Ears in the liveries of the various Theban families, bore them swiftly through the wall gates and along the way to the wharves, where, at different places, Ak-hor's Nubian Scouts took the chair poles on their shoulders and ran with their precious cargo to board the pleasure-boats and ferries that were waiting to take the Thebans across the River to the Valley Festival. On seeing the Royal Nubian Guard, our people kept reverent distance, and among the statues being carried, the chanting and processions of the Mortuary priests, the Necropolis workers and their children, and the hundreds of the visiting faithful invading from the Eastern Shore, sixty-four horses in ox-carts and carrying-chairs were as lost to the eyes as fleas on a jackal. As we crept along the side of the granary, I thought that our ancient rites, our traditions and even our domestic customs seemed to work for Kamose's plans; for the other arm of the secret passage led to the enclosed court behind the kitchens. It was here the ox-carts unloaded their meat and vegetables, grain and flowers, and returned with refuse to the River. They were heavily curtained against the ever-plaguing flies and hornets and no one went near them, nor wanted to. It is all so simple, I thought. Yet long night hours had been spent on every detail, and our tomb builders and carpenters had worked overtime, and with joy, since my father's reign, on the paddocks and passages underground.

Ahmose-Eb cut into my thoughts. He was crouching and talking quietly, almost to himself.

"They are so sure of their strength. It is not to be believed they can be so arrogant, so blind! And their women like Egyptian men. It is so simple."

"You have echoed my own thought. But let us beware, my Friend. When we openly doubt our enemy's strength, we double it. Let us rather remember what we heard in Council."

Ahmose-Eb sighed. "Two hundred and forty thousand soldiers, well-armed and well-trained, are this day manning the walls of Avaris, and that not counting the subjects within, who know well the use of weapons."

"And Ra-en-Ra! The traitor city!" It was hard to bring the word to my lips. "Neferusi is an arsenal."

"Its walls new-built and strengthened with all the might of Apophis," Ahmose-Eb said as we rounded the corner and came to the front of the granary. "But that will be later. This plan for the Cataract Fort, it is two plans in one . . . the tribute-ships, and the Fort. But our spies say the garrison is smaller and the men ever lazier."

"And Pery-em-wah's men have lived among them since we were children! They let down the rope ladders for Ak-hor's raiders. . . . How we used to tease him about his night raiding." As I took the key out of my sporran, I was thinking of Rai, and her hand in mine as she whispered, "There's something more in that old granary than durra for the cows." I opened the huge lock and stood for a moment lost in memories.

Ahmose-Eb closed the door quietly behind us and went to the foot of the silo steps. He moved the first two and stood aside for me to descend.

Soker-uff was frolicking about the enclosure. We-het is right, I thought, he is of a smaller breed. I will give him to my brother for his lead horse. I knew that, though I desired to, I could not sit on him. Through the months of training I had come to know that even the larger breed, from Teti-sheri's Golden Fiery One, and from Minirt, could carry a light-weighted man for only two hours, and already Tui and I had marked the horses and she-horses whose backs were strongest to breed together. I watched Soker-uff, then called him by name. He was night-black, and beautiful. "Rai's Ka will sit on you," I whispered, "and lead the King's chariot into the straight paths." He came to me, trotting and shaking his head. Then he nuzzled his soft hairy mouth against my bare chest. I scratched the white star on his brow with my fore-finger, thinking of Rai.

Ahmose-Eb, watching me, asked, "How many Companies have you now? Fully trained, and battle-ready?"

"Five companies of a hundred men and horses each . . . and the spare horses."

"Spare horses?"

Early in the work I had known they must be trained in pairs. "After the Sitters on Horses have made their swift, fiery rush through the city, the relays will be waiting for them. The men will sit on the fresh horses and lead the others to the secret stables. Thus, no horse's back will be overtired, and the speed of disappearance assured."

"My Prince, I rejoice that you are part of this last fight."

"Last fight, Ahmose-Eb?"

"Whether we conquer or are routed, this is our last fight. If we lose, the barbarians will rule the Two Lands for a thousand years. The boundaries will be moved at will, the measuring rods will be shifted and the Breath of Truth will not liven the nostrils of Justice."

"Ahmose-Eb?" I looked at him, and felt again the passion in him for all his quiet ways.

He looked at the she-horses in their stalls, a long row of heads, brown, yellow-brown and gray-black, like Kamose's chariot horses; then at the long-legged young, making antic play on the soft earth.

"Train them well, my Prince, for of a truth, a man upon a horse, in battle, will be as a god."

"I love these animals. The thought of them in battle breaks my heart."

"They will be the means of our victory," he answered, and as we walked to the north end of the paddock he told me that Pery-em-wah and Apophis' Chief Scribe, It-yu, were ever deeper in the king's confidence. "All his secrets . . . and his vices they share. And his vices are strange and involve dark rites." He lowered his voice. "Anat-neby has been made High Priestess of Set, and she is worshiped as a goddess."

"She is curled and oiled, Aknere says, and heavy-scented as a Hyksos woman."

As we came to where the horses were roped off, Tui came out of his square tent. "My Prince, I did not hear you." He bowed and, rising, pointed to Soker-uff. "Has he not grown?"

"He has. And Tui, you are right. He is a chariot horse."
I smiled at him. "We will train him for the King's chariot."
He bowed again. Then together we chose the young animals ready to be taken to the underground paddock on the
the Necropolis Shore.

We had rarely spoken of Rai, my mother, my brother and
I, during these months. There was no need. Our heart-
thoughts were too deep for words or tears. She was with us
in all bright and lovely things. I could touch her in a low-
slung star, in the sun-bird's shining coat and the strut of the
hoopoe-lark, the cry of the crane and the small darting fish.
Every pleasant place I walked, her hand held mine.

Kamose, aware of the disciplines of my Temple studies,
called me to the secret Council only when he needed me for
a special debate. He himself, as his envisioned plans ripened
and took form, was closeted there for longer and longer
spans, and the habit had grown in him to call our mother
away from her Lodge by the Sacred Lake to share in the
details. He made due act of presence, with Sek-met at his
heels, on the Balcony of Appearances, but the trials in the
Judgment Hall he left to Miutu, High Priest and Chief of
Visions. Each day he fought fierce mock battles, in chariot
and on foot, with Neshi, Ak-hor and Ahmose-Eb, and his
Company. He slept no more than four or five hours, and he
never lay with Nefertari.

Tetisheri was at first unbelieving, then outraged. When, for
the third time, she had come to her daughter's garden, she
was beside herself with righteous anger. ". . . the insult to the
Queen. . . . By the Great Cackler! She is the Royal Wife. . . .
Her beauty is told the length and breadth of the South
Land . . . and her body ripe to bear us Royal sons . . ." For
a whole hour's span our grand-mother raged.

"I longed to bring coolness to her heart." My mother's sigh
was deep and sad. We were sitting together, in the star-light,
on the steps of her garden-house. "Ahmose, your grand-

mother is truthful and courageous, but this grim truth must be kept from her. She could not contain it. Akh! Ra-en-Ra . . ." Then she told me that, against her own willing, when Kamose had come to her garden at sun-set she had spoken to him of his grand-mother's rage. "Ahmose, your brother put no guard on his face. He listened, silent. Our understanding was a flame between us. . . . My Young One, with quiet and almost disinterest, your brother said, 'If Am-mit, Devourer of Carrion Souls, awaited me in my bed, I would liefer lie with her. . . . I am King, and that is my word to Tetisheri, and more! Ina has given birth to my child. I shall make her secondary wife. The Queen-Grand-mother speaks in innocence, I know, but she will speak no more of this . . . nor will the half-sister who apes to be Queen. This I will secure.' Then, Ahmose, he looked at me, and his eyes drove the soul out of me." She clasped her hands to her face. "Rai." She lowered them and looked up at the stars. "Rai . . . Rai . . ." She did not try to hold her tears but let them spill down her cheeks like a child.

Our grand-mother spoke no more of the King's bed. The tall, pale-skinned girl was made secondary wife, and sometimes she sat on a stool in the Center-court and ate with our company. She was graceful and quiet and sat with her eyes downcast. Kamose loved his baby girl, and spent his rare rest hours with her and his gentle wife. Our mother smiled on her, and on her first grand-child, but Tetisheri turned away from her with less than queenly grace.

Nefertari watched, and smiled as she dipped the black grapes that she loved into an alabaster bowl, golden-rimmed and jewel-studded, and pulled them with her long-nailed, hennaed fingers, one by one, while Thuty gazed on her and his eyes were the eyes of a man whose longing is insatiable and whose desire will gnaw and grow. Often I felt my half-sister's gaze on me, and once I looked her full in the face. She smiled at me. I smiled back, wondering at my own strange calm. Nefertari always behaved as though she were Royal through both her father and her mother, and now that she was Queen, she thought herself a Goddess. She was ever jealous of our mother, who was true Priestess and had the Opened Eye and the All-giving Heart, and who, since Nefertari had been Queen, lived more and more beside the Sacred Lake in the small House of the Priestesses. She had opened the road to my soul with her love, her wisdom and her Knowing, and joyous were the hours we spent together. But I knew that I was still far indeed from the soul-strength that would release my Ka in sleep to be with Rai in a life more deep and true than we had known together on earth. I rejoiced that now my work with the Sitters on Horses was almost ended, my work in the Temple would not be curtailed.

Then, three days after the state arrival of Hur and Mayebre the Libyan, at which I took my brother's place and greeted the tyrants, I was walking with my mother beside the Sacred Lake. We were watching the water-birds.

"Sit down here with me, on this seat," she said, and her eyes were eager. "Three days! The Feast of the Valley! And Kamose's plans for the capture of the Cataract Fort are sprouting!" She looked like a young girl. "I am to make a Royal Passage to my estates at Ed-fu, and the King will accompany me in the Royal Yacht."

"What of the tribute-ships?"

"Akh! By Hapi! This is Ahmose-Eb's task, and Aknere's, with Hori, who is Cataract-bred."

"Hori, I have not seen him since he taught me to sail when I was ten."

"He is Captain now, under Ahmose-Eb, of *The Wild Bull*, and four other prime ships."

I had not been in the Councils, and I asked, "What of the Hyksos spies? They swarm as summer gnats in the southern nomes. And Hur? He and the greasy Libyan still intend to sail in the tribute-ships?"

My mother shrugged, laughing. I wondered at her, and smiled. My father's plans had not brought this light to her eyes.

"Kamose has feasted them, as only Kamose can feast!

Spending his time with them, carousing. They are lazy now, and depleted with women. . . . At the evening meal you will see, Ahmose. Tonight you will see." She was still laughing and her eyes were mischievous. "And Ahmose-Eb, so stalwart and serious and quiet! Last night he took the oily Libyan aside and, feigning and flattering, told him that the people of his nome and other nomes south of Thebes were grumbling and irritating for a sight of their new young King, and he explained how a Royal visit could be a simple way to keep the southern nomes in check, and take their minds off the tribute. . . ." I was listening in amaze at all she knew. She had not, nor had Nefertari or our grandmother, taken part in the feasting for the visiting Hyksos. "Pen-aati told me," she said, "and then on the second night, as had been planned, in the middle of the feast, Ahmose-Eb said to Hur, 'And why do I not lead your tribute-ships in my flag-ship, *The Wild Bull?*' And at the same time prepare for the King's visit, for Kamose Whadj-Kheper-Ra?"

" 'Kamose Whadj-Kheper-Ra!' Mayebre the Libyan laughed aloud in the Banquet-court. 'Ra, it seems, has two sons,' he said. 'This young and lusty toy king, and Okenen-Ra Apophis! Lord of the Scimitar! Living Image of Ra on earth,' and he raised his goblet.

" 'And doubtless more sons, many more! Fathered in the Temple chambers,' Hur said."

My mother's face clouded. "In the rites of Set," she said, "the Royal Women and the priestesses lie in the darkness with all who come and any who come are the God."

"They laugh at us for our piety." I smiled.

"Amun be praised that they do. For whom they hold up to ridicule they do not fear, and this is as Kamose plans."

That evening it was I who must take the mocking homage of Hur, whose cruelty and greed were a reason for shame even in the North Land. But his place was secure, and Aknere said that Apophis himself stood in awe of his Overseer of the Revenues, and It-yu, the Chief Scribe, openly toadied and hung on his arm. Only Herath, the daughter of the king, Aknere told us, had laughed in Hur's face when he would have taken her to wife. "She is young and beautiful," Aknere said in Council. "And there is no love lost between her and her step-mother. Apophis is besotted with his new young queen, and Anat-neby is but four years older than Herath. . . ." And Kamose had asked, "Is this a Council? Or a gossiping harem?" I looked at Hur, coming across the Court-yard, and I thought that Herath had courage to laugh in his face. He was less oily then the Libyan, and his hair had fewer ringlets. But his eyes were pale blue and cruel-cold as the name he was given, and his skin had a yellow tinge. He bowed briefly, his hand on his heart.

"So tonight I am honored to sit with the young Prince? Last year, Prince Ahmose, you were naked as a boy." His look said that a shaven head and a belted loin-cloth had made small difference. "But I hear you are to be Priest." He shrugged and, without asking my leave, sat down beside me on the Royal dais. Neme's wife came to him with a bowl of scented water to lave his hands, but with a sharp gesture he refused her, and with the same rude flickering of his fingers he called a slim girl to him.

"Ita." I breathed in the name and would have sent her away on some errand, but the hated guest said, looking full at me,

"Few women rouse me. Even virgins brought, fresh and beautiful, from the nomes." And he held out his hands to be washed, looking around the while with an arrogant stare and eyes as bleak as a desert storm. But when Ita dried his hands on the linen towel, he looked at her and his eyes glowed, and as she handed him the lotus flower, he held her by the wrist. I knew that the slender love of Neme's son would know that a man could have the tearing cruelty of a beast, and nothing of tenderness. Hur smiled and bade her dance, flicking his fingers at the harpists. She did not raise her eyes. Her face was smooth, cool as amber and apart, as though it did not belong to the graceful movements of her body.

"She will serve none but me." Hur did not deign to turn

to me as he spoke. His cold eyes were watching the ripple of Ita's arms and the bow-curve of her body as she bent backward till her hair trailed, black and shining, along the painted tiles.

And when the meal was ending, and Ita was dancing again, and had laved his hands thrice, he turned to me. "It is a weary journey to the Cataract Fort, anchoring along the way to lade the tribute," he said. "I shall allow the fawning son of Ebana of El-kab . . . he is the Captain of your"—he paused, openly sneering—"your Royal Fleet? Yes, I shall allow him to lead our tribute-ships south. . . . Our North Land sailors are not Cataract men. . . ."

"And by Set's Boar!" Mayebre the Libyan had been listening on his cushions at the base of the dais. "Let their toy monarch play king." He raised his cup, spilling wine down his beard.

Hur looked down at him, though half-turned toward me. "And let this young priestling go along with the ships." He drew a slow breath. Then, letting it out with a small hissing sound, he said, "His mien has annoyed me since I set foot in Thebes."

For the first time, even though Kamose had sent me to meet him at the Royal Wharf, I looked full at him and my gaze was locked in a blaze of pure hatred.

The Libyan's thick voice broke the taut stretch of our gazing. "And the young . . . holy one's presence may ensure that last year's covert rebellion is not repeated . . . and he will not cheat! His God will be watching him. . . ." Mayebre the Libyan and his cronies were loud in their drunken mirth.

"There will be a hundred of our scribes to tally the grain" —Hur moved his weight onto his other hip as he sat watching Ita's dance, speaking the while—"to the last ear of corn, when the ships return. Meanwhile"—he paused, staring at Ita under lowered lids—"I shall await them in Thebes."

"A decision with merit!" Mayebre the Libyan was searching with his thick red lips for the mouth of one of Sen-ut's Young Eyes and Ears.

I turned away, sick, and when Ita ended her dance, I retired. As I walked slowly to my room I thought that Kamose's plans were thriving. Hur the Cruel One and Mayebre, with their brute-companions, were to stay in Thebes! And Neme's son? Ita, his bride? I lay atop the cover of my bed, seeing Hur's eyes again. The misery, the bite, the plundering that the South Land still suffered! Sen-ut's maidens! They were warriors. Where is Sen-ut? I will ask Thure tomorrow. Far into the night, I lay on the edge of sleep.

"We can stand their ridicule," my mother said. I was with her in her Lodge by the Lake, after the Morning Rite. "But it is neither just nor true that the Cruel One should have Ita." She clenched her hands and shook her head slowly. "She was here with me at dawn. . . . 'I am a warrior for the South Land,' she said. 'As the maidens of the Lady Sen-ut.' She is proud that her beauty helped to lure Hur into Kamose's trap. 'Without you,' I told her, 'Hur might be sailing himself. Without you, he might not have let *The Wild Bull* lead his tribute-ships to Assuan.'" My mother touched her amulet collar. "Amun-Ra be praised," she said quietly. "Oh, my Son, the Lord of Creation has lent his strength to Kamose. The King's soul beholds the Serpent of Flame on his brow." She turned to me and took my hand. "And you, Ahmose, you are to sail with Ahmose-Eb in *The Wild Bull*, did you know?"

"No, I did not. Why must I sail? Because my mien irks Hur? Are we such vassals?"

She shook her head. "No, but Kamose hoped for that. 'The Little Brother,' he said to me, 'has a gentle gaze more deep-searing than contempt.' That is why he sent you to meet the tyrants at the wharf. . . . And, Ahmose, the King would have you see the working out of his plans for the tribute-ships. . . ."

"But I know! They will be transformed into battle-ships and left to guard the Fort, and check the River traffic from the Land of the Nubians, while we attack the North Land. I have no part in these plans. Why should I go? I have done my work with the Sitters on Horses, and my whole heart was in that work, and in the secret Councils, when Kamose called me. It is my desire to give myself wholly to my work in the House of Life, while you are away . . ."

"A gale of speech, my Young One! But speech is swift when the heart desires. . . . Hor-min will stay in Thebes as scribe for the secret Councils . . ."

"But there will be no secret Councils. Kamose will be sailing south on the Royal Progress."

"Dispatches and messages come through almost every day. There will be heavy work for Hor-min, sorting and preparing them, written and spoken, for the King on his return. Pen-aati or Miutu will hold Council while we are away."

"Why should I not hold Council? I am Prince of the South Land."

My mother smiled. "You are as yet a fledgling tree . . . and the King wills it. 'Ahmose must learn more of his Land and his River,' he said, and he needs you!" She nodded. "With twenty of your best trained Horse-men."

"Why?"

"They will choose fifty from the three hundred horses we know are in the Cataract Fort, and your men will train them. They will leave *The Wild Bull*, when you have safely passed Assuan, taking rafts in the darkness to the Western Shore, where they will join with Ak-hor. His Nubians will be gathered in the Western Desert one day's march from the Fort . . ."

"But where will they train the horses they capture? How will they keep the training a secret?"

"In a secret ravine in the midst of high granite cliffs that rise from the desert on the eastern side of the Cataract!"

"How is it secret?"

"Your father and I came upon a note about it in an old papyrus of Mentu-hotep's. It had been secret for so long, we

kept it to ourselves. When Kamose was planning this venture
I told him of it."

"It seems that our ancestor has a potent part in this fight,"
I said.

"All our ancestors! And the gods."

"And I see that my work is not ended."

"Our work for the God is never ended, and, my Son, you
will come forth from the Cataract at the Cave of your beloved Osiris. . . . Pray to him, Ahmose, that Ak-hor and his
Nubians, and the Eyes and Ears inside the Fort, will have
the strength of the gods. It must be in our hands before you
and Ahmose-Eb come with the captured tribute-ships. If it
is not, then all our plans are as chaff in the khamsin wind!"

I looked at her, marveling at the scope of her knowledge,
and after a moment I said again, "The enemy laughs at
Kamose. They have no fear of him and his carts full of
virgins . . . and this is our strength. Apophis, at a banquet in
Avaris, squashed a black grape in his fat, oily palm and said,
'I can squash this lusty young Theban who plays king in the
South Land . . . like this!' And Aknere said that the dark
red juice ran through his fingers like blood, and Anat-neby
bent down and sucked it with her lips, and kissed him nose
to nose, and they kissed again and again in front of the whole
court."

My mother's face was solemn. "Ahmose, you are angry,
and you chatter," she said. "Where is your priestly calm?
Your acceptance? The King is the Royal Man, consecrated
by Amun. He is beyond greatness." She sighed and put her
arm through mine. "Live for a while under the Heavens,
and with the River, and the River will bring you closer to
the knowledge of Heaven."

"And Kheri-heb? He knows of this voyage that is planned
for me?"

"I bring a message from him."

"But I shall see him before I sail."

She shook her head again, slowly. "No, my Moon Child.

Kheri-heb is fasting, and you sail this day, at sun-set."

"Akh! Ra-en-Ra!" We both laughed a little. "Tell me, what is Kheri-heb's message?" I asked.

"Only he who is Brother to Water will Hapi guide through the Field of Reeds." I understood, and was silent. Then I said, "This voyage is one of those duties at which you said I would balk?" My mother raised one eyebrow and looked like Kamose. Then she said, "Aknere will sail with you in *The Wild Bull*. There is much work for him, and your brother wishes that you know more of this young man."

"I shall be glad to know more of him. He surprises me. So spare he is, and so wan of face, and yet Chief of our Young Eyes and Ears."

My mother turned to me, tall and slender in the morning sun-light. "Go with Ra." She held both my hands, and when I stood with her, I was the taller. "Your grand-mother is right. You will broaden with valor, my Moon Child." She smiled. "And may Osiris guard you, for this voyage is a hazard." Her smiled deepened. "Kamose and Kheri-heb knew you would balk at this voyage. But they are wise."

"Wise enough to let you be the bearer of the news!" I laughed softly, and we embraced. "My Mother," I said. "I go with good heart. What else can I do?"

In the golden light of Ra descending, Ahmose-Eb, Aknere and I went aboard *The Wild Bull*. Hori, the Captain, his shaven head bronze-shining in the sun-glow, bowed greeting to us at the bottom of the wood-slatted ramp, then followed us aboard.

The twenty horse trainers, who were disguised as rowers, made deep bows with the other sailors, not a flicker of re-membering, nor recognition in their eyes. I thought of the days and hours we had spent together in the underground paddock, of how sore our rumps had been, and I wondered how they would take to rowing.

Ahmose-Eb was in deep talk with Hori, and Aknere had

gone into the shelter-cabin, aft-center of the deck. I walked to the splash rail and looked away to the Western Crags. Tier upon tier of rock, they rose toward the red-gold sky. I thought of my father's funeral, and the long, hard walk to the place of the Rite; the walk back to the wharves after he had been sealed in his Everlasting House; and of the Thebans and the Necropolis Dwellers who had held festival. "Rai . . ." I had walked down the rocky path with her. Her hand had been cool in mine, and we had been thinking of our father, and the Rite. The laughter and chatter, the clash of cymbals for the male dancing, and the clatter of the metal pans, the hollow drumming of the tambourines, the singing and the feasting had echoed along the rugged edges of the cliffs, through the deep gorges and clear down the valley.

"Hat-hor of the West . . ." I murmured, as I watched the jagged, arid mountains, the darkening shadows almost to their golden summits. "My hand is in your hand, Ahmose," Rai had whispered. "I shall not go afar off."

"Rai . . . seven times sweet, and the thief of laughter . . ." When we had come to the wharf, she had held my arm and pointed to where a fisherman, on the brink of the shallowing River, had caught a hand-net full of binny-fish, tiny and silver-white and gold, that move by the thousands in the shallows. "Like a net full of early stars," she said as the man held up the net, dripping and shimmering in the sun-set, and together we had made the Blessing of Hapi, who is the burgeoning River, and the fisher had bowed, his hand on his heart.

"Hapi . . ." I prayed, as I leaned here, on the rail. "Bless this first time I have sailed far out on your wide bosom. Bless our sailing, and grant that we find the Fort in Egyptian hands . . . and Ak-hor safe, and our brave Eyes and Ears." I walked across the deck and looked toward Thebes. The Temple was filled with Light. It seemed to hover, and the descending God paved the avenues with gold and glanced bright dapples through the trees. "Thebes, City of the Hidden Name," I whispered, and thought of thousands of years of the Beloved Land, and felt, as I stood, the ancient heart-beat of the City; the Eternal City of the Unseen God, whose name in his Residence is Amun-Ra.

Suddenly the night herons, wakening to his last rays, flew out of the dom-palm trees, and with loud calls and wing-flappings circled about the boat and were away to their secret place to hide till the dawn. They brought me to myself again. I turned. Ahmose-Eb and Aknere were coming toward me. I crossed to meet them and we stood, as *The Wild Bull* pulled away from the wharf, and watched the dark shadows rising, encroaching on the last great shafts of light, and veiling the heights of the Western Hills to indigo darkness as Ra sailed down behind them to the Twelve Gateways of the Night. We stayed there silent till the River turned to gray, and the western sands grew pallid, waiting for the moon.

After the first obeisance, I was no longer Prince of the South Land, and on the morrow, when the River was running high, in yeasty waves, I was an ordinary sailor wearing only the tied loin-cloth and going barefoot. Soon I felt the joy we had known as children, when we were taught the ways of the currents and the storms, and of Shu, who is the air. A fresh breeze had risen with the sun and helped us all the day. The River was alive with cargo-boats, and *The Wild Bull* swept by them, her sail full-filled toward El-Kab, the city of Ahmose-Eb's family and heritage.

The five tribute-ships were one each side of us and three behind, manned by bearded North-men who knew the River. Their lead-ship, *The Black Boar*, to Hori's delight sailed almost alongside, and her Captain called out loud and arro-gant commands to him, while the Hyksos sailors shouted rude threats to our rowers. Hori's rejoinders were those of a Cata-ract man, and our sailors were at no loss for words.

Ahmose-Eb, Aknere and I shared the cabin. It was a strong shelter of native woods, covered with heavy reed matting, and the shield of Ahmose-Eb's city, the White Vulture of El-Kab, and the shield of his flag-ship were splayed to the sides of it. It was strong to withstand onslaught, and inside were four sleeping mats with goose-down cushions, and a low heavy table with two small wick-lamps. Aknere raised an appreciative eyebrow at the cushions, propped two up behind him and leaned deep into them.

He and I were alone as we sailed with the wind toward El-Kab. *The Wild Bull* stood off well ahead of the other ships, and I came to know more of the quiet, contained Chief of our Young Eyes and Ears.

He never seemed to feel he was in danger, that his work, at any moment, might mean his death. He looked upon death as a friend, almost as a lover, and he quoted the ancient poem to me:

> "Death, to me, is as the fragrance of myrrh,
> And the scent of the lotus-flower . . .

"Hundreds of years before this life, I am living," he said, and we looked at each other for the first time. His eyes are almost as merry as Hor-min's, I thought, but they were dark gray, and Hor-min's a deep-warm brown.

"Aknere," I asked. "Would you be Priest?"

"No," he answered. "I am happy in what I do. Death will be to me as the clearing of mist from the sky."

I said no more, and after a while we talked of the night to come.

"You are to stay in the cabin, my Prince," he said. "The King has so commanded. Hori will sail *The Wild Bull* on ahead of us before the attack."

"And you? And Ahmose-Eb?"

"He and I will lead the raiders."

"Our young Chief of spies talking secrets?" Ahmose-Eb pulled aside the reed matting. "You look as a young bird in its nest." He looked down at Aknere with a grin, then said, "We are nearing the appointed place, downriver from my city." There was excitement in his voice. "We shall take on bread there." His eyes glowed. He squatted down between us. "I shall enjoy the bread I ate in my childhood, and the honey from the bees that nest in the turpentine trees."

"Ahmose-Eb, you and your appetite! You think more of food than you do of the venture tonight."

"I shall be hungry as a wolf when the attack is over." He chuckled. "The crews of their ships are preparing to lade our corn. My city is the first tribute port." He turned to me. "We shall lie at anchor at the place where the River and the bank are almost level, which makes the lading easy . . ."

"And also our attack," Aknere added. "And there will be wine for the crews . . ."

"And two Companies of Mer-neb's Bow-men and Per-neb's Foot-soldiers, stationed and waiting for the darkness . . . and the prisoners."

"By tomorrow's dawn, the tribute-ships will be ours," Aknere said slowly and quietly.

"Tell me your plan," I asked.

And Ahmose-Eb answered, "My Prince, at the dark of the moon fifty armed men, of Pery-em-wah's Eyes and Ears and Per-neb's Foot-soldiers, will swim silently around each of the anchored ships, and board them. The Eyes and Ears among the crews will have heavily drugged their wine. They are arrogant and do not suspect, but there will be some skirmish with those on guard. They will be dealt with silently and swiftly; the others will be taken and bound while they sleep. Our drugs are potent. By dawn, as Aknere says, these worthy ships will be in Egyptian hands . . . and now, my Prince, this young spy and your servant here present, we should sleep awhile, for when the darkness falls we must be wide awake." He smiled as we both looked at Aknere. Already he was fast asleep against his goose-down cushions.

"I will go out on deck," I said. "May Osiris guard your rest."

The wind had dropped. No breeze rippled the water. Along with my Horse-men, who, as all born in Egypt, were River-men, I rowed till the first star came out. Then, in spite of myself, my eyelids grew heavy. Quiet as the smoke of the incense burning, I crept into the cabin and lay down, scarce taking a breath, that I might not waken the two men on whose prowess this night my brother depended. On the instant, I fell asleep.

I was wakened by a shout. I sat up and blinked my eyes. The full risen beams of Ra streamed through the reed matting and made colored rays through the weave and the warp of it.

I leapt up and ran to the splash rail. Hori greeted me from the prow of the captured *Black Boar!* And with their sails filled and billowing in the fresh wind that came with the dawn, the captured tribute-ships swept past *The Wild Bull*, manned by our own sailors!

We sailed on to El-Kab, where, for the first time, I would see the Great Girdle Wall. My father, and Ahmose-Eb's father, Ebana, had told me about it when I was a child.

I stood, leaning on the rail in silence, and as we approached his city, Ahmose-Eb came to lean on the splash rail beside me. He had caught up with us in the first ship captured, an hour before the dawn, and come aboard. We stood together in praise and thanksgiving as we watched the captured ships. Then he told me about the attack and the prisoners taken and sent to the places already prepared and guarded, so that my heart widened with a new understanding of strategy and the details of true planning, and I forgot the Great Wall till we turned toward the shore. Then, I stood spell-bound.

"Thirty-seven arms thick . . ." Ahmose-Eb murmured. "It was built in the Days of Splendor, and there"—he pointed to a hill that stood about a mile from the wharf—"there my father lies!" We were silent together. I thought of Ebana of El-kab giving me my first lesson with the wooden hand-ax; waving the huge fan over my father and mother on the Balcony of Appearances, and holding his fan stock still when Mayebre the Libyan held up the blasphemous ingot; then, his last words before his Ka left him: "To my son . . . my heart's love." Tears filled Ahmose-Eb's eyes for a moment. Then, still looking at the hill, he blinked and said,

"There I, too, shall build my House of Everlasting."

"When Kamose is victorious," I put my arm about his shoulder, "he will grant you your House of Everlasting, and endow it."

We stood by the rail together till the bread and goat's cheese and honey had been loaded aboard, and at noon we pulled away from Ahmose-Eb's city.

Our rowers sang as they plied the oars with good will and high spirits, to catch up with the captured ships, and when we came abreast of them, sailing each astern of the other, we saw with glee that our sailors were clad in the clothes of the Hyksos, and Aknere was Captain aboard *The Black Boar*!

"Where did he get that beard?" I laughed out loud. It was curly and long, and shining with oil.

"He has many disguises," Ahmose-Eb answered. "It must be an irritation to him."

"But necessary," I said, and with new insight, added, "We must get past Assuan and through the Cataract before we are suspected. Their spies are everywhere."

"Even on the River." Ahmose-Eb nodded. "I trust no cattle-boat, nor yacht, nor even the ferry-boat. Akh! By the Great Strider! If a wind would arise . . ." he said, but we rowed against the current in the still bright air, slowly making our way to Ed-fu, and when Ra was descending, my mother's city appeared in the distance. We had striven every hands' length of the way, Ahmose-Eb and I taking our turn at the oars, plowing a River as smooth as though the oil of the castor bean had been poured upon it.

Now we stood on the prow, and in the dusk we saw palms clustered green around the foot of the Temple slope, and, bright in the saffron light, the banners aloft in preparation for the visit of Kamose and my mother moved gently in the breeze that had risen with the sun-set. We slid past the city in the last of the twi-light. The breeze gathered strength with the stars and filled out our sail to billowing. It stayed with us throughout the night, and Aknere came aboard.

With the cabin curtains a-flap and the tiller scrouping and the creaking ship noises, we could not sleep.

"All told, sixteen of the enemy and fifteen of our men lost

their lives in the foray," Ahmose-Eb said. "The Hyksos we threw into the River. They will be carried on Hapi's breast to the North Land they invaded. Our own men we carried ashore to the Temple of the Anubis Priests, for embalming."

"And the large, new-built ships are ours." I thought how much had been brought to fruition while I was sleeping, and we talked of it, and of the Fort, the Royal Progress and Kamose.

"He is the Rudder and the Yeast of the Two Lands," Aknere murmured, sleepy against his cushions. "He quickens the hearts of his people as the fire in our marrow quickens all the organs of our bodies. . . ."

Drinking, now and then, a little wine, we talked of Kamose's Company, chosen from childhood, with perception and judgment, for qualities of heart.

"There is no guile, nor intrigue among us," Ahmose-Eb said.

"As among the Thirty Great Ones." Aknere put his wine-cup on the low table and leaned back again. "And the Council of Nomarchs."

We talked of Sen-ut and Res, and their young women who were Workers in Secret.

"For the first time in the history of Ta-mery," Aknere said, "we have women Eyes and Ears!"

"And for the first time in history," I said, "we have Sitters on Horses."

"Hur let us sail with his ships!" Ahmose-Eb whispered. "He allowed Kamose's Royal Progress. . . . They can have no knowledge of our strength."

"How unwise of Hur . . . and how blind . . ." Aknere's head fell sideways against the cushions with a wide yawn. He was the first one of us to fall fast asleep.

When we wakened, Ed-fu was far behind us and the strong wind was still blowing. Hori had come aboard again to bring *The Wild Bull* through the Cataract.

"Soon," he said, as we ate our morning meal of goat's cheese, honeyed milk and grapes, "we shall see Assuan."

Aknere stayed in the cabin all day poring over maps and

plans, and Ahmose-Eb and I sat on deck or leaned on the splash rail.

"See how our Beloved Land changes her countenance," he said, and I gazed at the huge black granite rocks that towered to the east of us. Then we walked across deck to the west, where great sand mounds rose, like a range of hills, and the banks of the River were edged with palms.

Onward we sped, past villages, small towns and small ports with boats lying moored at their wharves, till the bend in the River was rounded, and the last reach gained. Soon, with the five captured ships in our wake, we came to Assuan.

"This city is a nest of the Hyksos," Ahmose-Eb said. "And their allies from Nubia, just beyond the border, have swarmed into it."

We were watching the green Isle of Elephantine. It lay away from us, dividing the River. We sailed past. The wind had gathered to a storm. The sailors were all in their places, and Hori turned to us, showed his white teeth in a broad smile and pointed to Aknere, back again on the prow of *The Black Boar* and almost alongside, shouting a coarse, loud Hyksos curse at *The Wild Bull,* our own seamen shouting vile epithets about the enemy and their large tribute-ships to the wharf workers. Aknere, his false beard spreading in the wind, hurled insults at us in the Hyksos dialect, while our own Eyes and Ears in the other five ships added their Hyksos curses on all things Egyptian, getting back from us as good as they gave. In this way we sailed, as though the tribute-ships were still manned by the enemy, past Assuan in safety.

That night, at the darkness, the twenty Horse-men went ashore in their reed rafts.

I was silent with wonder as the River widened and I saw hundreds of islands, all as different as though each had been sculptured by a different artisan. Pylons, and columns, and rock-forts. A huge, humped island was green with palms, and a smaller one, square and high, was fringed with tamarisks and acacia trees, dom-palms and date-palms, and the rock-islands were of red and black and purple granite, planed by the waters of thousands of years, to shine back the sky's images as huge-looking bronzes.

"Hapi of the South . . ." I murmured, and looked at Ahmose-Eb.

"Though not a sailor, you are feeling the River, my Prince," he said. "And Hori awaits us. We are in his hands."

"And Hapi's," I said. "And yours and, perhaps, my useless hands . . ."

We went aft to watch the ships in our wake. The storm-wind was rising to greater strength, filling the sails as they followed a zigzag course behind us. I am a River-man, too, I thought. I had never known the wind-rushing joy of it.

The River, at the Cataract, did not narrow—but the rocks! Huge mountains of rock, thousands of rocks; boulders of granite and basalt, piled up on top of each other, or jutting singly, black and polished; and the water that surged, pouring off the towering summits in clouds of spray, and spinning and spuming over sunken rocks, eddying among smooth boulders, now shallow, now deep, bubbling over hidden whirlpools, fighting its way along paths and labyrinths to which, Ahmose-Eb said, Hori had the key. I knew that my namesake knew the Cataracts as the palm of his hand.

For two miles we sailed around the rocks, the wind howling and driving our ships into the current. We skirted the edges of foaming masses and slid, with a grating jar, over smooth stone lying hidden under the boiling foam.

"Always it storms," Ahmose-Eb said as we came to the place of the River passages that lead up through the rocks to the broad stream again. "The East Passage, Hori!" he called out above the sound of the wind and the water.

It was hard for him to stand aside and leave this to Hori, who stood watching the straining sail as we breasted the current and, amid shouts of laughter, *The Wild Bull* gave herself up to the River's rush. Then there was a roar from our crew and from that of *The Black Boar* as she almost rammed into us.

Ahmose-Eb wiped the sweat and the spray from his face

and brow. Then he turned swiftly. "By the Disc!" he said as Aknere scrambled aboard. "You are stronger than you look."

"You brought your *Black Boar* up along in fine fashion," I said as Hori, his bright yellow head-band dripping, went like a bird to the prow and the sailors to their places again. We came to a narrow passage, not twelve arms' lengths wide, where the water tumbled and poured from the broader stream higher up between the high rocks, foaming and roaring in a torrent around them and over them as well as between them, and *The Wild Bull* rushed, like the charge of her namesake, between the two boulders. Sailing here was an art that I had not known.

Hori steered us into an eddy and the sailors were singing, wild and harsh:

> "Sons of the River
> You are men! You are men!
> Your boat will not lag.
> Ra! strengthen us!
> Hapi! Wash us in glory . . ."

Ahmose-Eb was singing with them. Then he said, "Only by sheer lifting and pulling and hoisting can we get the ships over this!" And, as though gathering herself for the final effort, *The Wild Bull* seemed to settle, and the wind roared above us. "Come and watch!" Ahmose-Eb ran forward along the rail to watch Hori, who had dived overboard and swum to the rocks, then half swam and half scrambled ashore, where he stood for a moment to catch his breath. Now he stooped and picked up a handful of dust, and with a shout strange and wild he threw it up into the air. "Look!" Ahmose-Eb pointed, and on the instant, men appeared like afrits, from every part of the rocky River banks, deserted of human life a second before! Now the shore was teeming with people. Men, women and children crowded to join in the hauling. "And reap the rewards," Ahmose-Eb said as we watched them.

More than two hundred were swimming in the furious current, ropes in their hands, pulling and tugging, the waters raging around them and their bright-colored headkerchiefs bobbing like net-floats, clinging and laughing, choking with water, spitting and pulling as they towed us up and up with the ropes, while as many again, or more of them, stood on the rocks to push her away in a double effort of hoisting and hauling.

"Up! Up! Up! Ra strengthen us!" The people on the rocks were wailing and shouting, louder and louder the harder they pulled and they pushed, till, with a great heave and a long taut haul, *The Wild Bull* leapt up, the waters parting over her bow.

"She is a gallant ship," I said, holding on to the rail with both hands.

"I love her." There was deep pride in Ahmose-Eb's eyes as a great hawser was made fast around her. Men came all around holding on. "Now, my Prince, this is the great haul!"

And as Ra in his Sek-tet Boat descended, our crew and the Cataract dwellers fell to their work as gods of the River, hundreds each side of us, hauling and towing, swimming and clutching at the rocks, using the ledges as levers, in a strange strong heaving. Up and up, steadily we rose, and the great mounds of water rose.

"The Cataract men are a race to themselves," Ahmose-Eb whispered close to my ear against the roar of the wind. His eyes were gleaming. "I'm going to join them."

"I, too!" I took hold of the tow-rope he held in his hand. "By Hapi, my Friend," I said, as we jumped overboard into the cascading squall of spray.

I came up holding the rope. I was not even swimming, but bouncing like a ball, and laughing, till I swallowed a chest full of water, choked, spitting, and saw Ahmose-Eb rock-scrambling to a wide ledge. I held on to the rope as I crawled up beside him, and five men joined us from nowhere. Together we heaved and pulled with the others, then, as the tow slackened, swimming to another rock we hauled like giants, new-strengthened and sturdy again. I had no time to think, but the strength in my limbs rose in waves to my heart. I gave swift praise for the hardening work with the horses. This haul was my haul. It was my strength and my zest that moved *The Wild Bull* like a huge River-goose up and up through the rapid. I heard myself laughing as we swam out again and again till the sky darkened, choosing our rocks, proud with each pull, stubborn and mirthful in rhythm together, undying, soul-stretched eternal and upwards, plunging and heaving, our hearts like whirlpools, our vein-blood the River! And all the gods looked for was the rushing of the waters, the spray-spume and the flesh-tearing rocks, black in the moon-light.

Then, like a dream ending, the tow-rope slackened. I raised my wave-beaten head and looked around me. *The Wild Bull* was gliding, graceful as a pleasure-yacht, and the waters were pool-smooth. I lay on my back holding the slack rope, all energy spent, near swooning, weightless and all light within, and the Water itself, and the bodies of my companions, lazily swimming, half floating toward *The Wild Bull*, were all fashioned of the same bright, moon-lucent flesh.

Ahmose-Eb came swimming beside me. "You are a Sailor, my Prince."

"I am an Egyptian, my Friend, and a River-man." I knew, as we swam slowly back to the ship, that the gods had shown me a part of myself I had not known till this night, and I said in my heart to Kheri-heb, "I am Brother to Water." I climbed up the papyrus ladder and Aknere held out his hand.

"From the Two Lands into Nubia," he said as I climbed aboard, and we lay stretched out on deck while our ship sailed the last reach of the Cataract, and, her sail unfurled and filled with the billowing wind, swept on.

"The Cave of Osiris!" I sprang up. Under the high black rocks I saw the Cave and lay flat, face down, on deck. "Osiris, Lord . . ." I thought of my mother, and prayed, "Osiris, to whom the stars in the Celestial Heights are obedient, beneficent in decree, Osiris, Lord, smite the enemies of Ta-mery. Send fear into the bowels of our adversaries . . ." I rose, in astound at myself for my war-like prayer, and Ahmose-Eb said,

"The Cataract Fort is a half-day away."

"And all the ships safely through the rapids!" Aknere said. "They will be hidden close in to the granite rocks." His raiders and Eyes and Ears were still manning them, but the Cataract men had dispersed to their villages.

The Wild Bull, her sail furled, and seeming to rest after her long haul, was rowed slowly along, close in to the eastern bank.

"Your Horse-men should have joined Ak-hor by now," Ahmose-Eb said.

"And I have a meeting where the desert joins the village land. I will bring news of the Fort." Aknere gave a small salute and jumped over the side of the ship.

"Let us pray to Ra that by tomorrow the Cataract Fort will be in our hands," Ahmose-Eb said, and, too tired to talk more, we lay down and slept in the open.

The following day we lay at anchor in a sheltered cove, and though I was cool in the shadow of the towering granite cliffs, and tried, sitting alone on deck, to lose myself in meditation and prayer to Osiris, my muscles were stiff and sore from the swimming and hauling, and the fight that must this day be raging for the Cataract Fort filled all my thinking; our brave, patient Eyes and Ears, Ak-hor and his Nubian Scouts, and my Horse-men? The Sitters on Horses were, in Maat's Truth, a strong secret weapon. I felt a strange peace in the cool shade of the high-reaching rocks. Then, as lightning strikes, a new thought was born. "Messengers on Horses?" I sat up straight. "Messengers, trained as Eyes and Ears, on horses! Would the captured Hyksos horses be stronger than ours?" I was speaking aloud as I thought. "One small-boned young man on a horse, then running alongside, and sitting again that the horse would not tire, would be swifter far than a man on foot, or rowing against the current. . . . He could jump over canals, scramble up dike banks, his horse's feet padded, under the cloak of darkness . . ." The hours passed as minutes till, with the dusk, Aknere returned, and I saw from the look in his eyes that the Fort had fallen.

"Without a hitch," he said, "and none in the country around are aware of it." The Hyksos garrison, to a man, had been slain.

"Hy!" Ahmose-Eb climbed over the rail and ran across the deck toward us. "By tomorrow, four tribute-ships will fly the South Land flag and be all but equipped for battle." He came and squatted at my feet, looking up at Aknere. "What more?" he asked.

"Three hundred chariots have been captured, and, my Prince," Aknere turned to me, "six hundred horses! Your Horse-men have chosen three hundred from which you will choose your last Company."

"And my new Companies," I murmured to myself as Aknere was telling me that already they awaited me in the secret ravine. Then he gave a rare smile. "My Prince, I am commanded to row you, at night-fall, upriver to a place where a donkey and a guide will meet you."

Kamose was in his tent. He was half lying on a reed mat, his shoulders against a big goat's-skin cushion. Sek-met sprawled beside him. "Welcome, Little Sailor-man!" He turned to Neme, who had been my guide. "Thank you . . . now sleep. It has been a long day." He held out his hand, pulled me down beside him and told me how he had come as far as Assuan in the Royal Yacht, then ridden secretly, and in disguise, to meet me. "Most of the way in an ox-cart," he said, "then across the small stretch of desert on donkey-back."

Ak-hor was lying full-length on the ground. He was exhausted. In all the years I had not seen him look so spent; but the Fort was in Egyptian hands. We talked awhile, and I drank the Nubian wine. It was strong and prickled my tongue, so that my face puckered.

"It is a warrior's wine, my Prince," Ak-hor said.

"Not so much a warrior's drink as your blood and milk, Ak-hor." Kamose put down his empty cup. "Twice I have been forced to drink it. . . . Little Brother, Ak-hor's people slit the throats of their oxen and take out a cup of blood, as we would milk a cow."

"To strengthen us for hunting and fighting," Ak-hor added, and rose to his feet. "My King." He bowed to Kamose. "I must sleep." With a small bow to me and a drowsy smile, he left us alone.

Kamose looks older, I thought, as I finished my wine. He wore his hunting belt and sporran, and a short, fine-pleated kilt. The striped kerchief around his head fell square over his ears. His green, gold-flecked eyes were huge and dark, and his face was thinner. I asked of our mother.

"She is at her estate at Ed-fu. Let us go now," he said, "in the quiet desert night, to the high rocks."

Rodents scurried, afraid of Sek-met, to their burrows. A hyena howled, lonely.

"The ancient people of our Land would eat their flesh," my brother said. "Our grand-father told me that they fed them with goose-flesh till they were fat." I made a small disgusted noise, and he gave a soft chuckle. "And sterile women stewed their genitals in wine and ate them."

"Our grand-father told you that?"

"No, our grand-mother."

A late butterfly, white in the moon-light, flew around our heads.

"Tetisheri!" I said. "Her Ka knows that we are talking about her."

We came to a clearing between the high rocks. Here, even our breath seemed to echo from high cliff to high basalt cliff.

"To this valley our ancestors came," Kamose whispered. "They quarried here, and knew of this secret place. . . . One more turn in the path . . ."

We-het and my Horse-men were already in the wide

clearing. There were more than three hundred horses they had chosen from the six hundred captured from the Cataract Fort.

I refused only fourteen of them. Taking We-het and the Captain of my Horse-men aside, I told them of my new plan, and any doubts I had were washed clean away. We-het's eyes lit up, and the Captain slapped his lean thigh.

"My Prince . . ."

"Ra-en-Ra!" They both spoke together. Then the Captain said, "It is by the grace of the Lord Montu of the Animals that we captured more horses. . . ."

"And they are strong," We-het said. "My Prince, the Hyksos have been breeding their horses for a hundred years longer than we. They have mixed foreign breeds."

"And we now have their horses to mate with our own," I said. I chose fifty of the strongest for the Messengers, and fifty for the new Company of Sitters; the rest would be trained as spares. I gave orders to We-het to send the fifty strongest by our secret way up to Thebes, and after Kamose had talked with the men, praising them, we left them in the wide, rock-sheltered ravine to begin their training, and tasks, with the dawn.

The night hung, as a piece of dark linen, star-strewn. We made a fire of dried scrub against the cold and, sitting face to face, spent hours in talk. Then we did not speak, but lay prone on the moon-pale sands, and the vast calm filched our hearts. All was form; all emptiness, and our bodies were spirit, and timeless. We slept, Sek-met keeping watch, till a cold breeze shuddered our skins, and we were awake again. The moon was high, huge and silver-gold, and the sky above us and the desert around us had no beginning; no horizon. I looked up at the star-strewn heaven.

My brother sat up.

"I have left you alone with the work. How many men and horses have you battle-ready?"

"Ten companies of fifty."

"Do they know well, and fully, their mission?"

"They do! And more. They have been trained to guide their horses with their legs and buttocks. They can shoot arrows, and the short javelins they carry crosswise on their backs, in a larger sheath than their arrows . . . and they wear a short broad-sword in the belts of their plaited leather loin-cloths. They wear daggers, Nubian fashion, as you and Ak-hor, under their left arms . . ."

My brother laughed, and the sound broke the silence and echoed against the stone cliffs, and shivered the still air to crystal fragments.

"You have done well, Brother," he said, and after a while, "I may not use these Sitters on Horseback for the first forays. They, too, are targets for the hidden-swift arrows of the enemy. . . . I shall see how the battle goes . . . how they can best be used. . . ."

"And the chariots?"

"Our chariots are now a standard part of the army, and will be used from the beginning. We have pretended secrecy . . ."

"I know the number we now have underground."

"Hundreds more than they think they have secretly discovered in our hiding places above the ground. . . ."

"And now we have those from the Fort."

He nodded. "They are heavier, clumsier, than those we are building. Ahmose, of what were you and We-het and your Captain talking so deeply?"

"I have been waiting to tell you."

He looked at me, his eyes dark-ringed and shining, and a smile spread over his face. "Tell me, Little Brother."

I told him, and he looked strangely proud as he gazed at me in the light of the moon and the flickering fire.

"The Two Lands grew bright with your birth, Little Brother," he said.

The vast silence held us in thrall again. The full moon turned all things to stone. Time was eternity, yet swift as a bird's bright mating. The cool north wind swept through my heart, and I spoke my thoughts.

"I am a Sailor, Kamose." I pulled Ak-hor's woolen blanket over me. "I, myself! I, Ahmose, hauled *The Wild Bull*. I was drowned in the River, and—by Hapi!—the River flowed in my veins."

"Little Brother, Aknere told me of your swimming and hauling," he said, and we were silent again, and I seemed to bathe in his full-rigged, manifold heart. "To be in battle with me, Ahmose . . . to fight at my left hand . . ." He spoke in a whisper, and pulled his woolen blanket up about his shoulders and drew his knees up to his chin. "Gather some more scrub, Ahmose. The fire is low and the chill is bitter."

I rose, gathered an armful and brought it to the fire. Then I went back and gathered some more, and sat down, my blanket around me. "The tribute-ships? They will know that we captured them."

"No, they were lost . . . capsized! Word has already gone back to Thebes. . . . The Hyksos are not Cataract men . . . the ships were too large. Only one ship was saved."

"But the crew of that one ship?"

"Little Brother! In each of the five tribute-ships there were twenty of our Egyptian men. They have lived with the Hyksos for years. They wear their own beards! And oily they are . . ." He grinned. "They will bring back the one ship, laden with grain."

"And the other tribute?"

"They can send their own ships for it."

"And they will."

"That was a night of full worth, when you hauled through the Cataract," my brother said. "Nothing was overlooked. Our Eyes and Ears made great show of broken ship parts, and drowned hairy Hyksos rose to the surface of the water close to the shores, both eastern and western . . . those whom the crocodiles had not eaten . . ."

I sighed, and shook my head. "The Elders and Nobles are not anxious for war, Kamose."

"They become too friendly with our foes."

"Last summer, Thuty and the Chief Scribe sent their cattle to graze in the Delta Lands."

"For a fee."

"For a large fee! But the cattle grew fat and fleshy."

"And some of our Elders grow fat and fleshy, till the tribute must be paid."

"And their North-fed cattle are taken up North again. This time to stay!" Kamose chuckled. "They are few, the stupid ones . . . and the Nomarchs are loyal to a man."

"And the young are spoiling to fight."

Kamose nodded gravely. "Our people have stout hearts again. . . . On my return, I shall call the Thirty Great Ones to Council and Assembly."

"This Royal Council I shall want to hear."

"I shall need your Ka-strength, in Council and in battle, Little Brother." He pulled Sek-met's ears, and her purr was loud in the thin air.

After a moment, I said,

"My Brother, by harvest time, and by Osiris' Grace and the Strength of Ra, I shall have taken my vigil in the House of Life. I long for my trial, Kamose."

"I shall ask as little of you as I may." And he said again, "I shall need your Ka beside me, in battle."

"And our father's Ka, and Rai's and Ebana's," I said, and we sat for another while, silent.

Then Kamose looked up at the high rocks and, looking, stood up.

"Come!" I followed him. He took his dagger from under his arm. "Let us carve our names in the rock. Kamose and Ahmose, brothers, together in the Royal Rope." He put his arm about my shoulder and we walked together toward the high rocks. He searched till we found a smooth place. "Here!" He began to carve my name. I took the small dagger from my belt and began to carve his. Together, we worked in the moon-light quiet. For a while in silence, then talking, and his heart-thought was a hawk lofty-flighted through time and space, to stoop on a passion forgotten, a childhood prank we had played together, and on his Company. "My brilliant, brave, chosen Company!" The gleanings of his heart flickered from his tongue as flames, fearless, caressing, and old joys were bright again, but no brighter than his eyes as he carved, with untrembling hand, the clear letters.

In the high, full light of the moon we circled our names in the Royal Rope. And when it was closed, we stood back from the rock and looked at our handiwork.

"If we lose this battle," Kamose said, "we can become scribes to Ak-hor's wild, blood-drinking men."

Sek-met wakened, stretched and, with a great yawn, leapt to her feet and came to Kamose. He stroked her head, still looking at the two carved names.

I turned to him. "What is your plan? When will you fight?"

Without moving his gaze, he answered, "My Brother, in one year! When our South Land harvest is safely garnered into our own granaries . . . then! When Hur and his minions sail again from the North Land, thinking to bulge out their ships with our corn and our cattle, . . . then will battle be joined."

CHAPTER V

After the harvest, the earth grew dry and cracked with the heat, and so low was the River that only the top of Hur's ship-mast showed, as he and Mayebre the Libyan stood off from the Royal Wharf.

"In their one tribute-ship!" Tetaky said, his small-boned face beaming satisfaction. His unpleasant duty it had been to attend the barbarian needs of our unwelcome guests during our absence.

With Ahmose-Eb and the Twins, we were watching from the roof of the King's House.

"And manned by our own Eyes and Ears!" Per-neb said with joy. "By Hapi! Those men have lived so long with the Hyksos I was myself hard put to believe them Egyptian. . . ."

"Their manner, appearance . . . even their speech . . ." his twin added.

"Even their beards!" Tetaky grinned. "I was there when they told Hur their dire tales of the wrecked tribute-ships, and the perils and storms of the Cataract . . ." His eyes still held surprise. "Their gestures, their voices, were so native to him that, in spite of his rage and deep suspicion, the Cruel One believed all their story."

"But at first," Ahmose-Eb said, "when my *Wild Bull* pulled into the wharf with but one tribute-ship in her wake, Hur lost his cold arrogance, and his calm. . . . Ra-en-Ra! Was he a pattern for plunderers?"

"How he raged through this House! The King's House . . ." Tetaky said. "And into the Royal Quarters"— he turned to me—"to find you, my Prince."

"He found me. He strode, uninvited, into my room. Neme was dressing me. I did not halt my toilet. I was standing in front of the tall looking-bronze fixing my wig. I could see him, reflected, though I did not look at him . . ." I paused, remembering. "It was strange, as though his Ka, and not he, himself, stood there still as a stone. Not a word passed between us. As Neme put on my head the Fisherman's Circlet, he turned his back to us, and with a hard, quiet-harsh curse that was loud as a whip-crack in the silence, he walked away . . ." I shaded my eyes and looked at the lone tribute-ship sailing out to midriver. "And he is gone, back to the North Land again, he and Mayebre the Libyan . . . perchance for the last time," I murmured.

"My Prince," Tetaky said, after a moment, "Hur was not raging when he returned from seeking you. He was both cold and calm again, and he said to Mayebre—and in my presence! —'We must keep the lusty and whoring Kamose secure on the Theban throne. . . . I would not have this young priestling petty king in the South Land. . . .' My Prince, forgive me, but I almost laughed out loud."

I put my arm about his shoulder. "How the King will laugh when you tell him! Petty king, indeed . . . Whadj-Kheper-Ra, Kamose!"

"Their Set-dark faces will fall when this . . . petty king . . . this lusty, whoring Kamose . . . attacks!" Ahmose-Eb said, and we all smiled that we had kept our secret well.

"Even the Thirty Great Ones," I said, "and the Elders of Thebes are unaware of the depth and vision of the King's planning."

"And would not welcome the awareness . . ." Mer-neb's voice was sharp.

"You believe that they are truly against war? Set against battle?" I asked, remembering my brother's doubting, and thinking of the Council he would call at the harvest.

"My Prince, they are sleek and fat and comfortable." Per-neb blinked his eyes in disgust. "Thuty, the Chief Scribe, and four of the Elders have again, this year, sent their cattle to grow fat in the North Land pastures. . . ."

"The Chief Scribe should have sent Sittek!"

"Mer-neb!"

At the tone of his twin's voice, Mer-neb blushed. "Your forgiveness, Ahmose-Eb . . . my tongue runs amok."

"My Friend, say no more." Ahmose-Eb gave a faint rueful shrug and I remembered my brother, on a night in the underground paddock, telling me how the Chief Scribe had, on Ahmose-Eb's return from his father's funeral in El-kab, once again importuned him to marry his daughter. "But our Sailor has eluded the net once again." I had asked him how. And smiling, he replied, "With a battle to fight . . . to perhaps lose his life. What legacy that for a woman?" And I thought, but did not speak my thoughts, that Sittek and her father would be very pleased with the legacy of Ahmose-Eb's estates. Then, although chiding myself for my lack of charity, I could but think that if Ahmose-Eb's mother had lived to see Sittek grow to young womanhood, she might have released him from this youthful tie.

Ahmose-Eb's voice broke into my thoughts of him. "Next harvest time the River will be alive with our own ships," he was saying, and his gray-blue Sailor's eyes were bright.

"And four new ones!" I added.

We all stood watching, silent, as Hur's one tribute-ship,

looking small as a water-bird, sailed with the current, down-river to Avaris.

"Next harvest time," our Sailor repeated, and his rare smile widened into a grin, "the Royal Fleet will set sail for the North Land."

During the months of the Nile flood, when Hapi pours forth his Life-giving waters and our parched earth drinks its fill, had we been living in the Days of Splendor our farmers and fowlers and fishermen would have found work for their human strength, food and beer for their bodies and refreshment for their spirits in the building of beauty and majesty in stone to the glory of Ra. And though, through two hundred years of poverty and want, Theban Kings had created work for their people making the fine small things of everyday use, harps and sistra and double-pipes for the Temple, re-cutting old stone, mending the things of great worth and weaving fine linens, this year Kamose had a plan that killed two mallards with one throwing-stick. He recruited the eager farmers into the Army Reserve.

The clear-eyed and strong of arm were sought out by Merneb's Captains to train in the use of the new double-bows so that the walls of Thebes would be manned and guarded when our armies marched northward.

To those whose donkeys and cows were sleek and well cared for, Pen's Charioteers taught the care and driving of horses; and the lusty and strong, the fighters in taverns and the wrestlers for joy in their youth and high spirits were sent to Neshi, who shifted his School of Arms from the Battle-court to one of the large open parks behind the King's House. Here, the exuberant strength of young farmers, goat-herds and fishermen was tempered with the work that suited them best. They learned the art of the flat-sword and javelin, dagger and spear and the slinging of stones, and the best of them were sent to Kamose's command, to become, if they chose, regular soldiers.

The youths who were small-boned and nimble Tui gathered for my own new venture: the Messengers on Horses.

I took Montu-Thoth with me to the wide Stable-court above
ground, and as each one approached, the young Lector-Priest
knew, from the soul-color around him, whether he could
be trusted with the secret of the South Land's strength, and
to carry messages from the King to his Captains. Out of those
gathered we chose fifty-three, who were taken to be trained
by Tui in the underground paddock, and sworn to secrecy.
Eight of the others, who Montu-Thoth said were spies in the
pay of the enemy, when their guilt was proven beyond a
doubt were beheaded.

Tui and We-het and three Captains of my Sitters on
Horses worked with the new recruits, and four of Aknere's
Young Eyes and Ears gave them instruction in the secret
work. Sometimes at evening, after my work with Kheri-heb
and my visit to my mother, I would go down the hidden
steps of the old granary to share the evening meal with Tui
and We-het and my Captains, to ride awhile on Minirt and
to see the progress of my young Messengers.

We had raised fences in the vast paddock, put down tree-
trunks the width of a ditch and piled earth to the height of
the dike-banks, so that the horses would learn to jump, leap
and scramble. Aknere himself sent one of his own young
spies to me. "He makes up in courage what he lacks in stature, my Prince," he wrote. "And he is brother to animals."

The young man's name was Id-ne, but soon his prowess
with the horses in all exercises was so marked that, had I not
made him Captain of my Messengers, his companions would
have chosen him themselves; and they nicknamed him. After
a short while no one called him Id-ne anymore. They named
him Hir-ty, which means "Swift Traveler on Land."

Throughout the months of the ebbing River, and the sowing, the seeds sown in my own work with Kheri-heb burgeoned in the fertile soil of my spirit as the new seed in the
rich black earth. His first words to me when I returned from
the Cataract had both surprised and awed me.

"My son, you may now, without blasphemy, say . . . I am
Water." I sat at his feet in silence. "When you come to your

first place of trial you may walk unmolested past the Field of Reeds. . . . You are now One with our Sacred River. . . . Hapi is in you. You are in Hapi."

"In Hapi . . ." The words sang in my heart. I felt again the ecstasy when, with every energy strained, and every muscle and sinew stretched to breaking point, I near drowned in the Cataract waters.

After a while, Kheri-heb said, "You grow near to your first soul trial."

And he gave me no rest. Each day he set out for me, to inscribe and to meditate on, a principle from *The Book of Making Strong the Ka*, and always he left me alone with the same blessing on the work: "May Thoth, who is the Heart of Ra and the Begetter of Ra's Laws, and Maat, who is All Truth, mark out this day's course for you."

During these days my heart was led, pushed, carried aloft and dashed to the ground, and after a moon's span of travail and searching, for the first time in my life I saw the horizon not as a straight line, but as the Wheel of the Sun, and I on the rim of it, straining toward the hub. And Ra was the Hub, the Heart, the Blazing Orb wherein everything is held, contained, incorruptible, intact.

When I told Kheri-heb, he looked long at me, and from that day forward I no longer wrote out the verses, nor sat on the floor, but in a straight-backed chair. We sat together, without words, ofttimes far into the night, and my Ka hastened toward the Knowing. While I was absorbed in my Master's teaching, Kamose quietly and patiently was gathering the threads of his planning. The South Land seemed lazy and peaceful enough. Our mother lived simply, content and apart, in her Lodge by the Sacred Lake. Her beloved garden, and the lotus pool of our childhood joys, Nefertari had usurped. She had greatly enlarged, and furbished anew, Ah-hotpe's garden-house, which she used as almost a shrine. The maidens who waited upon her were dressed in cloaks of the finest Temple linen, and they rattled sistra as they danced attendance on her.

"And she holds her own sycophant court," Kamose once said, with sad scorn.

I could not believe it, for I rarely saw her. My evenings, after the days in the Temple, were spent with my mother, and during the last moon's span, after our evening meal, I had watched her and her young Priestesses making the Battle Crown Kamose had designed for himself.

"The enemy will see it and quake!" he said, when he gave Hor-min's drawing of it to our mother. "They will know that Whadj-Kheper-Ra, Kamose, comes against them in the Strength of Amun, and the sight of it will strike terror into their hearts."

She fitted the strong, supple, dark-blue-dyed leather clean-curving around his head and down to the nape of his neck. Then she lined it with finest linen. And when it was perfect, strong-stitched and close-fitting, she studded it with gold studs for glory and bronze for strength.

"He will wear around it the Fisherman's Circlet," she told me with pride. "And the Asp of Ra's Fiery Power on his brow . . . and every stitch," she smiled, "is a prayer."

When almost a year had passed in outward quiet and seeming content, yet full of underground labor, ceaseless preparing and constant vigil, my brother called the Council of the South Land.

Pen-aati was worried. "They are besotted with ease and sloth, the Elders of Thebes," he said, shaking his head. "My King, they are too comfortable."

"We are almost at harvest, Pen-aati, and the stars are benign. I cannot wait longer," my brother told his Vizir, and in answer to his command, the Thirty Great Ones of the South Land, the Elders, the Governors of the nomes, the Nomarchs who were visiting the Residence of the God, and the Princes in exile from the captured Cities: all the Nobles of Thebes gathered in the vast Court-yard of the King's House.

The Thirty Great Ones came in carrying-chairs, with their curtains drawn back that the Thebans, curious and merry, might see them and cheer them. A few of the Elders and the Nobles came in chariots, a new fashion taken from the conquerors, except that the Egyptians drove two onagers instead of horses. Kamose had taken quiet heed of those Princes among us who had taken to Hyksos ways.

In my brother's room, waiting to go to the Court of Audience, we could hear the noise and chatter in the Court-yard in front of the House, and I thought how surprised the Thirty Great Ones would be, and the apers of the tyrants, if they could see through the ground on which they were treading, to the training paddock and the chariot shops below them, and the she-horses and their young stabled there.

As Neme tied the Falcon belt around the waist of his fine-pleated kilt, Kamose said, "Your new Company of Sitters on Horses, from the Cataract ravine, have made the journey to Thebes in safety . . . and Ak-hor has returned!" He smiled. "I rejoice that he is here to bear the fan to my left hand, on this day. . . . Ahmose, we are in firm control of the Cataract Fort." Neme clasped the Lion bracelet on the King's right arm, while Kamose was saying, "Two of the captured tribute-ships, made battle-ready and manned by our Sailor-soldiers, are moored, hidden in a rock-cleft, across-river from the Fort. They will guard our southernmost border and keep strict check on the traffic from Nubia."

Then he told me of our precautions in the nomes to the south of Thebes. "All cattle-boats, pleasure-yachts, market-barges and every craft, even the ferry-boats, are boarded and searched. All traveling merchants, farmers with their produce, mendicants and people who can show no good reason for travel are kept in close view and constantly watched for Hyksos spies, who might have discovered that the Cataract Fort is now in our hands." He sat down while Neme tied on his papyrus sandals. "Aknere tells me that even if one of their spies did get through our network, it would be weeks before he could reach Avaris with his ill-omened news. . . . Notwith-standing, I told Aknere to keep constant vigil," Kamose said. "He left, with Sen-ut, for Neferusi . . . before this morning."

"With Sen-ut?"

"She and Res will enter Piopi's city to listen and watch and, with Ra's help, make friends with one or two of his maid-servants. . . . Disguised, one of them might even enter the traitor household."

"Thure?" I murmured.

Kamese looked up. "Their love could not be so deep and true," my brother said, "loved they not more the South Land's cause." The noise and bustle in the Forecourt was abating. "They have all gathered in the Court of Audience, agog!" My brother smiled and stood up. "Go to your place on the Dais, Little Brother. . . . No! Wait . . . first . . ." He went to the carved, painted cedar-wood box wherein, on a cushion, lay the Sacred Cobra of His Royal Majesty. It was fastened, with studs and wires of pure gold so finely wrought that the eye could not see them, to a thin golden circlet. Kamose picked up the symbol of Ra's Fiery Power and gazed long. Then he held it out to me. "You, Little Brother, place it on my brow, that Ra's Fire may take possession of me, set me ablaze and transmute me."

I was tall as he, though less broad of shoulder. I lifted my arms and put it on his head, setting it firm on his brow. Then, suddenly trembling, I was on my knees. I felt his hand on my head. It was hard and warm and heavy. Strength and heat came through his fingers. After a moment, he said, "My Brother, send out your Ka among the Elders, that I may have their ear. For while I play the whoring youth for the enemy's eyes, I am also thus to many of the loyal ones who are not in our secret Councils." He lifted me up, and put his arm about my shoulders. He was quiet and tense. "Now go, Ahmose, and take your place."

Followed by Hor-min, I came into the Court of Audience. There was a moment's stillness. The Thirty Great Ones rose from their chairs and bowed, as all there, their hands on their hearts. My chair was at the King's left hand. I sat down. Hor-min stepped behind me to where the Chief Scribe was already squatting with his papyrus roll and the gold-embossed palette of his high office. To quiet my thoughts behind the practiced calm of a Royal Son, I thought of Kheri-heb and Montu-Thoth and the Lector-Priests who were, at this hour, together in the wall chamber of the Temple, praying and watching. Then, as I had learned, I emptied my heart of thought that they might use my Ka for the strength and truth of God's will in the hour to come.

A stirring in the Court brought me back to myself. Nefertari, in jeweled magnificence and wearing, she, with whom Kamose had not lain, nor ever would, the Beautiful White Crown of the Beloved Royal Wife, came, with vain assurance, to her place on the right of the Throne Chair. Thuty walked, tall behind her, holding the widespreading fan, and I saw, with chagrin, that among the Thirty Great Ones and the Elders there were those who would jump to her bidding should she but crook her slim brown finger.

Then Miutu, Chief of Visions and High Priest of Amun-Ra, brought blessing to the Hall. He was leading my mother, and the chill in me vanished as the dawn wind when Ra's first beams warm the earth. Ah-hotpe came quietly. She wore the simple white linen gown of the Priestess, the age-old, long-shriven amulet of the God hung at her breast, and on her head was the Double Plumed Diadem of the First Adorer of Ra. Her eyes were large with prayer and vigil, and I thought how in our world there were all kinds of battles, and how we were thrown, each of us, at our birth, into the thick of the Quest. Then, as if in answer to my thoughts of fighting my fiery grand-mother came with swift grace, so that Senseneb, holding the tattered fan he had held at her Crowning, was hard put to keep pace with her. I smiled inside at his small sigh of relief when she took her chair next to the Queen; but when I saw the look of admiring love in her eyes as she looked at Nefertari, there was no smile inside me.

With the strange, sharp sound of breaths in-drawn, Kamose was there. In the silence, Sek-met at his heels, and Ak-hor and Ahmose-Eb, with their full-spreading fans, to the left and the right of him, he walked up the shallow steps to the Throne Chair. All assembled rose as one man, bowed low and stretched out their hands, palms upward, in adoration.

Miutu raised his hand in benediction:

> "Behold! He comes, the Beloved of Ra!
> The incense is laid upon the Fire.
> The Fragrance of Kamose comes to you."

And all there responded:

> "Amun-ra! Bless the desires of our hearts.
> Bless the words of our mouths."

Kamose sat as the God, his feet together and his hands, palms down, on his knees. His eyes were cool, and when he spoke, his voice was calm and deep.

"To what end this power of mine when one usurping Chieftain is in Avaris, and his puppet king rules to the South in Nubia?" No one moved, but I saw a few eyebrows among the Thirty Great Ones raise the fraction of a finger's width. "I sit between a Hyksos tyrant and a Nubian, and each holds his slice of Egypt." There was a murmuring in the Court, and glances of amaze at my brother's majesty and quiet. "They have captured Memphis, our ancient Capital and the birthplace of Queen Tetisheri, which properly belongs to us. They have massacred my people in Abydos and . . . Neferusi. . . ." At the word, Kamose moved from his ceremonial position, and clenched his fist. "Neferusi is a nesting place for the Hyksos. We are wasted in service to the barbarian." He leaned forward. "I shall grapple with them and slit open their bellies."

The low murmuring grew. Heads came together nodding and shaking. My brother glanced at me, a swift side-long look. Ak-hor and Ahmose-Eb lifted and lowered the light-trembling plumes above his calm face. I watched the Lord Chief Justice at the head of the Thirty Great Ones. I saw Thuty catch his eye, and thought that my half-uncle, even as Overseer of my grand-mother's household, had his cronies. The Chief Justice rose, stepped forward and bowed, his arms outstretched. Then, rising, he spoke.

"True, O Falcon, clothed in splendor! The Hyksos have retaken Kus, and have stuck out their tongues at us. But we hold our part of Egypt. We are at ease."

At ease? I thought. We have kept our secret well!

"Elephantine is strong," one of the Great Ones said.

"And spelt is sent for our swine," the Chief Justice added.

"At a price!" A young Nobleman raised his voice from the back of the Court. "And we drive home again but half of the cattle we send, and keep silent about the stolen." His voice was sucked into the maw of their ease, but I saw my brother's swift cognizance of him.

"A back is not broken by bending," one of the Elders said boldly, and the Chief Justice agreed.

"They hold the land of the Hyksos," he said. "We hold Egypt."

The land of the Hyksos! He dared to call part of the Beloved Land "the land of the Hyksos"! I could scarce keep my calm as he walked backward to his place.

As he made the ritual bow and resumed his seat, I saw that Tetisheri's small, thin fingers were grasping the arms of her chair till the knuckles shone white as, I remembered, when we were children and she told us of the Hyksos, and Memphis, the ravaged city of her birth. Her small body was trembling with the force of her rage. Then she rose from her chair and stood, in full ceremonial dress, tiny and regal.

"Hai! You Great Ones of the South Land! Hai, You Elders of Thebes! You who quail and veil your coward faces to bloody massacre in the Holy City of Abydos! When the crocodiles sink down into the Nile mud with Egyptian flesh in their bellies, craven! You close your rheumy eyes! To tyranny and pillage, plunder and rape, you stand unfirm of sandal! By the Thighs of the Sky Woman! If you, the Great Ones of Thebes, stand pigeon-hearted, and unmanned, then who will redress the dark evil of Set? To what dark god, to what tyrant king, will our children and grand-children pay homage? Akh! By the Eater of Shades! Are they The-bans I see, who sit here besotted with comfort and mouthing blasphemies worse than those spewed by Mayebre the Lib-yan?" She stood silent. It was as though she held each man there in the palm of her small, hard hand. "Are they Thebans I see?" she asked, and her voice was soft, "who were in this same Hall of Audience when their King, Seken-en-Ra, was insulted? Who kept Funeral watch for His Majesty, mur-dered? Do I see? Or are my eyes grown old? These are not men of Thebes! By the Phallus of the Apis Bull! These are not Thebans!"

They quailed before her. Kamose had resumed the ritual position. Tetisheri turned to face him, her head high. Then she bowed, her hands across her breast. Then bowed again, her arms outstretched in adoration, and all there rose to their feet, and once more made obeisance. Without a backward glance, the Queen Grand-mother left the Court of Audience, followed by Senseneb.

Kamose's face was a granite mask. Only the two fans above his head moved in the stillness. Not a whisper was heard. Slowly he rose and stood, his left foot forward. Sek-met rose with him, her mouth closed. She was as though carved in stone. In Ra's Fiery Power, his hands to his sides, his fists clenched, Kamose spoke.

"I swear, as Ra loves me, as my father Amun favors me, as my nostrils are rejuvenated with his Breath, my Majesty shall proceed to battle. Let him who wishes come in the fol-lowing of my Majesty. . . . Cover your face, Set-Apophis. The sword of Whadj-Kheper-Ra, Kamose, will cut you to pieces that you may never rise again."

With his Fan-bearers, Miutu, Chief of Visions, and Pen-aati, he left the Court of Audience, and his Royal rage, pent up and held in check during years of patience and planning, burst out of him. He called his Company to the Battle-court, and there, with the age-old long-bow that none but he could draw, he sent forth a stream of arrows, high-curving to the gardens, tearing the vines and the flowers from the trees. Then he threw down the bow and called for Ahmose-Eb to fight with the battle-ax, and wielding and striking and cleaving the air, their feet as nimble as dancers, they circled each other. Then he called for the broad-swords, and with thrust and parrying, flat-ringing, smiting and hewing, with strife and struggle they fought till Kamose drew blood, and wept at the sight of it, and his first rage was spent.

"He is Lord of the Bursting Heart," Tetaky said to me, as we watched.

Then they brought colored balls with bright feather-tails and threw them high in the air. With spear and javelin Kamose brought each one to the ground. He could not have missed the tiniest amulet; his companions missed three out of five. He called for the short double-bows, and Mer-neb vied with him in a test of distance and points, straight-shooting and swiftness of flight, till Per-neb challenged him.

"I'll fight you," he said.

"We'll all fight each other." Per-neb looked around him, and they called for their wooden training-swords and the whole Company, taking sides, fought. First with laughter, then in earnest and to win, till the night spread her veil.

Later, when Neme had bathed him and smoothed his golden skin with unguents, my brother called for me, and when we were alone together, he said, "Our grand-mother's words were a store-house of strength."

"Her words echoed to the stars and opened the eyes of our Elders to look at themselves."

"And I have gravely displeased her."

"This dotage on Nefertari . . . our grand-mother's blind love for her . . . it has estranged us."

"There is no reasoning in love, Ahmose. And Akh! Ra-en-Ra! She does not know the half-sister"—he paused, and closed his eyes for a moment—"as we do."

"Our tiny grand-mother is true Queen," I said, and we were quiet for a while. Then he raised his head.

"First Assiut, then Kus and then . . . Neferusi." I was dismayed. He smiled. "Little Brother, you think that my rage will betray me? Has already betrayed me in this decision? Ahmose, Neferusi is where horses are bred by the hundreds for the enemy's chariots. This city is an arsenal for the North Land. . . . And, Ahmose, . . . this you have known since our father's murder."

"But Abydos! Kamose, you will pass Abydos? Our father's plan was to free the Holy City. Our mother waits to share in the restoration of Osiris' Temple."

"Have no fear, Little Brother, the Beloved Osiris will be worshiped again in his Holy Shrine. But have patience. Abydos is filled with our Eyes and Ears, and since," his face grew stern, "since the massacre in that city, to a man the people are loyal to us."

"Then why not now? First?"

"It is not in my plan." He leaned forward in his chair. "I have today received a message from Aknere. Hur, he will sail southward again for the tribute . . ."

"Ra-en-Ra! That is no news."

"Akh! Little Brother, you speak too soon." He gave Sekmet a long, slow punch with his clenched fist against her cheek. She growled, then licked his hand and rubbed against his bare thigh. She was full-grown now, wide of shoulder, and her golden eyes glowed when she looked at Kamose. He was smiling a little. "It is news, Hur's sailing! He will put out from Avaris with six ships, and four of them will be loaded with treasure!" Kamose's eyes were afire. "With marble and porphyry and sacred woods, green ore of copper and turquoise from Sinai that the South Land has lacked these long generations. Myrrh from Ugarit and Byblos, fine resins . . . and gold! And arms! And, my Brother, all to be unladed at Neferusi . . ."

"For the murderer Piopi and," my voice fell to a whisper, "Teti."

"You can put your tongue to his name?"

"It is in my craw as a sharp pebble in a craw of a River-bird."

My brother laughed. "You are not yet Priest," he said. "Ahmose, these ships will sail full of gifts to the greedy Piopi from the Hyksos King." His eyes were gathered to points of cold light. "Apophis pays well for the murder of our father." Then he gave a quiet chuckle. "Now you see? Neferusi must be in our hands before these treasure-ships dock at Piopi's wharves."

I shook my head. "Praise be to Ra," I said, "that you are King of the Two Lands, and not I."

"The Two Lands . . . Ta-mery . . ." he murmured. "They will be one. Once again all Egypt will be one. How the gods do work strangely. These ships and all that is in them will be ours! As I promised to you, Little Brother, when we carved our two names in one Royal Rope, we are ready! We shall join in battle at the harvest . . . and for good measure, Ra sends us the treasure-ships!" He punched Sek-met again and she lashed her tail.

"When do they sail?"

"In one and a half moon's span. Their plan is to unload the gifts at Neferusi, then sail south to reload with our tribute."

"Four prime ships bulging with riches!" I shook my head again in unbelief. "How delighted our grand-mother will be."

"After today in the Court of Audience, I would see her pleased with me again. I would see her gray eyes sparkle. Hor-min must take scribes with him to tally this treasure."

"Hor-min? What place has he in your battle plans?"

"He will sail with me in *The Falcon*. I need him to record each day of each battle. I have given him his studded shirt, chariot and horses, and Ak-hor has assigned two Nubians to guard him. He will not fight."

I nodded. Then I asked, "What is your plan of battle, Kamose?"

"Before we attack these treasure-ships, three cities must be in our hands: Assiut, Kus and Neferusi." I waited, silent. "Thure, being Prince of Assiut, will himself take that city. I shall proceed directly to Kus."

"How are we deployed for both battles?"

He smiled. His voice was quiet, his face, drained of rage, was intent and alert. "Two Companies of Chariots, three regiments of Archers and four of Foot-soldiers are already in a hiding place in the shade of the Assiut Mountain, within sight of the city. At that place, tomorrow, Thure will join them to lead the attack. Our Eyes and Ears in Secret are among the people. They will make entry for us. The loyal sons of Assiut will be at their posts."

"And the Sitters on Horses?"

"We shall not need them at Assiut, nor at Kus. I would save them for Neferusi, which is a fort and an arsenal for the Hyksos. . . . But your Messengers! Ahmose, that was a thought from the gods, these young men too small of stature and too slender to fight, but with the courage of lions!"

"They are swift and sure, for they are trained also in the subtle ways of our Eyes and Ears in Secret." I laughed. "Aknere has already used them in his secret army, for their swiftness of movement."

"The swifter to come for you when I need you!" He raised an eyebrow. "Ahmose, the harvest is garnered into our granaries." He stood up, and I rose from my chair. "Tomorrow I sail with but fifty prime ships . . . easy to hide in the reaches and ravines of the River. They will be all armed and battle-ready, but disguised as though I were on a Royal Progress. We will keep our secret till the last moment."

"Which will come soon enough."

"Hor-min will be with me in *The Falcon*," he said again. "And Ak-hor. Pen and Tetaky will sail with Ahmose-Eb in *The Wild Bull* alongside. Mer-neb and Per-neb will be waiting for us, with their Archers and Foot-soldiers, in the desert to the west of Kus . . . and this time we shall not be betrayed." He put his arm about my shoulders. "And you, Little Brother, who have done for me, and for the Beloved Land, a deep and never repayable service"—he stood in front of me and put both his hands on my shoulders—"I will leave you here in Thebes, with Kheri-heb and our mother, to prepare for your own soul's battle."

"May your Ka strengthen me, Beloved of Ra," I said, and we stood by the pillars together.

"Our Kas embrace as One, as our names are carved in one

rope on the face of the granite cliff." He turned to me with a strange, deep gaze. "Somewhere, deeper than the River and higher than the heavens, Little Brother, we two are more twin then Mer-neb and Per-neb."

Early on the morrow, after the Morning Rite, Kamose stood on the Balcony of Appearances to proclaim to the Thebans that battle was joined. Nefertari, in full court regalia, and Tetisheri and Pen-aati, were as shadows behind him to the watching Thebans, for in the first full Light of Ra in his Atet Boat ascending, the metal studs in Kamose's leather tunic and the bronze threads in his warrior's belt glistened and shone. And his helmet! He was wearing the Blue Battle Crown! With two streamers behind for the ancient Fisherman, and on his brow the Fiery Cobra of Ra's Royal Power, it was a blaze of Light around his head as he told his people that from this day till the day of victory, Thebes was at war.

The vast crowd was silent. Each man there knew his place, his task, in this fight, and was ready. The people were reverent and quiet, till Kamose turned swiftly and descended to his waiting chariot. Then there was a murmur as the buzzing of millions of honey-bees.

I stood with my mother and the two High Priests on the steps of the Outer-court of the Temple, as Kamose drove through the high Pylon Gates of the King's House.

"His wings are outspread," Miutu said.

"He is the Dawn Falcon of rich plumage," Kheri-heb answered.

"Ra has made for him a ladder of his noon-day Fire Beams." As my mother ended the ancient blessing, Hor-min came to us. He bowed to her and to the two High Priests.

"I am happy to go with the King," he said, and Ah-hotpe embraced him. As I took his hand in mine, I saw by the light in his eyes that his words were true.

"May our Kas be together in sleep," I said.

"My Prince, may each hour bring forth its fullness to you," he answered. Then, with a chuckle, as we embraced he whispered, "Ra-en-Ra! Things will move with the swiftness of a falcon's stoop from this day forward." He bowed again. Then he went to his waiting chariot.

My mother watched him as he followed Kamose. "Friends are sent by the gods," she said. And without turning her eyes to where Nefertari stood on the Balcony, she murmured, "It was by the Royal right, and pure, that I stood there with your father."

"If base metal be overlaid to appear as pure gold, at dawn it is lead," I whispered, and though the new Queen stood vainglorious there, no Theban looked at her. Every man, woman and child was gazing at Kamose as he slowly drove the wide Temple way to the Royal Wharf. And as Sek-met, of a sudden, stood up on her hind legs, tall as the King himself, her front paws on the rim of the javelin quiver, lashing her tail and showing her teeth, a tumultuous roar filled the throats of the Thebans, and they dashed their red pots, inscribed with the names of Apophis and Hur and their own rude names for the tyrant scavengers, with a splitting and cracking and a smashing on the stone paves, that the enemy's bones might be broken and never come together again.

Then Kamose drove Soker-uff, two white plumes from Rai's ostrich fan nodding proudly from the crest-band of his bridle, up the ramp to the deck of *The Falcon*. He raised his arm in salute, and the people were solemn again, and the depth of their quiet and their loyalty was a throbbing, living, invincible strength. Still silent, the people of Thebes raised their arms Ka-square, to receive the God's Power.

As *The Falcon* pulled out from the wharf, I was holding my mother's hand. "The Blue Crown," she whispered, "with what majesty it reflects Ra's beams." Tears filled her eyes, and as we watched the fifty prime ships of the Royal Fleet, their sails billowing in a wind from the south, sail out to midriver, her tears fell down her cheeks as spring rain in the wadis. "I am a Priestess now, not a reigning Queen," she said. "I may weep."

I felt my own tears. My brother had left me for the battlefield. My heart was a storm of memories. "Kus!" The word rang inside me. Kamose went forth with our father, in the pride of his youth, and returned to weep at my bedside. "Osiris, Lord . . ." I silently prayed. "Osiris, Lord, is my brother so much a part of me?" "You have your own soul's battle," he had said. Suddenly I was filled with a great loneliness; a great fear, though to descend to the grave is a part of Life; to lie in a granite coffin alone in the deep-down sealed room. Heavy with my flesh, and laden with my sins— Akh! My Brother! How may my Ka prevail?

"My Young One." My mother's voice stilled my thoughts. I looked into her tear-washed face. "He is in the God's Hands," she said. "And you, Ahmose, you will come to me, as ever, at sun-set?"

I nodded, and kissed her nose to nose. Then I walked with Kheri-heb across the wide Temple-court to the small and quiet place of our learning.

He knew the depth of my fears. We passed between the Pillars of Silence, and as each day he led me along the Path of Un-knowing he created a circle of peace around me, to refresh and strengthen me for the first of my seven ordeals in the Caverns of the Underworld, where he who aspires to be Priest must first travel, walking upright, his spirit keen-tempered, to the place where the Light is submerged in the abyss, and the dread pall of a blood-dark sand-storm hides the Dwelling of the Lords of Terrors in Hearts.

I saw my mother each day. "With this moon's fullness," she said, as we gazed at the silver-gold burgeoning crescent, "will come your first Ka-trial, my Moon Child." The Sacred Lake, smooth as gray marble, reflected the stars. "Fear not Water. You are One with the Nile God. Dive into the Lake of Jackals. Fear not the dark beasts who feed on the bodies of evil men, though monstrous they be and the stench of them sicken you. Montu of the Animals will be at your side . . ."

"The God Montu? How have I earned his aid?"

"You have given of yourself to his horse-animals, given of your own heart and your labor."

"And my pleasure. Often I steal out to the underground paddock to sit on Minirt." Then, remembering, I said, "At my father's Funeral Rite I was one with the high crags; with a hair on the tail of the wolf that slunk to its lair; and with the sun-lizard's scale."

"Amun-Ra knows and feels the touch of the ant's foot," my mother smiled.

"And the Lords of the Terrors in Hearts?"

"Ahmose, before them you stand alone, in the armor of your own true heart."

Three days before the full moon, both of us aware of how close was my first time of proving, my mother and I were sitting together, looking out through the pillars of her lodge to the calm, sun-lit lake, when Ita came running, her eyes wide with excitement, to tell us that a messenger had arrived from the King.

"He asks leave to speak with you."

My mother's eyes widened. She nodded.

The young man entered.

"Hir-ty!" I said, and turned to my mother. "Hir-ty is the Captain of my Messengers on Horses."

"My Queen . . . my Prince . . ." Hir-ty bowed to us both.

"Speak to us, Hir-ty," my mother said.

"My Queen, Assiut is again a free city of the South Land."

"And Thure?" I asked.

"He rode through his own city in triumph. Jackal banners wave from every air-slit and roof-top and Assiut holds quiet festival."

"Sit down, Hir-ty, and tell us all." My mother beckoned to Ita that she bring wine and grapes.

Hir-ty sat on the edge of a chair, leaning forward. "The Hyksos garrison was unprepared for the attack," he said. "Our Eyes and Ears in Secret led Thure and his army into a city unguarded and unwatched. We had need only of the Second Chariots, and one regiment each of Archers and Foot-soldiers."

Ita brought the wine, and served it.

"And what now?" I asked Hir-ty.

"All forces, except the Sitters on Horses, are converging on Kus. Thure, with his unused hosts from Assiut, is already within a day's march of that city, Pen's Chariot Companies are hidden in a desert ravine behind it. Ahmose-Eb's Sailor-soldiers, three regiments of them, are with the Fleet. The King awaits with his own armies, to the south of Kus."

"And where are my Sitters on Horses?"

"Five Companies of them are on their way north." Hir-ty smiled. "They travel by cattle-boats and barges, some drive light chariots during the day-light hours, others seems to be relay horses. By these, and other unnoticed ways, not an hour is wasted, though often the going is slow. Only when darkness falls do the Sitters mount up and the going is faster."

"But where are they going?"

"To the underground paddock close to the city of Nefe-rusi." He bowed, and took a second cup of wine from my mother's hands. "All will be in readiness, my Prince. But there is no time to lose."

"And victory is hard to keep secret," I said. "Let us pray that the King's armies will come to Kus before the enemy spies can give warning," I said. Then I asked of Hor-min.

"He is hard at work in the King's ship."

"A joyful work! He is inscribing our first victory," my mother said with a smile, and then asked, "Have you other message?"

"Ak-hor's Nubians have been scouting the Western Desert, keeping safe the secrecy of our hidden forces. They will gather, and advance on Kus from the north. Swiftness and secrecy have been the watchwords, and the people all help us."

"Egypt is full of round hearts," my mother said. "Where is the King now, on this day?"

"His Majesty should be one day from Kus. He will sail this night. At dawn tomorrow, battle will be joined."

"He must first take Kus . . . then Neferusi . . ." I murmured. "This traitor city must fall before the treasure-ships from Apophis have time to dock there with their dastard gifts to Piopi."

"My Prince, though Hur and the treasure-ships have already sailed from Avaris, there will be time for the King's plans. The Cruel One sails in leisurely manner, feasting with the traitor Nomarchs of the North Land, on his way . . . But, my Prince, I come with a message to you from His Majesty." Hir-ty stood up and pulled a small scroll from the small leather satchel slung about his shoulders. "I am to put this into your hands."

I took it, held it for a moment of foreboding as I met my mother's eyes, Then slowly unrolled it, and read it aloud.

"Little Brother, come! I need you. Return with Hir-ty. When we meet, by the Grace of Ra, Kus will be ours again. Then Neferusi! I would have you there. Ahmose, your King commands."

I stood quite still. My mother lowered her eyes. Not now! Not this moon of all moons! I did not speak the words. I felt cold sweat break on my upper lip and my temples. The months of travail: seeking, working, praying, falling by the wayside, unworthy; girding my faint spirit and clinging with my soul to rare moments of vision. Not now! I looked at my mother. She stood up. Her eyes were sad. She turned to Hir-ty.

"Go with Ita. Bathe and refresh yourself."

He bowed. Then he said, "Your pardon, my Prince, but we should leave with the darkness. His Majesty wishes that you bring Minirt."

I nodded, and my mother said, "The Prince will join you at sun-set. . . . May the Grace of Ra go with you."

Hir-ty bowed, and was gone. My mother stood where she was. She did not embrace, or even touch me, but she smiled a little. "Take heart, Ahmose, and think on this! You will see the God-hills! Akh! What joy! To see them, dazzling white, illuminating the Two Lands . . . And perchance, Mem-

phis! Where Imhotep, thousands of years gone by, lived and
built and worshiped, and healed . . ."

"Imhotep . . . Kheri-heb-her-tep! First Lector-Priest, and
Mentor in spirit of Kheri-heb . . . Imhotep's God-hill . . ."
I was caught up in my mother's vision. "The first to be built
of hewn stone . . ."

"Akh! In the Eyes of Ra, a thousand years are as one
day . . . and, my Moon Child," her eyes were bright with
an infinite tenderness, "the Gods choose their own hour to
receive us."

Wearing the linen-lined leather loin-cloth that had become
the uniform of the Sitters on Horses under my pleated kilt,
and a loose metal-studded shirt, I drove my chariot, with
Minirt running behind me, to a day's march beyond Kus.
Hir-ty was well known at the relay posts and I was greeted,
when the people recognized me, with pride and homage.

As we neared the Royal Fleet, one of Pen's charioteers
met us, and following him in our chariots, as we came to a
curve in the River, one hour's sail from Neferusi, we saw
The Falcon rising clean out of the water. She was crescent-
shaped at bow and stern, and her rudders were attached to
two great posts with golden hawk-heads atop of them. The
shelter-cabin amidships was large; there were awnings for
Kamose's chariot and the horses, and two smaller cabins in
the bow. She was flying the pennants of the Royal Barge.
The Wild Bull and the other ships that lay around her
showed no battle array, and as we came close I saw Kamose
in his chair on deck. He rose when he saw us, came to the
splash rail and waved.

"Haja!" He called, then came down the ramp to meet us.
"Welcome! Welcome! Come in peace, Little Brother."

"What of Kus?"

I saw that his eyes were tired, and held no triumph. His
face was stern. But he said. "It is ours again." He embraced
me, and gave thanks to Hir-ty and the charioteer. "But come
aboard, and while you rest I will tell you, Little Brother,

what I have learned of warfare in this, my first battle, and a hard one it was. But first," he turned to Hir-ty, "I have messages for Ak-hor and the Twins. . . . Come."

While the messenger followed Kamose into the large cabin, I watched my chariot and horses brought aboard. Minirt and Soker-uff were apart from the other horses, all stabled openly aft and to port of *The Falcon*'s deck. I went to cosset the two animals I loved: Minirt, pale as first milk, and Soker-uff, night-dark except for the white star on his brow. I had no honey-cakes, but they made their familiar small, high noises and nuzzled me with their soft mouths, and I was, for a swift moment, one with them, and with Kheri-heb. "Montu of the Animals, guard all these brave and beautiful creatures. . . . Protect Minirt and Soker-uff," I prayed as I left them and walked to the rail. The huge curve in the River was a cove that hid our ships from Neferusi. The sun was westering and the air was still. Scarce a ripple broke the calm green-gray of the water, only the soft paddling of our Eyes and Ears in Secret and our Sailor-soldiers scouting the wide stretch of River in reed-rafts and fishing-boats. Then I heard Hor-min's voice and turned.

"My Prince!" He came running out of one of the smaller cabins, a small scroll in his hand. "My Prince, so it is that once again your own work is stayed at the crest?" His black eyes were bright. "But for me, your presence is a joy . . . and for the King! Time and again, in stress he has said, 'My brother should see this . . . I would that my brother were here.' "

"Hor-min . . ." I laughed softly at his spate of words, and we embraced. Then we leaned together against the rail and I told him, "Hor-min, at this full moon—this one!—I was to be left alone in the tomb chamber. Hor-min, already I miss Kheri-heb's silent presence."

"He is with you, my Prince, wherever you are, for with the Ka there is not time, nor space."

My brother came out of his cabin, followed by Hir-ty, whose shoulder-pouch was again full of small scrolls. "Our

Messenger leaves," Kamose said. "Let us pray he finds our various forces in the places they are meant to be, in the desert." He turned to Hor-min. "Have you the map?" Hor-min gave the small scroll he was holding to Hir-ty, and Kamose turned to the messenger. "Take cover till the darkness falls."

"My King."

"And may Isis spread about you her cloak of stars, for the orders you carry this night mean victory." Hir-ty bowed the Ritual bow, then, leading his two horses, he ran down the ramp to the shore. My brother turned again to Hor-min. "You have scribe's work to do," he said. "Come Brother, I would tell of Kus."

"And I would write of it." Hor-min bowed, his hand on his heart, and left us.

"There is a folding stool in my cabin," Kamose said, and when I brought it and sat down beside him, I saw, in the sun-set light, that his face was thinner and he looked older, but his eyes were panther-bright and deeply intent as he looked at me and said, "Ahmose, we could have lost Kus." I listened in silence. "On the night of the attack, ten thousand of our seasoned Foot-soldiers and Shock-troops, five regiments of Mer-neb's Archers and three thousand of Pen's Chariots were in array. Ak-hor's Nubians, after scouting the desert fastnesses, had gathered to the north of the city, and six other war-ships had joined with the Fleet. At moon-rise, according to our plan, the Eyes and Ears in Secret opened the gates to the westward and Pen led his chariot forces through them in a furious charge, hoping to find, as in Assiut, the people lining the streets and cheering! Ra-en-Ra!" My brother leaned back. He took a deep breath. "Ahmose, the enemy spies had preceded us. The town was a fortress. Every Egyptian—man, woman and child—had been shut in his houses on pain of blinding with hot irons. Had not the loyal ones among those shut in been well armed and long trained, we should have lost the day. But I am ahead of myself. The Hyksos raked our chariot charge with a storm of arrows.

From the roof-tops on one side they aimed at the horses. From the other side they aimed at the men. Our losses were grievous . . ."

"Pen . . . and Thure? The Twins?"

"By Ra's Grace they are safe. But Pen's horses were killed outright in the first on-rush, and Thure was wounded." I caught my breath. "Pen mounted another chariot and we tore through their ranks as gods. Step by bloody, death-dealing step we fought our way to the garrison. Their defenses were vicious! Ahmose, they shot flaming arrows at the horses so that they panicked, their manes and tails flaming. Our charioteers were all fighting aground with the Foot-soldiers, kicked by our own horses and run down by the heavy enemy chariots. My Brother! These things we had not given thought to, nor ever imagined."

"But to take deliberate aim, with arrows afire, at the horses?"

He nodded slowly. "I know! Ahmose, I know." Then he looked at me. "We, Little Brother, would give our lives for Amun-Ra, and for Ta-mery."

"But it is our own choice."

"I too have thought of that . . . and I have a plan that may help, perhaps in time for Neferusi. But Ahmose, to the animals we are as gods, and is it meant to be that they, in their own way, serve us as we serve our god . . . as Sek-met fights with me?" He clenched his fists. "She took an arrow through the skin of her back, a light wound, but her left forefoot was near severed." He saw my face. "Montu-Thoth has healed her. He has put on her the Sleep of Health, and the while, put sinew to sinew and bone to bone, and bound them together. She will fight with me at Neferusi." He leaned forward, his chin in his hand. "This is war! By the Disc!" His face paled. "It was almost a massacre." After a while he leaned back. "Then, as Ra loves us!—to our surprise, for while we fought for our lives we had quite forgotten them, the loyal ones inside the houses, through the slits in the walls as they had been trained, let fly a steady stream of arrows.

The enemy was astounded, and many a Hyksos charioteer was caught off guard as he turned in surprise. Then, again by Ra's Grace, our Workers in Secret at the northern end of the city, opened the smaller gate to the north and Ak-hor's Nubians poured through to our rescue. This gave Mer-neb time to regroup his Archers, and the tide of the battle had turned. Our Bow-men advanced, raining arrows. Our remaining chariots charged at the gallup, and our Foot-soldiers fought hand to hand with new heart. There was no doubt at all of the outcome." Kamose sighed. "Four thousand Hyksos were brought out of the city and set on their march to Thebes, and I . . . Ahmose, I was victorious. I rode my chariot at dawn through cheering crowds to the Temple, and as Ra in his Atet Boat flooded the earth with his Light, I celebrated the Dawn Rite in the Temple of Kus."

"And the city is garrisoned?"

"The young men flocked to our banners. I was till noon with the High Priests and Elders, and those in the city who had been working in secret for us were put in places of firm authority." Kamose got up and walked to the splash rail. "Hyksos arms were captured, a great mound of them. Their heavy chariots are clumsy, far too heavy to be carried on shoulders to the places of combat. But they will be of use in heavy shock tactics . . ." He swung around and looked at me again. "Tactics! Ahmose, by the Cobra's Eye! I have, during these months and years of planning, been deep in strategy. This, my Brother is the art of war. It covers the whole campaign. But tactics! Tactics! They are the art of each battle, and perforce must change with the tide of it."

"And your tactics have changed for Neferusi?"

"My plans remain. But we must be swift as falcons. Neferusi, then the treasure-ships, then Memphis . . ."

"For Neferusi, what is your plan?"

"It is simple, yet long thought has been given to it. One year ago, two hundred of Pery-em-wah's most seasoned Eyes and Ears, at different times and places, volunteered as traitors to Egypt, for archery duty on the new-built high walls of

Neferusi. About half of them were chosen, and the others are in the city, unsuspected.

"Aknere and his young Eyes and Ears have tunneled under the southeast wall. At the darkest hour before the dawn, Ahnere will light a torch on that wall. At the signal, our Egyptian men among the Hyksos archers along the top of the walls, aided by those in secret among the people, who will have taken their places at the base of the walls, will silently garrote or slit the throats of the archers and wall-guards.

"At the same signal, Mer-neb and our own Archers will come through the tunnel and man the walls of the city!" I listened to him almost unbelieving! He was absorbed, still seeking the slightest flaw. "Aknere," he said, "when he has lit and put out the torch, will steal through the dark city and open the great main gate for"—he put his hand on my shoulder—"for your Sitters on Horses."

"I have prayed they would play their part in the razing of Neferusi."

"A war-like prayer for a Priest, Little Brother."

I was suddenly tired. I leaned against the rail and asked for news of Thure's wound.

"An arrow in his shoulder and a sword-thrust through his rump, in the first foray. Montu-Thoth cut out the arrow-head and charged the wounds."

"Where is he now?"

"In *The Wild Bull*, and a messenger has been sent to Sen-ut."

"Where is she?"

"Still doing her secret work in the villages around Neferusi. She and Thure will come aboard for the evening meal."

"It will be a benison to see them."

"And for them, to see each other. They have been parted since before Assiut."

I smiled at the scope of my brother's heart-thought, and asked of Pen.

"Ahmose, how he escaped with his life, let alone a few

wounds, I am at a loss to know." Then, his brow drawn and furrowed, he said, "Mer-neb and his Archers should now be a few miles to the south-east of Neferusi. . . . Pray to Osiris, my Brother, that Hir-ty will find him, for he should be well hidden."

I smiled. "I will. But Hir-ty has Hor-min's map."

Kamose smiled back at me. "So he has! And you, Little Priest, you are weary."

"My eyelids are heavy."

"By the Hare! You have traveled far and fast, and I have talked long. We will talk more when we gather for the evening meal. . . . Go now and rest."

In the shade of the large cabin I slept for three hours, and wakened cool and refreshed in mind and body. Though I did not remember my dream, I knew that Kheri-heb had bathed my Ka in the Waters of Quiet.

At the evening meal we sat on deck in the bright starlight. A fresh breeze had risen with the night. Ahmose-Eb and Tetaky had come aboard, and Thure and Sen-ut were together, he on a chair with a hole in the plaited reed seat of it, for the wound in his rump, and she on a stool close to him. He was holding her hand against his shoulder-wound, content, and Tetaky, teasing them, quoted,

> "The hand of my love is a lotus flower,
> And her breast is a pomegranate . . ."

Then the sound of Pen's chariot broke the evening stillness.

He came aboard, lean and tall, and I thought that he, too, looked older. After his obeisance to Kamose and a short bow to me, he asked,

"Res? Where is she?"

Sen-ut looked up at him to speak, but Kamose answered.

"Res is in the house of the murderers. She is disguised as a maid-servant in the house of Piopi. . . . Tetaky, pour wine for Pen . . . Hor-min, bring a stool."

Pen took the wine and sat down. He was frowning and worried.

"She has many of us around and about her, Pen . . . she is not unguarded."

Hor-min came and sat with me at the King's feet. Kamose was less austere and the frown left Pen's face as we ate the heron's eggs cooked in wine, river-eels stewed in garlic and duck spiced with cloves; breads new-baked by joyful hands in the kitchen ship, fruits and the cream from the top of the milk. The news of our victories had spread, and our people from the villages around the towns we had freed lined the banks of the River with baskets of gifts on their heads.

"The enemy spies must have seen them. They are as the sands of the desert," I said, but Kamose shook his head,

"No matter, our easy victories are over. . . . And yet in Neferusi they do not fear us. Their city is a fortress, its walls as impregnable as those of Avaris, new-built and manned. . . . No! They are not afraid of the South Land's armies . . . Amun-Ra be praised."

"Let us enjoy this food for the gods, my Prince," Ahmose-Eb said to me, and raised his hand for fruit as Tetaky passed the dish of grapes and figs. "At this time on the morrow, we shall be in battle array."

"And this is no sailor's fare," Thure added.

"But we had sailor's fare at the Cataract," I told Sen-ut. "We ate of your dried water-fowl."

She looked up in surprise. "Was it good?" I nodded, and she turned to Pen. "Res it was who thought of drying the water-fowl."

"I know."

She put her hand on his knee. "Pen, Hat-hor will see that no harm comes close to her."

Pen smiled. "I know," he said again.

Kamose wiped his mouth on the linen napkin and Neme brought the bowl of sweet water to lave his hands. He seemed to brood. Then he held up his drinking cup.

"To this hour on the morrow!" His voice was clear and quiet. "May Amun-Ra, whose Flame casts down his enemies, hold the steering poles of our ships." And he drank deep, then held out his cup for more wine. Tetaky leapt up and, taking the wine-jug from Neme, filled the King's cup to the brim. Kamose looked at us all in turn. Then he said, "All that may be planned by the heart is planned." We sat silent around him. "Pen! Two hours before dawn, you will draw up your chariots in battle array outside the Great Gate of Neferusi, at five hundred cubits . . ."

"But there is no space," I said. "The trees?"

They all smiled, and Ahmose-Eb said, "My Prince, eight moons past my Sailor-soldiers, at the dark of the moon, paddled in reed rafts to the shore and cut down all the trees in six thousand cubits, leaving them where they fell."

"But the noise? The villagers?"

"My men were disguised as Hyksos, with beards and baubles, and the villagers helped when they heard it was at Piopi's command."

"And the Hyksos, too, when the Great Gate opened at dawn," Sen-ut said, "they came out and gathered it on sleds drawn by oxen to take to their work-shops." She laughed. "And no one at all thought to ask who had given the order."

I sighed. "Forgive my interruption," I asked.

"Your question had merit," Kamose said, and Pen added, "We would have used the good native woods for our chariots!"

Kamose smiled a little at him and repeated his words. "Pen, two hours before dawn you will be in array outside the Great Gate of Neferusi. Per-neb's Foot-soldiers will flank you, and his Spear-men and Fighters with the Broad-sword will be hard behind you, to join you. I have sent final orders by Hir-ty. When Aknere shows the torch on the south-east wall, Mer-neb's Archers will come through the tunnel and man the walls. . . . The traitors will have planned their means of escape, though they do not expect an attack. They are subtle. Every Egyptian man must keep his eyes open for them. . . . And whatever the cost, the walls of this traitor city must be manned and held."

"Our Workers in Secret are waiting and ready," Sen-ut

said. "I spoke with their Chief in the village this morning. When the torch is lit, the Hyksos wall-guards will be slain."

"By the Fire in the mouth of Ra!" Thure murmured. "Let our Workers in Secret be silent and thorough."

And after a while, Ahmose-Eb said, "My Lord, we should capture at least six or seven hundred trained chariot horses."

Kamose raised his head quickly. "Horses! Pen . . . the blankets?"

"My King, till this morning when I drove away, enough mailed covers for my first two Chariot Companies were lined and studded."

"That is good," Kamose said, and I thought of his words when we had talked of the horses at Kus: "I have a plan." Again I marveled at my brother. "Ak-hor's Scouts are scouring the desert that our hiding armies may not be discovered," Kamose was saying, "and you, Ahmose-Eb, may not be needed, but have your Sailor-soldiers in array to the west of the city, ready for action . . . or to carry the wounded to the ships when victory is ours."

"My King."

Kamose lifted his cup for more wine. This time Neme filled it, and brought the jug around to us all.

"At two hours after midnight we shall all fore-gather. . . . Silent as stalking panthers, in the gray-dark mist of the hour before dawn we shall attack Neferusi . . . and in the blazing Light of Ra at the noon-day, I shall kill Piopi of Neferusi and his Set-spawned son." He sat back, and slowly put the full wine-cup on the folding table beside his chair. Then he pulled the gold-hafted dagger from inside the sheath around his left arm. The bronze blade shone in the star-light. My brother held it in front of his eyes. "With this dagger I shall stab them through their ears! It is for this moment I have lived since the night of our betrayal in the camp at Kus." I saw the agony dulling his eyes as it had the night he came to my room and wept, and I knew that, as a thousand times in these years of planning, he was seeing again the mangled body of our father, and hearing Ebana of El Kab's last accusing breath. "Piopi, of Neferusi," Kamose whispered, and his face was gray as a Ka-less corpse in the pale light of the rising moon. He put the dagger back in his arm-sheath. Then he took up his wine-cup and lifted it, rising to his feet. "Ra! Fold us in the White-Heat of your noon-day Fire. Guide us to victory . . . Her-bak!" He spoke the word of the Falcon.

We stood up around him and held our cups high. Then we drank to the dregs.

"Send a player on the harp to me." My brother sat down again. "And you, my Goat-herd, make merry on your pipes."

We all sat down. Hor-min took his pipes from the pouch in which he carried his palette and scrolls and played where he sat for a while. Then he leapt up and, dancing about the deck, played ever faster and higher and merrier tunes, and Tetaky danced. How light his lithe body sped over the boards! And then Sen-ut danced, and then they danced together and Thure watched her, his love a living light in his eyes. I wanted to dance, but I stayed at my brother's feet. After almost an hour the King said,

"Back to your scribing, my Goat-herd. Or to sleep! For on the morrow you will write a story to be told for a thousand years . . . and what you write shall be carved by Neshi on a granite stela." He looked down at me. "Little Brother, I am grateful that you will come with me to Neferusi. It was beyond your duty. I am aware of the depth of my intrusion. But, Ahmose, it was strong in my heart that you should watch the day of doom for our father's murderers . . . and the first prowess of your Sitters on Horses." I looked up at him and our eyes met. Then he said, "Tetaky, take off my sandals." He looked at us all with love. "Now leave me," he said, and as I rose to my feet, he added, "all save Tetaky, my Poet, here. I have need of his heart-thought on the eve of this battle."

"My King." Tetaky's eyes were bright as he squatted on deck, close to Kamose.

I went to the splash rail as Pen dove over the side to bring

a reed raft for Thure, who, with his wounds, could not swim.
I stayed at the rail till he had paddled the lovers to *The Wild
Bull*. Then I turned to my brother. The harper was sitting
on his folding stool, plucking the strings and tuning them,
and Kamose said,

"Little Brother, you will have work to do in this battle.
The wounded will need you . . . and you need your rest."
He leaned back and stretched out his long legs, and I went
aft.

I sat down between the huge rudder and the back of the
cabin, leaning against the cool matting. My thoughts were
full of my brother, of the long day of waiting on the morrow
and the battle that lay at the end of it. Then, too tired for
thought, with the stars above me and the rippling soft music
of the harper in my ears, I stretched out on deck, and slept.

At dawn, Kamose celebrated the Morning Rite. Montu-
Thoth censed the ship and then, in a reed raft, he went to
all the other ships moored around us in the hidden cove.
After the morning meal, Kamose and Hor-min were closeted
together in the large cabin.

Ahmose-Eb had swum to *The Falcon* for the Morning
Ritual, and we were alone on deck. Our Eyes and Ears were
scouting the River, but the ships around us held a waiting
quiet.

"Yet few will sleep on this long-awaited day," he said.

"And a long day it will be," I added.

"We should find shade, my Prince. Ra in his rising is
fiery today."

"He is girded for battle," I said, and we were going to sit
behind the cabin when the sound of sweet singing came to
our ears.

"That is a beautiful sound," Ahmose-Eb said, and we stood,
listening.

> "The fisherman's net is leaping with fish,
>   And the night is cool,
>   But day is born again,

And I grind, and I grind
The grain . . ."

"Her voice is cool as the River in the season of sowing,
when the moon is new," he said.

She was singing a love song.

"I passed by the door of a young man who loves me,
The door was open . . ."

Ahmose-Eb went to the rail. I saw his shoulders stiffen.
I followed him and looked down on the kitchen-ship, with
its bakery and brewery and geese, and a cow in a pen near
the tiller. I looked at the gifts of the people in baskets and
boxes, and the long butcher's table, and, sitting amidships,
I saw the two women. An old woman and a girl; they were
grinding corn for the bread. The old one wore a dark blue
robe and she ground in silence, not looking up, nor to the
side, but swaying, and her rhythm was ageless. As I watched
her, I found myself lost in it.

"How old must she be?" I whispered to myself.

"About eighteen years," Ahmose-Eb answered, and I
laughed, but my friend was in no mood for laughter. I looked
at the girl. She wore a plain white shift fastened on one
shoulder and leaving the other one bare, and as she leaned
forward grinding the crushed corn to flour on the stone, her
hair, held back by a bright, blue-dyed string, fell thick and
heavy over her shoulders.

"He is a fine young man.
How he stared when I walked past his house . . ."

She sang as she ground, both her strong, slim hands holding
the stone. A young male servant emptied more corn on the
slab from a basket. She raised herself and pushed back her
hair. I heard Ahmose-Eb catch his breath. Then she raised
her arms, slender and golden, and she saw us. She stayed for
a moment, her arms upraised. Then, with her hands across
her breast, she bent again over the quernstone. I heard
Ahmose-Eb's breath again. It came out slowly with a faint

sweet whistle, and I saw, for the first time, desire in his cool brown eyes.

"Her arms are more splendid than gold," he whispered.

"Ahmose-Eb!" I had not heard him ever speak the words of the poets, and I would have teased him, but he turned and looked me full in the eye.

"I am going aboard the kitchen-ship," he said. "With your leave, my Prince."

"Why do you not send for her?" It was not the custom for the Captain of the Royal Fleet to descend to the kitchen-ship.

"I will never send for her, my Prince. She is not, nor ever will be, my slave."

My heart leapt toward him. I put my hand on his shoulder. "You have my leave," I said. "Though I doubt if you need it."

He bowed slightly, his hand on his heart, but he did not smile. He climbed on the rail, stood poised for a moment and dived into the water.

"The Glory of Hat-hor, Lady of Lovers, has come alive in a kitchen-ship," I said to myself, as I went into the shade by the rudder and sat down with my back to the matting. I watched the cheeky wag-tails perching, familiar and unafraid, on the tow ropes and twittering around my feet, and thought of the warm desire in the eyes of my friend, and, with a start, of thin Sittek! Then all else was lost in the crowding thoughts of this night's mustering outside Neferusi. "Osiris, Lord . . . Montu of the Animals . . . may Hir-ty have delivered safely his messages. . . ."

"The King sleeps." Hor-min came and sat down beside me, and as we talked together, the hours of this fateful day passed swift as a dream. "Assiut of the Mountain was an easy winning," he said. "But Kus!"

"The King told me. Their spies had warned them. Their muster was huge, and ready."

"My Prince, it was a murderous and a roaring rout."

"You have written all this?"

"Almost all . . . and there will be more to write, after the morrow . . . and, my Prince, I fought at Kus. Every Egyptian was needed . . . and, my Prince, I have given myself the task of seeking out the wounded and tending them, as well as performing my scribe's work."

"I would join you in that," I said, and on a sudden I thought of his uncle, the traitor who had lived in Kus, and was about to ask when he, himself, spoke of him.

"I sought out my father's brother to slay him. I could not. My Prince, he cowered in front of me. He bowed to me, his arms outstretched. I was sickened. Though he had murdered my father and mother, I could not strike off his head . . . bending there . . . Akh!" He shuddered, and a deep sigh shook him.

"What did you do?"

He was silent. Then he shrugged and said, "I had him shackled, with his sons and his household, to be sent to Thebes. His wife and daughters I left to their sorrows. The loyal in Kus for a while will show them small kindness."

"The King says our victories will be hard won henceforth."

"The Hyksos are long entrenched. They have mighty reserves, and foreign allies beyond the Two Lands. . . . But my Prince! What of your sailing? I heard tell that you swam the Cataract and helped haul *The Wild Bull* into calm water."

"Is that so great a thing?"

"By Hapi it is! Even for a sailor."

With a sigh of contentment that we were together again, and talking, I told him of the strange joyous feeling, beyond my limbs and my knowing, that I had felt in the last moments when my breath had left me and I was flowing like the water itself; the strange ecstasy of my self's surrender. "Kheri-heb said I was . . . in Hapi," I said, and stood up. "Come, Hormin." I dove into the cool, sun-lit water. He followed me, and we swam together, came aboard to eat honeyed dates and drink new fresh milk, and swim again and talk, and at last we slept.

We wakened as Ra in his Sek-tet Boat descending ringed the edges of the clouds in fire against a malachite sky.

"We must prepare," Hor-min said, and I thought of my brother's words: "All is planned that the heart may plan." I could not believe that on this night we should be in array for the long-planned, fateful battle for Neferusi. Hor-min bowed, and left me.

At moon-rise, we left *The Falcon* and, led by the Nubian Scouts, we drove our chariots along the silent dike paths, then with relief turned eastward to the desert, to circle around and come to Neferusi from the south-east, a mile away from the wall where the tunnel was opened.

The Twins were waiting for us, and We-het! He bowed, but I lifted him up and we embraced, and I felt the tremor that chilled us both. We were all in hiding behind a huge sand hill as high and wide as a mountain, in the boundless, fathomless desert quiet.

"The silence is stealing from star to star," Tetaky whispered.

The city of Neferusi was still as the tomb.

"Hiya!" Ak-hor came, silent as a cat. "This city is a bastion!" Kamose put his hand on his friend's shoulder. "My King, their ramparts are bristling with Bow-men and Guards."

"Two hours before dawn they will bristle with our own men, by the Grace of Ra," Thure murmured. After Montu-Thoth had put him to sleep and charged that his wounds should heal, he was almost himself again.

"The foul Piopi and his son have indeed made their city a stronghold for the Hyksos." Mer-neb shook his head.

"Since my father's reign," I added, and Kamose breathed through his clenched teeth,

"Today I shall wade in their blood." He was standing at Soker-uff's head, in full battle dress, tall in the moon-light. He had not yet donned the Battle Helmet and his brown-black hair curled crisp on his brow. He stroked the dark nose of his horse. Then he patted his arched neck and touched the white star between Soker-uff's eyes, and looked into mine.

"May the Ka of his mistress protect him in battle," he said, and Rai was in this fight, closer than heart-beats. Then he raised his hand and beckoned to We-het. "Your Companies? The Sitters on Horses?"

"They have left the underground paddock at Per-shak one by one, led by the Nubians in stealth to a desert hiding place. At this moment, my King, five Companies are gathering, as you commanded, outside the Great Gate of the city."

"They have studied the maps? They know each of the enemy defenses? The arsenal? The chariot shops, the barracks, their relays of weapons?"

"As the palms of their hands, your Majesty."

"And the torches?"

We-het bowed. "All is in readiness."

"Then to your command, and go with Ra."

We-het bowed again and turned to where I stood with Hor-min.

"My Prince, may your Sitters on Horses this day earn the Gold of Valor," he said, and disappeared into the darkness.

Kamose turned to Ak-hor. "The stables? You know what to do?"

Ak-hor nodded, his soft brown eyes bright as embers in the moon-light. "Their horses will be in Per-sak before the battle is over," he said.

"That is good. . . . Per-neb, our assault units? The Shock-troops for entry to Piopi's house? The enemy will have their archers at every air-slit and doorway. The traitors must not escape! Per-neb, that is the work of your special troops this day. . . . Surround the house, enter and hold for me . . ." His lips stayed still at the names. "Hold them for me."

"My troops are at the ready, my Lord."

"Mer-neb?"

"The tunnel is open. My Archers will be in their places on the walls of Neferusi, my King."

Kamose looked away to the Eastern Hills. "The hour approaches. Soon this darkness will be vanquished by Ra. . . . Pen, if my orders have been followed, is now in full array in front of the Great Gate . . . Ra-en-Ra! Where is Aknere?"

We all stood, tense and silent, waiting. Neferusi's new-built high walls rose, dark and close.

"Akh! Ra-en-Ra!" Thure whispered, as three wide red-gold circles lit up the darkness and were gone.

"Ak-hor . . . my Battle Crown." Kamose stood still while his soul-friend obeyed him. Then he said, "Let us lead our horses till we muster in array. Silent as desert foxes, let us draw close . . . for at this moment, our long-trained Eyes and Ears are slaying the wall-guards and archers, and Aknere is stealing through the sleeping city to open the Great Gate."

Silently we made our way over the gritty sand to the wide, tree-cleared space in front of the Great Gate.

"Osiris, Lord . . . Ra in your noon-day Fire . . ." I was praying as we stood together, Hor-min and I, in his chariot. His eyes were shining. Kamose moved close to us.

"You, Brother, and Hor-min will follow close behind the Sitters on Horses and find a place of vantage." He stretched out his hand and clasped mine. "Watch the battle from the walls . . . and watch the prowess of your Sitters on Horses, for on them our victory depends." He loosed my hand.

"And Sek-met?" I asked.

"Her back is healed. Yet her fore-foot, I wonder." He shook his head. Then, with a faint smile, he said, "She will fight with me." He raised his hand. "Hiya!" he said, on his breath, and turned Soker-uff's head toward the dark mass of Pen's Chariots.

"May Pery-em-wah's seasoned men have performed well their assault on the wall guards. . . . All is silent . . . is it too silent?"

"Silence is the watchword, Hor-min," I said.

He nodded, and patted his leather satchel where it bulged.

"I have bandages here," he said, and as the first pale vanguards of the fore-light turned the black world to dark, misty gray, I saw the muster of ten thousand chariots, and my heart swelled at what our years of planning had wrought. Then, "Montu, of the Animals," I murmured, for the first long line of chariot horses wore mailed blankets, and I saw

Kamose at the head of his hosts, and I saw that Soker-uff had no blanket.

"Ra-en-Ra!" Hor-min whispered, and I echoed his awe, for as we watched, five Companies of Sitters on Horses appeared out of nowhere, their quivers of torches strapped on their backs. Each had his bow threaded onto his arm, and a quiver of arrows to the left of his shoulders. Foot-soldiers with linseed-oil hand lamps stood at the ready to light the first torches. I felt a cold sweat breaking out all over me.

"You are calm, my Prince, at your first battle-waiting," Hor-min said, and my breath came out with faint sound through my tight lips, as I saw Kamose poised in his chariot, and Sek-met with him. She stood on her hind legs, strong and quiet. In the dim half-light I could not see her fore-foot. Behind the King, Pen and his Chariot Corps were mustered and waiting, their javelin quivers filled to bursting, and their arrows strapped to their backs; their long axes and short swords in slots to hand and their daggers at their waists.

Hor-min stood holding the reins. His horses were well trained and stayed still as statues. We watched, scarce breathing at all.

"Aknere! Osiris, Lord . . . Aknere?" I was praying, my eyes on the huge high door of the Great Gate. "Ra-en-Ra!" The whole place was coming alive with golden flames as one by one the Sitters on Horses lit up their torches, and— "Osiris, Lord . . ."—not breaking the silence at all, slowly, unbelievably, the huge doors opened!

"Our Eyes and Ears have used vats of oil," Hor-min whispered.

But I was staring like a child at the Sitters on Horses, who, five abreast and a horse length apart, swept as afrits through the gate of the city. Hor-min tightened the reins.

"Now we find our place," I said, and he drove our chariot in at their heels and, leaping out just inside, to the left, he tied the horses to the branch of a persea tree and climbed up the wall.

"Come, my Prince! Here we can see. We can follow their prowess from the top of the walls."

"If our Eyes and Ears have performed their task well," I muttered, and climbed up after him.

We scrambled to the top of the wall and looked down on the city. The Sitters on Horses were here, there and everywhere, and yet were too swift to be seen. Only the torches, in every place as though they had a life of their own! In a trice, it seemed, flames rose to the north and the south, the east and the west of the city. Then, swiftly and silently as they had come, they were gone, leaving the defenses of Neferusi in flames, and the town in a turmoil!

"The South Gate was opened for them," Hor-min said.

In the flame-lit dawn, the enemy chariots were gathering, with their spear-men and bow-men.

"They are well prepared," I said.

"They are all, or almost all, foreigners." Hor-min pointed to the man close to us on the wall. "Mer-neb's Archers! They came through the tunnel unseen. Our Archers are manning the walls! Eureka! The King's plans are working. . . . The King!" We stood still on the parapet.

Kamose, not giving the enemy time to array, came hurtling through the bronze-studded doors at the head of his chariot hosts. The Barracks were blazing and lost, but the enemy forces were strong and many, and as the first beams of Ra in his Atet Boat ascending lit up the faces of men, the battle was joined. Spears flew, arrows leapt from their bow-strings, horses broke loose, affrighted and plunging, wounded and bleeding, and fell as the chariots thundered together. Dust whirled in clouds and mixed with the smoke from the fires. Spear-men and Foot-soldiers fought at arm's length, shield to shield, and Per-neb's special troops, their shields as a wall, were fighting their way to Piopi's house.

"Come!" Hor-min said. "We are scribes. We must follow the King."

We ran around the wall, past archers and dead guards about whose throats were strong strings cutting into their flesh, and I knew why the silence of our vigil outside the city had not been broken when our Eyes and Ears had fulfilled their grim task.

"There is the King!" Hor-min said, and for the first time I saw my brother in battle. He was a god. His face was red-gold, and unsated of combat. I could not take my eyes from his Blue Battle Crown in the thick of the fighting. There was no hurry in his movements, but a rhythmic flow, like the River in spring, as he fought his way to the house of Piopi. Heads fell from their bodies, eyes were gouged out with spears, men fell to the ground with javelins quivering from their chests and throats. "A Falcon to scatter the starlings!" Hor-min's voice was awed, his eyes large with looking. I held my soul in my hand. The earth was slithery and wet with blood. The horses could not keep their feet in the slime. Then I saw Tetaky. He was close to his King, wielding his small lighter-weight arms like the sting of a wasp, subtle and swift. Amid the hurtling jangle of javelins and sharp striking of swords, and the crashing of chariots, breaking and splitting, their wheels rolling away knocking down all in their path, dauntless and mighty Kamose threw light spear after spear and each found its mark, yet no point reddened on him. As he fought his way through the bloodied ranks with death-dealing blows, his spears as the sun's rays, I knew he had but one thought in his heart. The Shock-troops in strict forma-tion, a huge wall of shields, had stormed the house of Piopi. "My Prince! This way!" Hor-min took my hand and pulled me along with him. Res had completed her task and opened the gates to the Shock-troops. They broke ranks and poured into the Court-yard, raked with a storm of arrows. Then I saw Kamose tear through the broil of battle with Thure and Tetaky, Ak-hor and ten of his Body-guard, and drive Soker-uff through the gate. He leapt from his chariot and bounded up the steps into the house. The sweat was cold in my groin and about my ears and my nape as, waiting, I watched. "His full rage is on him," Hor-min said.

"May Ra who has brought us forth act in his son," I prayed aloud. "Let him come pure to avenge his father."

All was confusion in the house of the traitor. Shouting and screaming, the women came rushing out of the doorways, their hair streaming and some still in their night shifts, and the men of the house were dragged out by our troops while their archers took heavy toll. Then Kamose came out of the house and his rage was a flame around his head. He stepped into his chariot. Sek-met leapt up beside him, and I saw that her left paw was encased in a hard leather glove the shape of a bottle. Kamose beckoned to Thure and Tetaky to drive each side of him.

"The traitors have escaped." Hor-min's face was gray. "Come, follow me, my Prince."

We turned a corner and rounded the ledge of a tower, surprising two of our Archers, who stood back close against the wall to let us go past.

"These walls should be wide as our Temple walls," one of them said, as with precision and deadly aim he let fly one arrow after another.

"They are wide enough," Hor-min said, but his voice was lost in the uproar of battle as we passed on to a place where we could see all that happened beneath us. Our Archers along the walls were raking the enemy with arrows as showers of hail, and our Shock-troops had formed again and were advancing, those who were left of them, a solid mass of high shields. "Look! Look! The horses!" Hor-min pointed at the stable enclosure. Already the Nubians' work had begun. "They will drive them through the South Gate," Hor-min said. The cries and shrieking of the women and children, the high-screaming animal sounds of the horses, sword-slashed, pierced with arrows and bleeding, and the groans of the wounded filled all the air, and I longed to run from the place of battle and seek peace in the desert. My stomach cringing, I forced myself to watch, and saw Kamose in full pursuit of a tight group of enemy chariots that had turned away from the fighting. "It is Piopi! Where did he come from?" Hor-min's voice rose. "He is trying to escape through the South Gate. Come, let us get onto a roof top"—he pointed to a house at the left of us—"for this I must see and record." He almost fell down the steep of the wall. I followed him, scraping my shins and my thighs. We stayed pressed to the wall, and dodging the heaving, growling, cursing men fighting around us, we came to the door of the house. A woman and three children cowered in the corner. She covered her face with her robe when we entered. I spoke to her.

"We are scribes. You will come to no harm." I touched the head of the youngest child. "We must watch and record." She lifted her arm toward the stair-way. Hor-min and I went three steps at a time up to the roof top, and I saw my brother. His Blue Battle Crown flashing in the sun's high rays, he was bringing swift death on every side of him, slashing his way to the fleeing Piopi. A spear, long-thrown, flew straight at his head. He ducked. Four enemy chariots closed in around him. Soker-uff seemed to guide himself. "Rai's Ka is sitting on him!" He bounded forward, his long mane streaming. Sek-met lunged with her mighty right fore-paw and caught the driver of the nearest chariot full in the face, her claws tearing his beard. Then she fell on his archer with the hard glove on her left foot and felled him with a blow, as Kamose plunged his spear and a fat belly opened. A warrior tried to jump his chariot, and three more closed in on him but fell back before Sek-met. Ak-hor speared them clean through their breasts, as two more chariots charged and Mer-neb, with arrows between their eyes, felled both their horses, then caught, with another swift arrow between the eyes, a bearded tyrant whose broad-sword was raised in both arms to cleave the Blue Crown on my brother's head. But Kamose leapt up in the air, his huge broad-sword flashing in the noon-day sun-light, flailing and swinging as he clove his path, slashing and parrying toward Piopi and his body-guard, who were lashing their horses toward the South Gate.

"Kamose, Whadj-Kheper-Ra! Kamose!" Hor-min's soft voice was a great shout in my ear as the flat of the King's razor-sharp blade shone like streak lightning. Thure and Tetaky were now up beside him. Tetaky seemed to be filled

with the God. His body was light as air, and as frail, and yet
he was ever there, his small sharp sword dealing death all
around him. I saw him shear off the head of a captain of
foot-soldiers three times broader and taller than he, and I
saw the blood spurt from the neck of the man, straight-standing and headless, before he fell. Tetaky stood on his body
and threw his javelin between the shoulders of a Hyksos
whose ax-arm was raised to smite Pen. Foam flecked his
lips. I felt hot, stinging tears. Frail Tetaky, his poetry and his
deep, clear thoughts. How much harder he had worked at
the arts of war. Again and again he swung his sword, his
flesh so agile it seemed all spirit. Again and again he saved
the King. Then a spear caught his flank, an arrow his shield
arm. I held my sick breath and would have leapt from the
roof-top. Hor-min held me back. "My Prince." He held me
fast. A second arrow had struck Tetaky. He recoiled, lost
himself and fell on one knee. A Hyksos, a dark man and
bull-like, with a yell of triumph jumped toward him, but
Kamose struck him down in full flight. Tetaky tried to rise.
Blood oozed from his shield arm. In fury he pushed Pen
away from him. "The stubborn young Theban." Hor-min's
eyes were wet. "The stubborn young poet." Tetaky rose.
Standing upright, poised and seeming tall as a god, he threw
a javelin sideways through the neck of a Hyksos who would
have felled Ak-hor, then caught in his own breast a Hyksos
spear. He stood for a moment, quite still, retching blood.
Then he lifted both arms, the blood streaming down them,
and his mouth formed the beloved word, twice.

"Ta-mery . . . Ta-mery!" And his frail body fell in the
bloody slime.

Piopi of Neferusi and those left of his body-guard were
thrashing and goading their blood-spattered horses to flee
through the South Gate. With a cry to awaken the shades
in the Dwat, Kamose took after them. Thure and Pen, who
had been fighting on foot, leapt into an empty chariot, and
Ak-hor, taking one of the enemy's, pulled Mer-neb up after
him. They hurtled after their King till Soker-uff reared and

the other horses all slid to a halt in the slime, as the fleeing chariots were stopped in their tracks! "By the Disc!" I spoke without sound. As though Lord Montu of the Animals had himself planned it, their escape through the wide-open Gate was blocked by their own herd of horses! The body-guard turned and fought. Kamose, using his javelin, caught one of them in the groin, overthrew a second by the sheer violence of his charge and sliced off the Hyksos' head, while Piopi, slashing his whip and screaming curses, had turned his horses toward the stables. Sek-met with a curving leap landed full on the body of the third charioteer, and the horses, shrieking high cries, reared up and overturned it as my brother swung Soker-uff around and swift as an arrow was in front of Piopi's chariot, while Ak-hor held the murderer's horses. Kamose leapt from his chariot and pulled Piopi of Neferusi to the ground. I saw his plump, familiar face, shiny with sweat, upturned in the bright noon sun-light as Kamose held back his head. All fighting had ceased. The thunder of their hooves as the last of the captured horses were driven through the wide South Gate died away. With the capture of the Prince of Neferusi, the battle was ours! As the River ebbing, all except his company, Egyptians and the enemy both, all drew back, away from the King. Piopi's fat arms flayed helplessly. He was sobbing. Kamose slit open the traitor's belly with his sword.

"That his viscera will be lost in the Dwat," Hor-min whispered in awe. "The King is thorough."

As though he performed a ritual, Kamose watched the murderer's bowels burst out of his belly. Then he stabbed him through the chest with his blood-wet sword and watched the life-blood flow out of him. When Piopi's Ka had almost left him, my brother cut out the heart of the traitor, and clove his head from his neck.

The circle of quiet around the King had spread through the city. No one moved. Even the wounded, it seemed, both horses and men, had ceased, for these dread moments, their agonized cries.

The King stood up, his bloodied sword in his hand. The noon-day Fire of Ra blazed down, and no man cast a shadow.

"The traitor and murderer, Piopi of Neferusi, is fallen and overthrown." Kamose's voice was as the mooring of a great ship. "I have taken his heart from its place. I have cut his vertebrae at the neck. I have annihilated his soul. His name is not. His egg shall not last, nor his seed knit together. He has no more a place in this Land."

Kamose turned away, and with Thure, Ak-hor and Pen, he went to where Tetaky lay. My brother looked grimmer than sudden night as he held the shoulders of our childhood friend. Thure held his feet and Pen carried his weapons. In silence, those left of the King's Body-Guard around them, they bore their burden to the ox-cart of Montu-Thoth and the Healing Priests.

"Tonight they will raise the Tent of Gold for him." My voice cracked and trembled. "Tonight they will begin the Ritual."

"He belonged to his hour," Hor-min said. "And the hour he belonged to was glorified in him."

I blinked the wet that was more than tears from my eyes. "We must look to the wounded." My voice was clearer.

He nodded slowly, but we stayed there awhile staring at the terrible scene. Then we descended the stairs.

The woman was standing up now. She was tall and young. Her younger children hid in her full dark-blue skirt, their wan faces and black eyes peering out at us.

"The battle is over," I said.

The city was carnage. Horses and men lay wounded and dying, chariots on their sides, overturned and piled up in heaps where they had smashed together, and in one, both its horses dead, a young soldier lay sleeping. The ox-carts of the Healer-Priests had already come into the town, and the young Priests with water-skins; our men were already gathering the prisoners; our scribes were counting the dead.

We threaded our way through streets crowded with

wounded awash in their blood. My stomach curled again at the sight of the pile of hands, growing bigger each moment, by the side of the scribes, whose folding chairs sank into the blood-wet ground, and my whole body retched and chilled at the mound of new-severed manhood. We tended the wounded of our armies and carried them to the ox-carts, to be taken to the clearing outside the walls where tents had already been raised and supplies stacked; and those of the city of Neferusi who were Egyptians our Priests healed, and took out the arrows that pierced them.

To the wounded of the enemy we showed mercy, and we cared for them but then left them lying on their cloaks against the walls to be tended by the people of the town.

All through the night we worked in the clearing where we had mustered in array at the dawn of this day, Hor-min and I, washing clean the wounds and salving them, while Montu-Thoth and the Healer-Priests charged the jagged holes where arrows and javelins must be cut out of the torn flesh with the Life of Ra. With the Looking, and sometimes by pressing their two first fingers between the soldiers' eyes, the Healer-Priests sent them to sleep that they might not feel the pain of the knife, and while they still slept, those who could be moved the ox-carts carried to the wharves, where they were put aboard the long barges waiting to take them South, to Assiut and to Thebes.

"Osiris, Lord . . . Charge these your children with your Life. They have earned the Gold of Valor, and proudly they fought. . . ." I had come, in the after-glow, to the River's edge, and was leaning against a date-palm, four trees growing out of one root, and reflected clear and still in the sun-golden water. I was spent, and in a strange way at peace. As silently, save for the splashing of the oars and the dip of the barge-poles, the ships with our wounded put out from their moorings, Hor-min joined me.

"My Prince, you have done the work of ten men, and the work of a Priest. There is food and a cup of wine in the house there," he turned. "There, beyond the tamarisk trees."

"First I would go to the edge of the desert where the Anubis Priests have erected the God's Booth for Tetaky."

"By your leave I will come with you."

I shook my head. "Leave me, Hor-min, and in a while find Thure and Pen and the Twins, and together we will visit our friend. . . . And the King?"

"The few scratches on him even now give no showing. He is as a god, and he does not tire. Ak-hor is with him. He straightway ordered a search for Teti of Neferusi . . . but he has escaped. None saw him in the fighting at all, nor did our Shock-troops find him in the house."

"The Set-pig."

"My Prince?"

"I am less than a Prince and far from being Priest when I think of that name. Hor-min, I am amazed at the rage the sound of that name arouses in me. . . ." I felt the cold sweat on my body again. I can hate, I thought. I, who would be Lector-Priest. "Teti of Neferusi." I shivered. "Go for the others, Hor-min." I put my hand on his shoulder. "I will meet with you at Tetaky's Tent of Gold."

Hor-min bowed, and left me alone. Slowly I walked across the wide clearing and along the village, past bright-painted houses, darkening now, and trees black as onyx against the saffron-blue sky. I stopped to talk to the wounded men, blessing them and praising them.

"You fought for the Light of Ra . . . and to free the Two Lands from the Darkness of Set, and our people from tyranny," I told them.

"And would fight again," was the answer I got, and I thought that some of them looked at me strangely, and that one of them turned his face away from me.

I walked on till the village lay behind me, bright with house-lamps and the torches among the wounded, till I came to the Tent of Gold where Tetaky lay. Montu-Thoth stood aside, and I looked down at my friend. He was smiling, and there were specks of dried foam at the upturned corners of his mouth. "The West is sweet," I thought. How often he had said the words: "Why anger your heart over anything that happens? Think only of joy, and wreath with flowers the girl that you love." As I gazed long at him, there was a tenderness, a mobility in his face, a mild, triumphant joy, and for a moment I was one with the unyielding grandeur of him. I blinked my eyes, and when I looked again, his face was still.

With the fall of night the Companions came into the Booth and stood beside me, and Pen said,

"Night is the thought of death, but Ra in his Atet Boat rising is the sureness of Life."

"Descend with the God," Thure whispered. "And rise with him in the Flame of the Morn."

I touched his brow. "Your heart is unangered." I thought of him dancing on deck with Sen-ut. Was it but last night? "You will join in the Dance of the Stars with Rai," I said softly. "Fine gold is not as the Radiance of you . . . Osiris, Lord . . . Osiris, Lord . . ."

"Osiris, Lord . . ." they all prayed with me.

"Whose fragrance the gods love. . . . Wash this your Beloved in the Heavenly River. Bathe him, Bright of Plumes, in your Love. . . ."

We stood rapt, as one, and knew that the Ka of our friend was in the midst of us, for the tent, still warm with the heat of the day, was suddenly cool: the Coolness of Isis' Breath. We were laved in it, and were refreshed. Then they stood aside, and I walked from the Tent of Gold.

Montu-Thoth was waiting for me. "His Ka was bright with joy . . . and his joyous blessing is around his King . . . and about your heads."

I took the young Lector-Priest's hand and held it against my brow. Then, with the others, I went to the house in the tamarisk clump, and on fresh reeds, half lying, half sitting, we ate with a will of goat's cheese and barley bread, fine leeks and cucumbers, and drank the wine of the South Land.

Our soldiers, forgetting the hazards and agonies of the day, were as lions with their spoil, dividing among them the herds, fat and honey, and drinking the good Delta wine captured from the house of Piopi. Kamose had ordered that it be given to the men who had fought and won the battle this day. "The traitors were always full to their gills of it. Till Avaris is ours, and the Two Lands are One," he swore, "I will not drink the wine of the Delta."

But the hearts of the solders were gladdened, and, drunken, they slept where they sat; and we fell fast asleep where we were, on the beds of cool rushes.

Hor-min had spoken true words. Kamose would neither rest nor eat. Guarded by the seven men still alive of his Body-Guard, and by the Nubians, in the Court-yard of Piopi's house he had questioned, with Ak-hor, all the prisoners, both men and women, till long after the darkness had fallen. Our Eyes and Ears were searching the papyrus marshes, boarding all boats, and under night's cloak our Messengers on Horses scoured through the villages. But none knew, or none would tell, where Teti of Neferusi was hiding. In an anguish of thwarted rage. Kamose had mounted his chariot and, with Sek-met and Ak-hor, gone back to the yacht made ready for him; and on this night he lay with the maidens fairest of limb and face, who had not been opened in childbirth, slaking his wrath and chagrin till, exhausted at last, he, too, fell asleep.

CHAPTER VI

After almost two hours of troubled sleep in the village house, Hor-min had wakened me, and together, in silence, we had driven in his chariot back to the ship. Still without speaking, he went to the small cabin with his palette and pens, and I to lie down in the space between the rudder and the main cabin. It seemed as though the short sleep on the cool reeds had released the horrors of this bloody day to gather behind my eyelids. "Osiris, Lord . . ." When I opened my eyes they filled all my looking! I tried to gaze upward at the myriad stars. My eyelids fell, heavy. A throaty laugh broke the night silence. I fell asleep.

Almost, it seemed, at the same instant, Montu-Thoth touched me gently on the shoulder.

"Awake in peace, my Prince." I looked beyond his calm face to the dawn sky. "The King is already awake, cleansed and shriven." I blinked, and closed my eyes again. "After sleeping for just one hour, his Majesty swam ashore from the pleasure-yacht, mounted his chariot and drove, in the hour before dawn, to the Tent of Gold where Tetaky lay. We prayed long together." My brother, I thought, the God and the man so strong in him! "Then," Montu-Thoth was saying, "in an ox-cart, the King drew the coffin behind his chariot to *The Southern.*" I opened my eyes and he answered the question in them. "My Prince, *The Southern,* with Tetaky's coffin on the center deck under a shelter, will lead the fleet with the captured treasure-ships and the prisoners back to Thebes."

"How his Ka will rejoice," I murmured, and thought how always he would rejoice: "Put music before you . . . bring flowers to the feet of the woman you love . . ." I lay there, lost in the memory of a day in our youth. Tetaky had teased a young girl in a ferry-boat. "Hai! Ist! Open your bodice! A beetle has run down your bosom." I felt the tears prickle at the back of my nose, and I thought that when we were young in Thebes, though we were poor as mice we were merry.

Montu-Thoth was bringing the Holy Ewer of natron water to lave me, talking quietly the while. "There is peace in Neferusi, my Prince. The quiet of men and women at peaceful tasks. All now within those walls are Egyptian. They are cleaning and repairing their city and their homes."

"And the wounded?"

"A few remain who are too ill to move. They are well tended in the healing-stations in the clearing outside the city gates."

"And the treasure-ships?"

"They anchored at sun-set yesterday. Two of Aknere's Young Eyes and Ears brought the news, and they told us, too, of the roistering and the drunken brawls of the sailors, of villages ravaged even in the North Land. Today, my

Prince, they were to unload the treasure at Neferusi. . . ."

"Where are they?"

"Around the next reach of the River. . . . Since the first star-lit darkness last evening, Ahmose-Eb's Sailor-soldiers and Shock-troops, on reed rafts and in fishing-boats, have been within sight of them." He smiled. "Trawling for fish." He held out his hand to me. "Come, there is no time to waste, my Prince."

I took his hand and, diving overboard, swam for a while in the cool, sweet water, then came back to have the young Lector-Priest pour the cleansing natron water in a shower over me. I donned a clean loin-cloth and went barefoot to the main deck where Ah-mose-Eb, Thure, the Twins, Hormin and all our sailors were flat on their bellies. I joined them, my nose against the hard wood.

Kamose was bowing in adoration, in thanksgiving and praise for our victory, and when Ra, God of All, in his Atet-Boat rising sailed upward behind the Eastern Hills, he, too, fell down on his belly, and as the God, the Beginning, the End, the Midst and the Continuance, granted to man the Gift of the New Day, every heart swelled with joy. We all rose and stretched out our hands to the Light.

Kamose turned toward us and spoke his own words. "Had we, each man here, ten thousand mouths, and ten thousand voices with which to glorify the Father of Souls, we should still be unworthy. . . ." He smiled. "Yet we are his children and we ask gifts of him, even though before we ask they are granted to us."

Then the sail was hoisted. The sailors dispersed to their places and tasks, and as we were eating our fruit and warm honeyed milk, Ak-hor swam to *The Falcon* and climbed aboard.

"My King . . . we must not delay. It is sun-up, and they plan to unload."

"They know nothing of Neferusi?"

"The reach in the River is wide and high. They anchored last evening at dusk, already full drunk."

"All praise to Ra!" Kamose chuckled. "Let not one grain of spice be unladed before these ships dock in a Theban wharf." He went to the prow.

We could see *The Wild Bull*. Already she was rounding the reach, the troop-ship behind her. Sailing with the current, a wind from the south in our sails, we were as birds streaming through the bright air, and soon we, too, rounded the reach. The River was alive with small craft: pleasure-boats from the North Land in the wake of the treasure-boats and tribute-ships; cattle-barges and kitchen-ships; hunting-rafts piled high with harpoons and throwing sticks; and I saw our own shock-troops in their fishing-boats, trawling their nets and fishing with hand lines.

Our troop-ship was filled with Mer-neb's bow-men behind a wall of rigged shields, and as *The Falcon* sailed into view, the seeming fishermen slipped from their rafts and, led by Ahmose-Eb, Per-neb and Thure, swam underwater to the anchored ships and silently, stealthily, boarded them. They slit the throats of the few sober guards and, by the Truth of Maat, they found all the sailors unwashed and uncleansed, still sleeping off their drunken carousing.

Our Sailor-soldiers went aboard the ships in minutes, and the Archers in array on our troop-ship rained arrows like hailstones, killing and wounding the fat, bearded Hyksos and scattering the pleasure-boats and hunting-craft like chaff in the wind.

As we sailed alongside the largest treasure-ship, Thure called out, "Ist! Ist! Behold! Mayebre the Libyan! Mayebre the Libyan is here!"

Kamose frowned, then threw back his head and laughed, and we watched while three of our soldiers tied a rope around the Libyan's fat wringing hands.

"Look at him! Look at him now! The arrogant bastard!" Ahmose-Eb had shinned on a line back to our deck.

The oily Hyksos envoy was no longer raising his harsh voice to mouth blasphemies; he was wailing and calling on Set and Astarte, stamping his jewel-sandaled feet and writhing with rage and despair. He fouled the air with his curses on the captains and all the sailors for drunkards and sluggards.

"Isti! Look at him! His very nails have turned pale!" Hor-min said. "This I shall write in the darkest red ink! How I shall relish describing this scene."

Ahmose-Eb came up behind me. "My Prince . . ." We walked across to the splash rail and, leaning against it, gazed awhile at the far shore and at the pleasure-yachts, small as toys in the distance, speeding downriver to the North Land.

"This news will have wings," I said, and he nodded. Then he turned to me.

"My Prince . . . I have fallen in love! I love this maiden . . . Atu."

"Atu?" I felt my face redden. In the stress and horror of yesterday's battle I had forgotten the girl in the kitchen-ship. "You spoke with her?"

"My Prince, she is lovely as her voice. She is the grand-daughter of an Oasis Chief whose village was ravaged by the Hyksos when her mother was a girl . . . I called on her to helped with the wounded . . . I would have sent her back to Thebes but she desires to stay with the Fleet and to serve the King . . . She is brave as she is lovely . . ."

"Ahmoses both!" Kamose called to us. He was in high spirits.

"We will talk of this again, Ahmose-Eb," I said as we crossed the deck.

"Thure and Per-neb are coming aboard," Kamose said as we approached him. "We must plan. Every moment that passes brings danger close. Come, Brother . . ." He put his arm around my shoulder. "The Little Brother is silent today. . . . So be it. When Ra descends to the caverns of night, you will be on your way, you and Hor-min . . . and it will not be to battle. . . . But of that later. Come, and you too, Ahmose-Eb, sit down and mark well what I am about to say."

Ak-hor, Mer-neb and Hor-min were already on their haunches around a large map spread out on deck. A thin acacia wand lay across it, and Sek-met sat up with her two front paws on it. There was only a small bandage now on the wounded one, and sometimes she would lie with her chin on it, or give it a small lick.

Kamose picked up the wand. "My plan for Memphis . . . Ahmose-Eb, you will sail to Avaris with me this night, when darkness falls, but . . . you will leave one prime ship and five Companies of your Sailor-soldiers to capture the shore villages that lie around Memphis . . . here!"—he drew the wand along a wide stream—"here along this canal. Choose two of your best Captains to lead them. Hor-min has a hand-map in readiness for them. The wharves must be in our hands lest the enemy, now alerted, come in secret by water, and that our wounded may be sent with all speed to the healing-stations outside Neferusi."

"There will be few wounded at Memphis," Ak-hor said.

"That is my hope. The people have long been loyal to Thebes and to Queen Tetisheri. As for the tyrants, Memphis is far north, and they feel safe. But you, Ak-hor, must be swifter than the falcon's stoop."

"I, my King?" Ak-hor's soft brown-black eyes were round with surprise.

"You, Ak-hor." Kamose looked across at me. "When the ancient city is once again free, you, Little Brother, and the Priests of Ptah will purify the Innermost Shrine and restore the worship of God, in his ancient Taurian aspect of Ptah, to his Holy Place. . . . By the Disc! I envy you, Brother, and Ak-hor, for my soul desires to set free the ancient city of Memphis."

I did not answer, but I thought that my brother also sacrificed the desires of his heart.

"My King, what are your commands?" Ak-hor's face was grave.

"You will march on the city from the Western Desert. Three Companies—the Second Chariots, the Fourth Bowmen and the Seventh Foot-soldiers—will swell your ranks."

"They are among the oldest and best of our army. . . . I shall scarce need them in this foray."

"This is my hope. I have other plans for them."

As we waited, silent, Thure and Per-neb climbed over the splash rail, both grinning like cats.

"Look! Look at these!" Per-neb had a bow strung on his arm and was carrying a slender bronze-headed ax. He threw the bow to his twin. "Catch! And there are four hundred more for you. And more than five hundred of these!" He brandished the ax and the razor-sharp blade of it shone bright red-gold in the sun-light.

"Stop gloating," Kamose said. "I would tell of my plans. Sit down."

Thure sat down on deck beside me. Per-neb, the ax across his knee, squatted next to him. Kamose's eyes were narrow with thought. He looked at Ak-hor. "The three seasoned Companies I am sending to you will form the core of my Memphian Army."

"My King! This is a plan with merit! A Memphian Army! My Lord, many men within this city are long trained in arms by our Workers in Secret." Ahmose-Eb's face was alight.

"For two generations, my Sailor-man." Kamose turned again to Ak-hor. "Your father will join you in Memphis. Neshi has no peer when men must be quickly and thoroughly trained. . . . Ak-hor! Quick and thorough you both must be. . . . I give you and your father one month"—he held up a long, slim forefinger—"to form and train an Army of ten thousand men."

"My Lord, and my King."

"Each man of the Companies sent to you will be given the wand of a Captain. Each of them will train a company of men chosen by Neshi for their natural bent . . . and Ak-hor, seek out the tallest and broadest of shoulder." Kamose looked down and shook his head slowly. "We lost all but four of our gallant Standard-bearers at Kus." He looked up. "Kus! The chariots we captured there . . . they are heavy, and you, Ak-hor, will train two fighting men to each of them. . . . Ahmose-Eb's Captains will unlade them when his Sailor-soldiers have made safe the wharves around Memphis. And

Ak-hor, the training of your army will proceed during the march southward."

"Southward, my King?"

"You will meet me at Abydos."

"Abydos," I murmured, and my brother looked at me.

"By the next harvest time, Little Brother, you will worship Osiris restored to his Place in the Temple of Abydos. This is a promise. But first Avaris. By the Disc! That fortress city must fall and fall quickly. We shall attack at the dark of the moon, silent and swift. . . . Again, Brother, your Sitters on Horses will mean our victory, and you yourself shall carry my orders to them. You and Hor-min, my Young Ones, you have had your bellies full of battle . . . for a time." He raised an eyebrow, then with a smile he said, "You will go north-westward to the House of Ameni, Nomarch of the Wall Nome. He has ever been loyal to Thebes, and the Fore-court of his House covers one of our secret underground paddocks, built two years ago." He turned to Ak-hor. "Your father is already a welcome guest in that House. He awaits my commands. . . . And you, Little Brother, you and Hor-min, after a visit of three days to Ameni, will make your way to Memphis. It is but one day's journey . . ."

"And by then Memphis will be free," Thure said.

"I am depending on that." Kamose nodded, and Ahmose-Eb said,

"When this vast city is in our hands, we shall have the stronghold we need in the North Land."

"And a loyal one!" Thure added. "The rape and plunder of the Temple of Ptah, and the slaughter of the holy Apis bulls for meat, have hardened the hearts of the people forever against the tyrants."

Kamose sat back in his chair. "Brother, you will await my messenger in Memphis. Then come with all speed to Avaris . . . Avaris! Pery-em-wah has sent clear knowledge of those impregnable walls . . . and those ramps!"

"Yet, their first strength is in archery," Mer-neb said.

"And we shall be open to their cross-fire," his twin added.

"It is murderous. We saw that at Kus," Thure said. He still showed the arrow scars on his shoulders.

"What news of Pen?" Kamose asked of Ak-hor. "Where is he now?"

"He awaits you, my King, at the appointed place. His whole force is hidden in a ravine, four thousand cubits deep, in the Eastern Desert to the south of Avaris."

"May Ra hold him in his Light. I wish he could have seen all the treasures we have captured. Hor-min, call a scribe. I would hear of this treasure from Retenu and the Isles of the Great Green Water."

Hor-min rose to his feet, went to one of the small cabins in the bow of the ship and returned with a scribe. "My Lord," he said. "The treasure is great, and not yet tallied."

"No matter, Hor-min. Scribe, tell us so far as you have learned."

"Your Majesty." The man made the ritual bow, and unrolled his papyrus. "Jars and vases of costly stone, and gold, and tribute chests full of silver and gold, onyx, turquoise and lapis lazuli . . ."

"And five hundred silver discs," Thure said. "I saw them myself. The size of Sen-ut's hand."

"This is indeed treasure." Kamose inclined his head toward the scribe. "Tell us more."

"Bronze coats of mail, one hundred of them, and tent poles, strengthened with metal . . ."

"To make chariot poles. . . . Proceed, Scribe."

"Staffs of ebony and ivory carved with human heads, Syrian-worked jars, flat plates, harps of ebony silvered and gilded . . . besides spices, myrrh-incense, and olive oil, and honey—and the kitchen-ships, bulging with corn and maize! And barges there are, Your Majesty, full of young cattle and goats, fat and sleek . . . and many more treasures as yet uncounted."

Kamose smiled. "The provender, all save the spices, we will

keep for our soldiers." He looked at the young scribe. "We are pleased with your diligence. It will be your task to see that this order is obeyed."

"Your Majesty." The scribe made the ritual bow, and Kamose raised his hand in blessing.

As the scribe left us, Ahmose-Eb said, "With my own eyes I saw more than a hundred large rounded platters, and wine-cups of pure gold . . ."

"More gold than I've seen since my birth." Thure laughed.

"For two hundred years they have mined our gold, Egyptian gold, to pay for the treasures of foreign lands," Mer-neb said.

"And put to slavery our Egyptian artisans." His twin nodded.

Thure sighed. "I wish Sen-ut were here," he said. "I have a gift for her."

"Is it a secret?" Kamose asked. "Or will you show it to us?"

Thure smiled. "My King, for that reason I told you." He opened the pouch in his sporran and took out two bracelets of such delicate beauty that even we, Thebans, used though we were to perfection in small things, gave gasps of delight. He handed one to Kamose, and the other was passed among us. There were seven strands in each of the bracelets. Four of them were of acacia pods carved in carnelian, beryl and amythyst, and three strands were threaded with tiny green-gold tree-frogs, so perfectly wrought that they seemed to move.

"Harbingers of Life," Kamose murmured, and Thure whispered,

"Sen-ut is my life."

We handed the two bracelets back to him. I turned away from the naked longing in his gray eyes.

"Thure"—Kamose's eyes were warm, and yet stern— "Sen-ut asked for this mission."

"I know . . . my little wild lioness." He sighed again. "But I would she had not."

"If anyone in the Two Lands can discover . . ." Kamose balked at the name and it burst out of me:

"Teti of Neferusi."

My brother said slowly, ". . . Sen-ut will find him."

My whole being rose against the thought. Since childhood the foul, fat-fingered Teti had hungered for Sen-ut, for the touch of her hands. "Let her not find him . . . Osiris, Lord . . ." I was praying inside me. "Let her not find him."

"Thure, my friend," Kamose said, "you will see your love before the siege of Avaris. She has orders to join and hide with Pen and his Chariot Companies, and to meet with us at the appointed time. By then, Thure, by the Grace of Ra, she will have discovered all the traitor's designs."

"She will be safe . . . and think of her joy in your gift." Mer-neb smiled. "Your beautiful double gift."

Thure answered his smile and softly quoted Tetaky's poem:

"The hands of my beloved are as a cool breeze
And her touch as gentle as dew . . ."

With the thought of Tetaky, I was praying for Sen-ut. "Hat-hor, Lady of Love, let her not find him . . ." Then I heard my own voice.

"Thure, Hat-hor guards the lovers who love her. She will guard and cherish Sen-ut." The words had a faraway sound in my ears and seemed to be lost on the bright air, but Thure was smiling again.

"My Prince, you have spoken few words this day, but these have gladdened my heart. Before the siege of Avaris, I shall place my gifts on the wrists of my love," he said, and his voice rang warm in the afternoon silence.

Mer-neb looked up and smiled at him. "Akh! Thure . . ." Then he said to Kamose, his eyes alight, "My King, even the skeleton of these bows is made of four woods!" He stroked the inner side of his captured bow with his fingers. "Four of them! See how pliable." He held it out. "Look at these strips! And the bands and the glue. My King, these are bows for the gods."

Kamose laughed. "Then use them well, Mer-neb. It is the gods who have given them into your hands."

"And the treasure-ships," Ahmose-Eb said.

"And best of all!"—the smile still lingered on Thure's face—"best of all things that this day came to pass . . . Mayebre the Libyan! How I relished tying up his fat, sweating hands."

"Hori will see that he does the dog-walk." Ahmose-Eb gave his rare soft, throaty chuckle, and Kamose turned to him.

"Let us row downriver till sun-set. It will ease the going for those of us who are bound for Memphis . . . and you, Little Brother, and Hor-min . . . and you, Ak-hor, my friend, will leave *The Falcon* at sun-down and travel by the desert." He looked at the others, then down at the map. "Tonight, after the evening meal . . . we who sail for Avaris will complete our plans. . . . Avaris! I shall raze the city of the tyrant king, the foul Apophis, so that not one house is left standing whole, nor a cubit's space of those vast walls unbroken. . . ." Then, as the sky before a desert storm, his face darkened. "Teti of Neferusi." The name came through his clenched teeth. "Sen-ut will find him. . . . All others have failed. . . . She will find him and I will cut out his heart." With a swift movement he was on his feet, tall above us, his golden arm stretched out toward the North Land. "Tonight, by the Grace of Ra, I lead my hosts to Avaris . . . and now, my Sailor-man"—he turned to Ahmose-Eb, standing wide of gait, his hands on his hips—"bring me my oar. I wil! take my heart for company and till sun-down I will row with the men."

Ahmose-Eb brought the ebony gold-bladed oar that was twenty cubits in length. Kamose took his place at the oarthole, and his stroke was as the stroke of ten.

At sun-set, Hor-min and I went ashore with Ak-hor, and

my brother, Sek-met at his heels, came down the ramp to the wharf.

"Ahmose, let us walk toward the clump of date-palms there." He took my arm. "Little Brother . . ." We walked on in silence. Then he said, "Your heart, since the battle, has gone out of itself, and the eyes of your soul have withdrawn their seeing. . . . Brother, I am sending you into the desert, the arid, vast Western Desert. There, lying alone where the sand and the sky never touch, and the silence is music, you will fill again the Barque of your heart. There your soul's eyes, stripped of human thoughts, battle-stain, slaying and carnage, will again see the Whole . . . and Little Brother, you will see the God-hills!" His potent gaze held me. The gold of the sky had turned to crimson. I marveled at the depth of his Knowing, his love. "Come," he said, "I would speak with Ak-hor. This is his first full Command."

"And a great one."

A flock of night-herons flew over our heads. Kamose looked up. "Be secret as they are," he said, as we came to Hor-min and our chariot. "You have four Nubians only. In the desert your small company will be as six fleas on a donkey." We knelt for his blessing. He lifted us up and embraced us. Then he turned to Ak-hor.

"My friend, many Egyptian men will be lost in the siege of Avaris. I shall have need of your Memphian Army."

"My King." Ak-hor fell to his knees.

"Go with Ra." Kamose embraced him. They stood for a moment, each with his hand on the other's shoulder. Then Kamose walked back up the ramp to the deck of *The Falcon*. He stood there with Ahmose-Eb, the Twins, Thure and Sek-met, with her paws on the splash rail. He raised his arm in salute, stood for a moment and went into his cabin.

Ak-hor took leave of us. "My Prince . . . Hor-min . . . give my father greeting. Tell him I shall await him in Memphis. . . . The blessing of Ra on us all." He mounted his chariot and rode away to recapture the ancient city from the tyrants.

A gray-blue mist rose from the River's edge as, with our Nubian scouts, we skirted quiet villages, then turned to the northwest, and when we came to the desert I leapt from the chariot and eagerly mounted Minirt.

Hor-min, in the chariot alongside, said, "My Prince, it is hard to be secret with Minirt. He is a silver horse and shines in the moon-light."

"Remember the King's words," I said. "We are lost as six fleas on a donkey!" I touched Minirt's sides with my heels. He bounded forward along the hard sand stretching before us, white-bright in the light of the new-risen moon, and I knew that he felt as I, and smelt as I, for his nostrils quivered. He made small high sounds, raised his head and shook it, his ears pricked forward. Then I smelt a jackal, but we did not come upon it for more than two hundred cubits, dark-out-lined on the ridge of a dune. I was far ahead of the others, but the sound of their coming was close in my ears, and I thought how strange and changed sounds were in the desert. Twice, so swiftly that I almost fell off him, Minirt veered, and, righting myself, I saw night-feeding snakes as they slith-ered away. "He sees in the dark!" I whispered. "Minirt's eyes are bright in the darkness." Night animals scurried away from us, rats and a desert hare. I waited on the crest of a hill-high dune for Hor-min, and in the hollow down the northern slope of it, the Scouts made camp for the night.

In the gold-and-turquoise dawn, restless and not inclined to company, even Hor-min's, again I rode on ahead, and when I could not see the others I waited in the shade of a dune. But I found no peace from the horrors that pushed themselves into the vanguard of my thoughts. Then a large lizard darted close, stood still as a stone and fixed me with his cold gaze. "They suck the milk of sleeping goats," Ak-hor had once told me. "And their bite is fatal." I stared back, unblinking, into the cold eyes. With a movement too quick to see, he was gone.

On the evening of the third day we came to the top of a wide, high, wind-driven sand-slope and halted, all six of us, spellbound. The God-hills! My heart stood still as I gazed at the mountains of stone so long imagined, so far beyond imagining. They rose purple-dark, in infinite, unchanging majesty against the changing sky of approaching night.

The Nubians were still as statues. Only their fingers moved as, in awe, they touched the cowry shells on their left wrists.

"Enduring are the Places . . . Pure is the Mountain . . ." I breathed the ancient names I had learned from the age-old papyri as a child.

As I gazed, my heart grew warm within me, and the eyes of my soul opened to a new, yet ancient vision, the vision of thousands of years of Ta-mery; and my thin breath gave sound to a name, "Imhotep," who in the dim past built the first God-hill of stone, and who was born near to Thebes. Imhotep: Adept, Architect, Physician and Master Builder, High Priest and Vizir. Then Kheri-heb was close. "Kheri-heb . . ." I called to my Master.

We stayed there, unmoving, till the darkness fell.

At first dawn I awoke and wakened Hor-min. We cleansed ourselves in the bright gritty sand and stood together looking toward the east.

"After the Rite we will turn and look at the God-hills," I whispered.

"As men have done for thousands of years," he answered softly, and after I had spoken the words of the Dawn Rite, we lay on our bellies in the sand, and as Ra in his Atet Boat rising brought gladness to all the earth, we rose to our feet and, turning to the westward, gazed again at the God-hills.

No two were the same, and the light and color of them, as Ra rose in the heavens, filled my heart to bursting with worship and love for the ancient Great Ones, whose vision had conceived and whose hands had wrought this glory in stone.

Hours and moments had no meaning. The nearest God-hill shimmered in the clear air as a mirage shimmers, yet was still, then seemed to tremble again, yet was a mountain of stone, man-built, shining there, golden–milk-white in the first Light of Ra. I remembered Kheri-heb and his teaching: "The four corners are the four elements: Fire, Water, Earth and Air, rising to the Point of Unity to gather Ra's Light. . . . And from this Point his Love and his Light descend to the four corners of the earth and spread throughout his Creation, into souls both general and particular, and into the nature of all things." Kheri-heb! Kheri-heb! My heart called again to my Master. Rai, my sister, my soul's love . . . come through the door of your Ka-house. The white light was consuming me. Kheri-heb, Rai, Ah-hotpe, my mother; Kamose, Whadj-Kheper-Ra! "I have built a Ladder to the Sky!" The ancient words had a new meaning for me, pure and active. "I have trodden a Ramp to the Heart of the Living God!"

"My Prince." Hor-min's soft words were as a great shout in my ear. "Your pardon, my Prince. We must not tarry longer."

I turned and put my hand on his shoulder. The leader of our scouts brought our chariot. Minirt was tethered to it on a long leash. Then suddenly Hor-min said, "Look, my Prince."

I tilted my head to follow his gaze. A hawk hovered, onyx-black against the yellow-gold sky of early day.

"Her-bak!" I whispered. "Horus Hawk of the South Land . . . Dawn Falcon!" And my brother was closer than the space between heart-beats.

The desert sands were as fields of pale corn. The rocks to our left rose high and huge, fretted by the wind and sand into pillars, great foldings and pleats, and they were pitted with caves. "The Beloved Land," I said to myself, and I thought of Tetaky as I saw the shadows, dark blue in the rock hollows, and the green shades on the sand-drifts. He would have made a poem to the beauty of Ta-mery. The distance was close. We drove across the shelterless sands, then along the zigzag desert road; and when noon had passed and the fiery heat of Ra was westering, Memphis rose, seeming high before us, in the far distance across the desert plain, and I thought of Ak-hor and the battle before him.

In the after-glow, we turned toward the River, and as in the red-gold of the dusk we drove through land-parcels green with maize and tawny with durra, and across a verdant fowling preserve where geese of all kinds and water-birds fussed to their rest, I saw ruddy shelducks with dark yellow beaks, cranes, green-beaked red bitterns, and green-footed avocets. Around pools we rode, and alongside canals abounding with fish, and there were goats and capering kids, and oxen lowed the night-fall in the pastures.

"The North Land abounds in green pasturelands," I said in amaze.

"In both summer and winter," Hor-min answered, as slowly, walking our tired horses, we came to the outer wall of the House of Ameni, Nomarch of the Wall Nome. We halted and looked at this House that had been a retreat and a hiding place for Pery-em-wah's Eyes and Ears in Secret since the days of my father, and, during the last three years of planning and preparing, the place of an underground paddock for my Sitters on Horses.

As we stood there in the chariot, a wall door swung open and we entered the Court-yard. Ameni and Neshi the Nubian stood in the door-way to greet us.

"Azanta! Greeting, my Prince. May the Grace of Ra be in your hearts." Ameni bowed.

"My Prince . . . Ahmose." Neshi bowed, his hand on his heart, then for all his years came with a bound and caught my hand as I leapt from the chariot. "My son? Ak-hor, where is he now?"

"By Ra's Grace, near to Memphis . . . if not already there."

"I would have joined in this fight."

We embraced, and I told him, "Neshi, Hor-min has the King's orders for you."

Neshi turned with a broad smile on his ebon face. "Hor-min . . . I would hear all that has passed."

"You will hear that from Ak-hor." Hor-min gave him a scroll. "Neshi, you are to leave for Memphis at the darkness, tonight."

I turned to our host. "With your leave, Hor-min and I will first carry out the King's commands."

Ameni bowed and led us down the secret way to the underground paddock.

"We shall await your presence, Prince Ahmose, at the evening meal." He bowed again, and left us.

Bathed and cleansed, I blessed the House and said the evening prayer before I sat down on the raised dais with Ameni and his wife, and looked about me. Flowers wreathed the pillars to the roof, garlands were twined around the table-legs and single buds lay on every dish of food. Male musicians were playing softly on their harps and pipes. Ameni talked to me but my attention was feigned, so rapt was I in the pleasant and gladsome sights all around me. Each stool and chair had its own small table, and two of the guests were already in wine, and were laughing and pretending they could not balance the scented cones on their heads. The Delta women wore colored linens, and their long pleated skirts were dyed blue as the kingfisher; paler blue as the sky at dawn; full green as malachite; pale green as the wings of light from the north; yellow as the new corn; and even pale red, like poppies far-faded, and their skirts were bordered with stitchings of flowers and fishes embroidered in gold and silver. I was lost in the natural riches and luxury of the North Land, and for the first time I understood why the tyrants cared so little for Thebes. We were almost a joke to them, I thought. They blasphemed. They desecrated my father's Throne, and when he was goaded to fight, they murdered him. "Toy monarch," Mayebre the Libyan had called Kamose. Our tribute was all they needed from us. Yet they had forced my father to fight. The reed pipes were playing. I let all thought go from me. Then a girl came toward me.

"My daughter," Ameni said.

Her skirt was pale purple and the linen of it fine as a butterfly's wing, so that her supple limbs gleamed, golden, through it, and about her slim waist was a belt of soft leather, dark purple and studded with jewels: carnelian, beryl and amethyst. She held a lotus-flower in her hand. Her fingers were henna-tipped, and her fragrance was a joy. She was smaller than most of our women, slender and golden as a reed in the sun-set, and her eyes were gray as river-pools in the swift darkening twi-light, and soft as does' eyes. I took the flower. She did not smile. I looked at her as a man ever looks on beauty, and asked, "What is your daughter's name, Ameni?"

"Inhapi, my Prince."

The blood coursed in my veins. "Inhapi . . . In Hapi . . . Inhapi . . ." With each beat of my heart I whispered the name.

She waited on me, and brought before me such a feast as in my life I had never known. I caught Hor-min's eye as he ate of flamingos stuffed with small thrushes, each stuffed with a mullet roe, and I drank in silence to my brother on his way to Avaris. "No more battle for you, Little Brother . . . not for a while," he had said. Had he known, too, of the beauty in the House of Ameni? I lifted again the fine porphyry cup and sipped the tangy dark wine. Inhapi laved my hands in water strewn with the petals of flowers, and dried each finger gently with linen. Then she served to me strips of gazelle meat in vine leaves, and quail stuffed with honeyed figs, and then she washed my fingers again, and her touch was cool as the Breath of Isis, and her hair was blacker than the moon-void night. Many moons had passed since my manhood quickened.

Then maidens came with small harps, and the oil-lamps were lit, and the torches, and the male pipers played an ancient tune, and Ameni said, "Our daughter would dance for Ahmose, Prince of the South Land."

"Prince of the Two Lands, my husband," his wife chided him, and he smiled and patted her hand, and nodded.

"Prince of the Two Lands . . . Ta-mery, by the Grace of Ra," he said, and called to his daughter. "Inhapi . . ." His voice held pride, and he looked on her as she came with a father's love.

"I long to dance for you, my Prince." Her voice was low and soft. "I long to clash my cymbals before you, and bend backward to the ground before you. . . ." She stepped back from us, her hands folded on her breasts.

My whole being leapt toward her. I turned to her father. "My heart is heavy till I see Inhapi dancing," I said, and he clapped his hands.

At first she sang to the music of the maidens' harps, swaying quietly the while.

"Sweet of love is the daughter of the King,
Her hair is black as the night's blackness,
Black as the wine grapes are the braids of her hair,
The hearts of men are water at her glance . . ."

Her father and mother listened, leaning forward in their chairs, and I saw Hor-min watching her. Then he turned his gaze to me.

"Sweet of love is the daughter of the King,
Red are her lips as red jasper . . ."

The reed pipers played alone, bird notes. She raised her arms, and they were as the golden corn when the dawn breeze caresses the fields. Tiny silver bells made silvery sound with the tremor of her hips, and her hair fell loose. "My Slender One . . . O Lovely Hips," my heart sang as I gazed on her. "O Lotus-breasts . . ." Then the harps, like water on the rocks in the wadis, rippled cool sound, and the castanets, with the play of her fingers, were as wild as the blood in my veins, and her body was music.

Her dance ended. I waited, and she was by my side with a fragrant cone. She leaned toward me and placed it on my head. I could have kissed her breast. She laughed, and the sound of her laughter left me weak. Then she was gone, and her father was talking to me of my brother's battles, his plans and matters of warfare till I could bear no more, and pleaded exhaustion from the journey.

"My Prince." Hor-min's voice snapped the tense strings of my thought as I lay on the bed in the high, wide room, awake and aching with desire. "My Prince . . . Inhapi sends a message to you." I lay there holding my breath. "She bids me say to you that if you will but come and speak with her, the moon of your face will destroy the darkness where she stands without you." My breath burst out of me. I sat up. "She is in her garden, beside the pool. Come, I will lead you."

I put a kilt around me and, barefoot, I followed him. The tiles were cold to my feet, and I was trembling. The night-blooming flowers were fragrant, and the herbs gave forth spiced smells on the clear air. Then I saw the moon-light, silver on the water, and the slender girl who stood by the pool. Silently Hor-min left me. Unable to move, I watched Inhapi. "O Lovely Girl . . . O Giver of Pride to me . . ." I walked toward her. Though my bare feet made no sound, she turned to me.

"Your footsteps are like the young of the antelope," she said, and held out her arms to me.

I touched the tip of her fingers with my own. "Inhapi . . . Inhapi . . . When I hear your voice I am snared. When I see you dancing I am a fish caught in your net."

"There is no snare in my singing." Slowly she came close, lifted her arms and clasped her hands at the back of my neck. Her lips were against my cheek. "Nor a net in my dancing. . . . But only my heart, and these lips and my feet . . ." She stood, her bare feet on mine. "These my palms, and my fingers and my breasts to caress you." She lifted her face to me. I held her, and drank the honeyed sweet of her lips.

"Your mouth is the lotus that opens to the sun."

"To the God," she whispered, and her lips were cool. "O Loved One."

With closed eyes we stood close. Her girdle dropped to the tiles with silvery sound. She stood, shining naked.

"O Wonder of Women." She trembled as a lute-string at my touch. I loosened my hold. She sank down, and I knelt beside her, gently caressing her. Then I slowly leaned over her. "Hold in your hand the torch of my love." Her face bore the smile that comes with the ardor of passion. Gently I lay on her, in a rapture that was hindrance to firm embraces. There was no skill in our love, but yearning and delight, and swift fulfillment.

She opened her eyes and gazed on me, and our bodies, entwined as wild grape-vine, gathered fire, burned and merged. Fragrant flesh, blood and soul, she blended with me, and I sent my energy wholly into her. "Inhapi . . . Inhapi . . ." We lay in a double, inseparable bliss till the stars fell, one by one, into the bowl of the fading night. Then, with a new smile, her eyes wet with tears and her body moist, she crushed her breasts against me and held me in triumph and a wild desiring. "Inhapi! Inhapi!" As the Cataract waters plunge down to the deeps, we drowned in each other.

On the fourth day, at dawn, we set out on our journey to Memphis. For three festal days, while I could see Inhapi and hear her voice, it had been better to me than food and drink. When I left the House of Ameni, I was riding away from a manifest joy, yet my soul was joyful as I took the leathers from Hor-min and drove the chariot.

The day-light hours passed in silence save for the rumbling of the chariot wheels on the rocky sand paths and the changing thud of the horses' feet as we left the farm-lands for the hard dike road.

Where the branch of the River skirts the plain, Ak-hor's Scouts met us, and Hor-min said, "Here the North Land and the South Land meet."

Then we heard the good news that the ancient city was again in Egyptian hands.

"The King's heart will rejoice." I spoke my first words that day, and after resting for a while we followed the Scouts toward Memphis.

We drove through groves of tamarisk and thorn, of acacia and terebrinth trees, and we saw our Theban soldiers standing around, or lazily sitting, their backs against tree trunks, watching the gazelles drink at the pools as we passed; and birds filled the dusk with their song.

I pulled in the horses to a walk, and, turning left toward the gates of Memphis, I gazed at the majesty of the Great White Wall and the God-hills around, towering, dark, in the twi-light. I seemed to see the reality that inspires all form, and I knew in my heart that on earth it is in Form that all Spirit moves, as the Spirit moved in the heart of Menes, Hawk Prince of the South Land, when he bound the Two Lands together, thousands of years gone by, and built the Great White Wall upon which my gaze rested; as the Spirit moved in Imhotep and transformed his vision to stone, to rise throughout all times from the desert sands; as it moved in my own seed in the womb of Inhapi.

"My Prince, the Scouts are far ahead of us."

As Hor-min spoke, I turned to him and saw that his black eyes were bright with tears. "It is homecoming for you! You return in your youth to the House of your ancestors."

"And the home of Queen Tetisheri," he said, and we stayed where we were, gazing long at the vast ancient city, the Wall and the high limestone cliffs rising behind them. Then I turned to Hor-min. "When the King is victorious, I would study here, in the Temple of Imhotep."

"Then make it your task to revive it," Hor-min answered. "For the ancient scripts have been long hidden from sight, and the Priests of Imhotep, those who escaped the sword of the Hyksos, are in hiding. My Prince, the desecration of this city was as great as that of Abydos."

"Hor-min, I would sleep this night in the Temple of Imhotep. Together we will loosen our Kas, and Kheri-heb will lead us in dream, for in the world of sleep he sojourns with Imhotep. The ancient Sage is his Mentor . . . and I have need of Kheri-heb."

"My Prince, we must press on." Hor-min tightened the leathers and our horse bounded forward.

As we drove through the Gates of the city and upward toward the Temple of Ptah, Ak-hor came to meet us. "My

Prince." He bowed, his hand on his heart. "The King's work is accomplished."

For almost a whole moon's span I sat at the feet of the Priests of Ptah, in the new-shriven Temple. Kheri-heb was close to my Ka, and he guided my dreams. Hor-min and I stayed in a small Court in the Temple of Imhotep, and sometimes we passed whole days in meditation together, or delving into the ancient papyri, and while he worked alone at his scribing and mapping, I went out over the Sacred Lake to the parks in the west, where the bulls grazed, walked the streets of the ancient Capital and took my leisure in the sacred groves; the size of this vast city, from the center of it, was a half-day's chariot journey to the north and the south and the east and the west. On a day, the Ptah Priests took me to Sitke-mose, my grand-mother's ancient estate, where the new Apis-bull had, three days past, been born.

"The first in seven generations," the Ptah Priest said. "It is a sign. His name is Horns of the Morning Star, and he has on him every true marking." He showed me the white square on his forehead, the eagle outlined on the pelt of his back, and with my two fore-fingers I felt the sacred scarab-lump under his tongue. Soft and wet his tongue was, and his eye was bold. "And look, my Prince!" The Ptah Priest held out his tail. Each hair of it was forked at the end.

"I would take three hairs to make a ring," I said. Inhapi . . . Inhapi, my heart sang as the Priest, with a flint knife, cut off three hairs.

"Per-du-Ptah the Dwarf shall make the ring," he said, and gave to me the three precious hairs. "Once again he is at work in his Temple work-shop, and his name means 'Gift of Ptah.' He is of great age, but energetic and virile. . . . And he would journey to Thebes. He has waited a long time."

"I will secure his safe passage."

"He has manifold gifts for the Queen Tetisheri, gifts hidden for two hundred years and kept bright, in secret, by generations of beleaguered Ptah Priests."

"How my grand-mother's heart will rejoice," I said, and we bowed to each other. Then he blessed me.

Per-du-Ptah the Dwarf drank wine with Hor-min and me, and partook of our evening meal. He talked in a deep, gruff voice, and his pale eyes gleamed. "I know the liturgies of the gods, the Ancient Canon. Perception of Cosmic Order, my Prince, is as constant as the order itself." He gazed at me for a moment, then drank wine and told us, "I know the attitudes for the statue of a man, how he poses himself to throw the harpoon and the look in his eye at that moment . . ." He waved his short, fat arms as he spoke. "The way that a spear-man lifts his arm, and how a woman sits . . . With my copper chisels I make jewels so fine that the eye is ravished. I know the secret of inlays that fire will not burn, nor water dissolve. The treasures I take to the Queen Tetisheri will be proof of the skill of Per-du-Ptah."

The hours we were not in the Temple at the feet of the Ptah Priests, or in the underground chambers of the Temple of Imhotep, browsing among the ancient papyri, we spent in his work-shop. He made the sacred-hair ring for Inhapi, and a hundred tiny jewels to nestle in the curls of my grand-mother's wig; gifts for Pen-aati and Senseneb; and for my mother he made a necklace. On a fine golden chain he hung three large golden flies: the Gold of Valor for her husband, Seken-en-Ra, and her two sons.

During these days which, for Hor-min and for me, were out of the flux of time, Neshi and Ak-hor were about the King's business. They had organized in Memphis twelve thousand men in addition to those who had been secretly armed during the long years of planning. They both, aided by the Captains of Archers and Foot-soldiers, trained them in shifts, night and day, and Neshi thoroughly garrisoned the city so that the Priests of Ptah and Imhotep would not be forced into hiding again.

On the twenty-fifth day, at the hour when the city was bathed in the golden rays of Ra, downing, holy and perfect to Night's Underworld, and the clouds were as streams of milk poured out from golden cups, we were drinking the sweet wine together, Ak-hor and his father, Hor-min and I, in our small Temple Court, when suddenly, through the pillars, I saw a small-boned, slim figure, gray as a ghost with dust and sand.

"Hir-ty!"

At the same moment, he saw me and came to us, running.

"The King's message, at last!" Neshi leaned forward in his chair.

"My Prince." Hir-ty bowed to me and gave me a small papyrus scroll. I greeted him and asked Hor-min to bring wine. "For Ra-en-Ra!—you look exhausted," I said. He bowed again, and seemed in great haste.

"Prince Ahmose, we must go with all speed to a secret oasis in the Western Desert."

"In the Western Desert?" We all looked at each other. "The King? Where is he? Is he not in Avaris?" We all spoke at once.

"His Majesty is with loyal Dwellers in the Desert . . . at the secret oasis."

Neshi, Ak-hor and Hor-min were staring at me, amazed and perturbed.

"Tell us, Hir-ty, of the Hyksos city. . . . What of Avaris?"

"His Majesty, after besieging from the water and from the Eastern Desert, was victorious. The Sitters on Horses had done magic work and the enemy capitol was in flames. Then the King heard, and this from the lips of Apophis' daughter herself, that Teti of Neferusi was not in Avaris . . . but in the Western Desert . . ."

"The King heard this from the princess herself?"

"From the daughter of the Hyksos king."

I held back more questions, but one came from my heart. "And what of the Lady Sen-ut?"

Hir-ty shook his head. "There has been no word of the Lady Sen-ut."

A cold shiver crept up my spine. "And Teti of Neferusi? Where is he?"

"Somewhere between the Oasis of Bahria and Kus, in the Western Desert. . . . But my Prince, it is his plan to deploy his forces in the Eastern Desert, a little to the north of Abydos."

"That is the reason, and a potent one," Ak-hor said, "that he could not be found in Neferusi."

"My Prince." I felt Hir-ty's urgency. "Our Armies are gathered again in the Western Desert. The Sitters on Horses were not discovered. They disappeared in the darkness. Traveling by night, they should by now be again in the secret paddock under the House of Ameni." I felt the warm blood rise to my face, but Hir-ty was looking at Ak-hor. "They will wait there for your orders."

"My orders?" Ak-hor asked.

Hir-ty turned again to me. "My Prince, the King's message is in your hands."

I unrolled the small papyrus and read it. Then I looked up. "Neshi, you are to remain in Memphis, to guard and protect this city. Ak-hor, you will lead your Memphian Army by the Eastern Desert to Abydos. The Sitters on Horses are under your command and will travel with your Memphian Army. Among your Chariot Companies, and your horses, they will be safely hidden on the march."

"And the King?" Neshi asked.

"The King, and his hosts from Avaris, will go by the Western Desert to Abydos."

"But Avaris?" Neshi's face showed the pall of his years, and I said,

"I see the King's plan. . . . But Hir-ty, you are weary. Drink your wine."

He took the cup from the table where Hor-min had put it, and drained it to the dregs. Then he said,

"The King said, 'with all speed.' "

I turned to Hor-min. "Let us hasten."

"I will call for the chariots." He quietly left us.

"Sit down, Hir-ty, and tell us more of this Hyksos Princess. What is her name?"

"Herath, my Prince."

"The same who laughed in the face of the scavenger Hur when he would have her to wife?" Ak-hor asked.

"She is the same."

"And she betrayed her own father?" I shook my head.

"By the Truth of Maat! She opened the Eastern Gate of the city, and the door of the Palace to his Majesty."

Neshi and Ak-hor were looking at the young messenger with a world of question in their eyes.

"Avaris?" Neshi asked again.

"The Hyksos city is greatly ruined," Hir-ty said. "It was for a time in our hands."

"For a time?" Neshi's voice was a whisper.

My heart was thudding in my throat. My mother's words rang clear inside me. "I am afraid for Kamose, that on a moment, he might lose all." Hir-ty was looking at me.

"What is it?"

"My Prince, when His Majesty heard that Teti of Neferusi was in the Western Desert, His Majesty drove out of Avaris on the instant."

"And the enemy rallied again?" Ak-hor half-asked, and Hir-ty looked at him. His young face was drawn and gray.

"The Hyksos Bow-men, those left in the city, remanned the ruined walls."

"And the others?"

"They fled to join Teti of Neferusi's hosts outside Abydos."

"How many of the enemy left the city?" I asked.

"About ten thousand, my Prince."

I looked at Ak-hor. "Each day your Memphian Army grows more vital to our cause!" I turned to Hir-ty. "And Apophis?"

"The Hyksos tyrant escaped, we believe to the Oasis of Bahria. At least that is what his daughter believed."

We were all silent. Our souls were as cold as the wind from the north.

"And Ah-mose-Eb? And the Fleet?" I asked, showing no sign of my inner unrest.

"They are regrouped and sailing southward to Abydos, keeping in to the western shore of the River. There are twenty-four ships. They are bringing Mer-neb and the Archers. Per-neb and the Foot-soldiers are behind the King, by two days' march."

"And Penekheb?"

"The Lord Penekheb is himself with the King. But his Majesty sent the Chariot Forces to join the Memphian Army." He turned again to Ak-hor. "They should be in Memphis by dawn tomorrow. The Lord Penekheb will re-join his command at Abydos. His Majesty is bent on seeking out the Neferusian traitor, and he desired that the Lords Thure and Penekheb be with him."

As I rolled up the scroll I heard the clatter of horses' feet and the rattle of chariot wheels on the tiles of the Temple Court, and I looked through the pillars at the sound of Min-irt's small whinny. But I did not see him.

"Where is Minirt?" I asked, and though since Hir-ty's coming the faces of Neshi and his son had been as funeral masks, now Ak-hor's splendid white teeth flashed in a broad smile, for Hor-min led toward me a black horse with white stripes.

"Here, my Prince."

"Minirt?" I went to him.

"He was a moon-white target for every arrow, and we are in the North Land, my Prince. The Priests of Ptah painted him."

"Minirt . . . you are a new kind of desert animal that the gods have created."

"He will become yet another legend," Neshi said with a smile.

Hir-ty, smiling too, said, "My Prince, your Sitters on Horses are more than a legend. They are talked of behind closed doors and whispered about in awe. There is a deep fear of them among the Hyksos, and the priests of Set are having amulets made. Both soldiers and the people wear them around their necks and wrists against the afrits who come in the darkness, with fire, from inside the mountains."

"And you are an afrit animal, my Minirt, by the Truth of Maat," I said, and, mounting Hor-min's chariot, I took the leathers. "Neshi, guard well this ancient city for the King. Ak-hor, the hosts under your command grow larger with each moon. We shall meet at Abydos."

"And by the God of the Innumerable Names, my Prince, may you and the King come upon Teti of Neferusi and slay him."

I smiled at the two Unique Friends. "Neshi . . . Ak-hor . . . the King will raze Avaris in his own time," I said. "Go with Ra."

"And may the star gods light your way this night," Neshi said. They both bowed, their hands on their hearts, and their faces were gaunt again, as though carved in ebony.

At midnight, Hor-min, Hir-ty and I, and our two Scouts, were met by the loyal Dwellers in the Desert who would be our guides.

"And strange guides they are!" Hor-min said, after half a night and a whole day's march.

But soon I came to know them, their voices and their movements, and they were a source of hidden mirth to me. The rise of an elbow, or a jutting out of the chin, or an over-solemn look in the eye contained a whole world of meaning. Fingers loud-snapped with a bent arm meant one thing; loud-snapped with the arm held straight out meant another. I came to know them all, and their leader was called On-kier, which means wolf.

"I bit my mother when I was a baby," he told us, and bowed with both hands to his brow in a way strange to us.

As I rode in the chariot with Hor-min over the huge, wide sand-slopes, my woolen cloak pulled close around me,

I found myself wondering why Herath, the daughter of Apophis, the Hyksos king, would betray her father. And Anat-neby? Herath was but four years younger than her step-mother. Anat-neby of the ivory skin, and blue-black eyes. Queen in Avaris. Had Kamose come upon his first love? Had she escaped into the desert with her husband? The Hyksos Princess, where was she now? And Pery-em-wah, and his supposed confidant and friend, It-yu, Apophis' Chief Scribe? Had the oldest of our Eyes and Ears in the North Land guarded his long-kept secret? But one thought stayed in my heart, as a rock over which all other thoughts flowed. Why? Why had Kamose, after years of patience and planning, given himself to the rapture of fury? Why had my brother, victorious, left the enemy fortress to regather and rearm? Was Teti of Neferusi worth more than Avaris? My thoughts spun wild. I longed to sit on Minirt, but our secret strength must not be revealed, even to loyal Dwellers in the Desert. Hir-ty was riding a donkey, his thin legs dangling. To quiet my thoughts I took the leathers from Hor-min.

On the morrow, in the fiery heat of Ra at the noon-day, we came to the place where Kamose awaited us. His tent was near to the dark blue water of the small oasis. Whispering date-palms grew all around, and trellises of vines in full fruit. The black grapes hung heavy, in clusters. There was a herd of small donkeys among the boats and the crane-birds, and beyond us the huge sand-slopes shone white as milk.

My brother came out of his tent. Hor-min pulled our horses to a standstill. Kamose looked tired, but his eyes were bright and his steps swift, yet without haste. "Come, Little Brother," he greeted me. "There is much to talk of." Hor-min jumped down from the chariot and bowed. "My Goat-herd scribe!" Kamose raised him by the hand and embraced him. "Join us for a cup of wine. . . . Though you are both tired from the journey, there will be less than two hours to rest." As we walked to his tent he looked at me, a swift, sidelong glance. "Lighten your tongue of the question, Brother," he said.

My tongue had a life of its own for, without my willing, I said the words I had self-sworn not to say. "Was Teti of Neferusi of more worth than Avaris?"

"Do not judge me, Ahmose. . . . Hor-min, you will share quarters with Pen. Come, both of you, I would hear of Neshi and Ak-hor and my Memphian Army."

"They are both about your plans," I told him. "Neshi has fortified Memphis. The High Priests of Ptah and Im-hotep serve again in their Temples—and Kamose! A new Apis Bull has been dropped! The holy young creature showed all the sacred signs."

"That is a good omen, and heartens me, for our fight has just begun. And Ak-hor?"

"He will amass your Memphian Army, Pen's Chariot Forces and the Sitters on Horses in the Eastern Desert, according to plan."

"There may be a change of plan."

"How? Why?" I asked.

"Sen-ut!"

"Sen-ut? I have already learned that she did not meet you before the siege of Avaris as you ordered. Where is she?"

Looking straight at me, he said, "Sen-ut has lured the traitor-pig of Neferusi and keeps him with her, on his way to join his hosts at Abydos. They are camped two days' journey from this place." He took a small papyrus roll from the wooden table beside his tent chair and handed it to me. "One of Aknere's Young Eyes and Ears crept into my tent at dawn."

I unrolled it and saw Sen-ut's small, neat script.

> My King, Kamose,
> I can hold him for six days, no longer. I am to go with him to Abydos. Five thousand men escaped from Assiut, Kus and Neferusi, both Hyksos and foreign mercenaries. They will swell his hosts camped to the east of Abydos.

He will be battle-ready. Capture him now, here in the desert. His one thought is your death, my King, and the razing of Thebes.

"The razing of Thebes! My Brother, forgive my questioning. The razing of Thebes . . ." I said again. I had not thought of this. "The Residence of the God." Then I thought of Sen-ut, and felt my fingers crush the tough papyrus.

Kamose poured out a cup of wine. "Drink this." He held it out to me but I could not move. My heart spewed out the thought of Sen-ut with Teti of Neferusi.

"A high price was paid for this knowledge," I said, without looking up at my brother.

"Ahmose, drink this wine."

I took the cup and poured the wine, without swallowing, down my tight throat. My anguish found words. "Always he lusted after Sen-ut. Always she stood away from him . . . Always she shuddered when his fat hands touched hers." I felt my lower lip stiff as a stone and drawn down to my chin as with a foul taste. "Sen-ut . . ."

"Little Brother . . . Ahmose." There was compassion in my brother's eyes as I held my retching stomach with my fists still clenched on Sen-ut's small scroll. He and Hor-min waited in silence while I gathered myself, and when the strings of my body loosened and I sagged, spent, in my chair, my lips formed a word.

"Thure."

"He has read Sen-ut's message," Kamose said.

"Where is he?"

"In his small tent, alone. Ahmose, if Sen-ut's plan succeeds, there will be no more bloodshed in Abydos . . . and if we are there with her, as we shall be, within two days . . ." He leaned forward and spoke with a terrible energy. "This time —Ra-en-Ra! I shall come upon this Set-hog-scourge of the Two Lands and slit open his belly. Thure shall cut out his heart." He sat back. His tense breath eased out of him, and he turned to Hor-min. "You, my quiet Scribe, are beyond exhaustion. Go to your tent, I doubt not that Pen is sleeping soundly."

"The Lord Penekheb has the Gift of Sleep," Hor-min said, stepping backward out of the tent.

"May Isis watch over you both." Kamose turned and poured out wine for himself, then said to me, "Ahmose, Thebes has no ramps, only her ancient walls against the brutal weight of the Hyksos battering-rams, their heavy chariotry and their hordes of Bow-men. . . . My brother, Avaris can wait! Whether I come upon the Neferusian pig here in the desert and kill him, or whether I put his forces to rout at Abydos, Thebes will be safe. Judge me now, Little Brother."

I stood up, Sen-ut's secret message still in my hand. Then I said, "Thebes, the Residence of the God, is of more worth than Avaris," my brother rose, and put his hand on my shoulder.

"It will take many moons for Apophis to repair and re-build the ruins of his city, and we shall return, swiftly, to the attack . . . more swiftly because of Sen-ut. It would have taken many moon spans to come upon the traitor with-out her."

"Kamose, why did Herath, the daughter of Apophis, be-tray him?"

My brother turned and poured two cups of wine. Hand-ing one cup to me, with a faint smile he said,

"She looked on me with desire." He drank the wine, put down the empty cup and went to his couch. "And she is beautiful," he said. "Now to your rest, Little Brother. We have but till the moon is high-risen, to sleep." He stretched out, full length.

Still standing, I raised my cup and drank to the dregs, and my heart was round with the knowledge that no lust of anger had prompted Kamose to leave Avaris, but his

Falcon-heart had weighed and balanced the Scales of Fate. As I put my cup next to his on the table, he said,

"We have a hard journey ahead of us. Ra grant the foul traitor is still with Sen-ut," and I felt the wine in my stomach turn sour again. Kamose rolled over on his side. "Sleep in the pupil of the Eye of Horus," he murmured sleepily, and slowly I went to the couch at the other side of the tent, and lay down.

I was still holding her scroll. "Her Ka is untouched," I told myself over and over again, lying there. "Sen-ut's bright soul is untarnished. But her body, Sen-ut's slim, boyish body, her beautiful hands . . . The body is the temple of the God within. . . . It is the linen shift of the soul. . . ." My thoughts were a wild ache, and I was praying that Teti of Neferusi would still be with her. "Osiris, Lord of Compassion . . . let her loyalty, her courage . . . her sacrifice . . . not be in vain. . . . Osiris, Lord, grant that no more blood be shed in your Holy City. . . . Grant that Sen-ut's plan will work. . . ." With the thought of her I almost groaned, but held the sound for fear of waking my brother. He was sleeping as a child sleeps, his Ka released, and guarded. Then the thought of Inhapi drowned all other thought, and the blood in my veins grew warm again. After a while, I, too, fell asleep.

"Wake up, Ahmose."

I opened my eyes to see my brother. He was in half battle dress, and did not wear the Blue Crown, but a wide striped kerchief, green, white and red, on his head, and the Asp of Royal Power on his brow. He looked as though he had slept for a whole night, fresh and young, and I did not wonder that Herath had looked on him with desire. Sleepily, and still clad in the leather loin-cloth of the Sitters on Horses, and the light, linen-lined, metal-studded vest to my hips, I followed him out of the tent.

The whole Company was assembled. Thure was in Kamose's chariot. I went to him and we clasped hands for a moment. His face was barren in the torch-light. Hir-ty was with Hor-min, and he was leading his horse as a spare till we left the oasis and said farewell to the Dwellers in the Desert. Pen was waiting for me with Minirt, the new, strange Minirt, tethered to his chariot. I leapt up beside him to ride and talk with him, and with the Royal Guard of ten chariots around us we set forth on our fateful journey.

Pen let our chariot fall behind the others as I, eager to hear of Avaris, plied him with questions.

"Where is Ahmose-Eb? Is it true we lost twenty-one prime ships?"

"He is with the Fleet. They are keeping abreast of us," Pen said. "And we lost twenty-one prime ships at Avaris. But they lost more. The Hyksos are not River-men."

"And Per-neb's Foot-soldiers and Spear-men?"

"All regrouped, and at this moment one day's march behind us. Our forces will be aligned as the King had planned. Akh! Ra-en-Ra! The King's plans! His tactics! Though our losses are great, the inside of Avaris is a ruin. No other plans could have worked, so strong a fortress is that navel of the barbarians."

"Pen, tell me of Avaris . . . I have a hundred ears."

"There is much to tell. Avaris is not an Egyptian city. It is a fortress. There is a moat around three quarters of it, and its walls, strengthened with the garnering of generations from Egyptian quarries, metals and strong foreign woods, are not walls alone. My Prince, around them, as though shoring them up, are long ramps: tall, smooth slopes, deadly to attempt; and at the gates, on each side of the ramp leading up to the huge, high, metal-studded doors, are ledges for bow-men, and bastions and towers that protect them; and they shoot their venom-tipped arrows through slits in the bricks. And Ahmose, at its height, the gate-ramp suddenly slopes steep down to the doors. The attackers are caught in a pit to be slaughtered like beasts. Pery-em-wah had warned us of this. Following the King's orders, Ahmose-Eb led his Fleet as far up the branch of the River as he could;

when darkness fell, he ferried his Shock-troops close to the moat and they swam underwater, their small round shields strapped to their backs, crept up the ramp to the Western Gate, keeping in shadow, near to the walls, and, where the ramp steepened down, they slithered on their bellies like snakes and set fire to the doors. We lost all but three men. But Per-neb's Foot-soldiers crawled up the ramp in a stream of crossfire and drew away the enemy from the east of the city, where the King's main army was in array. It was the King's plan to enter by the flaws and passages built into the walls by Egyptian captives. We know, to our sorrow, from Pery-em-wah, that five of our secret tunnels have been discovered, and of the Egyptian workers who were slaves in Avaris, sixty were rounded up, drawn and quartered and their heads put on spikes above the places where the tunnels had been . . ."

"After Kamose left the city?"

Pen nodded. "Rancor and revenge . . . and now they will look for more flaws and tunnels. . . . But Herath! Surely that was of the God!"

"Herath . . . a strange name."

"And a strange maiden . . . She sent the Overseer of her Household, the man Ben-arpath, of whom we know from Pery-em-wah . . ."

"Pen! She cannot know of Pery-em-wah?"

"My Prince, the oldest of our Eyes and Ears has been so long in Avaris that he is thought by all to be a Hyksos, even among themselves."

"And this Ben-arpath?"

"Herath sent him, in secret, to the King's camp in the Eastern Desert. I was with the King. We had waited a day and a night for Sen-ut."

"Akh! Pen . . . Sen-ut . . ."

"My Prince, let us send the strength of our heart-thought to Thure. He has not spoken since the messenger came."

We rode on in silence for a while. Then I asked, "And the man Ben-arpath? He came to the camp?"

"The Guards brought him to the King's tent. He had no written message. He begged leave to speak, and when the King had dismissed the Guards, he said, quite simply, 'The Eastern Gate of the city will be opened to Kamose, Falcon Prince and King of the Two Lands, at one hour before dawn.' He would say no more, and left as secretly as he had come. The King was wary. 'What strange trick is this?' he asked me when Ben-arpath had gone. 'Call five of my Messengers on Horses. Our plans remain. But the men in the tunnels must wait till the hour before dawn. If the gates remain closed, we attack according to plan. If the gates are opened to us, then they must stay in the tunnels till the darkness, and steal out by twos and threes, covering their tracks. If these long-planned and perilously built tunnels are not used tomorrow, they must remain a close secret.' Then he summoned We-het, and told him that the orders stood for the Sitters on Horses to be outside the Eastern Gate in stealth, with their torches. The King was quiet. He slept one hour. When he rose, he said, 'The burden of this foray may be lightened for us. We shall see.' And, my Prince, we saw! At the hour before dawn, the huge gates swung open and our Sitters on Horses, their bodies painted black and their torches aflame, raced through the city, firing the arsenal, the chariot shops and the weaponries, and causing rout and superstitious affright among both soldiers and people, except for five of them, who a few of the braver soldiers attacked!"

"By the Lord Montu . . ."

Pen laughed. "My Prince, they let out the unholy screams they had been taught by a Temple singer, and took out their small bows and killed their attackers. Still screaming as afrits, they escaped without capture. But, my Prince, our secret was almost discovered. . . . Had your training not been so thorough . . ."

"Then the King entered the city?"

"I was beside him as he led the chariot charge, and Merneb's Archers surged in behind us, loosing their arrows over our heads at the wall guards. Then our Foot-soldiers joined in the fray, and the battle raged at the gateways and along the walls. But the King had one thought in his heart."

"Two," I said. "Teti and Anat-neby of Neferusi. My brother thought him to be in Avaris with his sister."

Pen nodded. "As a streak of red lightning, with Thure and me the King tore through the defending ranks, a score of chariots guarding him, and entered the high-built house of Apophis through a gate in the outer wall: a gate that was open for us."

"Herath was thorough."

"And Herath was there! She was waiting for us at the top of wide steps in the first light of day, with Ben-arpath and four of her maidens."

"No guard?"

Pen shook his head. "The King leapt from his chariot and mounted the steps on winged feet, Sek-met at his heels. We followed him. The Hyksos Princess looked into his eyes as he stood before her. For a moment, they stayed still as statues. Then, in the Royal manner she welcomed him, and with grace welcomed us. Turning to Ben-arpath, she told him to stay the defense of the city, and to tell the people that their Princess held council with the Falcon of Thebes. With her hand on his arm, the King walked by her side into the Palace."

"And the Hyksos king? Apophis?"

"He had gone into hiding."

"And Anat-neby?"

"My Prince, she was waiting for us. It was a plan to trap the King."

"But Herath?"

"She went along with it . . . in her own way. My Prince, she is a subtle and courageous woman."

"And the traitress?"

"She had a feast for us, with wine and a table of such foods that our back teeth cringed, and music and dancing girls, fair-skinned, from Retenu. She was in the rich and shining dress of the Hyksos, and the ivory skin of her was sweet with scented oils, and on each of her toes was a golden bell. Flowers, both fresh and jeweled, were laced in her hair, long and straight and black as ebony, fragrant as night-flowers. We, each one of us, held our breath and prayed to Ra. We thought the King was lost. He stood, Sek-met beside him, gazing into the dark-flashing, long-lashed eyes of his first love. He seemed not to breathe, so still he was . . ."

"He would have made her Queen, though her blood was not Royal."

"She moved a step closer, her slim hips swaying, and when she saw how still the King was, and how gently he gazed on her, in her pride she thought it a man's weak flaw, and a gleam of triumph brightened her eyes. It was that evil flicker . . . the arrogance, the assumption of power in her, that released the King. I saw him let out his breath slowly. Then he smiled, and still looking at her with gentle gaze, his voice clear and quiet, he said, 'Take her away. Stab her through her traitor's heart. But give her the ritual burial of her own Land, that she may come to the Place of the Scales, to be weighed in the balance and answer to Osiris.' "

Pen was letting the horses walk as he talked, and the others were out of sight on the other side of a long sand-ridge. After a while, I asked, "And the King?"

"He went to the Hyksos Princess. She was alone with her maidens. She did not rise, nor bow to him, and her eyes, gray as the gray heron's plumes, were wide with question as she looked at the King and asked, 'What of my step-mother?'

"The King looked down on her in silence. Then he spoke the Words of Judgment. 'There was agreement between my Captains. She will answer to Osiris.'

" 'But she was Priestess of Set.'

" 'She will answer to Osiris,' the King said again, and Herath smiled. My Prince, her lips are red as the poppy. She rose from her cushions, looked at the King with straight glance and said, 'Her brother, Teti, thought she could with ease woo and seduce you.'

" 'And you, Princess?'

"Her bosom rose as she took a deep, happy breath, and with a long soft sigh, 'Kamose, Whadj-Kheper-Ra,' she said, and with her arms outstretched in adoration, she bowed the ritual bow. He took her hands and lifted her. They sat on the low couch together, and as her maidens ministered to our needs, and she herself poured wine for the King, she said, 'Refresh yourself, my Lord, for you cannot stay one day, not one hour, in Avaris.' As we ate with relish, and drank the sweet wine of the Delta, she told us where her father was hiding. 'He is at the Oasis of Bahria. . . . When Anat-neby had seduced you, he was to call you to Bahria to talk peace in the Two Lands.' She leaned toward the King. 'Lord Kamose, my father is false. He will kill you.' She was no longer a soft-fleshed, beautiful girl. Her round face was stern. Her words were clear and unembellished with flattery, as she told us the scope of the enemy's plans. 'Teti of Neferusi's main army, long-gathered and more than twelve thousand men strong, is encamped in the Eastern Desert, five miles to the north of Abydos. When you attack that city, the main forces from the camp will come in behind you.' She shrugged her smooth shoulders. Then she told us, 'Hur is in full command when Teti is absent, even over the seasoned Hyksos captains. He has led armies before and is both clever and cunning. My Lord, he has made of this camp a desert fort. The fence around it is impregnable! It is of tall shields and taller spears, razor-sharp. . . .' She poured more wine. The King asked no questions, but listened to her words as he ate and drank, sparsely. 'Teti of Neferusi has this day left my father at the Oasis of Bahria to wait for you, and to kill you, while Teti himself rides south with one chariot company to meet an army of five thousand men who escaped from Assiut, Kus and Neferusi, to swell the camp forces. . . .' "

"Sen-ut's message confirms that news. The Princess spoke truth."

Pen smiled. "And while she spoke words of dire import,

her bracelets jingled and made sweet sound." I smiled with him. Pen always saw the beauty of women. But Res was his heart's love. "This camped army is a menace," he was saying. "They are the long-trained, seasoned Hyksos, those who escaped from the cities we recaptured, and foreign mercenaries, and my Prince, Herath told us that they are armed with battering rams, long poles with torched ends and a new kind of wall-scaling ladder. 'My Lord Kamose,' she said, 'you must leave forthwith and put to rout this great force at Abydos. My father and Teti of Neferusi have but one thought: to raze Thebes.' Thebes! We all grew rigid with shock. The King did not speak. He neither ate nor drank more, and his face was drained of blood, cold and pale as the marble of the South Land. 'My father has a plan in his heart for the Ruler of Nubia to attack Thebes from the south, while Teti and the Hyksos armies attack from the north . . . after they have routed at Abydos whatever forces of the South Land may still be fighting . . . while you, my Lord Kamose, languid from the embraces of my step-mother, go as a mouse into a trap, to the Oasis of Bahria to talk peace with my father.' She laughed. 'I have heard since childhood the lusty tales of the Falcon Prince . . . of virgins in carrying-chairs . . .' We would have laughed, too, but the thought of Thebes attacked was new and terrible, and with it, my Prince, the King loosed Avaris. We were all watching him. He stood up.

" 'By my Soul and my Shadow,' he said. 'Lady, I take my leave of you. Stay here till I send for you. It will be within the hour. Your safety is more precious to me than fine gold.'

"Herath did not move. Unsmiling and grave, she watched us leave. My Prince, though she is soft, there is purpose and strength in her."

"Where is Herath now?"

"The King sent her, accompanied by ten of my Chariot Captains, to Ahmose-Eb, with the command that she be guarded night and day till the battle for Abydos is joined and won and we sail upriver, triumphant, to Thebes. . . . She is in her own Royal Yacht," he said, and there was a sound of relief, almost content, in his voice. "Ben-arpath and her four maidens are with her."

"And our Fleet will guard her well," I said. He used the long whip lightly, and soon we came up with Kamose and the escort.

The night was cool, and only the sound of the chariot wheels, like a lathe smooth-worked, and the steady thud of the horses' feet broke the vast silence around us. There were a few distant lights from the villages on the banks of the River, and sometimes the screech of a night-owl, far-carried and loud on the thin air, rose above the chariot sounds, or a faraway voice, lone on the water.

By dawn, we were farther south of Minieh than we had hoped to be. Kamose called a halt behind a huge ridge of sand, and as Ra in his Atet Boat rose in the east, he performed the Dawn Rite.

"Ra had a hard fight with the monster Apopi this dawn," Hor-min said, for the rising sun shed no beams of early light, but hung heavy, and the desert was still, palled with a weight of quiet. It seemed that no beast, no crawling thing, lived; only sand, huge, great dunes of sand, and our own small company, in the vast yellow-brown darkness.

Thure spoke, for the first time since he had read Sen-ut's message.

"The sand-storm," he murmured, as though he had augured it.

And almost with his words there rose the shrieking of a great wind. Without warning, huge clouds of sand whirled up from the dunes to the sky, darkened the day and the sun turned black. The horses turned their backs to the raging wind that grew by the moment stronger and colder, roaring against us with a fierce, wild beating. Sek-met buried her face in her front legs and curled herself into a ball. We wrapped woolen blankets around us and over our heads, and stretched out face downward. All the huge wind could carry was swept up into its embrace. Driving grains of sand cut our hands and our faces, gritted our lips, filled our closed eyes and coated our throats. Then, as suddenly as it had arisen, the wind died.

When we sat up and looked at each other, we were all yellow men. We watered the horses, then cleansed ourselves in the still leaden, sand-laden light. We had not lost our chariots. The charioteers had crouched down inside them. When all was checked and we were settling down to sleep in the shadow of the ridge, which was higher now, and of quite different shape, the Captain of the Guard called out,

"Isti! Hai! Look!"

And coming over the top of a new ridge, from the north, we saw a man on a donkey. We all stood up, and Pen said,

"He wears Hyksos dress."

Thure ran toward the stranger, followed by two men of the Guard, to halt him. He tried to escape, jumping off the donkey and pulling it back up the steep slope, but Thure easily caught him and, searching him, found the message he carried. He brought the small papyrus roll to Kamose.

"Let us see what Ra has put into our hands," my brother said, and read aloud that we all might hear.

"Okenen-Ra Apophis, Son of the Sun-God . . ." Kamose's eyes flashed.

"Son of a pig!" The words burst from Thure's mouth.

With tightened lips Kamose read on.

" '. . . greets his son, the Ruler of Nubia. Do you see what this petty king, Egypt, has done to me?' " Kamose's left eyebrow was raised. "At least he calls me Egypt." He read on. " 'This Egypt is attacking my cities. My land and Nubia he will lay to waste. Come, journey downriver. Behold! He will be here till you arrive. Your hosts will attack Thebes from the south. Then we shall divide the towns of this Egypt and enjoy prosperity.' " Kamose looked up. "Herath told us the very truth." He rolled up the papyrus. "By Ra's Grace, the Ruler of Nubia will receive no orders to attack Thebes from the south. One menace is removed! As for this trembling messenger, give him provisions and water. Feed his donkey and send him on his way back to Apophis." He looked at the scroll in his hand, then at us. "In this vast desert place, our own small Company, at this moment, come upon this lone and secret messenger . . ."

"By Maat's Truth!" Pen said. "The gods are with us."

We rested until the evening, and at sun-set we had broken camp and were ready to journey again with the darkness.

"Praise be to Ra," Kamose said again, "no message will go to the Ruler of Nubia." Then his face was grim. "May Ra's Grace fall on this night's essay . . ." And I heard him murmur under his breath, "Hat-hor, keep Sen-ut in your care." Then he called Hir-ty to him. "Go in haste to Per-neb and our Army. They should be a day's march behind us. Listen, Hir-ty! They will march forthwith, hiding by day-light, to Abydos. The Lord Per-neb himself will meet with me four days hence, in the secret ravine one day's march from Abydos. . . . Hor-min has two maps. Give one to Per-neb. Then ride with all speed to Ahmose-Eb and the Royal Fleet. He and the Lord Mer-neb will come by River to the secret ravine. Four days hence I hold council of war." He looked around at us all. "I know not where Aknere is, but it is vital that he know my plans for the Hyksos camp." He turned again to Hir-ty. "He and his Young Eyes and Ears must prepare an escape for the Sitters on Horses, to the southeast of the camp. Find him, Hir-ty, or one of his followers, within these next four days! I would meet with him in the secret ravine." He put his hand on the young messenger's shoulder. "It is vital," he said again.

"My King." Hir-ty knelt for Kamose's blessing. Then he leapt on his horse and was away in the twi-light.

Kamose turned to me. "Brother, this night, when we come close to where this Set-pig is camped, you will sit on Minirt, go swiftly ahead of us, find where he is. I would have no sound of chariot wheels. For Sen-ut's sake, we must be stealthy as desert foxes."

After four hours of swift travel, Kamose rested the horses, and at the dark of the moon I mounted Minirt.

We rode as though winged over the silver-white sand, till

he tired and I slid off his back and walked him, holding his bridle. The silence throbbed with the sound of our walking. Each step made strange music. In the pure air Minirt smelled sweet and pungent. I halted him and we stood together, scarce breathing and at one with the solemn, sleeping soul of the desert. It seemed to me that the tearing, roaring-wild chaos of the sand-storm had been gathered again to its place in the Whole, into the still heart of the One, the Nameless One, who created Heaven and Earth, and the Underworld and all that therein is. My own spirit yearned to be wide and quiet as the desert, yet to be tiny as one speck of gypsum on its vast surface. For an unmeasurable moment, standing there with Minirt, I knew the everlasting, shining solidness; the joyous peace of God; stable as his Creation, simple as Spirit. All One! Storm and war, murder and greed, love and sacrifice, all the heart's deep yearning, all One in the God who is One.

As the touch of a bird's wing, the moment was gone. Slowly I took hold of Minirt's black-dyed mane and swung myself onto his back. I sat athwart him, my bare legs feeling his smooth warmth, and his heart-beat. Then my knees tightened. Each hair in my nape hackled, chill. Minirt tensed, trembling, as a harsh clatter, a loud rattling noise, ripped through the clear desert air. I looked around me. I saw only the silver-white dunes. Though it had ceased, the sound rang in my ears. What was it? Chariot wheels! It was the sound of chariot wheels on the stones of a wharf. A wharf? Am I so near to the River? Sounds from afar are close in the desert. Teti of Neferusi's camp must be yet an hour away!

"Let us hasten, Minirt."

Riding swifter than I had known, it seemed but a thought's span when we turned toward the River, and coming up over a high sand-hill, I saw in the bright moon-light three square tents nestling in a wind-funnel at the base of the long, steep slope. I slid from Minirt's back and, commanding him to stay, quiet as a fox, each light step slipping in the sand, I came to the back of the middle tent. It was made of fine leather and richly embossed. Teti of Neferusi was ever rich and greedy, I thought, and a wave of sheer violence held me breathless. With my hand on my dagger, I crept around the side of the tent, to the wide opening, then flattened myself on my stomach. The tent was deserted. I listened for a while. No sound came from the two smaller tents. I got up slowly, and held on to the turned-back flap. In the light of a small oil-lamp on a tall stand at the entrance I saw the inside of the large tent. It was royally appointed, and on a table to the left were the remains of a rich feast: a gazelle haunch, water-fowl, leeks and gourds had been served on flat dishes of silver and gold. There were golden wine-cups, and a heavy wide bulging wine jug encrusted with jewels that gleamed in the lamp-light. On the right, I could see the outline of a curtained sleeping couch. I picked up the lamp and slowly crept toward it. I could see the fine needle-work, in patterns of flowers and birds. Slowly I drew back the embroidered linen and held up the lamp. "Osiris, Lord . . ." I covered my eyes with my hand. "Osiris, Lord . . . Hat-hor . . ." I opened my eyes.

Sen-ut lay in her short linen kilt. The head cushion and the cover were stained with her blood. There was a dagger deep in her throat, and her hands—Sen-ut's hands! I stared in cold horror at the slender, blood-caked stumps of her wrists, crossed upon her bloodied breasts. "Her hands! Sen-ut's hands!" Mad with a sick rage, I searched, and holding the lamp high, I came to the table.

On a golden platter carved with the Black Boar of Set were Sen-ut's hands.

"I will kill him." I heard my own words in the stillness. I gazed long at the severed beauty of them, gently crossed as she would hold them on her lap. My blood ran cold. A rage I had not known even when my father was murdered held me there, staring at the desecrated, lifeless perfection of Sen-ut's hands; a rage that harrowed my soul. "Teti of Neferusi is mine to kill."

A stealthy sound brought me back to myself. I turned

swiftly. Two desert hyenas, smelling the blood and the food, had come foraging. I strode toward them, the lamp in my hand. They slunk away into the darkness.

I went back to the couch and gazed long on the bright boyish beauty that was Sen-ut. Then I knelt beside her, in homage and deep loving.

After a while, I took the lamp and climbed up the ridge. I left it there to lead Kamose's Company to the place, and, leading Minirt, I came down again. In the star-lit darkness I went into the tent, and, kneeling on the ground beside Sen-ut, I kept watch over her till I heard the sound of our chariots.

Slowly I rose and went out of the tent. Dark figures were coming down the slope, slipping and sliding in their haste. Hor-min came last, the lamp in his hand. They stood still in front of me.

"He has fled. Teti of Neferusi is aboard a ship."

My brother was beyond rage. His face was a carven mask in the moon-light.

"A ship?" Pen shook his head.

"I heard the sound of his chariots on the stones of a wharf."

Thure was staring at me. A whisper broke from his throat, without sound. "Sen-ut?" He put out his hand and gripped my shoulder. "Sen-ut!" The loud cry sprang from the core of his being.

I stood aside, looking toward the big tent. Thure tore across the sand.

Kamose was looking at me. His eyes held the question and answer both.

"He cut off her hands," I said.

CHAPTER VII

My brother's face was set in a graven rage. Our spirits had gloomed. We had all scarce spoken on the four-day march. Now, in the deep-cleft, hidden ravine, one day from Abydos, we waited, unquiet, for Ak-hor and Aknere.

All save Hor-min and I were asleep. In the everlasting cold of the sun-less abyss, the small cooking-stove gave scant warmth. I looked at Hor-min, quietly scribing in the fitful light of a small oil-and-salt saucer-lamp. His face was grave and absorbed. Was he writing of Sen-ut, as I had been thinking of her during the long, silent march? And thinking, with a cold inside me deeper than the eternal chill of this benighted cave, of Teti of Neferusi. Twice foul purveyor of stealthy slaughter! Who—what thing—had betrayed Sen-ut's secret to him? Was her messenger a renegade Egyptian in the pay of the Hyksos? He had left the small oasis without food, and in haste. "He looked and spoke as an Egyptian," Pen had answered to my query. "He told us with precision the place where Sen-ut was. . . . The King commended him for his zeal."

I looked at Pen now, his long, lean body curled up like a child, his cheek in his hand. How Pen sleeps! Mer-neb was restless beside him. He lay on his stomach, twisting and turning, while Per-neb, his arms flung wide and his feet crossed, was lying flat out on his back. Ahmose-Eb slept sitting up, his back against the hard rock. It was the first time I had seen him since before Memphis. I looked at his square face, as calm in waking as in sleep, and I thought with surprise of his kitchen-ship love. Then words my father had spoken came back to me. "Even in wine," he once said, "Ahmose-Eb is too solemn for his years. He does not go a-whoring in the villages with Kamose and his Company, nor do I see him cast glances at the maidens of our Household, but on a day —by Hat-Hor!—our young Sailor will give his whole heart." With a sigh, I thought of thin Sittek, of her huge appetite and the small avaricious eyes of her father. He would loathe indeed to lose Ahmose-Eb's large estates in El-Kab. I looked up, almost startled! A thin streak of Ra's noon-day Light had pierced a tiny crack in the deep-hacked ridges of rock too high for the eye to see. It streaked down, pale, almost white, touching Kamose's dark, war-grown curls and the soft under-belly of the lioness where he rested his head. Kamose, Whadj-Kheper-Ra! I had marveled at his austere command of himself, that had dealt with necessity on the instant, in spite of horror and grief.

He had turned his stricken gaze from the tent where Sen-ut lay murdered, and straightway called for the Captain of the Guard. Speaking through tight, gall-bitter lips, he had ordered a kitchen-cart to be cleansed and prepared, and commanded the Captain himself to go with all speed to the Royal Fleet. "The Lord Ahmose-Eb will prepare a Funeral Barge for the

Lady Sen-ut, and assign four prime ships to guard her coffin on its journey to Thebes. Remind the Lord Ahmose-Eb and the Lord Mer-neb that they meet with me in council four days hence. Go with Ra."

The Captain of the Guard had bowed, and was away in the darkness. Then Kamose had turned again toward the tent. "Thure shall escort his love to the Fleet, and sail with her to Thebes."

"Brother, he fights at your left hand."

"He is verily my second shield arm." He lifted his head. With dry eyes, more tragic than if he had wept, he said, "Thure shall sail with Sen-ut's Funeral Barge to Thebes . . . and, Little Brother, in this dire moment the thought of our mother is as close to me as she is close to the God. She is High Priestess, and she shall have her part, and her joy, in restoring Osiris to his Place."

Again, I had been lost in amaze that he would send for our mother before the battle, against such great odds, had been won. I was thinking of those odds when Hor-min's voice broke into my thoughts.

"The Queen-Mother Ah-hotpe, and Thure, should now be but one day's sail from Abydos," he said, and as I turned to him, I saw that his black eyes were full of tears. Then I knew he had been writing of Sen-ut, and for a moment the space between us was filled with her: spicing mullet-roes for Kamose, and dancing with Tetaky on the deck of *The Falcon;* singing a merry love song with Thure as they ran hand in hand through the new black mud to the River, and a lullaby, her voice soft and warm, to Thure wounded. Thure! I leaned back against the rock remembering how he had stayed, from dark to light, and from light to dusk again, with his murdered, mutilated love, and tended her. With a linen napkin dipped in the half-full jug of wine he had laved the still soft-caked blood from her wrists, joined Sen-ut's small, God-gifted hands each to its place again and bound them with linen strips. Then he clasped his gift bracelets over the bandages. He had carried her in his arms to the cleansed and shriven kitchen cart, and laid her on the reed matting. She lay there as though she were sleeping, her lotus-hands clasped beneath her small pointed breasts.

As Ra in his Sek-tet Boat descended to the west, leaving a red-gold, green-gold sky, Kamose, High Priest and King, stood at Sen-ut's head and spoke the Ritual words. Then he turned to Thure, and his eyes were the Feathers of Maat.

"Sen-ut will be with you, if your rage and grief do not shut her out, in your sleeping," he said. "Your waking hours belong to me, Warrior on my left hand, and to Ta-mery. Thure, grief will not sweeten your bitter heart." His gaze softened. "You will guard your heart's love on her journey to our Fleet. Tomorrow you will sail to Thebes with Sen-ut's Funeral Barge, and return with the Queen Ah-hotpe to Abydos." Thure's brows creased into a frown over his empty eyes as he listened. "You and my mother will sail to the Holy City with Hori in *The Southern*. You will lead two of the captured treasure-ships, refurbished and battle-ready to swell our Fleet. My mother shall name them *The Offering* and *Shining in Memphis*, and they must be fully armed and manned, for we know not what the battle for Abydos may bring."

"And in this battle for Abydos, my King"—Thure's voice held no life, but was bleak as his eyes—"who will fight at your left hand?"

"Sek-met will guard my shield arm in this fight," Kamose said, and a shiver had cold-cringed my spine at the words. My brother stood for a long moment gazing at his friend with clear, cool eyes. Then he turned away, and called for a lighted torch. "Not one shred of this evil habitation shall remain to sully the clear calm of the desert air."

A guardsman came with the torch. Kamose handed the long, flaming reeds to Thure. We followed him across the sand and stood silent, watching as he put the first fire to the brazen opulence of the murderer's tents. Then he handed the torch to me.

"Henceforth, I am a prisoner of time," he said, and turning to Kamose he bowed, walked three steps backward, turned again, and went to his chariot.

We burned the three tents and all the things inside them, and Kamose ordered the men of our Guard to scatter the ashes to the desert winds.

"Here evil has flourished," he said. "This is a black fire, and the fiends of darkness rise in the smoke of it."

As we walked away from the stinking smolder, I said, "Our friend has drawn tight the strings of his heart."

"Thure is a man who would release his Ka with his own hand, and will not." Kamose spoke through stiff, scarce-moving lips. "Such men are bravest in battle, and guarded of the gods."

I was thinking of Thure's thin straight back as he walked to his chariot, his dull eyes and his words as he handed the torch to me: "Henceforth, I am a prisoner of time." I thought of Rai, and my own moment when, holding her Ka-less body, time was not, and I was one with the sweet solid soul of her. For a swift moment, sitting against the cold rock, I saw how Heaven is here and now for those who, as Rai, live on this earth ever shifted a little toward Heaven. Then Minirt brought me back to myself. He and Soker-uff were stabled in the back of the ravine. He snorted into his feeding-bag. It was not a loud snort, but it wakened Ahmose-Eb, always wary. He saw I was awake and edged closer to me. "My Prince," he whispered, "since before Memphis I have not spoken of my love. Only you are aware of Atu."

"My Friend, where is Atu?"

Ahmose-Eb blinked. Then, looking at me with a rare glint of humor, he said, "The Princess Herath has now five ladies in waiting," and I laughed out loud.

Kamose sat up, awake on the instant. Sek-met stretched and gave a deep hollow growl. "Akh! Ra-en-Ra! You have not eaten this day." He put his arm about her neck. "Neme has food for you."

"And for us all, I hope," Ahmose-Eb said.

"You and Sek-met are voracious." Kamose smiled. "And there is food prepared, I smell it. But eat lightly, and drink only one cup of wine. This night's work needs clear heads and flat bellies, and," he added, and his brow was dark, "none knows his lot when he plans for the morrow." I turned to him swiftly, but he did not meet my eyes. "Isti! Sek-met! Behold, food!" With a bound she was at Neme's hand, her tail lashing. Kamose turned to the sleeping twins. "Zatoo! So! You two!" They wakened. "Look to the water, and the wine." He leaned back, then forward again, listening. We stiffened, silent. The slight sound was now soft, even footsteps. "Ak-hor! Hail, and thrice welcome!"

"My King."

"Sit down, and while we wait for Aknere—for come he must!—tell me of my Memphian Army."

"Your hosts are fully trained and battle ready. They have been at the appointed place these last three days."

"And the Hyksos camp?"

"Strongly entrenched, my King. Hur the Cruel One is now captain of all the Hyksos forces outside Avaris. He is cold and deceitful of heart, and he has a remorseless strength. He has built up a fence around this camp that is strong as a rampart."

"Herath was well informed. Her words to me were the Truth of Maat," Kamose said, and he brooded while Neme served us food where we sat. Pen wakened. We all ate little and drank less. After a while, his voice low in the silence, his eyes dark and watchful in the torch and lamp-light, my brother said, "It is my wish that not one arrow be loosed, nor one more drop of blood spilled within the walls of Abydos." He drank his wine and put the cup down beside him on the gritty sand. "I will not besiege the Sacred City, nor the Temple of Osiris." He was weighing each word. "The people are loyal to us."

"Children of fifteen have seen their fathers massacred," Ahmose-Eb said, and Ak-hor nodded.

"They are cowed, but not craven," he said. "At a given moment they will turn on their oppressors."

Kamose turned swiftly. "By the Breaker of Bones! Aknere!"

Without sound of step, keeping by habit even out of the thin ray of light, the Chief of our Young Eyes and Ears was among us.

"Ra-en-Ra!" I murmured. Aknere had grown a beard! It was greasy, and his hair fell in ringlets. We all stared at him. Kamose shook his head. Then he gave a soft laugh.

"Sit down. Do not constrain your tongue. Aknere, the escaping place for the Sitters on Horses? It is accomplished? The Neferusian, where is he? What is the extent and measure of Hur's preparedness in the camp?"

"My King, Hur has the enemy well prepared. He is depending on the hosts camped in the desert to hold Abydos, put an end to our campaign and wholly rout us."

"By Ra's Grace that army will not exist after this night's work."

My brother looked ageless as he spoke.

"As for Teti of Neferusi," Aknere was saying, "he does not fight, he plans, and Res will know of his plans . . . and his whereabouts."

"Res?" Pen's face drained of blood. "Res!"

"She will not go near to him, Pen, have no fear. She asked for this mission. I, myself," he turned to Kamose, "have been, these last three days, inside the enemy camp. My King, they are well more than twelve thousand strong." He gave a small smile. "And not unharassed in these last days. My young men, dressed as Hyksos soldiers, have dug under the fence at the south-east of the camp, and emerging at dawn-light, unnoticed among all the others, they have loosened the hub-pins of their chariot wheels and slit the harness leathers half-way through. . . . My King, thirty of them will remain. They will be ready to pull up the loosened fence for the escape of the Sitters on Horses."

Under his hairiness, I thought, he looked older and thinner.

"But, Your Majesty, the ambush must be tonight! At dawn tomorrow, the Hyksos army will march to man the ramparts at Abydos, and to defend the city."

"And what of Hur? Is he already in Abydos?"

"I do not know."

"How did Hir-ty find you?"

"He did not. He sought, and found one of my Eyes and Ears in a village tavern."

"By Ra's Grace." Kamose's breath came out in a quiet sigh. "I no longer have the escape of the Sitters in my thoughts." Without raising his head, he said, "My whole force, all my hosts: my Charioteers, Archers and Foot-soldiers—and Shock-troops"—he paused, and looked up at Ahmose-Eb—"all except your Sailor-soldiers I shall use in this night's foray. But have your men at the ready, my Sailor-man! We may need you, too!"

"My King."

Kamose turned to Ak-hor. "The Sitters on Horses? They know their place, their ploy—the peril they face?"

"They are eager, my King."

"Will We-het lead them?" I asked.

"He will—and he sends you greeting, my Prince. Though he did not speak the words, it is his desire that you yourself see this night's work."

"And work it will be." Kamose raised his eyes. His gaze pierced my own as a spear. Speaking slowly he said, "Five Companies of your Sitters, Brother, on those horses best trained to the leaping." My heart stopped. My thought stretched back to Minirt's first fence-leaping in the park of the King's House. Out of that wild splendor of horse strength had come this night's dread essay. My blood ran cold, chilling my spine. "Ahmose," my brother said, his eyes full gazing into mine, "your Sitters on Horses have ever meant victory. Tonight men and horses both will earn the Gold of Valor."

We were quiet, solemn. Sek-met, her hunger appeased, came back to Kamose, yawned and stretched out. Each man's face bespoke his own knowledge of the battle to be fought this night. Then a bright young voice broke the silence.

"Hiya!"

"Res!" Pen leapt to his feet.

Kamose rose. We all stood with him. "Res, sit down . . . sit with Pen. Share our battle-fare and a cup of wine, and—Ra-en-Ra!—tell us what you have gleaned."

"Abydos is but lightly guarded till dawn tomorrow, when Hur and his armies will enter the city."

"By the Grace of Ra that will not come to pass," Kamose murmured.

"The people are cowed. They hide in their houses."

"Hide, or are imprisoned?" Mer-neb asked.

"Both, Mer-neb. Those able men not slain for their loyalty to Thebes are herded together, locked up and guarded."

There was a silence. Then I asked, "And Teti of Neferusi? Is he in Abydos?"

She shook her head. "The Neferusian murderer is on his way upriver to Thebes."

"By ship!" I said. "I heard the sound of his chariot wheels on the stones of a wharf."

Res nodded. "By ship and by land he is both cunning and careful. His army of Hyksos who escaped from Kus, Assiut and Neferusi await him to the south-east of Thebes, in the desert."

"Where it is easy to hide," Ahmose-Eb said, and Res smiled a little.

"He plans to await the outcome of Abydos, then join with Hur's victorious forces and attack Thebes."

"Akh! Ra-en-Ra! They plan to attack from the south while Apophis rebuilds and rearms Avaris," Mer-neb said.

"So be it—Avaris will be once more a fort when we return." Kamose turned to me. "Little Brother, it seems that I must put to rout the Neferusian murderer's army to the south of Thebes before I lay siege to Avaris." His gaze held us all. "After the victory of Abydos, I shall sail in triumph to Thebes. Our people need this rejoicing. For three days they will hold festival—but not my armies. On the third day of the feasting, I shall lead my hosts to attack the Nefer-usian's army." His eyes narrowed with thought. "Aknere, after your work in Abydos this night, you and your secret cohorts will discover the hiding-place of this sly and foul Neferusian and his Hyksos army, and report to me in Thebes on the second day of the festival." He threw back his head. "Zatoo! So! Teti of Neferusi awaits the outcome of the battle for Abydos?" He turned to face me again. Our eyes held. "Our mother will share in the Restoration of Osiris to his Place in his Holy Temple, in his Holy City," he said, and every doubt in me was dissolved in the intimate fire of his gaze. He swung around on his haunches. "But first this night's battle! Ak-hor! The sentries? The camp guards? Your Nubians have their orders?

"One hour before mid-night there will be no sentries to impede your plans, my Lord."

"Per-neb?"

"My army is already crossing behind the reach in the River, and will be at the appointed place to the south-west of the camp in the Eastern Desert."

"We must attack from the north and the south. May Amun-Ra grant that we well and truly rout this enemy host," Kamose said, "for on this night's battle rests the fate of Abydos, Thebes and the Two Lands." He looked across at Minirt and Soker-uff, whose noses were buried in reed baskets full of grain, and his face seemed to draw itself together as though it were carved in stone.

Ahmose-Eb leaned forward. "My King, this crossing at the darkness . . ." His voice was grave and held doubting. ". . . this crossing of the River to raze a camp of so vast a size, so long entrenched and fortified, to lose—perchance more than half of our forces? And the Sitters on Horses, my Lord . . . some of them will be impaled. They will be dis-covered—"

"Impaled"—Kamose's eyes closed for a moment—"but not discovered. We-het has orders that the men slip off the horses' backs and disappear into the darkness, finding their way as best they can. Our Foot-soldiers will remove the wounded horses before the camp can gather itself."

I felt the cold sweat around my temples.

"My King"—Ahmose-Eb's face was flushed red as a poppy —"I cannot but ask this question: Is it prudent?"

"My Sailor-man, let us keep ourselves cleansed of prudence! Let us allow no doubts to bridle us this night. And now, my Friend, tell me of your precious charge, the Hyksos Princess."

"She is well beloved, my King, and grows each day in beauty. Ben-arpath and her maidens are with her. She is cherished, my Lord." Ahmose-Eb looked at me with a faint smile. "And my King, she has another maiden in her train— one Atu—"

"So that Herath is well cared for, she may have a hundred maidens in her train," Kamose said, and looked at Aknere, who had fallen asleep after his meal. "Waken, my brave spy," he said. "I have orders for you, and for Res." Aknere sat up and yawned. Res leaned forward out of the shelter of Pen's arm.

"How many Eyes and Ears are in Abydos?" Kamose asked.

Res answered, "Nine girls beside myself."

"And between forty and fifty of my young Eyes and Ears; also some of Pery-em-wah's oldest and most special men," Aknere added.

"That is good. Have you a meeting place?"

"The underground rooms in the Temple of Osiris. Only the Priests know of them . . . and of the arms and weapons in readiness."

"Aknere, Res, this night you will drug the wine and beer of the Hyksos guards. Free the imprisoned men and arm them. By the Grace of Osiris, by noon on the morrow, the men of Abydos will have freed their own city."

"My King, we have already talked and made plans with their leaders. They are alert and waiting."

Kamose rose to his feet, and we all stood up. He held out

his hand to Res. She bent her head for his blessing. He raised his hand, then put his arm about her shoulders and turned to Ahmose-Eb.

"You will see that Aknere and Res go by River and are put ashore, in secret, close to Abydos. You will leave two companies of your Sailor-soldiers to swell, if they are needed, the ranks of the men of Abydos."

"My King."

"And you will have barges at the ready to take our wounded from the camp, and our dead, to the Holy City. Those who recover will sail on to Thebes. Those who give up their lives on this earth for Ta-mery will have their Everlasting House in the city of Osiris, for they are the fishers, the farmers, the soldiers and artisans, the sailors, the scribes, the priests, joiners, carpenters, butchers and rope-makers—the men of Egypt." The words rolled from his tongue as a poem. He looked at us all in turn. "Hours pregnant with bloody slaughter, endurance and destiny confront us this night." He embraced us, each one. "To your commands. At the second hour of the darkness, in the Eastern Desert, we will meet and join—to the Glory of Amun-Ra and Ta-mery."

"Amun-Ra . . . Ta-mery." We spoke the beloved words, and Tetaky's mouth, round with his last breath—"Ta-mery!" —was in our hearts, and Sen-ut was closer than breathing. As we all raised our left hands to our brows in love and homage, I thought of Thure on his sad voyage.

Then Kamose lifted his hand in blessing. "Vela! Farewell —go with Ra." He turned to Aknere. "And by the Great Hare! Be shaven of those greasy ringlets and that beard before the triumph in Thebes." Aknere bowed. Kamose lifted him and embraced him again. "So that you bring the news that I desire, you may come to Thebes as you will," he said, and Aknere took three steps backward, bowed again and was gone as a shadow. In silence, the others followed him.

We stood watching them. The thin ray of sun-light, more

golden now, had left the ground and was halfway up the eastern wall of the cave.

"Ra descends," Hor-min said. "Your Majesty should sleep."

"And you, too, my young Scribe. You have work ahead of you this night." Kamose went to his place by the wall and sat down again. Sek-met, with almost a whimper of content, lay beside him and put her huge, strong paw on his bare thigh. I thought of the tearing strength of her front paws in battle; how gentle now. Then my brother said, "Take turns with Neme to watch. There are snakes and scorpions."

"I will take the first watch," I said. "May Isis refresh you with the wind of her wings."

He gave me a grave smile, lay down with Sek-met and was asleep.

Hor-min and I watched the desert creatures on the rocks above us. A kestrel hovered, beating its clumsy wings, tail down and body curved; a stealthy bird. It had no grace or strength in its wings, as the hawk. "The hawk! Horus . . ." I whispered, and looked down at my brother. Sek-met was asleep, too, though her golden-green eyes were half open. "Sek-met . . ." She was stretched out beside him. Her soft downy underbelly was the color of goat's cream. Her black-tufted tail lay limp on the gritty sand, and I thought how she could clout a man on the head and crush his skull like a goose-egg. Then I looked at Minirt, munching grain from the basket. He was almost as black as Soker-uff, standing quietly beside him. Again my flesh cringed. The cold sweat broke out all over my body. "Osiris, who makes to live the son of the worm . . . Lord Montu of the Horses . . ."

"You should sleep, my Prince." Hor-min's voice broke into my prayer.

I looked across at him. He smiled, and I felt my eyelids grow heavy. My Ka pulled away from me. I lay tense. All my doubts, fears, had returned.

"Watch for me, Hor-min," I said, and sank down on the hard, cold sand, my head on my arm. I tried to think of

Inhapi, of her warm-breathing, perfect body, but the thought of her took her away from me. The shadow of her in my heart was not enough. Each memory was a denial. I heard Minirt give a lazy snort, and shuddered. Chill dread still holding my heart, taut with dark-heralding thoughts, I fell into an uneasy sleep.

We seemed to be alone on the dark River. The deep, curved reach hid sight of us, and sound, from the watchers at the camp—if Ak-hor's Scouts have left any sentries to watch, I thought. The water was still and black except where the oars whipped it up. Not a light showed on our barges and rafts. Along the Western Shore a few torches shone, honey-gold in the darkness. Kamose stood silent in the prow of the barge, Sek-met at his heels, and holding Soker-uff's bridle, gentling him. I stood with Hor-min, holding Minirt by his head-strap.

"When I write out the King's plans," Hor-min whispered, "I can scarce believe them. They are wild, but they work."

"This plan is wildest of all," I answered, and thought of Ahmose-Eb and his prudence. We were silent. For almost an hour there was no sound at all but the steady dip of the oars. When we came to the quiet meeting place, we pushed in close through a reedy shallow alive with frogs, and waded ashore.

"No trumpets will blare, no drums resound, for this night's foray," Hor-min said close to my ear.

"And the croaking of these good South Land frogs will cover the sound of our horses' feet on the sand," I replied, as a Nubian Captain appeared out of the darkness leading a chariot with thick woolen padding on the wheels, and drawn by one horse. Kamose himself led Soker-uff to the chariot and harnessed him, then beckoned Hor-min to join him. I leapt up on Minirt, and in the night silence we kept a good pace till, after more than an hour, we heard Ak-hor's faint owl-call and, veering slightly to the south, we rode toward it. A mile or more beyond the line where the plowland ended, at the second hour of the darkness, we came upon our Army in full array.

Ak-hor and Mer-neb came toward us.

"My King," Ak-hor said quietly, bowing, "from the top of that rock you may see the outline of the camp fence. The torches around it are two Royal cubits apart." He was pointing to one of the high rocks that jutted out of the eastern sands to the right of us. Two scaling ladders were propped up against it. Quietly, Kamose and Ak-hor climbed up one ladder and Hor-min and I up the other. Mer-neb stayed on the ground. Our eyes were used to the darkness, and now the moon had risen. We came to the top and in the first pale beams we saw the vast camp. "Can you see, my King, to the south-east inside, the darker mass? That is a camp within a camp . . . Hur's head-quarters. He has a body-guard of twenty chariots, the cream of the Hyksos captains."

I heard his soft speech but my whole looking was held by the huge, high fence of shields and long-spears that girdled the camp. The shields were four man's arms'-lengths high, and the tall spear-points a length higher. They shone red, like devil's teeth in the light of the torches. The marrow in my bones turned cold with the horror. "My horses . . . Lord Montu . . . my Horses . . ."

"Never have we met so great a foe, nor one so well prepared." Kamose's whisper was clear in the desert air. "Let us hasten. The faintest sound is loud in this vast night space, and they are alert."

I was last to the ground. Mer-neb and Hor-min waited for me. I took Minirt's bridle and we followed Kamose and Ak-hor to where Pen was waiting. The woolen binds had been taken off the wheels of Kamose's chariot and another was waiting for Hor-min and me.

"All is as you planned, my King." Pen bowed.

"The Sitters on Horses?"

"We-het has your commands. They are hidden in the cleft with the Torch-lighters at the ready."

"Mer-neb, your Archers?"

"Deployed to our best advantage on the high ridge to the west of the camp. It is less than an arrow's flight from thence to the camp's center. One thousand are there; one thousand are outside the fence to cover the chariots and fight inside the camp."

"So be it. Let no arrow fly before the Sitters on Horses have escaped." Kamose turned to Ak-hor. "Per-neb's forces?"

"In array to the south-west of the camp. They await the escape of the Sitters to make their advance. Three Chariot Companies are with them."

"That is good. When the camp is aflame, we shall attack."

Standing with Hor-min, I saw that we were using the heavy Hyksos chariots we had captured at Kus. Kamose had mounted. The leathers were around his hips. The quivers on his chariot bulged with weapons. He turned slowly and stood for a long moment gazing at the assembled hosts.

How can ten thousand men be so silent? I thought as Hor-min and I mounted our own chariot. I looked at Kamose, Sek-met a lion-shadow beside him. Huge and tall he stood, dark in the moon-light, his Blue Helmet shining, the Royal Asp on his brow. Slowly he raised his arm, benign and powerful, to bless. In a silence deeper than the desert's quiet, ten thousand Egyptians prayed with their King.

Then slowly, with ease and quiet, we moved along the path the enemy had smoothed out for us. They had cleared a wide stretch of stones and piled them up at the sides.

"They did not suspect that the King would cross the River to attack their camp," Hor-min whispered, as we walked our horses beside Kamose.

"They do not know of our Memphian Army, Hor-min . . ."

"Ra be praised for the thousand and one vast ravines and wadis in the Eastern Desert," he said in my ear as we passed the high rock.

Then Kamose held up his hand. We halted. There was no sound, and my fear and foreboding were lost for a moment of wonder at the loyalty, the training, the patience and the will to win of the manhood of Egypt. As we waited, a slight figure sitting a horse came silent as a shadow out of the darkness.

"Hir-ty," Hor-min whispered.

Kamose bent his head to listen to the messenger. Then he straightened and leaned toward us.

"Good news! By Ra's Grace, the Cruel One, Hur, is still in the camp." He turned to the messenger. "Hir-ty, stay with the Prince Ahmose and Hor-min for this night's battle. I may need to send you for Ahmose-Eb and his Sailor-soldiers to swell our ranks. We shall see."

"My King." Hir-ty bowed from the waist, and Kamose said,

"Brother, you and Hor-min and our messenger to your place . . . atop the high ridge above the array of our Archers. Go with Ra."

As shadows we came to the high dune and, leaving the chariot and the horses with the Nubian guard who was waiting, we climbed to the top of the ridge. All was quiet as the tomb.

"Ak-hor's Scouts have done their work well," Hor-min whispered, and Hir-ty drew his breath in with a hiss.

"By the Breaker of Bones! Look at the size of this camp!"

But now I had plainer sight of the tall spears. There was no room for the horses to leap through the space between them. "Scarce one cubit apart," I said to myself. To my agonized gaze the points seemed to have a life of their own, darting red as reptiles' tongues in the torch-light, lusting for blood. The silence grew heavy. The lines of our Bowmen seemed as statues, dark and still in the moon-light.

"The moon is fast rising," Hir-ty whispered. "The Sitters on Horses? Where are they?"

"Ra-en-Ra!" Hor-min said close to my ear as a hollow thudding broke the silence.

It grew louder. Closer! Then suddenly, out of nowhere, two hundred flaming torches came, swift-rushing as a desert windstorm, toward the shield-and-spear fence.

"Spirits of Fire they are!" Hor-min's voice held new astound.

The thunder of hooves filled all the night.

"Or gods!" Hir-ty said. "I have not seen your Sitters on Horses before. . . . They are gods!"

"Lord Montu . . ." No breath came through my throat.

The unseen thunder became living men, living horses. I stood still and cold. They rode as one man. "Lord Montu . . ." The first Company leapt! "Osiris . . . Lord Montu!" A torch dropped. Horse screams set me trembling. Two torches had fallen. Another fell! Four, five, six! With each of my heart-beats they fell! Then four all together! And the rest were away. Only the fires lit by their torches marked their swift passage as the second flight rose, their torches a high curve of flame, blazing—and descended all! Without hurt! "Montu, Lord, by thy grace." The third flight rose. Nine horses stuck, their bellies ripped open, screaming terror as their riders slipped from their backs and were away in the darkness. Amid shrill horse-shrieking the fourth and fifth companies together, with a fierce ragged cheer, rose in a wide curve. Some fell on the others, pushing the dying horses deeper down on the spears. The whole camp was aflame. Tents, large and small, weapons-shops, arsenals and chariots stacked high; kitchen-carts, storage-tents and stables were lost in the licking roar of the flames. The gore-choked screams of animal pain filled my veins like cold worms. My whole body was shaking. I could hear my teeth clatter like the rattle of drums.

Hor-min came close. "My Prince, but a few of them failed."

I closed my eyes tight. With my whole will I kept my teeth clenched and took a deep breath through my nose. "I am Prince of the Two Lands . . . Amun-Ra . . . Osiris, Lord . . . Let not my calm be broken. . . ." I opened my eyes and saw our Foot-soldiers, a thousand of them, pulling up the shield-and-spear fence. A Company of them, with a swift sword-thrust, killed the horses still living and straightway buried them in the sand. Others were hurling the shields at a few of the enemy who had recovered from their amaze, and killing them with their own spears. In minutes they had cleared a wide place of entry and I heard—above the roaring of the flames, the shouts of the enemy and the cries of loose animals running, their manes afire—the voice of my brother.

"For Amun-Ra and Ta-mery . . . Ta-mery!"

And our chariots charged! Under the high curving cover of our Archers' arrows they hurtled into the flaming chaos of the camp.

The enemy was rapidly gathering. Archers were forming in array. Spear-men gathered in close companies behind their heavy shields. Horses loose and fleeing, sightless with terror, were caught, and chariots saved from the flames and harnessed. The Sitters on Horses had vanished as though they had never been. I saw broad, stocky barbarians whet their curved sickle-swords on four of Pen's Captains. Two Captains of Archers, just below where we stood, fell, taking arrows, one in his throat, and the other through his right eye. In the bright light of the risen moon I watched the enemy swarming like hornets in every part of the camp. Amid flurries of dust and sand and smoke from the flames, yelling war-cries and in a cross-fire of arrows from the archers of both sides, the battle was savagely joined.

Kamose's Blue Helmet was a beacon. Sek-met did not leave his shield arm. Through fire-smoke and sand-dust I saw the fame of his feats; his pride and his battle-fury. His ax swung in circles, bright in the flame-light. Ak-hor at his left and Pen at his right hand were smoting and killing those who would slay them. The hand-to-hand fighting was vicious and terrible. Men, hewing and tumbling, crashing together, fell in death-grapple, the savage ones winning, as Kamose, Ak-hor and Pen cut their way through the locust hordes of the Hyksos toward Hur's guarded camp.

Then I lost sight of them; and of the battle! For with the stamping of horses, the grinding of chariot wheels and the in-fighting rage of thousands of men, the dust and sand rose, met with the char-laden smoke of the fires and gathered into a fog, choking and whirling and blotting out, as the flames themselves died, all sight of the mutual slaughter.

"My Prince." Hir-ty was beside me. "By your leave I will ride around the camp to the south, and bring news."

"You have my leave," I said, and with a swift small bow he turned and ran down the wide slope at the back of the ridge.

I stood, staring at nothing. Ears took the place of eyes. Out of the thick dark cloud, as more and more of the enemy swarmed, louder and louder the drum-thudding of hooves and feet, the clatter of chariots, the grinding of wheels, the crack of woods snapping as the chariots crashed; the thick noise of carnage gathered like thunder; a holocaust of butchery and burning. Then the smell of blood rose on sand-dust and smoke, and the sick-sweet smell of warm death.

As rivers of blood dampened the sand, the fire-smoke rose high and was lost, and I could see again the thousands of men, laying waste to life all around them, slashing, felling, battering in savage man-slaughter. Horses wounded, balked, staggering and falling to the ground, rolled helpless while men fought over them, sliding and slipping. Then I saw one horse at the base of the ridge. He reared up, two stumps where his front legs had been, and my stomach heaved. The cold sweat was a tight band round my head. My groin quivered. My knees shook. I held myself upright, pressed my tongue to the roof of my mouth. My lips felt rough and thick. I turned away and, turning, gave the horror full power. My queasy flesh yielded. I flung myself down on the sand and covered my ears with my hands.

In the dark of the moon, before dawn, Hor-min came to me.

"My Prince." I gathered myself, rose to my knees and stood up. I was cold. My skin was stiff with dried sweat. I felt my face grow hot with shame. "My Prince." Hor-min's voice was gentle. "We cannot quarrel with our bowels," he said, and at his awareness, his love for me, fiery shame filled all my being. Slowly I walked up again to the crest of the ridge. There were no archers arrayed below us. With dry eyes as sere as my soul, I stared into the wide space of waning moon-light, pale stars and dark mountains. In the midst of the silence the camp beneath us was a black pit, seething with movement, stealthy and full of purpose. "My Prince." Hor-min had followed me. "It is almost first light."

"This strange half-silence . . ."

"Both sides are regathering to fight at dawn—Hir-ty has ridden with all speed to Ahmose-Eb and our Sailor-soldiers, and Aknere's thirty young Eyes and Ears have joined the King's ranks. We have need of every man and every arm. My Prince, we have lost more than five thousand of our Egyptian men."

"Hor-min! Osiris, Lord . . ."

"But the northern half of the camp is in our hands."

"And our wounded?"

"Gathered behind our lines, inside the camp—below us, down there!"

I looked down. The healing wagons were dark and square in the last of the moon-light and the guttering torch flames. Our Healer-Priests and novices seemed as beams of pale light in their long white robes. "Come, my Prince, it is the King's command." I nodded. Faint streaks of the false dawn lightened the eastern sky as I turned to follow him down the back slope of the ridge to our chariot.

The fore-dawn had gathered into darkness again, and a chill wind arose as we drove around the base of the dune and through the camp, skirting our wounded, then across the blood-dampened sand to the place where our shrunken forces were in quiet array.

"This time we cannot attack," Hor-min said. "We must wait and hold. Hur and his chariot force are fresh and have not yet drawn swords."

"Hor-min, the King?"

"He is the Great Hawk of Gold! All that he is is with him, my Prince. He uses but half the strength that is in him."

"What are his commands?"

"We are to watch from the rock . . . there, to the right of us." I followed his gaze and saw the up-thrust of tiered rock to the south-west, inside the camp fence.

"But first he will see us?"

"No, my Prince. The King rests. He has planned his tactic, and now he sleeps." I asked about Per-neb's force, and Ak-hor's Nubian Scouts. "They are all gathered around the King." We came to the rock. It seemed to rise out of a sand-mound. We drove up as far as we could, then stood in the chariot and looked down on the gray-dark battle scene.

Kamose had drawn up his remaining hosts in sickle shape, our chariots in the center. Foot-soldiers were deployed to the right and left of them, and Mer-neb's Archers were behind them and behind the Foot-soldiers. Our Shock-troops stood across from the enemy spear-men, shield to shield, in close array. I gazed on a set battlefield for the first time. The torches gave pale light. I could see Hur's stronghold and his chariot guard. The other Hyksos chariots were arrayed in front of them: three companies of fifty, all fresh and un-tried! The deadly Hyksos archers were behind and around, as were our own. Their spear-men and the foreign merce-naries at the ready seemed legion, and in the shifting light of the torches and the first gray hint of dawn, their army seemed vast and dark, crouching, I thought, like a huge toad that sits in the slime, tense and watchful, sure of the moment to spit out his poison. Our Egyptians seemed almost as if they loitered there, as though they had accepted Necessity, and were all One, imperiled, exhausted, but unshaken.

"Aknere's Thirty excel with the catapult." Hor-min broke into my thought. "Look, my Prince, there they are! On that rock." He nodded his head toward a buttress of huge piled boulders. "As slingers of the jagged stone they have no equal."

"This battlefield—look at that forest of spears—we are truly outnumbered."

"Ra's strength is not in the number of weapons, my Prince, but in the hands that wield them."

We were silent again, and as I gazed on our Theban ranks, my mother and father were close. I saw them in my heart as they stood together in the sun-set light. I could hear again my father's words, "The Darkness of Set has drawn too close to the Shrine of the God," and my mother saying, "This is an honorable field." Win or lose this day, for the men of Ta-mery, this is an honorable field. "And for me?" I asked myself. "For Ahmose, Prince of the Two Lands?" I grew hot again in the cold dawn. "Osiris, Lord, what charge is on my spirit this day? Osiris, mutilated, resurrected Lord, in this last fight for Abydos, this dread assault, how shall I fare? How shall I act?" As I stood there, it seemed that a new energy was born in me. I felt a fire, not shame in my heart, a coolness in my limbs. I had no certainty of my actions this day, I knew only that my spirit would not again grow so faint that my flesh would quease and cringe. On this day of peril we fight uncertain, except that we fight! "And Osiris, Lord . . . we are so few."

As though he echoed my thought, Hor-min said, "It is dawn. Let us pray that Ah-mose and our Sailor-soldiers will be here before Ra in his Atet Boat rises."

"His rising is shadowed. The day dawns with strange omen." I looked at the rock mass of the Eastern Mountains. Both pointed and blunt tops were shrouded in dawn clouds, gray and opaque instead of milk-white. Sheets of lightning shimmered green-pale and I heard the faint rumble of thunder. The men of Ta-mery, in array, seemed as an ancient scene, painted.

"Warriors of Amun-Ra," I murmured, and with my words Hor-min gave a gasp. The enemy had moved! Like the wind in a sand-storm, with a hoarse roar, the Hyksos hosts were upon us. Our ranks walked forward slowly, grudging every inch that they gave. Our Shock-troops, their shields a solid fence, moved slow as turtles. Lances and javelins glanced off them by the hundreds, but tens of them found their marks. Broad-swords clashed and clanged against broad-swords. Armor-plates ripped from their thongs fell, jangling on the shields of the dead. Yelling with tumult and strength, the thronging Hyksos aimed wild at both horses and men. But as well as our blankets, Kamose's Guards with long shields were each side of our chariot horses, so that the enemy must take careful mark at the moving targets of head and neck. Most of our horses were saved, and their wild spears and arrows felled their own. Suddenly a whole Hyksos chariot company was in chaos! Their wheels rolled away and their horses broke harness.

"Our Young Eyes and Ears! They cut the straps and loosened the wheels! They grounded a whole company!" Hor-min shouted. "Eureka!"

Amid the high shrilling animal terror and the cries of the wounded and dying, with howls of wild rage the Hyksos attacked us and struck, drew back, and surged forward again and again, plying swords and spears without pause. The air was a network of arrows, and Aknere's Thirty were cata-pulting jagged and deadly small rocks till the air was thick with them as hailstones. The grounded charioteers in their fury fought with daggers and maces, stabbing and swinging wild and screaming their rage like ravens, and for the first time I saw the full use of the battle-ax, and near parted from my Ka as a huge, big-boned Hyksos clove a thin Egyptian back clean in two and, raging and swinging his ax around and around like a wheel, went his way like a reaper through corn till a tall Egyptian hurled a short spear at his neck and he fell, retching gore from his mouth. Heads fell and rolled, backs were ax-slit, necks broken and eyes arrow-gauged. I saw limbs hanging loose and limbs lost, and the horses, plunging and thrashing in the blood-sodden sand, hostile to all in their terror.

The line of our Shock-troops grew shorter and shorter as men fell and their comrades closed ranks. Our Archers, their line broken up, had gathered in small groups back to back and our Spearmen formed circles. The Hyksos, all around us, fell to their onslaughts with wild yells of victory. Some of the mercenaries threw down their arms. Then, as the first Light of Ra pierced the clouds, with a sound to waken the blood, our trumpets blared! Our Standard-bearers raised high their emblems as, majestic and manifold, Kamose came! Our drums rolled, and with a long moan that growled in her throat, and grew, Sek-met let forth an earth-shaking roar.

Kamose took his place at the head of his small host, and two Hyksos chariots bore down on him. One of their captains swung at his Blue Crown with a mace. But he did not see Mer-neb's drawn bow and fell, an arrow between his eyes, as Kamose's spear slit the groin of the other. Ak-hor, beset by three chariots, pierced one Hyksos through the belly, split the skull of another with his mace and one of his Nubians caught the third with a short spear clean-flung to his nape. Pen, his chariot alongside Kamose, fought with the broad-sword and then with his javelins, till his quiver was empty and he fought with the broad-sword again. The alchemy of Kamose allowed no chill, but fiery trial and whole endeavor, and our hosts were braced. As Ra's Light lit up our standards and our shirts of mail, it seemed that he breathed his Life into our men, for each man there fought as a god.

Our Shock-troops advanced step by dogged step in tight formation behind their shields, dealing death and taking it. The Thirty filled the air with rocks and our Archers, fine-trained, again held close ranks and their arrows, whistling like the sound of young birds found, each one, its mark. No sword, nor spear, nor death could hurt the men of Ta-mery, but only dishonor in each other's eyes. Our remaining chariots gathered around their King. The Cobra Fire on his brow linked heart with heart and forged them, for this battle-fate, into one Being.

"O Lion-heart!" I was one with that Being. Kamose was slaying right and left the warriors who bore down on him as a wolf-pack, and wave after wave of the enemy chariots charged. Pen took a sword-thrust into his back. It came out through his chest. Then an arrow pierced him through the left cheek. Per-neb leapt up into his chariot, pulled him out of it and, with the help of two Foot-soldiers, carried Pen out of the fray, then leapt again into his chariot alongside Kamose, fighting with ax and mace till his shield arm was caught with a sickle-sword from the side and near severed off at the elbow. Shieldless he fought on, his arm hanging useless. Mer-neb left his Archers, fought his way to his twin, jumped up on his left side with his shield and together they fought as one man. Surge after surge of the attacking chariots was repulsed, while our ground troops fought steadily, stubbornly on. Pen's young charioteers fought as though waves of some impetuous, greater life swept over and through them, and yet they were slain. One by one, their blood running rivers down the sides of thier chariots, they were felled.

"Hur? Where is Hur?" Hor-min's voice was harsh and hoarse. "He waits for the kill, like a vulture."

His words fell as black stones on my heart. Ak-hor had taken a spear through his shield arm, high near the shoulder, but he still held. Sek-met was lunging and clawing, bashing heads in and tearing limbs and flesh with her teeth, the blood flowing from cuts in her back and the side of her neck. Kamose's ax swung rhythmic and sure as the River. Sweatless and cool, his eyes unblinking, he fought. Hurl after hurl of his straight-arm javelin-casts kept the enemy chariots at bay. Then he took a javelin himself, through the thigh, and Soker-uff, speared through his neck with an arrow, gave a great leap, saving Kamose from a long spear thrust as he fell back to balance himself.

Our Standards had fallen one by one. Our Spear-men were forming in smaller and smaller circles. All ranks fought to the death as, yelling brute strength, the Hyksos and their mercenaries clove, cutting and slicing with their axes and sickle-swords through the blood-drenched ranks of Egyptian men.

Then a great shout arose. The Hyksos ranks parted, making a clear path between them for Hur and his chariots.

I could see his cold face, white as the lime-stone cliffs.

Swiftly Kamose had broken off the head of the javelin and pulled it out. The blood streamed from his thigh as he turned and with a well-aimed edge-stroke parried a Hyksos captain and split his poll. Two others attacked him. With fullness of skill he slashed cross-wise with his broad-sword and, in one swing of his body, he slew both, then sheared off the helmeted head of a bearded mercenary who tried to jump onto his chariot as Hur, his long spear poised and his face reddened now with the fever of slaughter, tore through the parted ranks of his army, took aim and flung his spear. Kamose leapt aside. It grazed his ear. Hur flung a second spear. It went wide and glanced off the shield Mer-neb held guarding his twin. Then Hur's charioteer reined in his horses, while the Hyksos chariots pressed around and behind Kamose to carry him, Ak-hor and the Twins in a swift rush toward Hur, waiting with his twenty chariots, avid and lusting to glut their carrion souls on the Royal blood of Egypt.

I felt a blaze between my eyes. My heart seemed to burst in a great flood of light that was a word, one word!

"Ta-mery!" I jumped on Minirt.

"Ta-mery!" Hor-min gave a great shout and drove his chariot, smiting each side of him. As I tore across the sand-mud I saw him cutting his way to Kamose's side. I jumped off Minirt, slapped his rump and sent him back, picked up a battle-ax from the ground and clove my way through the struggling, staggering mass of men. I could see their eyes glittering to kill, their wet, red open mouths, but no weapon drew blood from me. In the trance of battle I felt no fear, nor feared hurt. A barbarian came at me, sickle-sword raised and death in his eyes. A jagged stone hit him. His eyes grew wide with surprise like a child's and he dropped, his brains and blood gushing from the hole in his head. Then I saw a chariot close, empty and harnessed, its horses unhurt, leapt up into it and cut my way through two chariots. They swerved and hurled themselves athwart me. I pitched over the side and fell on a Hyksos. My ax flew from my hand and we writhed together. I saw the flash of his dagger, fumbled for my own and would have been stabbed but an Egyptian Foot-soldier speared him through the leg and, when I jumped off him, stabbed him in the heart. I picked up the battle-ax, leapt up into the chariot again and looked for my brother. He and his Company were fighting like gods, our sparse ranks all around them. The men of Ta-mery, each chariot warrior and each man on foot, fought as three men to keep their King from being thrust, by sheer weight of numbers, toward the waiting Hur. Ak-hor, his shield arm hanging useless, thrust an attacker through the gut with his broadsword. The blood was pouring from his arm and from wounds all over his body, and the Twins were in straits. As I fought my way through, I saw Hor-min throwing spear after spear till he had no more. Then he took up his bow. Kamose was alone among the enemy chariots. Sek-met lay spent, streaming blood.

"His left hand! There is no warrior at the King's left hand!" The Hyksos, at Hur's command, had cleared a path between him and the King. Kamose had slain two thrusting chariot warriors and was swinging his ax at a third. "Ra-en-Ra!" His back was turned to Hur! Exulting, the Cruel One, with a yell of triumph, hurtled toward him, his broad-sword raised high in both hands to split the King's back in two. I must have whipped up my horses. They bounded forward behind Hur. He was poised to strike.

"Eureka! Set-swine!" I heard a great voice inside me.

Hur swung around, the huge sword held high. His mouth dropped open. Our chariots were close alongside.

"The priestling!" Hur's teeth snapped shut and bared in a sneer.

As once before, the cold hatred in his pale eyes thralled me. Then his upraised arms tautened to strike me. As two of his chariot guard crashed into me, I felled him. With a side-swing of my ax under his upraised left arm, I cut through his heart.

His eyes crazed with hatred, he stood straight for a moment. Then his thin body crumpled and, his hands still tight-clenched on the broad-sword, slowly, as though still moved by his own will, he slid to the floor of the chariot and out of it, down onto the blood-soaked sand.

There were no chariots around me. The Hyksos hosts, stunned by the death of their leader, for a few moments were still as statues. Then they turned to meet the new menace. Ahmose-Eb and his Sailor-soldiers! With loud battle-cries, their Standards aloft, they surged into the camp from the south-east, behind the enemy.

I stood where I was in the Hyksos chariot, still holding the ax that dripped with Hur's blood. My brother was looking at me. His eyes blazed love, and laughter! We gazed at each other, peer to peer.

"Warrior at my left hand," he said softly. "Little Brother, with your stroke the City of Abydos is freed from the tyrants." Then he turned to the men of Ta-mery, and his voice was thunder. "Hur is dead!"

"Hur is dead." Our hosts took up the cry and breaking their ranks, they fought with a will, their battle-cry "Hur is dead! Hur the Cruel One is dead!" And among the Hyksos, assailed now from the front and the rear, the whisper grew,

"Hur is dead . . ."

Little by little they lost their thrust, and the mercenaries, craven, grumbled and muttered, "None can slay this Hawk of the South Land," and they scattered, calling him an afrit King, and fled, jumping, three or four of them, into one chariot, whipping up tired, bleeding horses. Bent on escape to the North Land, they drove through the camp over the bodies of our wounded, till our men formed a barrier of shields and no other barbarian escaped that way.

My limbs were nerveless. The bloodied ax fell from my hand. I was gazing down at Hur's body, slain among the slain.

Were slayer and victim knit together in a secret-eternal harmony? The thought was born and lost in a heart-beat, and Hor-min was beside me.

"My Prince." His black eyes were shining like stars. "My Prince," he said again, and for the first time, standing there in his chariot, his legs and back bleeding from dagger and sword gashes, he bowed deep to me.

"Akh! Hor-min."

"My Prince," he said, for the third time, and we stood and watched the chaos of the whole Hyksos army in rout. I could not believe my eyes. The cry "Hur is dead!" had grown from a whisper to a wild fear to turmoil and frenzied flight. The reckless, feckless, shouting and cursing mass was scurrying in disorder, scrambling for chariots and swarming southward out of the camp, whipping up horses covered with blood to follow Hur's guard and their chariot captains.

"They will hasten to join Teti of Neferusi's army," Hor-min said, "and he will not relish their dire news."

"They will but swell the Neferusian's ranks," I said, and watched them goading camp donkeys as though all the Fiends of Amenti were pricking the heels of them. "Hor-min, by Ra's grace, Aknere will discover their hiding place in the desert to the southeast of Thebes—after the triumph . . . the triumph!" I felt my head shaking slowly. "I will never doubt the King's word again." After a moment, I said, "But we must waste no time. On the third day of the triumph the King will attack. The Neferusian's army must be annihilated before we can plan the attack on Avaris."

"My Prince, your words remind me of our youth, when the King would ever call you from your studies to sit in council with him."

"Hor-min, let us clean ourselves of our battle-gore—and I must find Minirt. Then we will aid with the wounded."

But at that moment, out of the wild riot of the captured camp, Ahmose-Eb, in an enemy chariot, drove to Kamose.

"Ahmose-Eb in a chariot." Hor-min laughed as our sailor pulled up his horses so hard that they reared and, his shoulders heaving, his words coming out in great pants of breath, cried out, "O Master of Double Strength! O Double Lightning!" He threw back his head and laughed at our boyhood names for Kamose, and outside myself as I was I thought that love had released our solemn sailor to the gift of laughter. From chariot to chariot they embraced.

Then Kamose said, "My Sailor-man, you attacked at the Moment of Maat."

"The day is ours! The day is ours!" Ahmose-Eb turned to me, then to Ak-hor, who was sitting in his chariot, his long legs dangling out of the back of it, and his eyes weary, yet blazing victory. Their eyes met. With tired grins they nodded at each other.

Mer-neb, his battle tunic in shreds, was holding his twin's arm for Montu-Thoth to set at the elbow. Four Healer-priests came. Ak-hor went with one of them, and the other three tended Soker-uff, swaying in his harness and weak from loss of the blood that flowed from the wounds in his neck; and Sek-met, lying still as though Ra's life had gone from her, was bathed with charged water, and while Kamose held her, they bandaged her wounds. Then Kamose rose.

"Ahmose-Eb," he said. "You will take charge of this camp. Have the enemy prisoners remove their wounded to the shade of the rocks. Detail men to bury the Hyksos dead in the desert. Have all water-skins filled at the well in the wadi close by and, my Sailor-man, all loot is to be piled up in the center of the camp for our Egyptian soldiers . . . our valiant Egyptian men." He paused and looked around him at the men of Ta-mery, some too tired to move, some aiding the wounded and others gathering the prisoners into large silent groups of defeated men. Then he said, "The captured arms send down to the River to be shipped to Thebes. Take no tally of hands and manhood. And now, my Sailor, to your manifold tasks, and I to Pen, who is in straits." He turned in his chariot, and raised his right arm, strong as rose-granite, and it seemed we were bathed in his grace, in his cool Fire, and the men of Egypt stayed their tasks and gazed on their King, serene and clean of heart in the midst of chaos. Even the greedy ravens and scavenger-birds fell silent, and for a long moment there arose in us a peace, a Knowing that passes all things. Each man was solitary, pure, yet one with the Whole, and Kamose, his bronze-and-gold-studded battle-shirt, his Blue Helmet shining as though he were girt in the Living Flame of Ra, was the Core of the Whole.

CHAPTER VIII

I wakened slowly from a dreamless sleep. Ra was an hour
high risen. I had slept through the Dawn Rite! I closed my
eyes against the bright golden-blue of the sky. *The Falcon*,
at anchor, was moving to the swell of the rising River. Voices
called from ship to ship, and from the ships to the shore.
I lay, all feeling and energy spent, in my chosen place between the rudder and Kamose's cabin. Slowly thought returned. I slew Hur. I slashed him with a battle-ax and cut
through his heart. We won the battle for Abydos. I have
slain Hur. I sat up, thrusting the thought deep down till I
could be with Kheri-heb. Instead, I remembered the strange
quiet in the captured camp, after the night and day of blood-
letting; and I remembered my brother.

Without his Blue Crown, his hair curling about his nape

and ears, his skin golden in Ra's high afternoon light, Kamose had moved as a god among the wounded and dying men of Ta-mery. Their eyes lit with joy. Those who were able raised themselves up, breathed his name, or spoke it aloud, or sobbed, or just stayed still and gazed at him, letting his light and strength fill all their weary hearts, and for many of them lying wounded there, the love and faith in their hearts for their King, Ra's son on earth, was so clean and clear that their wounds were healed from that moment.

With the King, Montu-Thoth, the Healer-Priests and the novices, Hor-min and I tended the men who had fought with us, and as I knelt beside one or the other of them, I could hear my brother's voice in the ravine. ". . . the farmers, the stone-masons, the fishermen and scribes, the carpenters and priests and artisans of Ta-mery . . ." and I had breathed in the smell of their sweaty, hacked and torn, bleeding bodies, and the smell had purified me.

It had been dusk, a bright clear twi-light, when the last of our wounded, in ox-carts brought from the villages, were taken to the River and the waiting barges. The chariots drawn by the captured horses, the shields, spears, javelins, quivers full of arrows and hundreds of strong-bows, sickle-swords and metal-studded battle-shirts, were early collected and sent to the wharves. Hur's harness was studded with gold and bronze, ill-worked and crude, and his horse's head-strap was jewel-embossed. Ahmose-Eb showed them to me as we paused to drink a cup of cool water. "Gold from our mines," he said, "and jewels from our Eastern Mountains, but, my Prince, look at this bit! They are all made like this."

"It is little wonder the horses reared when I pulled on the leathers. . . ." It was made of bronze and had flat rings, sharp-spiked at each corner of the horse's mouth. I stared in disgust and thought that I had used no whip when my chariot horses lunged toward Hur. "They will all be melted down," Ahmose-Eb said, and looked around him at the strangely peaceful scene. The torn and bleeding bodies were no longer there to bring a plague of flies and to lure the greedy crows and vultures to darken the day. The camp was clean. Ahmose-Eb sniffed. "That smell makes a Sailor-soldier hungry," he said.

The enemy's feed animals had been slaughtered and were roasting on the large Hyksos spits. On the bright fires of the round cooking-stoves, caldrons of grain simmered, and in the center, the loot was piled high: bowls, cups and plates of metals and pottery; hides and water-skins, and reed baskets of grain; fruit and dates and huge vats of oil; lamps and torch sconces, chairs and stools and tables, cushions and painted reed mattings from Hur's stronghold, and silver dishes and cups with his seal engraved on them; all for our tired warriors.

They had cleansed themselves in the cool well-water at the wadi's entrance, and cleaned their weapons, and now, in the Light of Ra in his Sek-tet Boat descending to the west, and the glow of the stove fires, with weary good humor they divided the spoils.

Slowly I had walked to the ox-cart where Pen was waiting to be drawn to *The Falcon*. He lay on clean reeds, as still as a stone. The left side of his face was swollen and purple. I touched his brow. It was cold and damp. I looked at Mer-neb and Per-neb sitting together at the head of the wagon. Per-neb's left elbow was bandaged and his arm held in a linen sling. I asked him if it hurt. He shrugged and said, "Pen is in straits."

"He took a spear through his stomach." Mer-neb said. "It entered from the back—"

"And an arrow through his chest," his twin added. "But by Ra's Grace, the arrow missed his heart." They were both looking at me, with a hint of surmise, but the love in their tired eyes was the greater.

"That was a warrior's stroke, my Prince," Mer-neb said, and his twin nodded. I turned and touched the large piece of charged linen that lay across Pen's stomach and chest. "Montu-Thoth put the Looking on him, and staunched the blood flow." Mer-neb's voice was awed. "Montu-Thoth charged the Ka of Pen to heal the wounds inside his body."

"How long will he sleep?"

"For a day and a night," Mer-neb said.

"He is in the Hands of Amun-Ra." Per-neb's voice was tired. "Res will be waiting aboard *The Falcon*. She will be his own will to live."

"Res! Aknere and Res . . . the men of Abydos? There is news?"

"My Prince"—a swift smile lit up Mer-neb's wan face—"it was easy!"

"One of your Messengers on Horses came from Aknere. . . . The men of Abydos freed their own city . . . it was easy," Per-neb echoed his twin.

I shook my head, scarce believing. "The King will enter the City of Osiris in peace and amid rejoicing. . . ." My head was still slowly shaking. "After generations of cruelty, massacre, desecration and tyranny . . . it was easy." I felt a smile stretch my stiff lips.

"The quarrel was in their blood and their being," Mer-neb said.

"By the Grace of Osiris, all the drugged guards were captured. There is quiet rejoicing in Abydos, and a great preparing. . . ."

I looked at them both, alike as two peas, and felt the tears in my eyes.

"The God will be restored to his Place. . . . O Still Heart! Osiris, whose word is Truth before the face of his enemies . . ." I murmured. Then together we had spoken the words of healing and blessing, for Pen and all of our wounded.

"Osiris, Lord, Prince of the Living . . . King of those who are Younger . . . nourish Pen, and all who are in straits. . . . Sweet Breath of Life! Fill them . . . make them whole. . . ."

We were silent. Then I asked of Ak-hor.

"He is a man of many wounds, my Prince, deep but not fatal. His faithful Nubians and two Healer-Priests are with him. Montu-Thoth put the Sleeping on him, too, and he is on his way to *The Falcon*."

"As Pen should be," I said, and with my words a Healer-Priest, accompanied by a novice, had come to drive the ox-cart to the wharf.

"My Prince"—the Healer-Priest bowed slightly—"the King awaits you."

I had watched the large ox-cart driven carefully, slowly away. It cast a long, thin-slanting shadow across the sand, and the prints of the oxen-hooves were cups of dark blue shade. As I turned to look once more at the place where the battle had been, the sweet cry of a female antelope broke the sun-set silence. One night and one day! I closed my eyes. I saw Hur, his teeth bared in a last sneering laugh. I shook the thought out of my heart. One moon-rise, and one sun-rise! "In the Eyes of Ra, a thousand years are as one day. . . ." Slowly I walked to where Kamose and Sek-met, with Soker-uff, his neck and shoulders bandaged, and Minirt, washed clean, and gold-white, yoked to a light chariot, were waiting for me.

My brother held out his hand. I leapt up. Holding the leathers lightly, he had put his arm about my shoulders, and under a honey-gold sky we drove at an easy pace to the River. Desert martins circled above us, and two golden coursers whirled up and away into the saffron-green calm of the after-glow.

"The men of Abydos have freed their Holy City," he said, and I nodded. "Aknere and a group of his Young Eyes and Ears are even this night beginning their search for the Neferusian army."

"He will bring the news to Thebes," I said, and as we came to the plowed land, there were people lining the way. Kamose blessed them, and they bowed their heads, their hands clasped on their breasts, then looked up and smiled, and raised their arms high in praise and rejoicing.

Between the lines of our people, we came to the wharves. Ra's last radiance turned the River to gold that rippled and ran together, and through the bright chaos of splintered light, the large dark barges filled with our wounded clove a path, and in their wake, as the last beams of Ra, behind great purple clouds, spread all the sky over, the six long Funeral Barges slid silently out to midriver.

"Their last pilgrimage." Kamose's eyes had been dark and deep as he watched. "They have, each one, earned their place, side by side with the gods of the stars."

As the after-glow turned to porphyry gray, he had turned Soker-uff and Minirt to the wharf road, and we drove in silence along the banks of the wine-dark, rising River to *The Falcon*.

I lay, still sleepy, apart and quiet, and listened to the diverse sounds and movements around and about me. With thoughts of Inhapi falling like blossoms, I had fallen asleep; and I was refreshed, but still unquiet. The sounds seemed as though I heard them from a great distance. *The Falcon*'s rudder, huge between its two golden-topped posts, looked small as a toy, and far away from me. I closed my eyes again and saw Hur slain on the blood-soaked sand!

"Come, Brother." Kamose stood tall above me. He looked fresh and young. I knew he had been with Herath. In the first light of the moon I had heard our sailors bring the Royal Raft alongside. Kamose had been rowed to the yacht of the Hyksos Princess in a manner befitting a King. "Come, Ahmose!" I stretched, looking at the deep wound in his thigh, a purple weal, red-rimmed but purified of poison and pain by Montu-Thoth, and almost hidden by his pleated kilt. "Arise, Warrior on my left hand!" His smile lifted my heart. He wore his Horus-belt, leather sandals and his lion bracelet. His dagger sheath was on his left arm. I thought of Ak-hor and asked of him. Kamose laughed. "Our Unique Friend scorns bandaging. His whole body is a mass of cuts and gashes, and his left shoulder is held in a splint—but his ceremonial cloak will cover all!"

"He will wear his vulture feathers?"

"He will be resplendent! Would that Neshi were here, from Memphis—but come! Our mother is about to set her foot in the city of Abydos." He spoke the words slowly, with a joyful awe. "Come." He pulled me up and called for Neme to bathe me, and to bring the Fisherman's Circlet, my father's belt and my lion bracelet. In the quarter part of an hour we were driving together to the Royal Wharf to await *The Southern.*

The ships of our fleet had all been painted and were gay with flags. All along the ropes they fluttered and waved, the pennants of the North Land and the South Land both, in the cool north wind. Musicians played on their decks and the sound of sacred music filled the clear air.

Mer-neb and Per-neb, in full battle dress, were already waiting in their chair, and Per-neb had a brightly striped sling to hold his left arm.

"Here is Ak-hor," Kamose said, and raised his hand in greeting. The Chief of the Nubians in Egypt, Unique Friend of the King and Fan Bearer at his left hand, was indeed resplendent, and his Chieftain's ceremonial feathers covered the wounds on his body and his long ebon legs. His golden anklets were fringed with monkey fur, and one tall ostrich plume rose from his high-pointed cap of pig-skin. His Nubian bearers, the cream of his Captains, were almost as resplendent as he.

The Southern eased into her moorings, and Kamose, watching, said, "Our mother this day comes to the city of her heart." Then he smiled and leaned toward me. "The treasure-ships"—as they dropped anchors alongside he murmured one of the names he had chosen: *Shining in Memphis* —"When Avaris is razed," he said, "and the Two Lands are one again, our grand-mother shall sail in state to the city of her birth and her heritage—Memphis."

And I thought that the heart of my brother was a loom eternally weaving. "When that comes to pass, Brother, I would study the Wisdom of Imhotep with his Priests in Memphis."

He looked straight at me, his face grave but his eyes still smiling.

"Brother warrior, you have earned your solitude. When the tyrants are thrust out of the Two Lands, I will not stay your soul-searching. As King of the Two Lands, this I swear to you!" He turned his gaze back to the River and softly added, "But while I fight, you, my Brother, you will be Regent." I had not thought of this. He turned back to me, his eyes clear and cold. "Who else? Think on it."

Sek-met's grunt broke into my surprise. With a low groan she rose stiffly and painfully to her feet as our mother was carried down the ramp of *The Southern* in her old carrying-chair, long-remembered, of ebony, its poles of sesame wood overlaid with gold. Slowly her bearers lowered it to the ground, and when she rose and walked toward us, tall, in white and gold, I thought I had never before truly known the beauty and majesty of my mother. She held the silver sistrum of Hat-hor and wore the Menat collar of the Goddess, for Health and Beauty and the Power of Womanhood.

Kamose walked to meet her. She bowed to him, her hands crossed on her breast. He embraced her and they kissed, nose to nose, and the people murmured with joy and thanksgiving.

"My King, the love of you is throughout all the Land of Ta-mery," she said, and embraced him again, looking with pride and love at her son. Then I went to her, and her great dark eyes were pools in which I bathed, and her arms were cool and strong about me. "My Child of the Moon," she whispered as we stood embracing. "Akh! Ra-en-Ra! You have grown—in spirit, and stature." She drew back and looked at me. "Ahmose, my Young One . . ." She smiled and turned to Kamose, who led her back to her waiting chair.

Thure, who had walked alongside my mother's chair, escorting her from the ship, came toward me. His face was cold as stone. There was no light in his eyes. "Osiris, Lord of Compassion," I prayed in my heart. "Sen-ut's Ka cannot pierce with her love this wall of grief and rage. Osiris, Lord . . . Let his Ka see. Let Thure weep——"

He spoke, startling me. "Zatoo! So! You are blooded, my Prince. You slew the Cruel One—you slew Hur." His voice was empty. He walked with me to our chair, and it was as though the warmth of Ra's beams bounced off him, as a ball against a wall. In silence, we mounted our chair and sat down, and between lines of quiet happy people we followed the King and my mother along the broad road to the city, the feet of our bearers treading on flowers all the way.

The people, smiling, bowed their heads as the King passed by them. Some lay gently down and stayed for a while on their bellies. I watched my mother. She held out her silver sistrum, leaning sideways in her chair to those who reached out to her that some might touch it and, being blessed, touch others. In joyous quiet, we came to the Temple of Osiris.

"Thure, at last," I whispered, "we shall see the Holy of Holies, the Inmost Shrine of Osiris, for nine generations darkened by the black rites of Set and the Lords of the Shadow."

He looked at me with empty eyes, gave a slight nod for courtesy's sake and did not answer.

The Passion of Osiris and his Resurrection lasted four days and four nights. The King, our mother and the High Priests stayed in the Inmost Shrine, fasting and in prayer, while the people of the city, the pilgrims and visitors, all in good part took sides in the fight between Light and Darkness. There was vigorous skirmish on water and land. The nights, sad and silent, when the Door of the God's Tomb was sealed, gave place to wild rejoicing in his triumphal return, his mutilated body whole, in full glory, in the Barque called *The Great* to his shriven, purified Shrine.

Thousands gathered in the vast Outer-court, and when Kamose, his war curls shaven and not one hair on his golden-skinned body, clad only in a new woven loin-cloth, the Royal Asp on his brow, our mother and the High Priest, all three of them thin and wan with fasting, came out to the top of the wide shallow steps, like wind over a field when the corn is tall, all there sank down on their bellies and kissed the ground of their city: a vast matting of human holiness, thanksgiving and praise. At last, the high clear voices of the Priestesses rose in songs of rejoicing. The rattle of their sistra mingled with the pipes and harps and horns, so that all ears were filled again with the joyful sounds of worship and the God's adoration.

Then Kamose came forward. His gait was grave and sedate. With one foot forward, straight-standing, he raised his hand, and the men and women and the children of Abydos rose to their feet. When his people were standing before him, in a silence that was not of their bodies, but of their intent and listening souls, he spoke as High Priest and King.

"Osiris, King of Kings, Lord of Lords, Beautiful of Countenance, is in the Land of Holiness for millions of years. His son, Horus, has set him upon his Throne. Set has been thrust out. His evil soul has been restrained." Then he spoke the words of the Seventh Hour of the Night. "Hail, Osiris! Lord of Life! Thou livest in Thy Place. Thou dost exalt those who are in Thy following on their coming before Thee. Thou hast gained mastery over those who worked against thee. . . . O ye spirits who are hostile to Osiris, who have blasphemed against the Lord of the Dwat, your arms and hands are fettered and you are tied with bonds, and your souls kept underward. . . . Osiris, Lord of the Two Plumes! The Doors of your Innermost Shrine are open."

My brother's voice rang out on the ancient words. Then, with the blessing of Isis sung softly by the Priestesses, and the prayers of Osiris chanted in quiet voice by his Priests, the King stepped forward with his right foot, and he made his first law and proclaimed it.

"To all the people of the Beloved Land, to all who live in Ta-mery who may do an injurious thing to any statues, offering stones or monuments which are in any Temple precinct, or inside any Temple in the Two Lands: My Majesty will not permit their own property, nor that of their fathers, to remain with them, nor that they join the spirits in the Necropolis, or remain among the living upon earth."

And with this law, after generations of blasphemy and desecration, he excommunicated those who would desecrate and blaspheme. I had seen the majesty of my brother, and known it—at his Crowning; on the Balcony of Appearances, when he set forth to battle; when he carried the shoulders of Tetaky, slain; when he raised his arm, dark in the moon-light, to bless his silent hosts; and when he raised it at the noon-day, in victory—but never had I seen him, nor known him, so very King.

"His first law," Hor-min whispered, coming up beside me. "The first law of our freedom."

Silence held the vast crowd. Then a Priest called out.

"Hail to thee, Whadj-Kheper-Ra, Kamose, High Priest and King."

The clear words ended in a murmuring and a thousand low-breathed blessings till the throats of the people of Abydos, closed with long fear and cruel stress, opened their hearts' joy in sweet cool sound, then, over-brimming, voices long dumb to liberty's fierce cries soared proud from the earth to Heaven's high reaches, and straddled the winds with human jubilation, as the King and his mother walked down the wide steps to their waiting chairs.

Kamose rode alone through his thronging people. For the first time in two hundred years the Gates of Abydos stood open, and those who had been in hiding, and those whose lives in the ravaged villages had known no surcease of woe, had all crowded into their city. They waved colored scarves and shouted the words that only Egyptians can shout, for the gods put them into their hearts, and their tongues shout them and sing them and call them out loud.

"Kamose is a Flame before the Wind!"

"The Doors of the Sky are opened to his Majesty!"

"He is Ra at his First Appearing!"

"Lord of the Two Lands. Horus Hawk of the South Land!"

"Kamose, Whadj-Kheper-Ra!"

"Fine gold is not as the radiance of him," my mother said,

and in her face, drawn with fasting, was the calm of the gods. "My Moon Child, Osiris is again in his Place." She had beckoned to me to sit with her, in her chair, and as we followed my brother, I thought, We are a happy people. The broad smiles on every face seemed to be carved in granite to last for a million years, so deep from the heart they were, and my mother spoke softly her own heart's joy. "Osiris is peace—that radiant peace few earth men know. Osiris, mutilated, resurrected Lord—his peace has always been, and always will be. When men cease to believe themselves separate, with separate existences, we shall return, each fulfilling the task before him, to Osiris' Peace. We shall know joy and compassion, and love for God, the gods and men, and the Peace of Osiris will be felt and heard, and seen upon this earth."

We sat silent together in holy gladness till we turned toward the River and I saw that our ships had not only been painted but the metals on them polished and shining so that our eyes were dazzled. The rich trappings on the Hyksos yacht where Herath waited shone brightest of all except *The Falcon*.

"Kamose spends each leisure moment and his nights with the Hyksos Princess."

"Ahmose"—my mother's voice held quiet question—"what of the Hyksos Princess?"

"I have not seen her, but Pen tells of her beauty and courage."

"Herath . . ." She said the name softly. "I shall come to know her on the voyage back to Thebes. I owe her much that she aided my son—" She paused. "Kamose holds her in his heart." She turned to me and our eyes met with the thought of Nefertari. "The Queen—" My mother could not erase the cold scorn in her voice as she said the word. "Nefertari will not welcome the Hyksos Princess. Ahmose, your half-sister has grown in cruelty and power. Nefertari is secretive and subtle. She holds men, many men, in thrall—"

"But not the King."

"Only those closest to us in the King's Household know that she is not true wife. My Young One, with her sycophants and cronies, she watches the slaughter of divine animals to read their entrails and draw omens from the dappled figures of gall and liver. And always she smiles—and Thuty gazes on her, Akh! I talk around my thought. I am afraid. Ra-en-Ra! It seems I am forever telling you my fears."

"You fear for Herath?"

"Though Kamose has never lain with Nefertari, nor ever will, as you well know, few are aware of this, and she is fawned upon. Her pride, her inordinate pride is satisfied. But, Ahmose, a Secondary Royal Wife—and a Princess, not a concubine—Nefertari will not countenance this. Unless her pride can be saved——"

"Her pride! Her perfidy? She is a murderess! I care not for her pride."

"Ahmose, the King is 'The Two-fold Great House.' Pharaoh. Lord of the Two Lands. Till our battle is won, the evil within our Household must be contained within our Household. There must be no stain on the family of the Son of Amun, Kamose, King in Thebes."

"Miutu and Kheri-heb, Pen-aati, Senseneb—they know Nefertari's evil. The Old One! He is close to my grandmother—"

"Tetisheri is his lodestar. She dotes on the Queen, and he will not gainsay her. But he is watchful. My Moon Child, since I heard of Herath, and Kamose's love for her, I have prayed for long hours, and in meditation a thought has blossomed in my heart." My mother turned again to me, her eyes bright with thought. "Envy of me, my son, salts Nefertari's craving to be High Priestess—and now, my life's dream has been fulfilled. Osiris is restored to his ancient Shrine in his Holy City." She closed her eyes for the space of a long, deep sigh. Then she blessed a child held out toward her and turned to me again. "Ahmose, I have given grave thought to resigning the offices of High Priestess to Nefertari"—she held up her hand, as I would have protested. "I would welcome simple and secret worship," she smiled. "My Young One, Nefertari would then have all the outward glories she now apes! She would be truly Chief Votive of Hat-hor, and Bride of Amun-Ra."

"And the revenues? You would forgo——"

"All the lands and the revenues. Would she settle for less?"

"Would she settle at all?"

My mother spoke her thoughts softly. "I have watched her. My son, her deepest yearning is to be worshiped as a goddess—she believes in her heart that she is a goddess. Ahmose, the High Priestesshood is the only step she can take toward the unholy ambition of being worshiped as one."

"The Queen is drunk with power as lesser women reel with wine," I said, and added, "but she will never vomit on it."

"This thought of mine may well be of benefit to Kamose and his desires for Herath—but enough." She leaned toward girl-twins, held out to her, and touched them each on the brow, "They are so thin," she whispered.

After a while, I asked her of Ina, whom Kamose had found on a roof-top the day before he was crowned. "And how is Kamose's daughter?"

"Ina waits upon me," my mother answered, "in my Lodge beside the Sacred Lake. Kamose will love this child. Ina's daughter is strong and beautiful. She has the green-gold eyes of her father, and the pale skin of her mother." Ah-hotpe's eyes were warm again.

We came to the wharf. Ahmose-Eb was waiting for us. He bowed low as Kamose stepped from his chair and gave his hand to our mother to lead her to *The Southern*. "At evening, I will bring Herath to you," he said. Then he turned to us all. "My Brother, and my Company, you are bidden this night to partake of our meal with us on the deck of *The Falcon*." We bowed. Smiling a little, he turned to Ahmose-Eb. "At sun-down, we set sail for Thebes."

"My King."

Kamose raised his hand in blessing, then turned to our mother and they walked up the ramp.

Ak-hor and the twins went back to *The Falcon*. Thure had disappeared, and Ahmose-Eb was beside me.

"My Prince, there is fruit and wine aboard *The Wild Bull*." His eyes were shining and held a peace I had not known in them till he met Atu. I knew he was yearning to talk of his love. We went aboard and sat on cushions in the shelter cabin, and I watched, almost in unbelief, as he poured wine from the northern marshes into magnificent golden cups, inlaid with faience, amethyst and lapis-lazuli. "Spoils, my Prince," he said with a wide smile. "And taste the wine!"

It was the true sweet, tangy wine of the marshes. I quaffed the full cup, then held it and looked at it.

"They will never again mine our gold, nor enslave our metal-workers to fashion it," I said, and Ahmose-Eb took the cup from me and filled it again with the silver-white wine. "Is Pen still asleep?" I asked, and he nodded.

"He will sleep till sun-set. Res watches over him."

I leaned back. "Tell me of Avaris, from the water."

"Akh! My Prince, when the King first called retreat we were forced to leave many of their ships and arms uncaptured." He frowned and drew his heavy brows together. "The greatest battle is still to be fought, for now both sides will be aware of each other's strength, and well prepared."

"The Hyksos are still strong, and they have Nubia for an ally. And the foul Teti! His army must be routed."

Ahmose-Eb gritted his teeth at the sound of the hated name. Then he said, "Three times he has slipped through our fingers, the three times murderer!" His eyes were now pinpoints of cold light. "Our fathers both . . . and Akh! Sen-ut . . . Thure told me all. He blames himself that she undertook the perilous mission."

"Thure . . ." I murmured.

"He is ever alone. Hori tells me that even the Queen Ah-hotpe was helpless before the wall of his grief." He sighed, quaffed his cup to the dregs and looked at me with rueful glance. "I am almost guilty when I think of the joy in my own heart. . . . My Prince, Atu! She grows each day in beauty and grace. The Princess Herath delights to play the harp for her to sing, and she chooses Atu above all others to play with her the game of Dogs and Jackals."

I smiled to see in him the reverence of loving, and the joy. Then I asked him, "How came she to be in a kitchen-ship?"

Ahmose-Eb's square face reddened. His eyes were cold again. "A friend of her father's, who was no friend, though he housed her and mother, betrayed her father to the Hyksos. As Atu grew to maidenhood, the man who had treated her mother as his concubine came at her. My Prince, she stowed away in the kitchen-ship of a Theban Nomarch that was anchored for the night. The old woman—you remember her? She took Atu under her care. Grinding the corn for the bread and the beer, she was safe, and the old woman stout to defend her, and kind."

"How came they to the kitchen-ship of *The Falcon?*"

"The old woman is high ranking in her work, and when she was asked to supervise the King's provender, she took Atu with her." Ahmose-Eb's eyes were soft and glowing. "By the Grace of Hat-hor," he said.

"My Friend, what of Sittek?"

"Akh! By the Thirteen Crocodiles! I do not know."

"The Chief Scribe is a tyrant—and avaricious. Sittek still waits for you?"

"Akh! Yes. A message came from her with Hori in *The Southern.*"

"Then there will be trouble."

"Dire trouble, I have no doubt."

"It seems wrong. The marriage was arranged when you were but a boy."

"I have resisted——"

"Long! And with stubborn strength. Forgive me, but when I saw Sittek in the King's House, I understood your resistance. Ahmose-Eb, her voice! And you are so quiet . . ."

He laughed, but the sound lacked full joy. He quaffed the

last of his wine and put the cup down on the low table with a hard, sharp sound of metal on tile. "I will marry Atu! Atu . . ." He caressed the name. "My Prince—O my Prince! If you could know how love is . . ."

I leaned back, smiling to myself as thoughts of Inhapi filled my heart. Inhapi, desiring and desired. O Joyous Hips, that trembled as the leaves of the sycamore tree in the wind from the north, bewildering me! "When the Two Lands are one again . . ." she said, knowing my secret will before my tongue gave words to it, ". . . I will come to Thebes." Inhapi, the light breath on her lips in sleep. Inhapi.

"You are lost in thought, my Prince."

Startled, I said, "I am thinking of the hauteur of the Chief Scribe. The scribes are arrogant and strong." Without weighing my words, I asked, "Could not Atu be a beloved concubine?"

"No!" The word snapped like a bow-string. Ahmose-Eb's face was white. Then he took a breath, and with his hand on his heart, he said, "Pardon, my Prince."

"The question earned the answer. But Ahmose-Eb, it will not be easy."

He smiled a little and shook his head. "I know. In Thebes I will ask audience of the King to speak of this matter. . . . My Prince, pray to Hat-hor. She is powerful, and the ways of Ra are sometimes strange." He looked out of the shelter at the sky. "And Ra is sailing westward, down . . ."

I rose. "Let us go out on deck." I put my arm about his broad, hard shoulders. "Kamose will be just. But have no fear. Whatever it may cost you, Atu will be your wife."

"By the Grace of Hat-hor," he murmured, and we walked together to the splash rail.

Young girls were dancing on the wharves, acrobats leaping and sweetmeat vendors shouting their wares. Ships full of returning pilgrims were sailing out on the swelling River, northward or southward, home, and *The Falcon*, her seventy oarsmen at the ready, seemed to be straining, impatient, at her moorings.

The Wild Bull's sails swelled, full, and Ahmose-Eb went to the prow. I stood watching. The wind was fresh. The strong ships creaked and were loosed from their mooring, and in the sun-set, as Kamose had commanded, they seemed to spring out against the straining current like horses at the halter. *The Falcon,* the wood of her stained purple-blue, and the light-gathering gold on her reflecting Ra's last rays, to the rhythmic pull of her chanting oarsmen slid out on the rising River toward Thebes.

All along our way the people flocked to the River, and every kind of boat, even the ferry-boats, sailed alongside our ships and in our wake. In front of *The Falcon,* during the whole voyage, the River was strewn with garlands of wreathed flowers, and when we came, fighting the wind and the current all the way, to the mountain-girded curve of the Theban reach of the River, we were met with rejoicing.

All Thebes and the villages around were making merry. Along the shores all who were able, old and young, were jumping and waving scarves and garlands, and as we drew near to the Temple Wharf, all manner of reed rafts, barges and yachts, all flying scarves and pennants and flags, painted bright colors—yellow and red, blue and reed-green, striped and spotted and cubed with every mixture of hue—rowed out, sailed out and poled out; youths and maidens came swimming out into the wide-risen sweep of the River to meet and welcome and to praise Kamose, their colored head-bands and their black polls bobbing on the wind-flecked water; and the King's name was in every mouth.

"Kamose has eaten the hearts of the Hyksos!"

"The lifetime of Kamose is Eternity!"

"The morning star is a Green Falcon!"

All along the shore they opened their mouths to shout, then fell silent, in awe, as Kamose came to the prow of *The Falcon* and stood there in full battle-dress. The gold-and-bronze studs of his Blue Helmet shining bright as the God's Flame in the full risen Light of Ra, he stretched forth his right arm, raising his great bronze sword high and straight toward the heavens to slant down the Rays of Ra to his Land in promise and golden blessing. He was the Eater of Shades, and Long of Stride in the Holy Places; Son of the Sun, embraced by the Flame.

It was the first time the Thebans had known their King victorious. Not in their lives, nor in the lives of their parents, nor their grand-parents' parents had they seen their King triumphant on the prow of his flag-ship. As we hove into the Temple Wharf, they stayed silent, still, standing and gazing, lost in wonder.

"Kamose, Whadj-Kheper-Ra, Kamose!"

They stood, their hands crossed on their breasts. Then slowly they bent their heads, and there was a murmur of homage so deep that I, too, bent my head, and said out loud the words of Osiris, forever in my heart: "And he caused a reverence to spread over the Land."

As we came with a thud to the wharf-stones the solemn silence broke, and all along the wide road up to the great Pylon Gate of the Temple the joyful sounds of welcome gathered.

"Yah! Amun! Yah! Yah!"

"Yah! Amun-Ra!"

"Kamose! Ra's son in Thebes!"

"Kamose, victorious—Yah! Yah!"

Hor-min touched my arm. "By the Eater of Shades!" he said. "Behold! My Prince, see who will be roped behind the King's chariot!"

"Mayebre the Libyan."

"A short beard becomes him," Ahmose-Eb said. "And he must smell more agreeable."

The leading rope was about his waist and held by a guard.

"It will be hooked to the King's chariot," Hor-min said again, with a wide grin.

The Libyan stood, fat-fleshed and broad-buttocked, and shorn of his arrogance.

"He wears a loin-cloth ill!" Ahmose-Eb said.

"His memories are bitter," I replied, and we walked

toward our ramp as Kamose drove Soker-uff, Rai's white plumes bobbing on his head-strap, and Minirt, down the shallow ramp of *The Falcon*.

All along the way our people stood, wearing flowers in their hair and waving garlands, and the men had collars of flowers around their necks. Three hundred deep they lined each side of the long way, as we rode in procession through the pennanted Gate to the Fore-court of the God, where Miutu stood—and Kheri-heb! My heart leapt at the sight of him.

Kamose stepped down from his chariot and with firm, slow stride led the captured Libyan and the Hyksos captains up the wide shallow steps, followed by his own Captains, their pennants waving in the breeze. Then Kamose Whadj-Khe-per-Ra, victorious, with Ah-hotpe, his mother, Queen and High Priestess, the two High Priests and myself, the Royal Brother, went into the Holy of Holies. Falling down on our bellies, we prostrated ourselves in thanksgiving before the Shrine of Amun-Ra.

After a long silence, the faint clear notes of pipes rose from the Shrine's cool shade. We rose to our feet as the Temple music swelled, echoing around the soaring pillars of the vast Temple courts in waves of triumphant sound.

Kamose came out alone. Merry and mute, all Thebes smiled on him as he led our mother to her chair, then leapt into his chariot, Sek-met beside him, and waited for us to mount ours, while the smaller Pylon Gates of his House swung open to receive the King.

The Court-yard was lined with the Nobles and Elders of the City of the God. The Thirty Great Ones came in their carrying-chairs, and those who lived within the confines of the city came on foot, their fan-bearers behind and at their sides. Some had their dogs with them, and some their monkeys; others had brought their favorite hunting cats on leashes of leather, embossed, or papyrus leads, all garlanded with flowers. I saw monkeys with colored caps and bright pleated kilts, and beads, and the Court-yard of the King's

House was a place of excitement and chatter and unrestrained gladness.

Kamose drove, swift and straight, through the cheering crowd to the wide terrace, where, at the top of the steps, our grand-mother, in ceremonial dress, the hundred curls of her wig bright with precious stones and a golden circlet around it of fine-carved flowers with turquoise drops, her gray eyes bright and young and glad, sat in her chair to the right of the Queen.

Nefertari wore a diadem of gold, and the Golden Globe of Hat-hor between two horns! I caught my breath at the sight of her. She had almost usurped High Priestesshood, and she held the ancient scepter! I looked at it in her blaspheming hand, newly fashioned of gold and ivory, and thought of my mother's words: ". . . her deepest yearning is to be worshiped as a goddess." Ten maidens stood behind her, and in their fine linen cloaks, flower-garlanded, they seemed to be, but were not, Priestesses of Hat-hor.

Nefertari stood up. The Great Royal Wife! My childhood's fear thickened around me. In the bright sun-light my whole body shook at the sight of her, and the blood in my veins was chill. Amazed at the depth of my feeling, I held on to Hor-min's arm and in a moment had gathered myself. Kamose jumped from his chariot and ran up the steps to our grand-mother. He stood looking down at her for a moment. Then, as our father used to do, he picked her up in front of all there assembled, swung her around, held her up to his face and kissed her nose to nose.

Then, in courtly manner, he turned to Nefertari, bent over her outstretched hand and held it till she was seated again. Then he sat in the King's Chair, and I went up the steps to embrace my grand-mother.

"Ahmose, my little Priest, I hear good things of you—I thank you for the Memphian dwarf—but most of all, I am proud of you." I looked into her shining, triumphant eyes. "Ahmose," she said slowly, "you have a stark look. Akh! My grand-son! You are a worthy battle scribe, and by the

Horns of the Apis Bull"—she put her hard, small hands on my shoulders—"you are a blooded warrior!" She stood on her toes and kissed me.

I turned to Nefertari, lowering my eyes and head in a sparse bow. Then to my brother, Kamose, Whadj-Kheper-Ra, the King, I bowed low, my arms outstretched in adoration.

For three days and three nights the City of the God held festival. Thebans feasted, merry on the shores of drunkenness, and every jaw laughed. The faces of men were bright and the gods rejoiced. In the King's House on the first evening of our home-coming, there was a great feasting. My grand-mother, joying in the treasures of the captured ships, called me, at the beginning of the evening meal, to sit next to her in Nefertari's chair. The Queen had not yet made her entrance. Obeying Tetisheri, I left my own chair.

"Grand-son, look!" She touched her necklace. But I was looking at the chair in which I sat. It was of ebony, rich-embossed with Hat-hor symbols, inlaid with gold and lapis-lazuli, and the purple leather seat of it was held with golden nails. "Hat-hor . . ." I spoke the name inside me. "Lady of Love, this is blasphemy."

My grand-mother leaned toward me. "Ahmosè!" I looked now at the jeweled collar around her slender neck and shoulders. "The Ptah dwarf from Memphis . . ." she murmured.

"Per-du-Ptah." I smiled. "His work is of the gods." I gazed with true delight at the disc-heads, barrel-heads and drop-shaped beads in gold and amethyst, faience and rock-crystal. I touched the tiny birds and the subtly wrought tree-frogs in green gold, and said, "Rai had a necklace of tree-frogs . . ." And for a swift moment she was there on her small stool on the Dais. Then I saw her running toward me in her short white kilt when Minirt and I had leapt the pasture fence. Rai, whose earthly face was like stilled lightning. "Rai, my soul's love . . ." Since my return she had been close as my pulse, and the thought of her assuaged the guilt and pain I had held in my heart since the day of battle.

"Ahmose, you are distrait."

"Thure had two bracelets made for Sen-ut—with tree-frogs."

"Akh! Ra-en-Ra! Sen-ut—" We both looked at her empty stool. "She is with Rai . . . they are sharing Rai's Everlasting House." I looked up. "Thure did not tell you?" I shook my head. "Strange, Rai and Sen-ut . . ."

"Murdered." I heard my own whispered word.

"Ahmose? What did you say?" I shook my head again. Then she said, her voice low with hatred, "That fat little traitor pig . . . Teti of Neferusi." Then she shook the thought away, and the jeweled periwinkle shells and tiny flowers among the tight curls of her wig glinted and gleamed. "Where is Thure?" she asked.

"He would not come to the feast. He is with his father in their small house."

"I spoke with him when he brought Sen-ut back to Thebes. He lives now only to fight the Hyksos and to find Teti of Neferusi—Ahmose, hard fighting still lies before us." She put her small hand on my knee. "But Kamose has promised me my own estate in Sit-kemose—just outside Memphis."

"I drove out to it. It is verdant."

"I know, as all the North Land, green and fresh. The Holy Bulls graze on it."

"I saw the new Apis Bull. He has all the signs."

"It is an augury! He is the first for a long age." Her eyes were bright with joy. "Akmose, look! The golden cups! Hidden for two hundred years underneath Ptah's Temple. Grand-son, we drink our wine tonight from golden cups, fine-carved and jewel-inlaid more than a thousand years gone by, in the Days of Splendor." She cocked an eyebrow at me. "From my own city," she said, and tossed her curls again, laughing like a girl. I laughed with her, and, leaning toward her, I kissed her, rejoicing that for the first time since her childhood she had around her the treasures she remembered in her heart. She looked at me with pleased surprise. Then her eyes looked past me. "Ra-en-Ra! Here is Pen!"

I turned to look. "He is pale and weak," I said.

He came, holding the arm of Res and wearing the long robe of a priest to cover his bandages. He is well, I thought, he will follow Kamose to fight Teti's hosts; and my heart was lifted as he sat gingerly down in a chair next to Ak-hor and the twins, and looked up at me with a wry half-smile, for there was a deep scar on his cheek.

"And here comes the Queen!" Tetisheri sat up in her chair. "What radiant beauty enters with her!" My grandmother's gray eyes shone. "To your own chair, Grand-son," she said.

But Pen-aati had taken my chair, and he and the King were in deep quiet talk. So I went to where the stools for Kamose's Company, each with its own small table, had always stood, to the left of the dais, and took Thure's vacant stool.

Though a hush fell, and all eyes except Kamose's were turned toward her as she entered with her retinue, I did not watch Nefertari. I turned to Pen, who, pointing to cushions richly bright, said, "Look, my Prince—from the North Land."

Huge and soft and filled with goose-feathers, they were strewn about the floor. I smiled and gazed about me. The pillars of the Center-court were wreathed with flowers: peonies, wine red, and frailer poppies, all intertwined with the stronger, bright acacia flowers. I thought of the feast in Ameni's House, and the flowers of the verdant Delta. "Inhapi—O Festal Body—" In my own man's flesh I felt the shiver of her hips, the cool smooth of her breasts. "Inhapi, sweet in love is the daughter of Ameni. . . ."

"My Prince." Res left her stool to sit at Pen's feet on a cushion. "We now have two warrior Princes."

Pen turned slowly in his chair. "I would that I had seen the blow that saved Abydos." And though it hurt to stretch his scar, his smile grew wider.

I shook my head. I was not able to speak of the pain and

guilt in me till I was with Kheri-heb. "I have the King's word," I said. "He will not stay my Temple studies."

We all turned to look at him. Pen-aati had left the Dais, and Kamose and Nefertari were receiving the Great Ones and the Elders and Nobles of Thebes. I saw that all gave equal homage to the Queen, and that she and Thuty were guarded in the meeting of their eyes.

Kamose sat in our father's ebony chair, its ram's feet clawing the Dais, as they had clawed the floor of his room when I played about him as a child. "Seken-en-Ra II, the Brave!" The thought of him brought my mother close, and suddenly my desire was to be with her in her small Lodge beside the Sacred Lake.

Mer-neb, Per-neb and Ak-hor were talking war plans, their heads together, and Res was wreathing her lover's neck with corn-flowers, Hor-min sat with the Priests and Montu-Thoth. Their cushions were hard, of bright blue leather, and they sat on their heels, as Priests sit, by the short-legged tables. Behind them, stiff as the high-backed chairs in which they sat, the Chief Scribe and his daughter, he fat, she thin and angular, watched the scene. They did not talk to the guests around them, nor to each other. I found it hard to look at her, and instead I watched Miutu. He was talking with the Old One on the Dais behind Tetisheri. "High Priest and Chief of Visions." I thought he had not changed since my father's day, and he was ancient then. He turned around, and our eyes met in friendship and in love. I remembered his smile on my first day in the House of Life, when he had walked away with Hor-min and Aja was barking.

"Being at home again," I said to Pen, "fills my heart with memories."

As we drank the tangy first wine, Kamose's mullet-roes were served, plain and faintly spiced, as he would have them, and Tetisheri laughed, her eyes bright with tears as she looked upon the King.

"Mullet-roes," she said, "at a triumphal banquet!"

And all there laughed and relished the fishermen's fare,

except Ahmose-Eb! On his stool beside Ak-hor, he was looking at his plate and eating nothing. I saw the sharp eyes of
Sittek narrow as she looked at him. With a tight smile, she
spoke, and the sound of her voice grated on my ear.

"The Lord Ahmose, Ebana's son, is far too thin," she said.
"And where is his appetite?"

"It is a wife he lacks," the Chief Scribe said, holding out
his fat hands to be laved before the next course. "It is, of a
surety, time that he married."

Seeing Ahmose-Eb's disquiet, I beckoned to him. "Come,
take Tetaky's stool here, beside me," I said, and he was
blushing when he sat down.

A serving maiden poured out new wine for him and we
drank together. Then, his blushes fading, he whispered, "My
Prince, I thank you. I am ashamed before Sittek and her
father—yet I am fallen ill of love for Atu. My heart is
heavy."

I sighed and thought it was true. He was thinner than I
had ever seen him. "Have you spoken of this matter to the
King?"

"He said he would speak with me during this feast."

"Then he will summon you to sit with him."

"When his mind is whirling with plans of battle—and
Herath?"

I smiled. "You know he will not forget."

We watched our household maidens, slim and naked save
for a belt of colored beads and the Menat-collar each one
wore to the glory of Hat-hor. "Hat-hor, help Ahmose-Eb,
for he is sick of love," I asked of the Goddess, and looked
at my brother.

He wore the short white kilt, his golden Horus-collar and
his lion bracelet, and he looked around him with radiant
grace. Though ofttimes he turned and spoke to the Queen, he
did not meet her eyes, or touch her, and I saw my grand-
mother shake her head with a frown, and sigh. But Nefertari
smiled. She is more regal in manner than the King, I thought,
as she who would never be truly Royal clapped her hands

and the music rose, and three girl dancers came to their place before the Dais.

The music softened again and was haunting and far away as they began the ancient dance of the Wind and the Reeds. One maiden, tall, in a full linen cloak thin as insects' wings, was the Wind. The other two were Reeds, and they were swaying to the gentle wind of Perit.

Then the Wind stood straight and tall and slim, her arms upraised, waving and weaving, a fair, healthy wind, and the Reeds swayed with her. As the music died away, she sank slowly down to the ground and lay inert, a wind no more. The Reeds rose tall and straight with sap and the life-giving water at their roots, and stretched upward to the sky. The music rose. The Wind quivered. She raised her arms, cloud-skimming like birds' wings, and leapt from the ground with a rush, high into the air. The Reeds shivered now, and rippled. Bending low, they lay almost flat on the ground as the harps and the pipes played shriller and faster, and ever stormier grew the Wind, bending the Reeds backward, their long hair trailing the floor and rippling along the tiles as waves on the River, till all three of them, with a sigh of gentle motion, were still, and the Court was silent.

Then a strange music sounded, a different tune, and it was merry.

"The Hyksos Princess!" Ahmose-Eb leaned toward me. "I have heard this music since we sailed from Avaris—and my Prince, you will see Atu."

But I was watching my brother. He straightened in his chair and his eyes glowed as, with the soft, joyful sound, Herath, followed by six maidens, each playing on a small sharp-angled harp, came, with youthful dignity into the Court.

"She brings her music with her," I said to Ahmose-Eb.

He nodded. His eyes were deep with love, and his face was now quite pale. "It has a thin, sweet sound," he said, "unlike that of our long curved harps."

Herath walked with flowing grace to the Dais. Her gaze

was lowered till, in front of Kamose, she bowed with reverence. As she rose, she looked full into his eyes. Then, lowering her gaze again, she bowed to Nefertari and, with deeper homage, to our grand-mother. I saw that she was beautiful. Her thick black curling hair hung long, to her waist, and was threaded with jewels. She wore rich robes of a soft and gently shining stuff, not linen, that covered her rounded body but revealed as much as the moth-wing linen our Egyptian women wore. I found delight in looking at her, and as she rose and smiled at Kamose, there was a hint of mischief in her smile that made me think of Rai. My heart leapt. I wondered how two women, so different to look upon, could have the same brightness of spirit, and I understood why my brother had spent his nights with her in the Hyksos yacht. I rejoiced that he had found a woman of double beauty to share his love and his life. Then, as I watched her, Herath startled swiftly as a bird, and I, too, looked at Nefertari. I had seen pride and rage, envy, chagrin and desire in my half-sister's eyes and the darker things of my mother's and my own foreboding, but never had I seen, nor hope to see again, a malice so baneful as now darted swift as an adder's tongue from the pupils of her long eyes. In the space of my glance, she was smiling. She smiled at the Hyksos Princess. But all I could see was her long brown back as she knelt in her garden, herb-gathering, and the death that had come to the living loveliness that was Rai.

Kamose stepped down and held out his hand to Herath. She laid her hands in his and he led her to a chair next to Pen-aati and his pleasure-loving wife, who put her hand on the arm of Herath's chair and leaned toward her. The Vizir's wife chattered without ceasing, but her words held naught of guile, and she was kind. Pen-aati bowed to Herath, a rare smile in his eyes, and I saw a flash of fine white teeth.

"Pen," I said, "in all these years this is only the second time I have seen Pen-aati's teeth—the second time I have seen him smile."

"He has something to smile about," Pen said. "I told you Herath was brave and beautiful."

"Ay! Yah!" Res eased her cushion nearer to him, and he looked down at her and ruffled her short hair. "But not as you, my Little Spy." She took his hand and held it against her cheek, then asked, "Ahmose-Eb? At whom are you staring so?"

He flushed again, and turned away from Atu, sitting among Herath's maidens, playing her harp. I leaned over to him. "She is lovely," I whispered. "You must talk to the King." I looked at Sittek, but her small eyes, bright with curiosity, were on the Hyksos Princess, as Kamose, standing by her chair told all there assembled, "This is the Princess Herath, daughter of the tyrant king, Apophis, in Avaris." He looked down at her. "Her words, advice and actions brought victory to the South Land."

There was a murmur of welcome, and manifold smiles. Herath bowed her head and with a slow smile beckoned her maidens to sit on cushions around her, as Kamose went back to his chair and the house-men, to the roll of drums and the applause of the merry and hungry guests, came into the Court with huge golden platters held high on their heads. I saw, with joy, that Ita was serving us again, and her eyes were bright with happiness.

"I should be drooling," Ahmose-Eb said, and I thought that love had, of a surety, taken my friend's appetite. "No remedies avail me—when Atu is mine, I shall be well."

I put my hand on his shoulder for a moment. Then Ak-hor, still talking with the twins of battle and tactics, said, "There is a secret Council tomorrow." I thought of the hidden chamber underground, where since my father's day our plans had been formed. "You will be there, my Prince?"

I shook my head. "I am no longer a battle scribe—tomorrow I go to the House of Life, and meet with Kheri-heb."

"That was a warrior's stroke," Ak-hor said, and his soft black eyes shone with a strange admiration. His wounds were almost healed and he was eating with relish. "I have never seen such a feast as this," he said as he eyed the stall-fed beef our maidens were serving, and the cucumbers stewed in wine.

"And peas dried in the sun since the harvest," Res told us.

The gazelle meat and haunches of wild deer were served with a sauce of figs stewed in honey, with lettuce boiled, and radishes, and on each platter there was a flower.

When they had served each course, our maidens sat on one knee in a row in front of the long table, and tapping their mouths with their hands they sang and made warbling, quavering mouth-music. I was laughing and warm with wine, and I forgot Nefertari as Kamose beckoned to Ahmose-Eb to sit in the chair next to him.

"Plead your case well, Sailor-man," I said as he rose, and Hor-min came and sat near to me. I saw Ahmose-Eb lean forward, tense. Then I saw my brother's eyes light up with laughter, though he did not smile, and I thought that our friend would marry his Atu, who sang in a kitchen-ship and played a small harp as she sat on soft cushions at the King's triumphal feast. She was small and slender, fair-skinned and dark-eyed, and I was happy for him. Then Res opened her eyes in surprise.

"The Blind Harper! My Prince—he must be a hundred years old!"

"Not quite," Pen laughed, and Mer-neb said. "This is the first time he has come into this Court since the days of your father, my Prince."

The youth attending him led him to the place in front of the Dais, and when he was sitting, with one knee raised, he gave into his hand the ancient harp. Tawny yellow it was, and I remember it since childhood, with its markings of red, black and yellow, and the Eye of Horus painted on its base. His bony fingers touched the bright red strings. Looking with sightless eyes toward the King, he sang to him:

"Your eye is clearer than the stars of heaven.
Your eyes see farther than the sun.
Voices spoken afar off, you hear inside your ear,
And hidden deeds are plain to the Ka-eyes
    of the King.

"The God of taste is in your mouth,
Maat, Goddess of Truth, is in your heart,

Your tongue is golden with the words
    of your desiring,
And the God is seated on your lips. . . ."

He sang in an ancient rhythm and cadence. It was as if the words and the music were the twin births of one passionate meeting, and his voice seemed never to grow old, as the Nile never ceases to flow and nights for lovers are ever young.

Res, gazing at the tall, thin old man, her voice soft, said, "My father told me that once, long ago, one of his harp-strings snapped and for a moment he checked in his music. Then a cicada made the sound of the missing notes and the Blind Harper was not troubled at all by the broken string."

We were all smiling. The Blind Harper sang the Song of the River:

"Hail! All greeting to Hapi,
    Giver of gifts,
    Bearer of All Essence,
    Guide of seeds, nourisher of grains,
    Provider of breasts and udders,
    O River of Life!
    No man knows thy secret caverns.
    No writing has ever revealed thy Name.
    But all the fruits of the earth are of Thee. . . ."

The feasting had ended. The last merry, chattering guest had left the King's House. Only the wild, harsh scrawl of a he-cat rent the silence, startling me, though I was not asleep. I lay, cold, under the linen cover. The merriment and the wine-warmth of this festal night, the love in us all, one for the other, as we sat in our old places, battle-worn and triumphant, simple and close, amid the rich spoils of our victory, should have brought peace to my heart. But not even the hidden thoughts of Hur, slain, and of my confession to Kheri-heb on the morrow, were as strong as the stress in me, the encroachment, of Nefertari. The stark malice in her eyes went beyond human malice to the Evil of the Shadow that summons unquiet spirits from the Nether-place and calls up the Dark Kings with Four Heads who are the minions of Set. I could not wipe her from my thoughts. The over-whelming chill that had all but sent my Ka out of me when we drove into the Court-yard held me in thrall. The evil resplendence of her! This evil waited. For whom? For what deed? I feared for Herath. "Osiris, Lord . . . Watcher Who has gained mastery over the workers of desecration—Osiris, Lord, watch over the King's House. Hold us all in thy hands away from hostile forces. . . ." I was trying to gather, to husband my strength, with the sacred words. "Osiris, Lord of Life, guard Herath——"

"Brother!" Kamose came into my room. "I am going to make the Princess Herath Royal Wife." My fear leapt up into my throat and choked me. "What is wrong? You start as a gazelle at the first arrow-prick."

I sat up. Almost without my willing, so deep inside me was the cold abyss of my fear, my lips formed her name. "Nefertari."

"Akh!" My brother stiffened. Then he walked around the foot of the bed and back again, and came close, looking down at me. "That is the other name my tongue shall never honor with utterance—I could put her evil in front of the High Priests and the people of the Two Lands, for I have proof of her crime." He sat down on the bed. Then, as the sun through a storm-cloud, his face broke into a sudden broad smile. "She is beautiful, my little rebel Princess! Her body is soft and strong. She will bear me sons——"

"And the people will love her that she gave us warning."

"Soon they will love her for herself. Ahmose, I leave Thebes on the third day, as we planned. Neshi will strengthen the garrisons of the freed cities and hold Memphis, while with all speed I put this Neferusian army to rout—by Ra's Grace! And let us pray to Ra that Aknere will be at the secret Council tomorrow with the news that I desire."

"Aknere will not fail," I said.

"Then to the Cataract Fort—and Nubia."

"What news from Pery-em-wah in Avaris?"

"Apophis has put it abroad that Herath was captured by the Hawk Prince of the South Land, and this has aroused every man to be warrior."

"This is an old ploy! It worked on the Theban men when Anat-neby was thought to be captured by Apophis."

"How strange is Fate." My brother mused for a while. Then his face grew stern. "There is other news. They have discovered the secret tunnels in the eastern wall." He stood up. "As Ra loves me, this evil city shall not stand in the Two Lands! But first this army the Set-pig has mustered outside our walls . . ." He walked around my bed again, talking half to himself. "Ten thousand of our Home Army, whose land is flooded, have already joined our regular forces awaiting me in the Eastern Desert." I looked at him in wonder. He stood still, grinning at me. "Though my nights were spent in Herath's sweet trap, my days were spent in plans for this new desert battle—at the Council tomorrow, you will hear it all."

"Kamose, I go to the Temple at dawn."

"So do I . . . the Dawn Rite."

"Then I go to Kheri-heb in the Court of Learning."

He laughed and lay on my bed, his bare feet at my head, his head at my feet. For a while I thought he slept, but quietly, as my eyelids grew heavy, he began to tell me the plans he had made, and my heart rejoiced. I was no longer drowsy. They were daring plans, wild and wise, and my heart was eased.

"The Set-pigs will be thrust far out of the Beloved Land. I will pursue them to Saruhen and the other cities they have caused, with our riches, to flourish and threaten our borders. . . . In three days the new battle begins . . ." He sat up. "While they think we are celebrating our triumphs, the Neferusian's army will be destroyed." He breathed the words slowly, and I thought, He is very King! King and Protector. "But first my marriage to Herath, so that the child in her womb will be a Royal child." He saw the fear return to my eyes. "Ra-en-Ra! Little Brother, I shall not have the half-sister beheaded—though the thought pleases me! No! I will not disturb the Royal House of the Two Lands. We will contain our own evil." He raised an eyebrow. "The half-sister has many who fawn on her."

"The friends of the wicked shall fall away like poisoned flies," I said. "She may refuse to countenance Herath as Secondary Royal Wife. . . . Mayhap persuasion . . . riches and lands . . . Akh! No, that is as likely as horns on a hare."

We fell silent awhile. His face was grim. I saw that his heart was set and I thought of my mother's words in Abydos.

"Herath will be Secondary Royal Wife." My brother sat with his chin in his hand.

"Our mother has a thought." He looked up at me. "She knows, as we all know, that our half-sister has long desired to be High Priestess. She has long been filled with envy of our mother. She covets the powers and riches that go with the Office—and more! Our mother says she yearns to be worshiped as a goddess."

Slowly, thoughts taking form in his eyes, he nodded. "That Crown—Hat-hor's horns! The priestess-aping maidens . . . when I saw them I thought it an arrogant game. Ahmose, my wise one! My wise Little Brother! Surely Hat-hor inspires your heart."

"No, our mother's," I said, and told him all she had said to me in the carrying-chair at Abydos. He sat on my bed cross-legged, his elbows on his knees and his chin in his hands, listening to every word.

"By the Serpent of Hat-hor! The half-sister shall become the Bride of the God—Ra will understand. . . ." He laughed. "She shall reign over an establishment richer than she has ever dreamed . . . within the Temple precincts! And sit there weaving her spells and counting her revenues . . . and lying with her lovers." He laughed again and the sound echoed through the still House and glanced against the pillars, back and forth from one to the other like sun-light thrown bright from leaf to leaf of morning trees; and after the night air had held it, the great triumphant sound died away, and there was silence, not a stirring in all the House. It was the laughter of a god, and only the gods could hear it. "I will speak to our mother at the Hour of the Perfuming of the Mouth, after the Dawn Rite . . . and before the evening meal, I shall pay my first and my last visit to the garden of—" His eyes held a scorn too deep for words.

"The garden of the new High Priestess of Hat-hor," I ended for him, then added, "Our mother, when she first heard of Herath, prayed long—she has already spoken to Miutu."

"Miutu, High Priest and Chief of Visions—Little Brother, how will he consent?"

"It will be only in the worldly sense that Nefertari is Priestess. She will not be allowed nor will she have interest in fasting and the Holy retreats of the true Priest. She covets power and adulation. Our mother's plan is a true one. Nefertari will have all the vast revenues, the outer trappings, of High Priestess, and she will still wear the Great White Crown of the First Royal Wife. A small pride will be lost, that Herath is Secondary Royal Wife . . . ."

"You have persuaded me. It is a wise plan—the only plan."

I felt full of joy again. "Our mother will persuade Miutu."

Kamose pushed me down into the bed, his strong hand on the top of my head, and pulled the linen cover up to my chin. "I miss your side-lock," he said. "What would I do without my little Priest-Brother, who with one warrior stroke slew the cruel Hur and freed the city of Abydos?" He stood straight, looking down at me. "And now, I must be cleansed and shaved and shriven for the Dawn Rite." Laughing softly, with long swift strides, as quiet on the reed matting as Sekmet's padded paws, he left me.

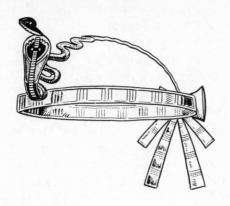

CHAPTER IX

Kheri-heb was waiting for me. Tall, familiar and beloved, he stood in the bright early sun-light between the dark blue shadows of the pillars. We did not embrace, but he put his right hand on my brow and his left hand on my heart, in welcome and blessing. Then we sat down, our spines straight, on our square stools, our feet together and our hands, palms down, upon our knees, in the cool silence of the small and ancient Court of Learning.

Not a word passed our lips. My Master was the Stillness itself, inside me, and my soul was washed in the waters of the Quiet. When, at high noon, a web-priest brought grapes and honeyed milk to us, the hours had seemed but a swift moment.

After the priest had laved our hands Kheri-heb bade me speak the stress in my heart.

"You know all my heart," I said.

"Put your guilt into words."

"I killed a man. Though it was Hur the Cruel One, and he would have slain the King . . . I have killed a fellow man."

"Your words lack wisdom." His gaze was a spear through my whole being. "With what sad righteousness your face is lengthened. When you say, 'I have killed a fellow man,' you speak as one who nothing knows. Life cannot be slain. The Life within all things stands beyond harm. Life cannot slay. Life cannot be slain. The end of birth is death. The end of death is birth. Not you, nor I nor Hur can ever cease to be." His eyes held mine. "But the living soul can be smirched and come to infamy, and man be less than man, if the task at hand is not accomplished to the full, be it in peace or war. Let no man leave the duty that stands before his face, though it seem to bear blame. For every work on earth is blamed by some of the men of earth, as fire is wrapped in smoke." As though he read the thought in my heart, he waited for me to speak.

"I stood looking down at Hur's body . . . and for a swift moment I felt—strange word!—a harmony between the slayer and the slain."

Kheri-heb was silent. Then he said,

"There is deep upon deep of mystery here . . . and words are clumsy tools. Prince Ahmose, by your virgin blow you released the Ka of Hur. His one grace, after his life of greed and rapine here, is that he fell in battle, and by the first stroke of your hand, innocent of slaying. Your ax touched not Ra's life in Hur. No weapon can touch that life, nor fire burn, nor water drown It. The man new-dead is as the man new-born: still-living man, one same, existent spirit. Hur goes toward the life he sought in his life here. My Prince"—Kheri-heb's amber eyes burned into my soul—"it was a spark of good in him, so small amid his evil, that drew your virgin ax into his flesh . . . and, my Son, a good in you!

You rose to the task in front of you." I closed my eyes. His words had touched a spark in my understanding. I listened, my eyes still closed. "Hur will go before the Judgment of Osiris, his heart dark-heavy with his evil thoughts and deeds. Had he lived longer in this flesh, they were too great even for Osiris' deep compassion."

"Osiris, Lord . . . !" I said the beloved name deep inside me, opened my eyes and met my Master's gaze. "Osiris would not have us in array against our fellows."

He smiled. "Osiris is peace . . . the unchanging, radiant peace in each man's soul. A time will come when we are not in array against our fellows."

"And till that time?"

"There is work and war, and full travail."

My stubborn tongue formed the question in my heart since boyhood. "Master, are not all men created by God, in love?"

"In Eternity, when all is fulfilled, men shall find, beyond the peace of Osiris, each man his own Self, in Amun-Ra!" His gaze purged my thought, changing it. I felt a pain at the top of my head. "There are two Paths for men. The Path that saves by true work; and the Path that is attained by meditation. Yet, Ahmose, these two Paths are One! No man shall escape from acts by shunning action, and none—nay none!—shall, by mere renouncing, find his soul. He who abstains from the task before his face in Ra's created world is shameful, and his life, more precious than fine gold, is vain. My Son, be not cast down in sorrow, nor over-full of joy in happiness. Take evil things and good neither desponding nor exalting. Ahmose, Neophyte and Prince, know the Changeless Spirit in the changing flesh. Know how action may be rest . . . rest, action!"

"As the King in battle . . ."

"As the King in battle . . ." His voice was not an echo of my words, but a fulfilling. "Kamose was born Initiate, and Warrior of Amun. Before the Cobra's Fiery Power was placed upon his brow, he was Initiate . . . Pharaoh . . . Per-aa! Two-fold Great House. Seat of the God-thought in man, becoming, unfolding, throughout thousands of years. Ahmose, those who have glutted their hot appetites on the beloved Land must be, till the end of this Ram's Age, thrust out, that this Land's work for piety and the ancient faith be unabated till the work is full accomplished. . . . O Prince of the Two Lands, Ahmose, this Egypt is the Image of Heaven. . . ." As I watched, his body grew rock-still. The sun's light seemed to gather in him. His skin grew pale, as at my father's Funeral Rite. His eyes gazed into realms beyond men's sight, and his voice was not his voice. "Ta-mery, the Land Beloved, is the reflection below of the Celestial Order. . . ." My flesh seemed to loosen on my ˙bones as I sat there, still and cool. "The time will come when it will seem that this battle for thousands of years against the Powers of the Shadow and the Darkness of Set—our victory, our faith and piety—have been in vain. Darkness will be preferred to Light, the pious man thought mad and the impious hailed as Master. The evil-hearted one, lusting for power and mouthing clever blasphemies, will be applauded as the best of men, and every holy voice will be condemned to silence. O Egypt! O Ta-mery! Use well the centuries yet granted unto you! For the time will come when this Holy Land, hallowed by ancient shrines and temples, will be filled with the sepulchers of the dead. Only words graven on stone will bear witness to our adoration of the God, and our long devotion. Men, long ages hence, will ponder them, and smile and not believe. The gods will return to Heaven, and in the Beloved Land the few Egyptians who remain will be alien, and their ancient speech and piety held up to contempt and sneering. O Lamentable Rift between the God of Gods, the gods and men!" Slowly his gaze came back to me with human warmth. "My Son, we must win this fight. At this needle-point in time, Egypt is threatened. The forces of Set must be contained within the Two Lands, as the evil in the King's House must be contained, that the destiny of Thebes, and the work, the initial mission of Ta-mery may be fulfilled. . . ." He stood up, a lone Priest-man, apart, Initiate, and held out his right hand to me. I rose and stood in front of him. "Ahmose, born Prince, and seeker of the Truth, the gods have their plan for you . . . and for the King." His eyes held mine, but I could not fathom the depth of his Knowing, nor read the message in his gaze. I waited for his words. Yet when he spoke, standing tall in Ra's westering light, his outstretched hand upon my shoulder, his words were trite, and their content already known to me. "Two days hence," he said, "the King will lead his hosts to battle."

Still in the golden light of Ra descending, my soul bathed in my Master's grace, I walked away from the small Temple Court and around the Sacred Lake to my mother's Lodge. She was waiting for me on her seat at the edge of the water, and in her hand that rested on her knees she held a looking-bronze. Smiling as I approached, she held it up and I saw myself. My shoulders were broader and more square. The roundness of youth had left my cheeks.

"My Moon Child," she said. "You left this place, when the King sent for you, a boy. When I saw you in Abydos, you were a man . . . and a warrior." I remembered how I had thought the same of my brother when he returned from Kus with our father's murdered body and knelt, weeping, beside my bed. "How like your father you look, Ahmose, at this moment." My mother turned the looking-bronze away from me and made dappled light with it on the smooth surface of the water. "Sit down beside me. My Young One, it is well that you are strong in body. To be Regent, with all the duties of that Office, and Initiate both, you will need all your new-found strength."

"I have been all this day with Kheri-heb." My mother's smile deepened. "All through the morning hours, silent we sat together, and my soul was washed of corroding guilt, and my heart refreshed. . . . Then, my Mother, Kheri-heb prophesied! His Ka sought realms beyond my power to follow . . . and his eyes! Before I left him they held a Knowing I could not fathom. But when he spoke, he said only, 'Two days hence, the King will lead his hosts to battle."

"All will be resolved." She took my hand. Her own was warm and strong. "The evil in the Royal Household, Ahmose, it will be contained within the Royal Household . . . by Ra's Grace. Miutu has been closeted for three hours with Nefertari. High Priestesshood, with all the offices, lands and revenues, has been offered to her."

"And she will still be Great Royal Wife. . . ."

"But she will accept the Princess Herath as Second Royal Wife, as befitting a Princess." My mother's eyes glowed. "And a beautiful one . . . Akh! Here is Miutu!" Our High Priest and Chief of Visions was walking slowly toward us. "From his aspect," my mother whispered, "it would seem that Nefertari has accepted the Holy Office." She stood up. "My Young Warrior"—she put her hand on my shoulder—"I would be alone with Miutu. . . . We have much to ask of the God, of wisdom . . . and forgiveness."

I kissed her nose to nose, and with a bow to the High Priest I left them together. As there hung an hour before the evening meal, I walked slowly, and without firm willing, to the Old One's Study-court.

Senseneb was squatting on his mat beside the ancient Hour-vase of the Night, and as I came through the pillars he looked up, held his stiff neck and smiled. "Iwi! Iwi! Welcome! Welcome!" he said. "It is a long time since my young ones come back to the Court of Learning." He looked up at me. "You have changed, Ahmose." His eyes narrowed, searching. "You have been all day with Kheri-heb . . . it is all about you. But my Prince, your manhood and your Priesthood are not yet full reconciled." His merry eyes gleamed bright amid their mass of wrinkles. "You will be ready for your Ka trials at the new moon?"

"Senseneb . . . I know not."

"And your valiant deed! A warrior! My Priest-Prince, I am proud of you . . . and your grand-mother! At last, she sees you a very grand-son after all." He laughed, and I joyed in the familiar sound of it, strangely deep in the throat of so small a man. "The Queen Tetisheri has given me the pleasant task of listing the treasures captured from the Hyksos ships and from the traitors' houses in Kus and Neferusi . . . and the treasures from Memphis." He put down his palette, still holding the worn rush pen. "She is as a child with toys known aforetime, and imagined all her life, as in a dream. . . ." His eyes were soft, and his wrinkles seemed to smooth away. "She left me but a few minutes ago. . . . Sit down, Ahmose." As I sat down on my own childhood stool, he was saying, "She came to tell me news of great moment. Nefertari has made her decision to be High Priestess."

"I saw it in Miutu's eyes as he came toward us. I was with my mother. What says my grand-mother?"

He drew his brows together like a woman threading a needle. "To be Spouse of the God is the highest office in the Land, and Nefertari will have great power. She will also still be the Great Royal Wife"—he looked at me, his black eyes darting under their drooping lids—"but the Princess Herath is Royal . . . and she is beautiful."

"And the King loves her."

The Old One's face was suddenly blank as the clean sheet of papyrus that lay across his bony knees. "Nefertari has always longed to be High Priestess. She has accepted with all piety and humility," he said and, turning, looked me full in the eye. I saw his deep foreboding. Then he took up a pen. "Zatoo! So! I must to your grand-mother's lists."

On the third and last night of the feasting, at the evening meal Herath had a chair beside me on the Dais, to the side, a little behind Kamose, and this evening Ben-arpath was welcomed and sat with Pen-aati. The meal was joyful, but it was a solemn joy. Kamose had called an early end to the feast in his Household, for the dawn would bring great Ritual: a new High Priestess, a new Royal Wife and the day of battle. Laughter and quiet changed places often, and the men of the King's House danced the ritual dance of the Slaying of the Enemy. Our half-sister was resplendent in the jewels of the Great Royal Wife, but she wore a simple linen shift with straps that crossed between her bare breasts, and a collar of gold-and-carnelian that caught the light of the tall lamps. Her eyes were ebon pools, her eyebrows like the wings of the raven that nests in the Western Crags, and her skin was as polished copper. She was grace itself to Herath, smiling and making her famous puns, and Kamose, when he turned to her, was gentle. Herath, shy, sat in her colored robes and rarely lifted her eyes from her hands, folded in her lap when she was not eating.

I looked at Nefertari, searching for a glance to awaken again my fear of her, my fear for Herath! But she met my eyes as though she were waiting for my look and smiled so softly, and with such clear humility, that her face, serene and goddess-like, drew an answering smile from me. With a start, I thought, This is the first time in my whole life that I have smiled at Nefertari. She was all beneficence, quiet and tranquil. Then I thought of Rai, and my face stiffened. If my half-sister saw it she did not alter her glance or look away. I turned in disgust at my sudden weakness and wondered at her strange power, and while I wondered, I understood, for the first time, the love our grand-mother had ever felt for her son's natural daughter. She is like a snake with a hare, I thought, and makes people think and feel and do that which is foreign to them. Then I looked at Kamose and I knew that she could never have power over him. His power is of Ra. "Initiate . . ." I smiled, remembering Kheri-heb's words, and my smile broadened as I drank my wine with the thought that our half-sister, though she was beautiful and desired him and though she had used the dark magic, she had not lured the King to her bed. He had not lain with her, nor ever would. In her own pride and lust for power she had consented to be High Priestess and to accept a Princess, whom the King loved, to be Secondary Royal Wife. "Royal Wife . . ." I whispered and looked at Herath, and a shiver chilled through me with the thought of chattering Neme as he dressed me and my smile was gone. "Her Majesty, Queen Nefertari, seeks omens in the genitals of crocodiles, my Prince. . . . She mixes them with madder roots and the seeds of leeks, and her house-boy brought to her the feet of a young cock raven and the belly of a fat young tortoise, and she burned them all together, and she poured a putrid-smelling syrup into the fire, breathed in the smoke, called names and writhed and clutched her breasts—my wife was near to die of fear. . . ."

I shook away the thought and looked again at Nefertari, and as I looked, she turned in her chair. My hair-roots hackled. I held my breath. "She is with child!" I spoke the words inside me. "Thuty." I was still with shock. The child of two Royal bastards! Nefertari's first-born! Sweat broke out around my nape and temples. Except for the few in the King's Household, all Egypt will believe this child to be the King's! I found that I was staring. Then, covering my shock, I gave fervent praise to Amun-Ra that Kamose was so ordering his affairs that his own son or daughter by Herath would be the Royal Child. "And not the bastard child of Thuty." I almost smiled again. This my brother would never countenance. "Nefertari's child will be born in the Temple, and there the child will stay," I thought, and looked at Thuty. His long pale face showed no emotion, but in his eyes there was a light I had not seen before. He was quiet and did not, as was his wont, keep lusting eyes upon the Queen. "The Queen . . . with child . . ." The King away at the wars. Suddenly I was cold again with fear for Herath.

"You look as though the food has not agreed with you, Brother." Kamose turned around to me. "You will be appointed Regent tomorrow, at the Audience. . . . You are happy that these battles for Avaris will be written by Hormin? You will have time, Ahmose, for your Temple studies. . . . It is good that you stay in Thebes. I need a Regent I can trust." He lowered his voice but his face did not change. "Mer-neb and Per-neb have already left Thebes to join my

Army waiting in the Eastern Desert. This morning, Aknere at last brought news of the Neferusian's hiding place . . . the map of a secret way through the wadi. With Ra's help, we shall surprise them."

"Aknere never fails. May Ra keep him in his Light," I said.

"Ahmose, after the two Rites are performed, my marriage to Herath and the half-sister's High Priestesshood"—he could not keep the contempt out of his voice, though his eyes were deep and peaceful—"I shall ride out in my chariot to the Eastern Desert to join my hosts. Pen, Ak-hor and Thure will ride with me—and Hor-min." He smiled. "Ahmose-Eb will not see this desert fight, but look to his marriage with Atu and the preparing of the Royal Fleet for the attack on Nubia."

"I shall joy to see him wed."

"And he to have you stand with him. . . . You were in his confidence from the first—he told me. Akh! Our Sailor-man is deep in love." Kamose grinned. "He will sail southward to meet me after the desert battle, at Ed-fu. We shall surprise this desert army and conquer swiftly. Hir-ty and five other Messengers on Horses I shall keep with me that my orders may quickly pass from Captain to Captain. Little Brother, you are Guardian of our city. Look well to Herath—she is my own and very dear. Have Ina in your care, and my young daughter." His face was gentle. He loved the fair-skinned girl-child who had climbed on his knee and put flowers in his wig as he pored over the maps and plans for our first forays. "She brings good fortune," he said. "Guard well the City of the God." He put his hand on my shoulder. His fingers were strong and hard, but his eyes were warm. "I am remembering a desert night . . . and two soul-names in a single loop . . . carved in the granite rock. In these two names together, is our strength. . . . Brother, our Destiny is Ta-mery." As we talked together in front of all gathered there in the Center-court, it was as though we were again alone in the desert beyond Assuan, and I prayed with all my heart to prevail in my Ka-studies that I might be with my brother in sleep and know how he fared in each battle. We sat for a while in silence. Then Kamose turned away from me and called to Pen-aati, and I leaned forward to Herath. She was quiet as a lily in a pool, but her yellow-brown eyes sparkled with thoughts like darting fish, and as we talked, she glanced between her long lashes at Kamose and touched, without knowing, the sweet weight of her breasts. Then she smiled as her maidens came, half dancing and playing their small harps, into the Court; and I saw Atu.

She was third from the left and her face was alight with joy. Her eyes sought and found Ahmose-Eb with a gaze that brought the red blood to his happy face. It had not been easy. I looked across at Sittek. She had a satisfied smirk on her thin face. And well she might! I thought. Kamose had judged her father's plea before the evening meal on the second day of feasting.

In front of the King, she and her father had pleaded for redress. Looking at Sittek now, simpering, gloating, I could not believe her rancor and her tears, nor the pompous outrage of the Chief Scribe.

He had read his plea from a papyrus scroll. With acid, well-chosen words he had denounced Ahmose-Eb and demanded compensation. And Sittek! She had had ashes on her brow. A weeping, rejected figure she stood, her shoulders slumped despairing, and while her father, with tears in his eyes, told of her youth wasted in waiting for her faithless betrothed, she had quietly beat her flaccid breasts and moaned.

Kamose had ended the unpleasant scene with swift, sure grace. "Your plea is just," he said and, calling a scribe to his Throne Chair, he spoke the words of his decree. "Ahmose, son of Ebana of El Kab, Fan Bearer on my right hand, and this day honored by my Majesty as Keeper of the Halyard in the Boat of the King, gives greeting to you and to your daughter, Sittek." He had not smiled at the weeping woman. Ahmose-Eb's face had been set and pale. "Ahmose, son of Ebana, has gifted to you, in compensation for his rejection of you, one half of his inheritance, and all his estates in Nek-heb." I saw Ahmose-Eb's fan quiver, so tense and tight were his fists, and the twitch of Ak-hor's lips, though his black eyes glanced at his friend with swift sympathy. "And further," Kamose was saying, "he has transferred to you his second largest house, the parks around it and the animals bred in those parks."

The Chief Scribe had lowered his eyelids, but not quickly enough to hide the glint of greedy triumph in his eyes. Ahmose-Eb's face was wan, but his fan was steady. Sittek had walked backward from the Throne Chair, her weeping and pleading forgotten. It seemed to me, looking at her now with the scented cone on her narrow head, that the satisfied smile would be forever carven on her thin face, and I was again lost in amaze at my brother's wisdom.

Herath's maidens had ceased their music, and Kamose and Pen-aati their talk. My brother held out his hand to Nefertari. She rose from her chair, stately tall, and we all rose with her. Together they walked through the lines of bowing courtiers and out between the pillars. As I watched them disappear, I thought that Nefertari had gained her long-coveted honor, High Priestesshood, with its revenues, land and power, and had lost nothing but her woman's pride. Herath rose and put her hand on my arm. I saw the courtiers turn toward her. As they looked on her young, soft loveliness many of them inclined their heads and smiled, and my thought came back to me as a ball bounced off a wall. Nefertari's pride. Her woman's pride! All in the Two Lands would now know of Kamose's love for the Hyksos Princess. Egyptians had already cheered her yacht, knowing the aid she had given their King, as she sailed with our Fleet to Thebes. All Egypt would know that Nefertari, for all her tall bronze beauty, now shared the King's love. "And Herath is no concubine . . . but a Princess who, tomorrow, will be Secondary Royal Wife." As we walked down the steps behind Tetisheri and the Old One, I was chill again. "Her woman's pride . . . She is with child! Why? What can she wish for this bastard child? Kamose will proclaim his own and Herath's child, whether boy or girl, the Falcon-child and Heir, unless . . ." My fear for Herath burst out of me in a cold sweat. Her hand was warm on my bare arm. I put my own over it for a moment and made to myself a solemn vow. "While I am Regent in Thebes, no harm shall come to Herath, my brother's own dear love."

I was lying on my bed, eased by my resolve and the knowledge that I could rely on the two High Priests, my mother and Pen-aati. "Not for one moment will she be un-watched," I swore again to myself, and with the abating of my fear, I lay and let Inhapi fill all my thought. I had bid her, commanded and begged her that she would come to the place where I would be. "I will sail upriver to Thebes," she had promised, "when the battle is won." "Come now . . ." I spoke the words softly as though she could hear me. "In-hapi, red as ripe figs are your lips . . . Come to Thebes now. I am Regent . . . Inhapi, like a night lily in the moon-light you waited . . . your girdle fell, Inhapi . . . the golden cups of your breasts . . . O Cool Breasts . . . Inhapi . . ." I lay, drifting into sweet half-slumber.

"Hiya! Little Brother!" Kamose's voice and the sound of sandaled feet on the garden tiles brought me back to myself. "Ahmose, get up!" Kamose was wearing a square-cut car-penter's wig, a loin-cloth and sandals, and Herath, her long, heavy, soft-waving hair coiled up on the top of her head like the maidens who carry the water-jars, was wearing a long dark-blue village girl's robe. Res, in her short kilt, and Hor-min, his reed pipe stuck in his loin-cloth, came, almost dancing, past the pillars of my room. "We are joining, on this last night of the feast, in the revels of the Thebans. . . . Come!" Kamose stood with his arm about Herath's waist and there was no more joy on Ra's earth than the joy in her eyes. "Come, Little Brother."

"We shall not leave without you." Pen still wore his long robe, but his wounds were healed. He was able to pull me up from the bed to my feet, and together we went out among the roistering people.

It was the first time in my life that I had been in the City of the God when the people were making merry, and my eyes were large as Thebes itself, watching them. The wrestlers, painted red and black, in girdles of bright-colored leather, tumbled each other, bracing themselves with great shouts and groans, jumping away, gripping each other's waists and toppling one over the other to the shouts and jeers and encouragement of the crowd. And the acrobats! There were three groups of them in bright beaded loin-cloths. We watched as three stood, their sturdy legs sprung wide apart, while the others, running, leapt onto their shoulders, three, two, one, forming a pyramid! Herath gasped as they loosed their hands and stood there by sheer balancing, and laughed and let out her breath as they seemed to flow to the ground like water at the Cataracts, and leap high, like frogs, one over the other.

A group of weight-lifters, each for a prize, were lifting heavier and heavier bags of sand aloft over their heads. Two teams played with balls, three to each side, catching them with one hand, their other hands tied to their chests. One tall, fair-skinned boy won every catch, and amid praise and laughter drank a whole jug of barley-beer without taking breath, while male dancers with tall reed helmets crashed their cymbals and leapt up in the air, to fall down on their loins, their long legs spread out flat to the front and the back.

"They have no joints at all!" Res cried, and turned, laughing, to watch some young boys swinging each other around, then letting loose and landing in ever more comic and vulgar postures, holding them till they rolled on the ground holding their bellies in riotous mirth.

We walked along hand in hand, avoiding the lurching ones already drunk on the dark, potent beer. Coming to the Market Place we paused at the edge of an open space where a young man and woman were holding their hands, crossed, and whirling around so that they were a blur in the eyes of the watchers; Kamose took Herath's hands and they, too, whirled around and around till her hair fell loose and he caught her, breathless, in his arms and kissed her.

"I am dizzy with looking," Res said to Hor-min, who was watching two youths sitting back to back and trying to rise up without touching their hands to the ground.

"Remember?" I turned to Pen.

"Tetaky! He was the best of all of us. He was the lightest-built and seemed to raise himself as though he were a feather. . . . Let's try our hand at this!" He picked up a pointed knife from a row of them on a rough table, took aim and hurled it at the eye of Set's Boar crudely painted on a square block of wood. He missed the eye.

"Too much wine, my Beloved," Res teased him, and he took another knife. "Ring it against the first one," she said, and took one herself. She hit the eye! I threw after her and rang her knife, Hor-min rang mine and Pen rang his. After ringing each other merrily for a while we pushed through the crowd to watch the conjurers, who were making small red leather balls disappear and appear from under cups of red Nile pottery.

Then we saw, in a space alone, ten cubits from the crowd watching him, a man squatting on his haunches, a thin black rod in his hand. He was tall and lank-haired, and the crowd around him was a pool of silence amid the lusty rejoicing.

"Let us listen to him," Res said, and, taking two reed mats from the pile propped up against a dom-palm tree, she gave one to Herath and they sat down and curled their legs underneath them. Hor-min and I sat down beside them, and Kamose and Pen leaned against the tree.

"He is telling of the afrits," Hor-min whispered to me. "Let us see if he says aught of the Sitters on Horses."

The story-teller, or whatever he was, had a small ox-dung-and-wood fire in front of him, and as he spoke, in clear words and with deep voice tones, he threw herbs into the embers. They would flame for an instant, then a sick-sweet, pungent smell would fill the air around. I did not like the smell. It choked me.

"The afrits can appear and disappear," he was telling his wide-eyed listeners. All ages they were, mothers and babes, young and half-grown children, lovers sitting close together and old men in a group, all silent and scarce moving. "They come from inside the mountains. . . . Animals can see them . . . cats more than others." He looked up and poked the embers with his rod. "Why does your donkey stick his toes in the ground, refusing?" He looked around. "And why do you not prod, nor whip the beast? You turn away and go around the place. . . . You know your donkey sees an afrit there. Akh! By the Worms who feed on blood! It is good that you turn away." He nodded slowly.

"It is as though he puts the Looking on them, so still they sit," Res said under her breath, and the man turned his face full at us.

"Sometimes they are huge dark men, the afrits," he said. "And sometimes women, talon-fingered, with long, clawed feet. And sometimes they are the bristling Boar of Set who has been since the Waters of Chaos." He threw more herbs on the fire, and the smell was a stink. I wondered that all there did not loathe it. They seemed not to smell it. "Sometimes a cat, sometimes a wolf, a black donkey, and they cast no shadow and they gather at the desert wells with slavering lips, these dread hare-hounds bred of the wanton-dark thoughts of men . . . of you . . . and you . . . and you!" He pointed his rod at the men and women in the half-scared crowd.

"Akh!" Herath shuddered. Res took her hand and held it while they listened to a young man shouting that he was a fisherman.

"The afrits fly in terror from me!" he boasted.

"And from me!" A woman lurched forward with drunken looseness. "When I am unclean."

"Show us an afrit! If you are so clever, raise one up from the brick floor of this Market Place!" The young fisherman laughed.

"When you need help," the man said, and his voice was soft, and startled me, "come to my dwelling place."

"Then prophesy. Tell us of the victory to come!"

"Akh! That is a good thought!" The fair-skinned boy who had won the catching game came to the rim of the group. "Tell us the outcome . . . for tomorrow we go to war."

"He's no seer! By the Cruncher of Bones! He is no prophet." The drunken woman was swaying on her feet in the middle of the open space. "Come! Wily man! Burn some hoopoe-lark feathers and show us something . . . if you can!"

"Put the oil of the castor-bean in your nostrils. Tam-it!" He smiled at her, calling her whore and she-cat. Then, throwing more herbs on the flames, he stood up, taller and straighter than twi-light shadows in the desert, dark and thin. She cowered away. He raised his rod. He looked bigger, dire and dark. "By the Power of Set, Lord of Transcendent Night, and of the seven kings under the earth, there will be victory! Victory for the Queen of Transcendent Night! Victory for the beautiful Woman of Spells!" He laughed, and it was the laughter of hell.

"Ra-en-Ra!" I made the holy sign.

"Give me your hand." Res shivered, and Herath jumped up and ran to Kamose. "Let us go," Res said. "I do not like this story-teller."

"The evil magic finds its putrid places even here in Thebes," Hor-min said, and rose to his feet.

"Let us go back through the village." I linked my arm in his, he linked with Res and she with Pen, and together, in step, we walked, half skipping, out of the Market Place.

Kamose and Herath lingered behind us. I turned to look at them. Slowly, their arms about each other's waists, their faces solemn and radiant, they followed us along the palm-bordered shore, past color-washed houses, their bright flags flying from air-slits near the roof, and in our nostrils was the smell of goats roasting on spits and pigeons on the round stoves under the palm-trees. Past tavern doors open and flower-decked we skipped, till we came to a clearing and, breathless, leaned against the dom-palms, to wait for Kamose and Herath.

A boy and a girl were dancing a love dance, his sash about her waist. Still out of breath, we stayed there to watch.

"She is good," Res said as the girl's belly jerked up and down and she danced around and around the boy to the rhythm of the sweetmeat-vendor's rattle. Hor-min took his pipe from his loin-cloth and joined in the music.

I watched two old men playing Dog and Jackals on a low table of unbaked Nile mud. It had four stumpy legs and the crude colored animals were coated with shining wax. "Thebans . . ." I whispered the words, and felt the tears prickle behind my eyelids. Old friends walked arm in arm, talking. Old lovers met again with familiar, husky laughter, and three boys were playing dice with three-cornered knuckle-bones, shouting fortunate words as they threw, and snapping their fingers like castanets.

The dance of the two young lovers was faster now and the girl was using the crotols. The sharp clicking sound of the wooden shells laced to her fingers filled the night air with merry sound, and Res took Pen's hands.

"Let us dance."

"Aya! No! No!" Kamose came running, one arm around Herath's waist. "Let his wounds heal! He rides to battle with me tomorrow."

"Then you!" Res turned to me with maiden-cool laughter and whirled me at arm's length. I had not danced since I was a youth, with Rai. Thinking of my sister, I lifted Res, dancing heel and toe, high in the air, and the women under the trees stopped their chatter to watch us. Then I swung her around and down. We loosed hands and, dancing heel and toe, we circled each other while Hor-min played his reed-pipe and Kamose and Herath and Pen stood clapping their hands, and I wondered while I danced if Hor-min had yet drawn Kamose's battle-maps of the Delta streams around Avaris. Were there at least some of our tunnels still un-

discovered in those massive walls? Then I wondered at myself for thinking of war as I danced, looking into Res' small
face, earnest and pale in the bright moon-light. She whirled
away from me and danced with the village girl. Slowly,
solemnly, their faces rapt, they circled around each other,
their bellies shivering, their hips a joy. One of the women
shook a small gazelle-hide tambourine, making quivers of
inebriating sound, and the boy dancer leapt high in the air.
I followed! With great leaps we changed places behind the
gently swaying girls. We both leapt straight upward. Then
upward again, twisting our bodies around in the air, to
change places and leap straight up and land on our feet in a
perfect pose, and pausing, give each other a small salute for
our prowess.

As I paused, catching my breath, I saw Kamose and
Herath, under the dom-palms a few arm-lengths away. His
arms were around her waist, her hands clasped behind his
neck. Hushed with passion, they stood amid the reveling
throng. In the moon-light and torch-light, I saw that her
face was wet with tears. Slowly they kissed. Her hair fell
all about them. Her dark robe had slipped from her shoulders.
Then, wrung with passion, lips still clinging, Kamose lifted
her up in his arms as a child and strode with her through
the palms and acacia trees down to the River and her yacht.

Res left the girl and danced toward me. "Come, dance!
Dance, my Prince."

We danced. I felt dexterous, wing-footed. The faces
around me were the faces of unknown gods, the gods of
Egypt, and my body was a flame. My heart took flight.
Boldly I danced. "The dance shall not vanish from Ra's
earth! Put a cap on me, rush-pointed . . . Res, Star-girl . . .
Stitch beads of turquoise on my loin-cloth, for my feet are
like kid's feet on the high crags and my heart is as free as
the young roe-buck. . . ." And the night-land of Egypt was
Res, my fertile doe, smiling grave and full of light, sweet
and wild.

Breathless, I closed my eyes. Res came close and held my

hands, and swaying gently with her I smelt the damp night smells: the earthy smells of flesh and beer, meats cooking, ripe fruit and the River. Then, our arms about each other, we went, laughing, back to Pen and Hor-min, by the long table.

"My Prince," Hor-min handed me a cup of barley beer, "no frontiers can hold you when you dance."

And Pen, gently but with strong holding in spite of his wounds, took Res as she stood there breathing fast and laughing, and, lifting her up in his arms, looked down into her flushed eager face and kissed her. She flung her arms around his neck and, laughing still, put her mouth to his. Then he put her down and she stood in the circle of his arm, a bright small craft in his heart's wide harbor.

"Come, Ahmose . . ." Pen used my name, and our eyes gazed deep in memory's well.

"Pen." I looked at the scar on his cheek and remembered my fear for him as he lay on the reed matting in the ox-cart after the battle.

"Come, my Prince," he said again. "Soon the stars will fade . . . and tomorrow . . ." His face was calm as he bent his head and leaned his cheek against Res' smooth, bright hair. "Tomorrow, we follow the King into battle."

Three hours before the dawn, the whole House was astir. I lay listening to the horses of Kamose's Guard in the Battle-court and the faint murmur of the Thebans, all feasting ended, who were already gathering in the vast Outer-court of the Temple to receive the King's blessing after the Morning Rite, and to show forth their heart's love for him at the noon-day, when he rode out to do battle for them and for their spirits' weal. I listened to the sounds of Neme and the housemen cleaning the armor. Shields, broad-swords, spears and javelins, they cleaned and scoured them till they shone. I heard the sharp-edged noise of spear against spear as they were dropped, razor-sharp, into the long quivers that hung outside the chariots, battle-ready for Kamose, Ak-hor, Pen and Thure to mount after the Double Rite. Suddenly I shivered. On this day not yet dawning, as Ra in his noon-day Fire changed Boats in High Heaven, Nefertari would become High Priestess of his Rite. "Spouse of Amun-Ra," I whispered and understood my mother's words: "We have much to ask of the God, of wisdom . . . forgiveness." It is blasphemy, I thought. And Herath? "Herath." I spoke her name. She of the mischievous eyes, round breasts and strong desiring would be the Secondary Royal Wife. I wondered if they were back from the yacht. I remembered her passion-stilled, tear-wet face. I moved the head-rest and lay flat out on my back in the darkness. This day the King rides out again from Thebes. "Kheri-heb!" I had waited for his words, beyond myself, lost in his gaze, exalted, and he said, "Tomorrow, the King will lead our armies to battle." And tomorrow is today. I turned over on my side, thinking that the Neferusian armies would be as dust beneath Kamose's golden feet! The thought warmed me. I knew his plans as the palm of my hand. After the Double Rite he would drive his chariot to join his hosts, gathered and waiting on the fringe of the desert, where the Black Land ends. An army twice as large for the fishermen and farmers, fowlers, husband-men and boat-men, gardeners and canal-diggers workless in the wake of the flooding River, long trained and well armed, who swelled our depleted ranks. I smiled and pulled the linen cover up to my chin against the fore-dawn chill. Each man would bring a goat, a cow or a donkey, grain, dried fish and vegetables to stock the cook-wagons and the kitchen-ships. And Ahmose-Eb! I felt my smile widen. The Keeper of the Halyard in the Boat of the King would tomorrow marry Atu. Then, after three days, with one hundred prime ships, troop-ships and barges, all refurbished and battle-ready, he would sail southward from Thebes to Ed-fu, await the King after the desert battle and set sail for the Cataract Fort and Nubia. There had been messages from Aknere's Young Eyes and Ears that a host of Nubians were gathered below Assuan awaiting the commands of Apophis and Teti of Neferusi. But our Fort was manned, armed and impregnable, and four battle-ships were already guarding our Assuan border. I lay remembering our attack on the Cataract Fort. How wise were Kamose's plans. How far-seeing his vision. How reluctant I had been to leave Thebes and my studies! How much I had learned in the Cataract waters! How I learned from my brother! Nubian hosts, massed! "Teti of Neferusi . . ." My whole body grew fiery with rage, then cold as the north wind. I shuddered at the blood-lust in my heart. "Your manhood and your Priesthood are not yet reconciled." The Old One's words were the Truth of Maat. I closed my eyes tight as my fists were clenched. I lay tense, willing my thought to Kheri-heb, forcing the fresh memory of his peace, and with a long, deep breath I fell asleep again.

The fierce rat-a-tat of a practicing lead drummer wakened me, and the thud-thud of two smaller drums answering him. There were noises now inside the House. Voices, harsh-bright and unhushed, shouted orders sharpened by good-natured cursing. Suddenly there sounded the high, sweet notes of a battle flute. My blood stirred. A boy laughed. The King must now be back in his House, I thought, and when I moved Neme came through the pillars. But I feigned sleep awhile, strangely loath to arise to this day. He stood beside me with a lamp. The flickering light of it was bright behind my eyelids. I opened my eyes and stretched.

"Your bath is prepared, my Prince," Neme said. "The King is already shaven and awaits you in the underground Council Chamber."

I got up and went to the bathing-room. Neme poured the sweet, cool water over me and rubbed me with light turpentine mixed with incense, and a fine sage-scented powder to keep my body fresh. Then he dressed me. In a short white kilt and jeweled sporran, I stood as he clasped my father's belt around me, and thought how I had found it there on the first day of my manhood, and on the stool my brother's gift, the lion bracelet! I remembered my heart-lift as Neme clasped it, now, on my arm, then put on me the broad collar. It was wholly of amethysts, all threaded to a Tet-pillar of bright blue faience in the center. Then I sat down while he put on my wig and tied the Fisherman's Circlet around it. As I stood up, I saw myself in the large looking-bronze and thought of my mother's words. I had grown broader in the shoulder, and I was tall as my father. With the thinning of my face, I looked more like my brother.

In the ritual dress of Prince of the South Land, I went down to the secret underground chamber.

Kamose was already sitting behind the long table, maps spread out in front of him.

"Ahmose!" He was clad only in loin-cloth and sandals! "Before I go to the Temple I would speak with you. Come, take Pen-aati's chair beside me." I sat down, smiling as I looked at the large map.

"Hor-min has done his work well."

Kamose pointed. "Isti! All the canals and marshes around Avaris!"

In clear outline and coloring, Hor-min had marked the depths of each, and the places where the papyrus clumps were vast and thick enough to hide our ships. The secret underground paddocks were marked by steps going neither up nor down, and the whole map seemed to be a thing of art and pleasure. But flowers were chariots, and trees were battleships! And the heights of the rocks and mountains told the number of men deployed. Our code was simple and could not be suspected. Kamose had been marking our positions in black ink, and the Hyksos in red, on a copy of the map in front of him. He pointed to the eastern wall of Avaris, and I thought that his reaching heart was already in that city: the Neferusian army routed and Nubia contained. "Where we wrecked the wall, to the east, they have built it out into the desert and filled in all our tunnels. The walled enclosure is now ten miles square, and Pery-em-wah tells us that sixty thousand soldiers are gathered inside those ramparts, apart from Apophis' subjects. But here!" He pointed. "Here, Ahmose, and here . . . and here . . . and here, our underground paddocks form a ring around Avaris!"

"These are new."

He nodded, laughing. "Brother," he said, "the work never ceases. With those secret gathering places for the Sitters on Horses so brief a span from the city, we still have the weapon of surprise." He turned and looked at me. "Akh! Ra-en-Ra! How you trained your Sitters on Horses! And in the course of our battles their uses are legion. Akh! Little Brother, if there were no Rites to be performed this day—by the Feathers of Maat! I would mount my chariot now, this moment. My Ka urges me to join my hosts. Ahmose, I have a vast impatience to be gone. I spoil for this fight." Sek-met rose to her feet, growled and put her fore-feet on the table. Kamose stood up. "By the Fire in the Eye of Horus! I would mount my chariot now, this moment!" he said again, and Sek-met growled deep and pressed close against him. He stroked her head, and his face softened. "But Herath, she must be Secondary Royal Wife, and the child under her bosom the Royal Child." He turned to me, his eyebrow raised. "The more so as our half-sister's womb is also heavy. By the Disc! Herath was unforeseen by the half-sister." Before I could speak, he said, "Come, Brother, it is almost dawn. Akh! These days in Ta-mery that shine before sun-rise! Ra is fervent this day. Come, let us greet his victory. Ahmose, share with me the Morning Rite." He broke into cool laughter and put his arm about my shoulders. "You are almost Lector-Priest, come!" As we walked together along the secret passage to the small outer room of the Inmost Shrine, he said, "Together, Little Brother, we will pray that Amun-Ra will fight within us, and that we smite our enemies."

Only Miutu and two web-priests, who censed the air around us, met us at the Sanctuary. After the King was purified with water from the Sacred Lake, and the web-priests had lustrated me, Miutu censed me that I might follow Kamose to the portal of the Holy of Holies.

I watched my brother, in new-woven loin-cloth and new-threaded sandals, myrrh-anointed, take in his hand the golden censor and walk into the narrow darkness of the Inmost Shrine.

My brother's voice held quiet rapture, and echoed.

"Iwi! Iwi! Welcome! Welcome! O Eye of Horus!
Rise, glorious, and unharmed.
Youthful, arise!
Ra shines forth below the horizon.
The power of Set has hidden itself."

I could see his tall dark figure in the light of the Sacred Fire. He censed the sealed Shrine Doors three times.

"Amun-Ra! At whose rising the gods exalt!
Amun-Ra, reborn each day.
Who has made the serpent to fall headlong down.
Amun-Ra! Who illumines Ta-mery with Rays
    of Turquoise Light.
True is the triumph!"

He broke the clay seal, cut through the papyrus string and flung open the Doors of the Shrine! As he spoke, and his voice filled all the place, a mystery of creative sound, the first rays of the God in his Atet Boat rising streamed through the slits in the wall of the Shrine and pierced the darkness, striking the figure of Amun-Ra with the new day's first golden Light. and Rai was close as the Light itself! I shivered. "Rai . . . gather your God-essence . . . Open the doors of your Ka-house . . . Rai . . ."

"The Doors of Heaven are opened!
The heavens are opened . . ."

Kamose's voice was golden sound answering me.

"The Company of the gods shines forth!
Thy beauties are thine own, O Amun-Ra!"

"Rai . . . guide Soker-uff in battle today. Lead the King's chariot through the dire maze of the enemy hosts . . ."

Kamose fell down on his face and lay prone. I lay on my belly behind him. Nine times we kissed the ground in front of the Shrine, and I knew they were with us, with Kamose and me: Rai, and our father, Ebana, Tetaky and Sen-ut, sharing in the Rite. Five bright Kas to aid the King in his battles along with the gods of the Stars. "Rai . . ." I called all their names aloud. In a profound all-embracing Wholeness, we were all One. I looked up. The God's Image, gathering the bright beams, sent them back to their Source, and Kamose, a huge diffused figure, rose and lifted his arms.

"Adoration to Thee, Amun-Ra!
Thou, only Form! Maker of all that shall be.
One only! The Creator of all that shall be.
Thou One! Only One! Whose Names are manifold.
Grant us victory over the dark forces of Set.
Hike! Hike!"

Kamose took up the broom of beben grass. He brushed away his own footsteps, as he walked backward away from the Shrine of the God.

When he came to the Door of the Inner Temple, he turned to face us. His eyes were all Light, his body huge and chaste. We lay on our bellies before him, and when we arose, the face of Miutu, High Priest since my grand-father's time, was the face of a youthful man.

Without speaking, Kamose turned toward the Outer-court. His body seemed to gather the outpouring of radiance into itself again, and he was man-size. In a thrall of joy and worship I followed him to where thousands of Thebans stood silent, waiting.

Kamose, naked except for his loin-cloth and sandals, hairless and shaven, stood and gazed on his people. Not a bird's twitter broke the silence. It seemed all breaths were held, all hearts stilled. Then he raised his hand in blessing. In silence they fell on their faces, then rose, each one to his tallest height, and raised their arms Ka-square, and the moment was as a thousand years.

Still silent, we went back into the Temple and made our way along the King's Passage underground to the door of his bed-chamber. He sat down in his high-backed ebony chair.

"All is done that may be done," he said. Then he raised his head and looked at me, a clear, all-seeing glance. "You shared the Morning Rite, Little Brother?"

And I answered slowly, still enthralled, "With all of you."

"We are all One in Amun-Ra. We do not fight alone." His voice changed. He crossed his legs and sat at ease. "Our grand-mother is delighted with the honor to be bestowed upon the Queen. Akh! This dotage!" He shook his head. Then, leaning forward, he said, "One hour before noon-day we shall assemble in the Court of Audience. There and then I shall announce the two solemn Rites to the Great Ones and the Elders, and forthwith we shall proceed, in state, to the Temple . . ."

"And Herath will be Secondary Royal Wife . . ." I murmured, and thought, Kamose from divine sources draws his being. He brings causes forth from their secret chamber to the light, and hides under bright ceremony that which must be hidden; and I was joyful at the ease with which his will was accomplished. But when I spoke, the words my tongue formed half denied my joy. "I wish that these two Rites were already performed," I heard myself say, and my brother sat up straight, impatient,

"And I! Brother, I would be at the head of my waiting armies. . . . But first the Audience, then the Double Rite. At the Audience, I shall first extol our half-sister's own desire to become High Priestess, ask homage for her with appropriate words and have Miutu and Kheri-heb lead her to the Temple, with all pomp and state, before I bring Herath into the Court. Akh! By the Golden Cow-horns of Hat-hor! How I shall relish the truth on my tongue when I speak to the Great Ones of Herath. Ahmose, rarer than emeralds found in sandstone is my Hyksos Princess." The words were warm in his throat and mouth. "But come! These morning hours are filled with duties." He looked at me. "You will be a Regent the King may trust, little Warrior-Priest," he said, and embraced me. "But hasten, we have a meeting with Pen-aati. He will be at your side always." He put his hand on my shoulder. "In his wisdom, the God did not make you wholly a warrior"—he raised an eyebrow—"nor wholly a Priest." His fingers pressed hard into my shoulder. Then he released me. "I am leaving Thebes well armed."

"There will be no need for defenses here." I knew in my soul that the words were true. Then I thought, Only in the King's House must Herath be defended. But I said, "Brother, the gods are with us."

"It is an honorable field."

The well-remembered words brought the thought of our father and mother, and as we stood there, Pen-aati came into the chamber. He bowed.

"They are assembling, the Great Ones of Thebes," he said. "And they are all agog. Curiosity and surmising about the Hyksos Princess are rife."

"Both their curiosity and their surmising will soon be satisfied," Kamose said, and he smiled at Pen-aati. "She is beautiful, my Herath?"

Pen-aati's face broke into a broad smile, and for a while we sat together talking of my Regency, the business of the nomes and the new ordering of the Cattle Census.

"A heavier work, my King, but a welcome one," Pen-aati said. "Since we no longer pay tribute to the North Land, our granaries are full, our corn overflows the sides of our barges and the wild gazelles are once more tame in the South Land, eating their fill of our maize crops." Kamose's face was young and eager as he nodded agreement, and I found that my heart was clear, and I understood and found joy in my new duties. There was peace in Pen-aati's tired eyes, and a deep love for me. With a small sigh, he said, "The Prince Ahmose is ready for his Regency."

Kamose rose to his feet. We stood with him. He looked at the old Vizir. "A musician knows another man, whether or not he is a musician," he said, and I did not see my brother till, two hours before noon, he came into the Court of Audience.

I was in my place, to the left behind the King's Throne Chair, with Res and Hor-min standing behind me. The Court of Audience was full. Ra's golden beams glanced through the pillars and lit up the seated assembly with rays of light. Tetisheri, beside the Queen's Chair, the jewels in her filigree golden crown sparkling and hanging like water-drops from silver chains thin as ox-hairs, sat straight, proud and regal. Her eyes were huge and dimmed the jewels in her collar and the gold threaded into her sandal-straps. I looked at them in wonder. They were finely wrought, tiny and perfect. The Ptah Dwarf, I thought; his work is of the God. Then my mother came.

She sat on the King's right hand in her ancient Throne Chair, austere and plain in its beauty as Nefertari's, in front of me, was richly embossed and jewel-encrusted. Thure stood behind her, holding her fan, and my throat closed with a sudden lump as I saw her jewels. She wore only the amulets charged with the Life of the God for the protection of her children: her amulet collar, her four plain golden bracelets, two on each arm, and her three golden flies; the Gold of Valor for my father, Kamose and me. Her presence brought beauty and peace. Her simple robe was of the finest Temple linen, with pleats so narrow they could scarce be seen. She had one shoulder bare, in simple majesty, and her breasts were covered. She wore the Royal Cobra on her brow, for she had been, and still was, full Queen. Her eyes were deep and bright, clear and unseeking as she turned her gaze toward Nefertari.

Under a huge, wide-spreading blue-and-green-dyed ostrich-feather fan held over her head by Thuty, and wearing the ceremonial robes of the Great Royal Wife, slowly, in lambent magnificence, she came into the Court of Audience. She stood for a long moment. All rose to their feet. As she walked up the steps of the Royal Dais she looked full into my eyes. My body shrank. My heart stretched out cold fingers as she sat down in her chair and there was a murmuring tumult at her beauty, like the rustling of small birds and animals when a serpent slithers around the papyrus roots.

Tetisheri leaned toward her, then stretched out her dry, small hand to touch her. I turned away from the adoring love in her eyes. The Great Ones were straining their ears, nodding their heads together in hearsay and surmising one with the other. Then the whole Court was suddenly quiet. Time stretched and passed, then stretched again. Kamose was Ra on earth. Only those touched by the gods can cause this hush at the hint of their coming.

With Ak-hor in full battle-dress on his left, and Pen, taking Ahmose-Eb's place, full-girded in spite of a few bandages, on his right, their tall purple-dyed fans held high over his head, with Sek-met at his heels and Miutu and Kheri-heb together behind him, Kamose came to his Throne Chair. All there assembled rose, then bowed low, their arms outstretched in adoration, palms upward against the radiant majesty of their King.

"Thebans! Unique Ones of my heart." He sat down in his chair and with a quiet smile gave them leave to sit. Then he spoke to them. "For this day the gods themselves have waited. Though at the Hour of Ra's noon-day Fire I go forth to battle, before he reaches his zenith we shall thrust beyond war, beyond valor, beyond earthly endeavor, to the will of the God, and to two holy Rituals." He turned toward Nefertari, but he did not look at her; his gaze was on the jeweled knob of her chair-back. Nefertari smiled, her eyes lowered. Kamose turned again to the assembly. He told them of the Queen's long will and desiring toward Priesteshood, of her acts of piety, and I thought, He does not speak one word of untruth; her outward acts are pious and she has long been envious of my mother. "The Great Royal Wife," he was saying in measured words, "wearer of the Beautiful White Crown, will this day become High Priestess of Hat-hor, and the Bride of Amun-Ra." There was a different murmuring, the sound of swift breaths indrawn, and some lips shaped a silent "O!" and others "Aya!" or "Zatoo?" So, indeed? And all eyes were as big as Thebes. I saw my brother's eyebrow raised. "A seat is prepared for the Queen in the Boat of the Sun-God! Amun-Ra, Who is True of Voice, hails her! He sees her for her own true self." I shivered at the hidden meaning of his words. Nefertari sat stately there, benevolent, serene; and like a vile dream, forgotten on waking and suddenly remembered at noon, I saw again the stark venom of her gaze as she looked at Herath on the first night of feasting. Again I gave silent tribute to my brother's wisdom that Nefertari would have left for the Temple before I went to bring Herath into the Court of Audience.

"Arise, Great Ones and Nobles of Thebes! Rise all, in homage to your Queen!" And all there rose and bowed, arms outstretched in adoration. As the two High Priests came to stand behind Nefertari's chair, Kamose turned slowly toward her, and though it seemed that he made a slight gesture of reverence, as to a Priestess-Queen, I, standing there, saw in his eyes a fiery scorn beyond the scorn of men. Then he held out his hand to her. Nefertari gazed up at him. Her heavy lids, green-painted, were almost closed. Her long eyes gleamed. Swaying as a tall lily's stem, she rose, and with Queenly, yet unassuming grace, not smiling but laughing a little in his face, she clasped the King's outstretched hand. I looked at her bracelet of amethysts, and the large amethyst ring on her finger, and I felt distaste for my own beaded collar. Still clasping his hand, she stood tall beside him. "The Great Royal Wife," he said, "Queen, and soon to be High Priestess," and I thought as he spoke, Even now his tongue will not form her abhorred name. Then I saw my brother's body shudder. He loosed Nefertari's hand. He stood still as a rock. Then he put one foot forward and, his arms straight down at his sides, his fists clenched in the ritual stance, he said, "The God speaks to Kamose, Whadj-Kheper-Ra, his son on earth." Then he turned to Kheri-heb. "Escort the Queen to the shriving room of the Priestesses, beneath the

Inmost Shrine. Surround her with Priests." I saw a knowing I did not understand in their eyes. My brother turned full around to me. "Come, Brother." His commanding gaze swept all on the Royal Dais. "Come! I hold Council." He looked down at Tetisheri. "Grand-mother, you will hold court here." He stood for a long moment gazing on the assembled Thebans, and his smile was a grace. Then, his face stern again, he said, "Await my commands," and with Ak-hor and Pen holding their fans high above him, and my mother and Res, Thure, Hor-min and I following, he walked with swift long strides toward his room.

As we left the Court of Audience I heard Miutu's words, clear and solemn. "The Flame of Ra has pierced the heart of his son. . . . Await the King's pleasure and his desiring." He gave the blessing of Ra and Osiris, then he joined Pen-aati and slowly they followed us.

Halfway along the wide passage Herath was waiting to be presented to the Great Ones of Thebes. Her maidens around her, she stood gentle and lovely in her long robes, her hair piled high and wreathed with jewels and flowers. Her eyes widened in wonder when she saw Kamose. She raised her arms toward him, then, her eyes bright with sudden tears, she crossed her hands on her breast. Almost savagely, Kamose caught hold of her and held her, whispering and kissing her soft nape. Then he put his hand, in blessing it seemed, on her belly. Tenderly, deeply, he kissed her and went on his way. As I made to follow him I saw the stark terror in her eyes before she swooned into the arms of her maidens. Shocked out of my joyful calm, I stayed to hear my mother tell Res to bring a Healer-priest. Then she went to Herath, knelt down beside her and smoothed the hair from her brow. Filled with foreboding, I ran after my brother.

When I came to the inner room of his quarters I saw the tall purple fans propped up against the wall, and the hidden door in the painted wall was ajar. I pushed it open and ran along the King's Passage to where the secret steps led down to the underground Council Chamber. The heavy drop-stone door was wide.

Kamose was not sitting at the long, wide Council Table, but in our father's high-backed ebony chair, facing the length of the room. Ak-hor and Pen, Thure and Hor-min were standing around him. I looked at my brother sitting upright, his feet together and his hands on the rams' heads carved on the chair arms, and I breathed again. Kamose is Ra on earth. I thought, The God spoke to him. This is one of his swift, sure changes of plan. Herath, as all women, was afraid of change. I almost laughed as I walked toward him.

"Ahmose." The word was like the crack of a whip. I held my breath, and bowed. "Brother, I have been poisoned. I cannot long hold on to my Ka." At the blanching of my face his eyes blazed God-fire. "Be not puny! And listen." His golden body shuddered. He clenched his hands on the curving horns of the ebony rams. "Ahmose, you are King of the Two Lands! My first command is to you. You will lead our hosts and join in battle with the Neferusian force, and when you have routed it you will proceed to Nubia, according to my plan. When our southern border is safe, you will lead our hosts to victory in Avaris . . . and beyond! To Saruhen, outside our borders." I longed to throw myself at his feet in a raging storm of grief such as I had never known, and clasp his golden knees and scream to the heavens that no mordant herb could venom the blood of Ra's son. His intimate gaze held me. I stood mute. "Ahmose, Little Brother, your shoulders have broadened. You will don my battle-dress, use my arms and wear the Blue Helmet of the King Warrior of Ra, who now you are! You will mount my chariot, and swifter than sound in the desert you will ride, this high noon, to the head of your hosts." There was love and laughter in his all-seeing gaze. "They fear Kamose! It is a deep dark fear in their vitals! The armies of the Neferusian pig will fall before the truth can be whispered. After Nubia, Little Warrior, you will be feared for your own King's valor." He looked at us all with a sweep of flame. "Hor-min, my Goat-herd scribe, you will drive the King's chariot this day. Thure, you will be, as you have always been, warrior at the King's left hand in every battle. Though you would release your Ka from the prison of your flesh, your life on earth will be long, and your life is the King's." Thure bowed low. Then he turned to me and I saw the first spark, since Sen-ut was slain, of warmth in the fealty of his gaze.

Kamose looked beyond us to Miutu and Pen-aati, who stood together awaiting his commands. He lifted his hand to beckon them closer. "Miutu . . ." The High Priest, at last, showed the bourn of his years. He put his hand to his brow and lowered his tall, thin body. "Miutu, High Priest and Chief of Visions since my grand-father's reign . . . Pen-aati, Support of the South Land for three generations of my House . . ." Pen-aati's face was drawn and gray with growing horror.

"My King." He bowed.

"I charge you both! Accomplish wholly my bidding, for each word is a pillar within me to uphold the Two Lands! Miutu, at noon you will summon the Anubis Priests to raise my Tent of Gold, here in this secret underground chamber. This, my body of earth, will remain hidden here——"

"Kamose . . . my King, my Son?" Our mother, entering, heard his words and came swiftly to him.

He held up his hand. "Wait, Mother, I snatch moments from time." She stayed a moment, still, then came to my side as Res, who had followed her, went to Pen and held his arm, her eyes wide with fear. No one of us could take our gaze from Kamose. His breath was growing thinner but his voice was clear and deep. "My body will lie hidden here till the Neferusian army is put to rout. Ak-hor! My soul-friend, you will escort, after that victory, with all state and proper grief, an ox-cart bearing a coffin to Thebes. It will be put abroad that I was slain in battle. Only then shall my earth body have ritual burial. Miutu! You and Pen-aati will break the dire tidings to the Thebans. You will proclaim Ahmose King . . . in absence! For you will tell them thus: 'Wasting no time in following the battle-plans of Kamose,

Whadj-Kheper-Ra, the King, Ahmose, Neb-Pethy-Ra—
Hik-towy!—has already joined with our Fleet at Ed-fu, to
lead our hosts into Nubia . . . Akh! By the Disc! My Ka
pulls away from me . . . Pen-aati . . ." The Vizir, his face a
thousand years old, bowed again. "Pen-aati, I proclaim you
Regent." Speechless, Pen-aati knelt and kissed the King's
hand. Kamose helped him to rise, stood up and embraced
him. "Go now with Miutu." He turned to the High Priest.
"Tell those assembled in the Court of Audience that, according to the Word of the God, I am this moment being
shriven for battle. Tell them, Miutu, that, as Regent, Pen-
aati commands their total allegiance. . . . Send them contented
away, to pray for the King and victory . . . and send the
Queen Tetisheri and the Old One down to this secret chamber. . . . Go you now." He raised his hand in blessing, sat
down again in his chair and seemed to labor with his breath.
Then he raised his hand, palm upward. We saw the double
row of prong-marks in the veins of his wrist, and two
larger marks on the outside of his palm. Angry pricks, pale-
rimmed and swelling in his golden flesh, where the venom
had entered his blood-stream.

"The amethysts! the bracelet . . . the ring!" I tore the
collar from my neck and flung it away from me, and with it
my Royal calm. The collar fell with a hissing crack on the
flag-stones of the floor, sharp in the silence, and I saw
Kheri-heb. He was standing inside the secret doorway.

Kamose looked at him with question.

"The Queen is in a room under the Inner Shrine. She is
well guarded." As the Lector-Priest made the Holy Sign,
he looked at me.

Then Kamose turned his burning gaze on me. "Ahmose,
Brother . . . in the Name of Amun-Ra, of your beloved
Osiris and of the whole company of the gods, I ask of you
one duty . . . one sacred, bounden duty for the weal of the
Two Lands." Bile rose, bitter in my throat. My mother put
her hand on my arm. "On your victorious return from Nubia
you will be crowned, and after that ceremony, Brother . . . I

ask of you that you follow our Royal and ancient custom."
My whole soul balked. As I stood, sweat beading my brow,
silent, quick footsteps sounded on the secret steps and,
breathless, Tetisheri and the Old One came through the wide
drop-stone door.

"Grand-son! These strange commands? Pen-aati . . . he is
Regent? It should be the Queen!"

My brother's gaze stayed her where she was. His flesh
surged. His poisoned blood flowed on. He leaned forward,
his eyes on me. "Ahmose, Brother . . . on the day of your
Crowning you will wed with the half-sister."

"His crowning? Wed Nefertari . . . Akh! what mad-
ness . . ."

Kamose turned the fury of his gaze on his grand-mother.
Her small mouth fell open. Her face was a bloodless mask,
hollow, empty and loose as though no bone nor muscle
held it. Kamose's voice was a golden gong. His eyes still
burning into hers, he spoke to me. "Akh! By the Blood Drops
of the Phallus of Ra! You need not lie with the murderess!"
A small, high wail, like that of a wounded animal, came
through Tetisheri's open mouth. "She has already coupled
. . . with the God, she will say . . . and she shall be Queen
in name, in ritual and in public!" His eyes, pitiless and fiery
cold, did not leave his grand-mother. "The half-sister has
twice murdered for it!" Tetisheri's small body sagged like
a doll, broken. The Old One held her, but she turned away
from him and staggered, moaning like a lost child, into my
mother's arms. Ah-hotpe gathered her close and held her,
soothing her agony. Kamose sat still as a rock, and holding us
all in his soul's grip, he spoke again.

"No living being, save you here, the Two High Priests and
Pen-aati . . . the Twins and Ahmose-Eb . . . and the murderess herself will know, till after the Neferusian battle,
that my Ka must answer to the Ferryman. Akh! Miutu, you
return . . . it is accomplished?"

"My King, the assembled Great Ones are on their way,
content, to their homes." The High Priest bowed low and

went to my mother's side. He put his hand in blessing and comfort on Tetisheri's trembling shoulders.

"Ak-hor . . . Pen." Speechless, they bowed. Kamose's mouth eased into the hint of a smile. "Res . . . my brave Res, you three, and all my Company, you will wait upon your King. Be his guard and escort as you were mine. . . . Grand-mother!" The word was ringing sharp as the clash of sword on shield. "Queen Tetisheri!"

My grand-mother slowly squared her shaking shoulders, stilled her trembling, stood for a moment straight as a lance in her daughter's arms, gathered herself and turned toward him, her head high. Tragedy, scorn and resolve had drawn her small face together. Her eyes were tearless, cold-bright as crystal. "Grand-mother,'" Kamose said, "you will deal with the Queen."

Tetisheri took three steps forward and stood, ravaged and regal before him. "Kamose, Whadj-Kheper-Ra . . ." Her voice was low and harsh. "Lord of the Two Lands." She bowed low, her arms outstretched in adoration, then stood straight again. "Grand-son . . . between my daughter, Ah-hotpe, the Queen Mother, and the two High Priests"—she flicked a glance at Kheri-heb and Miutu—"and Pen-aati, Regent, and ever watchful . . . and me—Tetisheri, Queen Grand-mother of the Two Lands!—the natural daughter of my son, Seken-en-Ra II, Nefertari, twice a murderess, will not, from this day forth, be free, waking or sleeping, from watching eyes. From this day forth . . . By the Everlasting Devourer, I swear it, Grand-son . . . the King's House will be a golden cage and . . . Nefertari . . ." She spoke the name again as though it were strange to her, slowly and with sick distaste, then slowly repeated it. ". . . Nefertari will be, for all the days of her earth life, as a bright plumed bird . . . with aching, useless, close-clipped wings . . . and yet, to all outward seeming, she will be a beautiful and Royal Queen."

"And, Grand-mother . . . to the child in her womb, she will always be a beautiful and Royal Queen."

"This I swear!"

Then, Kamose's eyes held mine. "The fates are kind to you, Brother, that the half-sister is already with child . . ."

Tetisheri bowed again. "This child, gotten by the bastard son of my husband, Seken-en-Ra I, on the natural daughter of my son, Seken-en-Ra II . . . will have the Royal warp, and will be a well trained and worthy heir . . . to this I give you my vow," she said, and though she had aged before our eyes, her face had a new-found splendor.

Kamose looked on her with love. Then his eyelids lowered. "The poison seeps into my veins as fire, yet I am cold as deep water."

Her eyes dry, adoring, Tetisheri stood. "The murderess, from this day, will not know one moment's respite from my scorn and my loathing." She clasped her hands and shook her head, the hundred curls in her wig in crisscrossed disarray. "By the Thighs of the Sky-Woman, I have been a fool! A stubborn, doting fool . . . and what is more, Grandson, an ancient fool!"

Kamose laughed. Then he stood, picked her up and kissed her, put her down next to Senseneb and embraced the old tutor. "So! My Old One, it is your little Priest-Prince the gods have chosen to lead the South Land to victory? Leave me now! Grand-mother, hasten, begin your life's work. . . . Deal with the Queen."

Bowing low together, they walked backward, then the Old One held out his arm and they walked to the door.

Kamose watched them. Then, sitting down again, he said, "Miutu, hie you now to the Outer-court of the Temple. Tell the beloved Thebans gathered there that my morning blessing suffices them of my presence for this day. Tell them their King rides to join his hosts. Disperse them happy, to pray to Amun-Ra for our victory . . . Miutu, High Priest and Chief of Visions." My brother held out his hand, but Miutu lay flat on his belly and kissed his King's feet. Kamose helped him up. His eyes blind with tears, the aged High Priest left the Council Chamber.

"Kheri-heb!"

"My King."

"Go forthwith to the Inmost Shrine. Have all in readiness, spiritually and temporally, to shrive the King and array him for battle." Kamose stood up. Each bowed to the other. Then they stood tall together, Masters manifest, Initiates. Each touched the other's heart with his right hand. Then, swiftly, Kheri-heb was gone.

Kamose sat down. In glowing fullness of heart he looked at each beloved man and woman, and it seemed, in this torch-lit chamber underground, that the air grew brighter, as though his eyes had set it afire. "Leave me alone with my brother." His gaze caressed each one, and blessed them. "You are souls of my soul. We shall meet and dance with joy in the Fields of Celestial Grain, and sail the Celestial River. . . . This is the Truth of Maat."

One by one, their containment lost and their tears flowing silent, each in turn lay on his belly and kissed the feet of his King. Then, walking backward, they left, each on his errand.

"My son . . ."

"Mother, come close." He held out his prong-pricked hand.

Ah-hotpe knelt at his feet and put her lips to his wrist. He stroked her shining hair as our father had done. "Look to Herath," he said. "Take her as your daughter. Rear her child as a Royal child, in line of succession . . ."

"The true line," she murmured.

"The gods have spoken. The fate of the Two Lands is held in the King's Household. . . . The years of our lives are as but a moment in the Eyes of Ra. Ta-mery . . . is Holy." He looked down at our mother. "Cherish my warm, brave and beautiful Hyksos Princess. She is my treasure. Guard her well."

"With my heart's love." My mother stood up. Kamose rose to his feet. They looked at each other. Then I saw that my mother was looking, not into his eyes but above him, to the left, and I heard her whisper, "Maat-Kheru . . ." and it was as if her whole soul burst into praising. Without touching him again, she bowed low, her arms outstretched in adoration and her face alight with a strange joy. She walked backward to the door and stood for a long moment gazing on us both. Then she left to bring comfort to Herath.

Kamose went back to his chair. "Take my hand, Ahmose." He sat with closed eyes. His hand was cold and wet. Sekmet, who had been still as a statue, now weaved about his chair, growling and nuzzling his knees. "My Guardian Beast." He laid his other hand on her head. "The Little Brother is your King." He looked up at me. "Till the Neferusian army is destroyed, you are Kamose . . . we are One. When they are beaten to their knees and flee in terror, you will be feared, Ahmose, for your own God-valor. . . . Little Brother, my last command to you. You will lay me, in one of the coffins piled up in the carpenter's shop, in our father's House of Everlasting. Thebes will mourn, but mourning will turn to joy when Neb-Pethy-Ra, Ahmose sails downriver from Nubia, victorious to Thebes. They will rejoice when you marry the Queen. You know all my plans. I think my Ka knew of this happening, for I have trained you well. Akh! By the Great Strider! This Ka of mine is strong and pulls away from me." His hand grew dry and colder. I loosed it and pulled the lion bracelet from my arm. I tried to clasp it on his. It was too small but it held. His eyes blazed green fire through a river of unshed tears. "I would stand," he said, and rose. "My legs are stiff as pillars." I looked at Egypt.

"Whadj-Kheper-Ra, Kamose . . . Brother." I fell on my belly and kissed his cold feet. I tasted the salt tears his friends had left on them and washed them with my own. Then I rose to my feet and looked full into his eyes.

He raised his hand in the God's blessing and, taking the Golden Cobra from his brow, he removed my Fisherman's Circlet and put upon me the Fiery Symbol of the true Priest-King. I felt a heat, as though a flame licked up along my spine, then a strange cool, as the Royal Cobra passed from Ra's son to Ra's son on its ancient, predestined way.

"O Great Hawk of Gold . . . Her-bak! Horus, whose Love has been since the beginning . . ." My heart breathed the words. We stood together in unchanged, unchanging love.

Kamose sat down again, his feet together, his palms on his thighs. "Leave me, Little Brother. The venom is now more than my blood can endure." He looked down at the lioness. "Follow your King." As on the day of his Crowning, she lay in front of him and licked his bare feet. "Walk away from me, Ahmose. No! By the sweet smell of Amun! Not backward! You are Neb-Pethy-Ra, Ahmose. Protector of the Two Lands, Hiktowy!" His eyes were cleansed of their flames, wide with infinite departure. The blood-pulse in his throat had ceased. His Ka had left his golden body before I walked, backward, to the drop-stone door.

Epilogue

The capture of Avaris about 1567 B.C. marked the end of the Hyksos rule in Egypt and the inauguration of the great era in Egyptian history which we call the New Kingdom. At Thebes the throne had passed from the redoubtable Ka-mosĕ to his younger brother, King Neb-peḥty-Rē' A'ḥ-mosĕ I; and it was he who in the third or fourth year of his reign besieged and sacked the enemy capital, breaking the power of the Asiatic rulers and depriving them of their last foothold within the boundaries of Egypt. Our only eyewitness account of the taking of Avaris is a somewhat subjective version preserved at el Kāb in the tomb of one of the king's marines, A'ḥ-mosĕ, son of Ebana, who, in itemizing his own deeds of valor, lets it be known that the city fell after a series of assaults by land and by water and provided, when finally taken, a very gratifying amount of plunder.

King A'ḥ-mosĕ I, hailed by posterity as the father of the New Kingdom and the founder of the Eighteenth Dynasty, was evidently a man of exceptional vigor and ability. Characteristic is the manner in which he followed up his victory at Avaris by his three-year siege and capture of the Hyksos base at Sharuhen in southern Palestine and by his pursuit of the enemy northward into Syria, moves successfully designed to forestall once and for all any recurrence of the disaster from which Egypt had just extricated herself.

William C. Hayes,
—*The Scepter of Egypt*